"What the hell's going on?" Claire demanded of her reflection.

The last thing she expected was an answer.

"You're one of them now," a gravelly voice said.

Claire spun around, a scream lodged in her throat as she peered into the far corners of her room. He was a shadow. A large, motionless form occupying her wicker chair—presumably where he'd been sitting since the minute she awoke.

Pressing a hand to her pounding heart, her gaze darted wildly in search of a nearby weapon. Despite his marble-like stillness, an energy emanated from him that only heightened her agitation. He sat there like a deadly snake, frozen and still before the attack.

"Who are you?"

"Gideon March." Something flew through the air to land on her bed. "You forgot that."

Certain she detected amusement in his deep voice, she glanced at the object on her bed. Her purse. She looked back at the intruder's shadowed features. "It was you in the alley," she said slowly. "You saved me. . . ."

◆ ◆ ◆

"A thoroughly tantalizing tale! Sharie Kohler knows how to deliver a riveting plot, steeped with sultry sexual tension and unforgettable love scenes between an irresistible hero and heroine—outstanding paranormal romance."

—Kresley Cole, author of
Wicked Deeds on a Winter's Night

Also by Sharie Kohler

Marked by Moonlight
Kiss of a Dark Moon
To Crave a Blood Moon

Marked by Moonlight

Sharie Kohler

POCKET STAR BOOKS
New York London Toronto Sydney

The sale of this book without its cover is unauthorized. If you purchased this book without a cover, you should be aware that it was reported to the publisher as "unsold and destroyed." Neither the author nor the publisher has received payment for the sale of this "stripped book."

Pocket Books
A Division of Simon & Schuster, Inc.
1230 Avenue of the Americas
New York, NY 10020

This book is a work of fiction. Names, characters, places, and incidents either are products of the author's imagination or are used fictitiously. Any resemblance to actual events or locales or persons, living or dead, is entirely coincidental.

Copyright © 2008 by Sharie Kohler

All rights reserved, including the right to reproduce this book or portions thereof in any form whatsoever. For information address Pocket Books Subsidiary Rights Department, 1230 Avenue of the Americas, New York, NY 10020

First Pocket Books paperback edition January 2008

POCKET and colophon are registered trademarks of Simon & Schuster, Inc.

For information about special discounts for bulk purchases, please contact Simon & Schuster Special Sales at 1-800-456-6798 or business@simonandschuster.com

Cover design by Min Choi.
Cover art by Craig White.

Manufactured in the United States of America

10 9 8 7 6 5 4 3 2

ISBN-13: 978-1-4165-4227-8
ISBN-10: 1-4165-4227-2

To my little princess,
whose fascination with the paranormal
already rivals my own.

I promise,
one day you can read Mommy's werewolf book.

Acknowledgments

This book has been a long time coming. That *Marked by Moonlight* has found its way into the hands of readers is due to the support of many. Sincere thanks go out the following people:

Tera, Leslie, and Ane, you were there for me at the very beginning. Thank you for patiently reading and rereading every page and listening to all my plot woes.

Robin T. Popp, who assured me this manuscript was destined for publication—your support was the encouragement I needed to push myself through the hard spells.

Sandra K. Moore, whose full manuscript critique sent me into a weeklong migraine—thank you! Without your input, who knows when the lightbulb would have gone off?

My husband, for understanding when deadlines arose and the laundry baskets piled—I love you.

My agent, Maura Kye-Casella, for singling out this manuscript from her slush pile, sinking her teeth into it, and, in true lycan form, never unlocking her jaws—thank you doesn't begin to cover it.

And to my editor, Lauren McKenna, whose guidance and insight helped bring this manuscript the final stretch home—you rock!

Marked by Moonlight

Prologue

Never turn your back on an unfamiliar dog.

—*Man's Best Friend: An Essential Guide to Dogs*

They were coming. The 911 operator's voice droned steadily in his ear, urging him to stay on the line, to wait, to remain as he was, crouched in a ball at the side of his bed. But when a second howl rent the night air, the phone slipped through his fingers and thudded softly to the carpet. Gideon drifted to the bedroom door as if pulled by an invisible string.

They were coming. But not soon enough.

With a shaking hand, he grasped the doorknob, the brass cold and slick in his sweaty palm. His family was on the other side of that door. He couldn't wait. Filling his lungs with a deep breath, he pushed open the door, the creak of oil-hungry hinges a familiar sound in an unfamiliar night.

His sister stood alone in the moon-washed hallway. Moonlight limned her blonde hair silver, giving her an unearthly aura. Her ragged bear dangled from one hand, its foot grazing the hardwood floor in rhythmic sweeps as she gazed in silence at their parents' door.

"Kit," he called, trying to keep his voice low.

She glanced over her shoulder at him before lifting a small, pink-nailed finger to the door in mute appeal. He hurried to her side and grabbed hold of her pointing hand while silently vowing to shield her from whatever lay within.

"Momma," she whimpered.

His gaze skittered away, then back to that wood-paneled door. A man's tortured cries echoed from the other side.

This had to be a dream. A horrible nightmare he would wake from at any moment. Only the bite of Kit's nails digging into his hand told him this was real. His parents would expect him to protect his sister, to get her far away from here.

With that sole thought burning in his mind, he closed his ears to his father's cries and swung Kit, light as a feather, into his arms and fled.

He didn't get far. The sudden splintering of his parents' door immobilized him. Clutching his sister close, he turned.

In that moment, he learned monsters were real. Horrifyingly real. *They did exist.*

This one bared its fangs in greeting. The tawny fur at its mouth and neck glistened black crimson. A glint of gold flashed in the hair of its chest, catching Gideon's eye. But only for a moment. That wet fur surrounding its mouth recaptured his attention, its exact nature unmistakable.

Blood.

He released his sister. Her gangly legs slid the length of his body to the floor. He shoved her behind him. She clung to him, locking her arms around his waist in a death grip. Tearing her hands free, he flung her back.

"Go," he commanded over his shoulder. "Get outta here!"

Her slight body shuddered where she stood, but she made no move to obey.

Never taking his eyes off the creature, he raised his voice and pushed her again. "Move!"

Maybe it was his sudden movement. Gideon would never know, but at that moment the monster attacked, surging forward like a spring uncoiled.

He had no chance. But his sister did. Against his every instinct, he turned his back on the beast and shoved Kit in one final attempt to save her.

A sudden, cracking pop pierced the narrow hallway, blending with Kit's high-pitched scream. Both sounds buzzed in his ears. In a quick, jumbling assessment, he surveyed himself and found his limbs intact. The beast had not ripped him to shreds. Turning, he watched it crumple to the floor inches from his feet, groping its chest with wild, frenzied movements.

A smoking pistol cast its shadow over the wall. Gideon turned, his gaze sliding past the pistol to the young man in police blues who cast an even larger shadow than the gun.

"Silver bullet," the officer said flatly. "Works every time."

The distant song of sirens congested the air, growing

steadily louder. The officer's eyes, as dark and flat as his voice, drilled into him. "Don't say anything, kid. There's gonna be a lot of questions. Let me do the talking."

Gideon nodded, unable to speak, and looked back at the dead beast littering his hallway.

Only it wasn't a beast.

The beast had vanished.

In its place sprawled his mother—naked except for the familiar gold cross nestled in the indentation of her collarbone.

And through the open doorway of his parents' room lay his father's mutilated body—a mangled, broken toy, blood pooling around him in an ever-enlarging circle.

Chapter One

Beware the silent dog.

—*Man's Best Friend: An Essential Guide to Dogs*

Stepping out of her car, Claire Morgan sniffed the smog-laden air warily. Locking her door, she faced the run-down apartment building and sighed. Brushing the salt of French fries off her slacks—evidence of her weak-willed drive-through detour—she eyed the gray building made all the more ugly by painted-on shutters framing every window. Even armed with her city map, it had taken her over an hour to find it. Apparently in this neighborhood, when street signs went missing, no one bothered to replace them.

Distracted, she failed to notice the two adolescents on skateboards launching themselves down the center of the street in her path. One of the skaters clipped her hip, nearly knocking her to the pavement.

"Hey!" she cried.

One of the youths turned back and flicked her an obscene gesture.

"What am I doing here?" she muttered, shaking her head.

But she knew the answer to that question even as she asked it.

She was here for Lenny.

By all accounts, Lenny Alvarez had been a lost cause. Seventeen, repeating his sophomore year, he'd originally sat in the back of the class with his head down, buried in his arms. Gradually, as the year progressed, he'd started paying attention, even staying after class so she could tutor him for his SAT, which he was scheduled to take tomorrow. It was the one test he couldn't miss; he would be there if she had to drive him to school herself.

Squaring her shoulders, she faced Lenny's apartment building. A radio played in the distance. The Tejano music that echoed off the row of apartment buildings lining the block had a liveliness that contrasted with the eerie stillness of the neighborhood. Sweat dampened her nape and she lifted the hair off her neck to let the faint breeze cool her skin.

Normally, she would be popping in a movie right about now, a plate of pizza on her lap like most Friday nights. A Saturday of grading papers would follow, and then a Sunday of church and dinner with the parents. She shrugged one shoulder. A break from routine wouldn't hurt.

And this was Lenny.

Stepping onto the sidewalk, she prayed she wouldn't have to confront Lenny's drunken foster father.

A dog hurled itself, spitting and growling, against the filth-encrusted screen of a ground-floor apartment.

Jumping back, she dubiously eyed the tiny screws holding the screen in place—the only thing preventing the animal from mauling her.

Gripping the iron railing with a clammy palm, she fled up the steps, doing her best to ignore the sudden memory of her cousin's mastiff attacking her when she was only eight.

The barking grew fainter as she neared the door of apartment 212. The sound of a television blared through the steel-framed door. She rapped on the door. No answer. She tried again, harder this time.

Suddenly a hard voice demanded, "What do you want?"

Claire spun around, clutching the stinging knuckles of her hand. An elderly woman with sagging jowls and deeply carved wrinkles peered from a cracked door across the way.

"I'm looking for Lenny. The boy who lives here. Do you know him?"

Small, piercing eyes studied her above the sagging chain lock. "You a social worker?" Before Claire could answer, the woman rushed forth with, "'Cause you should've taken that boy away a long time ago."

"I'm not a social worker." Claire shook her head vigorously. "I'm his English teacher."

The old woman snorted. "What kinda teacher makes house calls?"

"He's been absent three days." Three days. And Lenny *never* missed class. "I'm worried. Tomorrow's his SAT, and I want to make sure he's there." Claire didn't voice her other concern—that she feared his foster father had harmed him.

The woman absorbed this. Her disdain seemed to abate, and the hard glint to her eyes softened. She peered cautiously to the left and right before undoing the chain and opening the door wider to stick her salt-and-pepper head out. "The boy's gone. Forget 'bout him."

"Gone?" Claire frowned.

"Yeah, gone." The woman shooed Claire with her wrinkled hand. "Now you go on home. You shouldn't be here." Her head bobbed up and down. "Go on now. Leave. And don't come back here again."

She blinked at the strange command and jabbed her thumb at the apartment behind her. "Has something happened to Lenny?"

Those piercing, ancient eyes narrowed. "I seen the boy. These ol' eyes seen a whole world of things." She paused, pointing two gnarly, arthritic fingers to each of her eyes. "I seen the boy. And he's gone. Just forget 'bout him."

Claire gave her head a small shake, suspecting the woman with her strange words wasn't quite right in the head. "Thanks."

"You see that boy, run the other way! Hear me? Run the other way!"

Her smile wobbly, Claire moved toward the stairwell, pausing on the top step. "Er, yes, ma'am."

The dog's frenzied barks followed her as she crossed the street to her car. Disappointment squeezing her chest, she dug for her keys, noticing a figure streaking across the empty playground in front of her car. Suddenly he tripped and fell, stirring up a cloud of red sand. Resting her elbows on the roof of her car she waited, the teacher in her compelled to see the youth rise to his feet.

The sun had disappeared below the rooftops, tinting the sky a hazy purple. Visibility fast fading, she squinted across the distance, watching the boy rise. He glanced over his shoulder to check behind him.

And she saw his face.

"Lenny!"

Their eyes met across the playground. Recognition flashed in his face. He slapped a hand in the air, batting her away before sprinting off in the opposite direction.

Oh, I don't think so. She hadn't tutored him hours after school and paid his testing fee so he could blow her off and skip his exam. Stuffing her keys in her pocket, she slung her purse over her shoulder and took off after him. He was taking his SAT tomorrow. She would see to that. Few teenagers could turn their lives around so late in the game, especially at her high school, where the students were predominantly "at risk." She wasn't going to let Lenny slip through the cracks.

Her khaki-clad legs ate up the ground, her sensible shoes pounding the earth as dusk sank into night. Darkness encroached and the shadows took on a life of their own, pressing all around her. Only streetlights kept night from swallowing her entirely. Up ahead, Lenny passed beneath one, its beam a spotlight on him as he turned and disappeared between an all-night Laundromat and a nail salon with pink blinking lights. Halting, she peered into the alley's dark, cavernous depths.

Panting for breath, she lifted her face, watching as the clouds parted, breaking to reveal a full moon. The alley was suddenly awash in a pearly glow. A lone Dumpster sat against one wall, its putrid scent reaching her nostrils. The alley looked empty. No sign of Lenny anywhere. A dead end loomed ahead, so he couldn't have escaped. He had to be on the other side of the Dumpster.

Legs aching from her run, she moved the toe of one shoe into the alley.

"Lenny!" Her voice bounced off the two buildings on either side of her. "It's Miss Morgan! Please come out. You're not in trouble."

A low, anguished groan answered her.

"Lenny?" She advanced one sliding step at a time, concern for him swelling in her heart. Had his foster father hurt him? "Are you okay?"

"Stop! Don't come any closer," came his muffled voice, almost indistinguishable. "Can't stop it, can't help—" His voice faded into a moan.

Then nothing.

Silence.

Nearing the Dumpster, the soles of her shoes scraped over loose gravel, the only sound in the unnatural silence. She heard nothing beyond the rasp of her breath, and she could not help thinking the city was never this quiet.

"Lenny? Are you hurt?" Her voice cracked on the air.

Shadows pressed in, closing upon her. Her nape tingled and she trembled. The world beyond vanished, the narrow space becoming a tomb, blotting out all life, trapping her within.

A desperate whisper flew through her mind. *Go! Get out of here!*

Her feet rooted to the ground, unable to obey the silent command. She stole another glance at the sky. Her breath caught. A red-tinged moon. No longer pearl white. Blood moon, her mother called it. *Blood moon, someone's dying soon.*

As that litany echoed in her head, her feet shuffled backward. She hugged her leather purse to her chest, the strap slung limply over her shoulder.

Abruptly, the moon's glow vanished like a candle snuffed out. Darkness descended. With a shuddering breath, she searched the dark sky for a glimpse of moonlight to get her bearings. The tiny hairs at her nape tingled anew. She squinted against the murky air just as a large shape materialized in front of her.

"Lenny? Is that—"

Pain exploded in her face. She staggered and fell, her head hitting the ground with a sickening smack. Tears sprang to her eyes.

A massive weight fell on her, so crushing she couldn't draw air. She raised hands to push it off, encountering only fistfuls of coarse hair. Dazed, she wondered how the dog had gotten loose and followed her.

Then all thought fled.

There was only agony.

Pain ripped into her shoulder. She screamed as she was hoisted off the ground. The pain sharpened into a million pinpoints of fire as she was shaken side to side, her mouth opened wide in a silent, frozen scream.

Stop. Oh God, make it stop.

As if in answer to her prayer, the stabbing pressure in her shoulder abruptly ceased. The weight bearing her down vanished. She lifted her hand to clutch her shoulder and encountered the slippery stickiness of blood.

Using her uninjured arm, she flattened her palm against the pavement and struggled to her feet, eyes straining to see through the gloom.

She made out two figures locked in struggle moving deeper into the alley, away from her. One was definitely a man. But the other? She shook her groggy head. A dog? No. It was too large.

Whatever it was—she was leaving while she still had the chance.

She staggered off, but even numb with pain something nagged at her, niggling in the back of her mind. A memory flashed in her head with crystalline precision, like an old reel-to-reel home movie.

A blinding, bright day. The kind of hot, thick air she could grab with both hands and taste on her tongue. The prickly, sharp edges of freshly cut grass scratching her ankles as she ran, then her face as her cousin's growling and snarling mastiff tackled her to the lawn. The heavy paws on her back. The rank, hot breath on her neck. The paralyzing fear as sharp teeth sank into her flesh.

Tonight marked the second time in her life a dog had attacked her. Except tonight the animal had been silent. No barking. No growling. Not a single sound to warn of its attack.

As if it had been lying in wait.

Gideon March had killed before. He'd faced stronger than the one before him and come out on top. Tonight marked another victory.

Squatting, he inspected it with clinical dispassion, one hand braced on a hard, denim-clad knee. He pulled the nine-millimeter from its holster and with a few deft twists screwed on the silencer. The silver-bladed knife protruding from the creature's burly chest would only impede it temporarily. There was just enough time to finish the job before it was on its feet again.

Pointing the gun, he fired. The eyes widened, transforming from icy silver to dark brown as the bullet penetrated a thick pelt of hair, muscle, and bone. Sitting back on his heels, he waited, observing his quarry thoughtfully as the creature shifted one final time.

This one had been alone. The older and more experienced never left themselves open to ambush, but Gideon had spotted him a mile away. The instant he'd entered the pool hall, Gideon had marked him. His eyes stood out, a beacon among mortals. No colored contacts to camouflage his silver eyes from hunters.

Gideon glanced over his shoulder to verify they were still alone. Just as he thought—the woman was long gone. Turning, he watched the shifting complete. The dark fur disappeared and the musculature shrank, revealing a scrawny adolescent body clinging to the last moments of life.

"Ah, hell." He ran a hand over his face, suddenly feeling older than his thirty-two years. His dispassion slipped a notch as he suffered a stab of regret. In the smoky pool hall, he had appeared young, and now Gideon saw he was just a kid. No more than eighteen. The naked body lying on the pavement looked barely out of puberty. This did not bode well. He knew the nature and habits of lycans well, had spent half his life making it his business to know. They would never bring someone so young into their fold and then leave him to roam alone.

Had he been accidentally infected?

The kid coughed, trying to speak, but blood gurgled in the back of his throat. Too bad. Gideon wished he could press him for information. Instead, he placed his hand over the kid's brow, compelled to end his suffering.

"Don't talk. It'll pass soon." He pressed the barrel to the kid's forehead.

A hand shot out, circling Gideon's wrist in a hold surprisingly firm for one weakening in death.

His finger stilled on the trigger. They never lingered like this. The kid was a fighter.

"I— I didn't mean to hurt her." The boy coughed violently, blood spattering from his lips and spraying Gideon's hand.

Gideon reasoned that he referred to the woman who'd run off. Damn fool. She had signed her own death warrant. Even if she didn't believe in things that went bump in the night, basic self-preservation would keep a lone woman from strolling down an alley in the Fifth Ward.

The fact that the kid was sorry didn't change a damn thing. It was done.

And the woman would have to pay.

"I know," he murmured.

And they weren't just words. He did know. Better than anyone. It was never intentional. The bloodlust simply overpowered the will. It corrupted the soul, stealing both conscience and free will. To kill was inescapable.

Which was why he had to find the woman.

"Miss Morgan. Help her." The boy squeezed Gideon's wrist in a final surge of strength, lifting his head to glare at him fiercely. "Before she changes. Save her."

His fingers slipped from Gideon's wrist, and his head fell back to the pavement. "Finish it." The kid's voice was hollow as his gaze lifted to the sky.

Gideon complied. With another muffled zing, the kid lay dead. He stood and looked down at the wasted life. Although he had delivered the fatal blow, he suffered no guilt. Gideon had destroyed him, but the kid had been murdered some other time, in some other place, by an embodiment of evil that walked the earth even now, hunting its prey.

He unscrewed the silencer and holstered the gun. Then he pulled free the knife and wiped it clean before returning it to the sheath beneath his jacket. Flipping open his cell phone, he dialed. One ring and a brusque voice picked up.

"March here. Got another one. Holcomb and Delcorte. Between a Laundromat and a nail salon." Without waiting for a reply, he clapped his cell shut and snapped it back on his belt. Those terse words sufficed. The body would be disposed of without sending the local police into a frenzied search for a mad gunman.

As he walked out of the alley, a small bundle caught his eye. He bent and picked up the handbag and rummaged through it. Flipping open the wallet, he quickly scanned the driver's license behind the protective plastic cover. A piece of cake. His hunt just got easy.

Claire Elizabeth Morgan stared back at him, a plain face framed by hair so neat and perfect it could have been a plastic wig. *Frigid*, he couldn't help thinking, suddenly reminded of the nuns at St. Ignatius, where he had attended school until his parents' deaths.

He scanned the rest of the information at a glance. Age: thirty-one. Hair: brown. Eyes: brown. The address was clear across town, in the burbs. What the hell had she been doing here? He snapped the wallet shut and stuffed it into the purse. The night was still young.

Might as well get it over with.

Chapter Two

The birth of a pup can be a tricky thing; it must be monitored closely, especially the first night.

—*Man's Best Friend: An Essential Guide to Dogs*

Gideon located the light switch in the apartment. As light flooded the small space, he took a good look at the home of Claire Morgan: age thirty-one, street sense nil. The tidy living area's sparse furnishings reflected a modest life. From the worn, floral print couch to the brass-hinged old chest that functioned as a coffee table, everything pointed to the humble, unassuming nature of its sole inhabitant.

A green-eyed cat blinked at him before jumping down from the couch and disappearing into the bedroom. Gideon's lips twisted in amusement and he wondered how ol' tabby was going to welcome her new mommy home tonight.

Family pictures lined the walls. He surveyed the photos, immediately picking out his quarry posing with family members. Dad, mom, grandparents—he identified these easily, pausing to more closely inspect Claire's husky father. The man's hard eyes demanded a second look. In every picture, he gripped his wife's shoulder or arm—but not lovingly. More like he was afraid she might bolt from his side at any moment. Gideon inspected the rest of the photos. No boyfriends. At least no one important enough to grace a frame. Good. It improved her chances of returning home alone.

He could do what he had to and leave.

Of course, she could have called a friend or family member and be staying the night with them. Depending on the severity of her injury, a loved one might insist on looking after her. Yet she'd been able to walk away. Her injury could not have been too great and no matter the severity, she would recover. Sooner than humanly possible. Her newly altered DNA possessed tremendous regeneration ability.

Two strides took him to her bedroom. A captivating scent assailed him. He lingered in the doorway, inhaling. Gardenia and something else . . . faint and powdery. He flipped on the light and beheld a room as clean and orderly as the living room.

Several small burgundy- and plum-colored pillows were tossed at the head of the neatly made bed, a splash of color against the ivory comforter. A small desk sat against one wall, an obsolete IBM on top of it. Stacks of papers littered the surface, the only visible sign of disorder.

Curious, he stepped closer and selected a paper off the top of one stack, an essay of some kind with her name in the header. The neat comments in the margins undoubtedly belonged to her. The depth of her feedback told him she had a lot of time on her hands.

He shook his head and began to feel the pricking of his conscience. Most of his prey lacked identities, but a very definite picture of Claire Morgan began to form in his mind.

He shrugged off the uncomfortable pang of conscience.

His eyes landed on a photo on her desk. With a heavy heart, he picked up the heavy wood frame. The words *World's Best Teacher* were inscribed at the top of the frame, and behind the gleaming glass smiled a group of kids. The kid from the alley was there, one arm draped over Claire Morgan's shoulders.

Gideon gazed at the two of them for a long time, willing the image of the boy with the bright, hopeful smile and the woman with the timid eyes to disappear—if not from the photo, then at least from his mind.

"Shit," he muttered, dropping the frame back on the desk, wishing he had never set eyes on it.

Claire Morgan had been in that alley to help a student. Of that he felt certain. How could he snuff out little Miss Mary Poppins?

He reminded himself that her goodness no longer existed. She was one of them now. He shouldn't look at her differently from any other kill. He hunted. He destroyed. It had never been complicated before. It didn't have to get complicated now.

But she hasn't taken blood yet. There was still a chance. His thoughts turned down another path, one rarely ventured. Could things have been different if someone had given his parents a chance?

Shaking his head, he dragged his hands through his shaggy locks. He couldn't risk it. There was too much to lose. Too many lives at risk as long as she lived. He lowered himself to the wicker chair in the corner of the room. A ragged, one-eyed teddy bear nestled amid the pillows of her bed stared back at him, reminding him of his kid sister's old bear. The one their parents bought her their last Christmas together.

"Ah, hell," he swore as something long dead stirred to life in his gut. He was finished speculating. It was too late. Things just got complicated.

"Thanks, Maggie. Hope I didn't ruin your Friday." Claire rolled her shoulder, testing it carefully as her friend and coworker unlocked the apartment door for her. She winced at the shooting pain and flexed her fingers around the small, white pharmacy bag, eager to down one of the pills within.

"No problem," Maggie replied, tossing her purse onto Claire's couch. "The kids are with their dad this weekend anyway."

"Well, I still owe you."

Having left her purse in the alley, Claire lacked her insurance card and money for the co-pay. Thankfully, Maggie had been home to take Claire's call and come to the rescue.

"Sure. And don't worry. I won't tell anyone at work what happened. Not even Cyril."

Claire looked sharply at her friend. "Cyril?"

"Aren't you two dating?"

She should have guessed that her one date with the

band director would have made the rounds and been exaggerated into more than single, innocent date status. Cyril was a new teacher and word spread fast when an available man arrived in a largely female-populated workplace.

Cyril was a nice enough guy. At her age, and in her profession, she should latch onto him like bait on a hook. But there was no chemistry. Not that there ever had been. With any man.

"We're just friends."

"Mind if I give him a shot, then? I'm always on the lookout for an available guy." Maggie waggled her eyebrows.

"Go for it." Claire shrugged, and then sucked in a breath at the resulting pain. "But I have to tell you, I don't think he goes for the aggressive type."

Maggie settled her hands on generous denim-clad hips, her red lips curving into a grin. "Are you saying I'm aggressive?"

"No," Claire hedged, "but he's asked both me and Jill Tanners out."

"Tanners? The counselor?"

Claire nodded, trying to hide her dislike. Jill Tanners was the at-risk specialist. The counselor was supposed to help kids, supposed to keep them in school. Yet she hadn't done squat for Lenny or blinked an eye over his uncharacteristic absences.

"That cold fish?"

To drive home her point, Claire answered, "Yep. Miss Morgan and Miss Tanners. The mouse and the cold fish."

"You're not a mouse," Maggie argued, averting her eyes.

"Please." Claire fluttered a hand. "How many fights broke out in my classroom this year?'

"Uhhh . . ."

"Six," Claire answered, having no doubt that Maggie knew the number. "How many fights have you had?"

"I dunno." Maggie shrugged. "Can't remember."

"You can't remember because there weren't any."

"So what are you saying?" Maggie asked. "Cyril likes his women . . . soft?"

"Spineless would be a better word."

"You're not spineless," Maggie disagreed, slapping her hands together as if suddenly struck with insight. "You survived a dog mauling, right?"

"Yeah," she grumbled, glancing at her shoulder and plucking the bloody shreds of her blouse in distaste. "A little worse for wear."

"Smarts, huh?" Maggie's face screwed tight with sympathy. "Pop a couple of those pills and you'll feel better."

Reminded of the money she had borrowed this evening to pay for those pills, she said, "I'll pay you back on Monday."

Maggie waved a hand dismissively. "Hey, you lost your purse. Pay me back whenever."

Hardly lost. The vision of her purse lying in that dark alley flashed through her mind. She would have to go back in the light of day on the off chance her purse was still there. Tomorrow. When the sun was up. The alley wouldn't look so frightening in daylight. The dog would be long gone. The stranger, too. Whoever he was, she owed him her gratitude and she hoped he got away unscathed.

Claire sighed. At the moment, she needed relief for

her throbbing shoulder. Maggie must have read some of the pain in her face because she went into the kitchen, poked her head in the refrigerator, and resurfaced with a carton of juice. Shooing Molly, Claire's cat, off the counter, she poured a glass.

"Here you go. Take one of those pills," she ordered, extending the glass.

"Thanks." Claire ripped open the pharmacy bag, glanced at the instructions, and popped a pill into her mouth, chasing it with a swig of juice. "I really need to wash up and change." She held her blouse out from her shoulder in distaste.

"Why don't I stay until you're out of the bath and tucked in for the night?"

Accustomed to living alone and taking care of herself, Claire felt the stirrings of impatience. "It's late. You've already done enough. I don't think it's necessary—"

"Hey." Maggie raised a hand in the air to silence her. "I'm a mom. Let me mother. Besides, I don't want you hitting your head and drowning in the tub."

"All right." She gestured to the kitchen. "There's leftover Chinese if you're hungry. I won't be long."

Closing her bedroom door, she moved into the bathroom. Sitting on the edge of the tub, she gave the faucet a twist and let the water trail through her fingers until she was satisfied it was the desired warmth. A couple of bath oils. A swish of the hand. Relief was on its way.

Standing, she pulled her blouse from her waistband and moved before the mirror, watching as she gingerly slid her arms out of the sleeves and let her blouse flutter to the carpet like a wounded moth.

The severed left strap of her bra hung like a limp noodle. She gave it a disappointed flick. Ruined. Her areola peeked out from the sagging cup of the pink satin bra. Damn. It was one of her favorite bras, too. Her lingerie was the one area of her wardrobe where she permitted herself to be feminine and fashionable.

Carefully peeling back the dressing, she eyed the angry red puncture wounds decorating her shoulder, a stark contrast to her pale skin. She re-covered the wound, glad to conceal the nasty sight.

A bone-deep weariness closed its fist around her. She clumsily removed the rest of her clothes. Kicking free of her khaki pants, she stumbled, instinctively stretching a hand to the nearby closet door for support. Only her hand groped a fistful of air. She caught herself just before falling into the open closet. Straightening, she stared in silence at the dark hole of her walk-in closet. She was sure she had closed the door this morning. As usual. Otherwise, Molly tended to shred her clothes.

Claire shook her head, trying to shake the not altogether unpleasant fuzziness that appeared to be rendering her stupid. She probably forgot. No surprise, considering the kind of day she'd had. Hopefully, her clothes had fared better than the ones she had just removed. She would check for casualties later. For the moment, a bath beckoned.

With a delighted groan, she lowered herself into the tub, taking care to keep her shoulder above water level so she did not soak the wound, per the emergency-room doctor's orders. She forgot to pull her hair back and was too lazy to get out of the tub for a hair band. The ends of her hair tickled the tops of her shoulders, skimming the surface of the water like pale brown seaweed as she sank lower into the tub. She sighed, welcoming the codeine's effect as the burning in her shoulder subsided into a mild tingling.

Steam wafted from the water like tendrils of smoke, surrounding her in a protective shroud. Her tongue darted out to lick at the salty sweat beading her upper lip. Incapable of resisting, her eyes fluttered shut. And she began to dream.

Or maybe hallucinate. Too real to be a dream. All five senses were alive, stretched taut and sizzling with awareness despite the dulling drugs coursing through her blood. If this was a dream, never had she dreamed so vividly. Trees and brush surrounded her, their branches grabbing her like clawing hands. Whenever a break in the brush appeared, a thick fog rose to fill the space.

But she wasn't alone.

The others weren't visible, but she felt them just the same. In the wild thrumming of her blood, they called to her, summoning her wordlessly. Impossible to resist. She answered their call, running to meet them, propelled through yellowed fog. The moon glowed overhead, a huge pearl in the black sky, guiding her, revealing where to place her feet on the opaque forest floor.

Shadows crowded her, widening and lengthening as their presence grew. She felt their silent breaths, smelled their heat, tasted their hunger. Their eyes, tiny torches of silver fire, glinted like beacons of light through the hazy mireland of fog and forest, signaling her home.

She no longer soaked in a steaming tub but resided in

an unearthly realm that both tantalized and frightened. The fog was a tangible thing, cupping her face with yellowed fingers. The wood filled her nostrils with its earthy tang. The pads of her feet sank into the moist soil. It was intoxicating. More acute than arousal. Her flesh sizzled. Pleasure bordered pain as she drew closer and closer to them. Her family, her brethren, her pack.

At last, the shadows materialized. Faces took shape surrounding those eerie eyes—eyes so silver no human could possess them.

And no human did.

As the faces came into focus, Claire's body jerked in terror.

Her head slid off the tub's rim. She plunged into the warm, scented water with a gurgling shriek.

Coughing and sputtering, she shot up from the tub, hands slapping water as she sought something solid. One hand found the edge of the tub while the other wiped at rivulets of water streaming down her face. Chest heaving, she lifted her gaze. Through spiky wet lashes, she noticed her cat perched on the back of the toilet, black pupils so dilated the green could hardly be seen. The old tabby arched its back and released a long, moaning meow that twisted into a sharp hiss.

"Molly!" Claire reprimanded, feeling like a disappointed mother as the cat jumped off the toilet and bolted from the bathroom.

"Claire!" Maggie's muffled voice carried through the bedroom door. "You okay in there?"

"Yeah! Getting out now," she called, an unmistakable tremor to her voice. "Glad I never did drugs," she muttered. Who could predict their effect if a mild painkiller reduced her to this?

Claire rose from the tub, taking extra care since her legs felt as steady as rubber. Slipping on her blue terry-cloth robe, she emerged from the bathroom, weaving a crooked line from the door.

"Maggie, I'm going to lie down."

With a clucking sound, Maggie slipped an arm around her waist. "Those painkillers sure pack a punch."

They staggered together the few feet to the bed. Claire collapsed on top of it and tried to pull the comforter down, but her arms felt like two leaden weights, so she gave up, leaving them stretched above her head like a swimmer in dive.

"Wait here." Maggie's voice sounded underwater and far away. Seconds later, Claire felt the throw from the couch draped over her. She tried to voice her gratitude but her tongue was thick in her mouth and she couldn't form the words.

"'Night. I'll call to check on you tomorrow. See you Monday."

She thought she heard the front door open and shut over the roaring in her ears. Her eyes drifted open, then shut, and then open again. She regarded the whirling fan blades above until she grew dizzy. Squeezing her eyes shut, she opened them sometime later to a darkened room, preternaturally still.

How did the light go out?

Ribbons of moonlight crept in through the blinds, saving her from utter blackness. Claire shook her head as though the motion could clear it. No luck.

Before sleep swallowed her and robbed her of all thought, a man's voice rumbled through the air, rolling over her.

"Sleep now."

She managed to lift her heavy head with a mewling grunt. Her eyes focused for a brief moment. In that split second, she made out a man's shadowy form looming over her. Too weak, her head collapsed back on the pillow, and she surrendered to sleep.

With a sigh on her lips, darkness rolled in, the second whisper lost to the night.

"Sleep . . . forever."

Gideon brushed the back of his hand against her brow and winced at her fiery flesh. She didn't stir. Initiation had begun. The fever raged inside her, the poison spreading, eating its way through her, consuming the old life to make room for the new, but she slept peaceably.

He lifted his gun and pressed it to her head. She wouldn't feel a thing. The time was right. He had to do it now. There would never be a better moment. His finger curled around the trigger. In his mind, he heard that trigger click, heard the soft zing of the bullet whiz through flesh and bone, saw her body jerk—

She sighed softly and rolled onto her side. He bent his elbow and pulled the gun back, waiting for her to resettle before he placed it to her head again, this time directly on her temple where her hair fell straight and smooth, brushing the mouth of the barrel.

Do it. Do it now!

It was nothing he hadn't done before. Nothing he

wouldn't want done to himself if he were in her shoes.

He had pulled the trigger on other NODEAL agents, members of the National Organization for Defense against Evolving and Ancient Lycanthropes, like himself who were unlucky enough to become infected in the course of their duties. Men like him. Men he called friends.

So, why couldn't he pull the fucking trigger?

It was what he did. Who he was.

She snuggled deeper into the bed, rolling on her side and curling her legs. Her robe parted, revealing well-shaped calves and supple-looking thighs that would feel like satin in a man's hands. His cock grew hard, pushing against his fly, and he swallowed a curse. The thought of gliding his hands over her legs, of wrapping them around his waist as he buried himself in her soft heat, grabbed hold of him and wouldn't let go. Shaking his head, he decided he'd been too long without a woman. A matter he needed to correct if it stopped him from lusting after his targets.

Her arms reached out, instinctively searching the area next to her until her fingers met the sought-after object. She tucked the tattered teddy bear to her chest, triggering a flood of memories best left forgotten. Memories of home, of family, of a happy, unfettered life . . . before he'd known lycans existed in anything other than Hollywood movies.

She smiled in her sleep. A soft, dreamy smile that did strange things to his insides.

"Shit," he muttered, repeating the NODEAL code in his mind like a mantra. *Destroy them at any cost.*

Chapter Three

Some dogs take longer to train than others.

—*Man's Best Friend: An Essential Guide to Dogs*

Claire opened her eyes, blinked once, and was instantly wide awake, surging upright in bed. Astonishing alertness for a woman who deliberately set her alarm thirty minutes early just so she could hit the snooze button three times. Her body required that extra half hour to adjust to the idea of waking.

From the darkness enveloping her, she knew it was still morning. The bedside clock read four fifteen.

She had slept only four hours?

Strange. She had been so exhausted.

Her belly rumbled. Thoughts of swinging by Krispy Kreme wormed into her head. Hmmm, or breakfast tacos from Tia Rosa. Her growling stomach made the decision. Both.

Lifting her arms, she stretched, remembering too late to have a care for her shoulder. But surprisingly the stretch didn't hurt. She rotated her shoulder gingerly, waiting to feel her muscles' protest. Nothing happened. She moved her shoulder more vigorously, delighted to discover no pain at all. It felt fine. In fact, every last inch of her felt fine—great, even. Like a woman reborn, bounding with energy. The alien impulse to don some sweats and take a Saturday morning jog seized her.

"Some drugs," she muttered.

Then another urge asserted itself. Claire bounded from the bed. Arms outstretched, she made her way through the gloom to the bathroom.

Moments later she emerged and noticed the blinking light on her answering machine. Apparently, she'd slept through the ringing telephone.

But who would have called in the middle of the night?

She pushed play and returned to the bathroom. Flipping on the light, she squinted against the glare. As the messages rewound, she accustomed herself to the fluorescent lighting and gave her reflection a cursory glance, then reached for her toothbrush.

Her gaze flew back to the mirror and the face that was her own. Yet not. She leaned forward warily, as if the woman in the mirror might leap out to harm her.

Her face was . . . different.

She stared hard, trying to put her finger on the difference.

In the background, the first message began to play.

"Claire, it's your mother. Wanted to see if you want roast or spaghetti this Sunday. I can do either. Let me know. 'Bye."

Tearing her attention from the mirror, she gave the machine a peculiar look.

Like clockwork, she ate dinner at her parents' house every Sunday, and although her mother often checked to see what she preferred to eat, she had never called in the middle of a Friday night to verify. Shrugging, she returned to scrutinize her face, at last pinpointing the difference.

Her eyes. They weren't the same mousy brown that looked back at her every day. They were silver. No light blue or grayish blue either. Silver. A startling silver, reminiscent of ice . . . and something else. Something familiar. Something recent. A memory niggled at the back of her mind, but she couldn't quite touch it.

Her fingers lightly grazed her cheekbone just below those strange eyes. Could drugs alter one's eye color? Was this some sort of allergic reaction to the codeine? Or the tetanus shot?

Maggie's voice blared from the answering machine, penetrating her racing thoughts. Kids whooped and screamed in the background. "Just checking in. Call me if you get around to it. See you tomorrow . . ."

Why would Maggie think she was going to see her today? On Saturday? Shaking her head, Claire grabbed her remote control off the dresser and flipped on the television, clicking through channels until she found the local news. A human Barbie doll reported the early morning weather in cheery, singsong tones.

"Looks like it's going to be a gorgeous day today. A great way to begin the week. Maybe it will make those headed-back-to-work-Monday blues easier . . ."

The remote control slipped from her suddenly slack fingers and thudded to the carpet. She backed up, sinking onto the bed as realization washed over her.

She had slept two nights. As impossible as it seemed, it was four fifteen *Monday morning*.

"No one can sleep that long," she whispered over the drone of yet another message from her mother.

She jumped up and rushed back to the mirror, gripping her hands around the edge of her sink until her knuckles turned white. Inhaling through her nostrils, she lifted her face and met her gaze dead on. It was like looking at a stranger. Those eyes chilled her.

"What the hell's going on?" she demanded of her reflection.

The last thing she expected was an answer.

"You're one of them now," a gravelly voice said.

She spun around, a scream lodged in her throat as she peered into the far corners of her room, searching for the owner of that voice.

He was a shadow. A large, motionless form occupying her wicker chair—presumably where he'd been sitting since the minute she awoke.

Pressing a hand to her pounding heart, her gaze darted wildly in search of a nearby weapon. Despite his marble-like stillness, an energy emanated from him that only heightened her agitation. He sat there like a deadly snake, frozen and still before the attack.

"Who are you?" She plucked a curling iron from the basket of rarely used hair products next to her sink.

"Gideon March." Accompanying that less-than-enlightening introduction, something flew through the air to land on her bed, making her flinch. "You forgot that."

Certain she detected amusement in his deep voice, she glanced at the object on her bed. Her purse. She looked back to the intruder's shadowed features. "It was you in the alley," she said slowly. "You saved me from that dog."

Still brandishing the curling iron in her hand, she inched closer to flip on the bedside lamp. A soft glow filled the room, reaching its corners and granting her a better view of the man sitting so casually, so relaxed, in her bedroom—as if he had every right to be there. His large frame dwarfed the chair and she worried it might collapse beneath his weight. The muted haze of light did nothing to soften the hard planes of his face. Even as she acknowledged his arresting good looks, she had the distinct impression he rarely smiled. Lean bodied, stone faced with pale eyes—the exact color she couldn't yet detect—a regular Marlboro Man.

Gideon March nodded at the curling iron in her hand. "Planning to curl my hair?"

"What are you doing here?" Her fingers flexed around the curling iron's steel grip, ready to club him over the head if he moved her way. "I don't think you broke in to my apartment to return my purse."

"How's your shoulder?"

She ignored his question. "I don't have any money. Whatever I had was in that purse."

"I'm not here to rob you."

"Then what do you want?"

He sighed. "Someone's got to explain what's happening to you."

She scowled at his cryptic answer, then rushed on as if she hadn't heard him. "Listen, if you leave now, I won't call the police. You brought my purse back, now—"

"Don't you want to know what's happening to you?" He leaned forward, his hands—large like the rest of him—dangling off his knees. "You're one of them now," he continued, "and more has changed than your eye color."

She knew she should concentrate on getting this intruder out of her home, but what he said resonated within her. How had he known about her eyes? She couldn't resist asking, "One of who?"

"Remember the kid you followed into the alley?"

"Lenny?"

"Your student, right?"

She could only nod, wondering how he knew she was a teacher and then remembering her school identification was in her wallet.

"He was one of them. He attacked you. Bit you. And now you're one of them, too." He spoke as if he were explaining something very basic. As if she were a child. As if she were stupid.

"A dog attacked me. Not Lenny," she said in a voice that left no doubt which of them she considered mentally deficient.

"It was Lenny," he said with quiet certainty, then repeated as vaguely as before, "and now you're one of them."

What on earth was that supposed to mean? Had she been involved in some sort of gang initiation and didn't know it?

"What are you talking about?" She shook her head, trying to clear it. "One of who?"

"Lycans," he said as though the term might ring a bell.

When she didn't respond, he explained, "Sort of like a werewolf. Only not like in the movies. Werewolves are Hollywood. Lycans are the real deal."

"Werewolves," she echoed, her gaze darting about again, renewing her search for a weapon, something better than a curling iron.

"You're a lycan," he said blandly, lacking the passion such a declaration might warrant—especially shouted from the padded room of the insane asylum where he must normally reside.

She didn't move, didn't speak, afraid anything she chose to say might set him off.

"You're a lycan," he repeated in the same mild tone. For all the emotion in his voice he could have been the anonymous voice taking her order at a drive-through. "In a very short time you'll be a perfect killing machine."

"I see." Her tongue darted out to moisten dry lips. With the utmost care, she adopted a slow, placating tone and said, "Let me get this straight. I'm a werewolf. And Lenny—" She stopped cold, recalling his exact words. *Was*. All need to placate fled.

"What do you mean *was*?" she demanded, fighting back the urge to shout. "What happened to Lenny?"

"He's dead." Again, the flat voice.

"Dead," she murmured, her arm falling lifelessly to her side, her fingers loose around her weapon. *Dead*. The word rolled over her in a numbing fog. No. Not Lenny. He couldn't be dead. He never got a chance to live. Not the kind of life he deserved, anyway.

"And you will be too if you don't start listening to me."

"Lenny," she whispered, shaking her head.

"Listen to me." His biting command cut through her spinning thoughts, through the sorrow threatening to swallow her. "You don't have time to grieve. I need—"

"How do you know he's dead?" Her gaze leapt back to his face. Why should she believe this nutcase?

His mouth pressed shut and he glared at her.

Heedless of her own well-being, she lurched nearer, jabbing the curling iron in the air. "How do you know?" she demanded.

"Listen." He clutched the fragile arms of her wicker chair as if battling for patience. "Your life is in danger. You need my help."

Why couldn't he just answer her question?

"He's not dead," she charged, shaking her head vigorously. "No way." A fresh-out-of-the-asylum trespasser living under some very unhealthy delusions could hardly be counted on as a reliable source of information.

"He's dead." His voice broke through her denial with the viciousness of a whip. "And you will be too if you don't get a grip and start worrying about your own ass."

She tapped her chest with the curling iron. "Why am I in danger?"

He didn't answer her. Again. Funny how he had a way of doing that whenever she asked a direct question. When her students didn't immediately answer her, it was because they had something to hide. Her eyes widened, sweeping over him and suddenly she understood. She knew. *She knew*.

"You killed Lenny!" How else would he know for certain Lenny was dead? She staggered back and bumped into the wall so hard it rattled the picture frames.

"No," he corrected, then added in a somewhat quieter voice, "I destroyed a lycan who *used* to be your student."

"You're insane!" Her lips worked silently as she struggled for an epithet foul enough to hurl at him.

"Listen. Lenny was a lycan. And as of Friday night, so are you. If you need proof, look at your shoulder where he bit you."

Yeah, right. As if she would take her gaze off him to inspect her shoulder.

"Go look in the mirror," he snapped, unfolding his great length from her chair. "See how insane I am."

She slid farther along the wall, creeping slow inch by slow inch toward the bedroom doorway. "Stay back!"

He gestured at her shoulder impatiently. "Just look, damn it!"

She flinched at his raised voice. His sheer size coupled with his not so minor confession of murder left no doubt that the time for talking was over. She flung the curling iron at his head and bolted. His muffled curse told her the curling iron made contact.

Door, door, door. The word pounded through her mind like the heavy beat of a drum. She had to reach the door before—

A hand slammed down on her shoulder and spun her around. His other one muffled her scream as he hauled her against him, muttering, "Lady, don't make me regret helping you."

Helping her? Right. He was a regular Good Samaritan.

Keeping one hand on her mouth, he locked his other arm around her waist and lifted her off the carpet, imprisoning her against the rock-hard length of him. She landed a couple solid kicks to his shins with her heels. He grunted but still managed to carry her to the bathroom and drop her in front of the mirror.

Her pulse hammered at her neck in rhythm to the beat of his heart pounding at her back as he trapped her between his body and the counter. Hard body pressed behind hers, his hips pushed her into the counter. Staring at their reflection in the mirror, she saw with clinical dispassion just how good-looking he was. Even in the unflattering fluorescent lighting. And this, Claire mused quite irrationally, was vastly, horribly unfair. A manhandling brute should be ugly as sin.

His broad hand covered the bottom half of her face, his tanned skin a dark contrast to her paleness. Her lips parted and she tasted the saltiness of his skin with a dart of her tongue, detecting the rush of his blood just below the surface of his palm. Her breasts tightened and grew heavy and she had to resist the urge to take them in her hands and squeeze them.

Her gaze moved to his eyes. Green. A pale green. At the moment those lovely eyes—unbefitting such a cold, harsh man—glared at her in the mirror. She focused on the tiny flecks of gold, too numerous to count near the night-dark pupils.

The hand on her waist moved to the opening of her robe and yanked it open, giving further credence to his utter ruthlessness. She gave a tiny gasp, mortified when the robe parted down to her navel. Thankfully the sash was belted tight enough to keep at least some of her business private. But not all. A single breast spilled out of her robe. She grappled to cover herself, but he was bent on his own agenda. He bared her shoulder and thrust it forward until her head almost banged into the mirror.

Her gaze dropped to her shoulder. With a single, ruthless yank he tore off her bandage, and she quickly forgot about covering herself. Smooth, unblemished skin was all she saw. Not a scratch in sight. It was a miracle.

"Holy shit," she muttered into his warm hand, doubly shocking herself at her use of profanity. She rarely swore. Her father insisted ladies did not curse. Yet if there was ever a time for profanity, this was it.

"There's nothing holy about it. Your DNA regenerates at a greater speed now," he replied, apparently able to decipher her muffled exclamation. "You're facing eternal damnation unless you start listening to me." He dropped his hand from her mouth and cocked an eyebrow in question.

Their gazes clashed in silent struggle: his urging her to accept the impossible, hers steadfast in disbelief. Although more disturbed by the disappearance of her wound than she was willing to admit, that didn't mean she bought into his outrageous claims.

His gaze scanned her face and then dropped, examining the rest of her. All of her. He pushed his hips harder against her and she moaned far back in her throat. Belatedly, she recalled that more than her shoulder was bared for his inspection. With clumsy hands, she yanked her robe back in place, but not before his gaze burned across her exposed flesh and her treacherous nipple pebbled and hardened, rising in salute to his silent appraisal.

The hard length of his body tightened like a wire behind hers, singeing her through their clothes. A sudden rush of moisture gathered between her legs, so sudden, so immediate, she almost came on the spot.

A telltale hardness swelled against her lower back, prodding insistently. The temptation to turn around and rub against that hardness insinuated itself. Her gaze shot up in the mirror. Twin flags of red stained her cheeks. Mortified at her body's reaction, she wiggled free from the hard press of his body and the wedge of counter, taking refuge in the far end of the room. Putting several feet between them, she fought for breath in the charged air.

His scent followed her. Earthy smells. Cedar, pine, and aroused male filled her nostrils. Clearly her imagination worked overtime. No way could she *smell* him several feet away.

The throbbing ache between her legs alarmed her, but not nearly as much as her longing for *him* to assuage that ache. Her body had never reacted this way before.

He had to leave. Immediately.

"Get out!" She pointed a shaking finger in the general direction of the front door, her voice shrill and unsteady. "Now," she hissed.

Their eyes clashed in a battle of wills. At last, Gideon March turned to leave, but not before pausing to say, "I'll give you some time to think. This is a lot to digest. But this isn't over. On the next full moon, you will shift. And you will kill. I need your cooperation if I'm going to help you."

"Go away," she urged, resisting the urge to weep from the inexplicable *want* that burned her blood. "I'm not a—" She couldn't even utter the word aloud, wouldn't give it that much power. "I don't need your help," she finished.

He nodded slowly, his pale eyes strangely regretful. "Then that's too bad for you. Because without it, you're dead."

Then he was gone.

Legs suddenly too wobbly to support herself, she slid down the wall in a boneless pile. Her entire body shook. Yet strangely enough, not from fear. Her body thrummed for sexual release. She ached in places that had never experienced sensation before. Another second and she would have torn off her robe and pounced on him, wrested off his clothes, and investigated to her complete satisfaction that throbbing erection she had felt at her backside. What the hell was wrong with her?

With only one past lover, she didn't feel those sensations any longer. Didn't have those needs. Right? She didn't indulge in primitive urges. They were things other women felt. Not her. Those urges were too wild, too primitive, too beastly. Especially to feel for a self-professed killer who broke in to her apartment and spouted insane allegations.

His smell swirled around her as if he were still in the room. She even thought she heard the echo of his steps well past her apartment door now.

She rose and moved toward the phone sitting on her bedside table, thinking she would call the police. Her hand hovered over it for a moment before pulling back. What would she tell them? Some guy returned her purse and warned her that she was going to turn into a werewolf on the next full moon? They'd lock her away in the same insane asylum as Gideon March, and then where would she be?

Besides, Claire had other problems. Like finding out what had happened to Lenny. No way did she accept that he was dead. He probably just took to the streets to get away from his foster father. And she needed to come up with an explanation for missing Sunday dinner. The flu seemed the easiest excuse. The way her body ached and throbbed, she certainly felt as though she were recovering from some malady.

She opened her nightstand drawer and pulled out a little blue booklet. Monday was off to an ominous start and she wasn't taking any chances. Picking up the phone, she dialed the automated substitute system and reported her absence for the day.

She hung up the phone and made her way back to the mirror. The stranger with the wild, silver eyes was still there, waiting for her, preventing her from hiding and pretending everything was okay. As much as she longed to crawl back into bed, pull the covers over her head, and forget Gideon March, her desire-flushed face and tingling body wouldn't let her.

She could, however, take care of one nagging ache, even if it wasn't the one between her legs. Grabbing her purse off the bed, she headed for the nearest Krispy Kreme.

Chapter Four

> Self-grooming is an instinctive trait for many species, most often employed when trying to attract a mate.
>
> —*Man's Best Friend: An Essential Guide to Dogs*

Standing in her closet, Claire tapped her lip and contemplated her wardrobe. Lounging in her bathrobe and stuffing her face had been the perfect therapy yesterday—preceded, of course, by a cold shower to wash away the aberrant yearnings that had plagued her body long after Gideon March's departure.

Krispy Kreme had been only the start. Her hunger couldn't be sated. It was an insistent pull on her stomach, demanding satisfaction. Almost as demanding as the sudden, inexplicable ache of her body for a green-eyed nutcase.

After Krispy Kreme, she decided to stay inside. For some reason the smells and sounds of the city overwhelmed her, made her head spin. The early morning streetlights shone brighter, the horns and blares of rush hour traffic rang raucously in her sensitive ears.

She'd ordered takeout three times: Ding Lung's, Domino's, and KFC. She almost ordered a fourth time from her favorite Italian place, Angelo's, but they always screwed up the order. The elderly woman who answered the phone never got it right. Yet Claire never complained—just paid for her food and ate whatever she found inside the tin containers like a good girl. Yesterday would have been different. Things would have gotten ugly with the deliveryman if she got anything other than her correct order.

Sadly, reality nosed its ugly head through the take-out debris and her soap opera marathon. The gray light of Tuesday morning dawned outside her window, reminding her that duty called.

An array of khaki, brown, and white garments filled her closet, a safari adventurer's dream, but certainly not the most inspiring of wardrobes. Her hands slid hangers down the bar one after another, searching for something more inspiring, something with a bit of color, a bit of zing. Everything she owned was dull, dull, dull. Dissatisfaction knotted her stomach. How could she stand out when she blended in with everything?

Her hand stilled on a hanger and she felt a frown pull at her mouth.

Stand out?

Since when did she want to stand out? Unable to answer that question, she brushed aside her unease and continued searching for something provocative and eye-catching even as her nose twitched at the offending odor of the litter box in the next room. She had dumped it several times yesterday, but the smell still bothered her.

Considering the contents of her closet, she had a real challenge on her hands. She stumbled upon a black, sleeveless, V-neck knit top at the very back of her closet. The tag still dangled from the collar. Naturally. She never wore anything that revealed so much as a hint of cleavage. Must have been a gift. She pulled it over her head and moved to the mirror. Her lips curved in a smile. It was snug, clearly defining the shape of her breasts and the shadowed valley between.

Claire smoothed a hand over her torso and twisted to assess her profile. "Much better."

She might have to wear it with khaki slacks, but at least she wouldn't blend into the background. A fact that was suddenly very important to her.

That left her hair. She stared at the neat, shoulder-length bob. Hopeless. It hung limply around her face even after a full night's sleep. She ruffled it with both hands only to growl with frustration as it drifted back into place, every hair falling into order. Limp and flat. Still hopeless. Well, that's why God created hairdressers. After work she would find one capable of performing miracles.

Grabbing a hair band, she pulled her hair into a sleek ponytail and nodded. Not bad. With her startling eyes, the effect was striking.

Clasping her silver bracelet around her wrist, she finished dressing. She had to get moving if she wanted to stop by an ATM to pay Maggie back.

Fully dressed and even wearing makeup, Claire emerged from her apartment. With a definite bounce to her step, she headed for her Taurus, a strange sense of anticipation humming inside her.

The sky was tinged a predawn purple, the air already thick with typical Houston humidity. Her nostrils quivered at the noxious aroma of smog. As she unlocked the car door she noticed a gently purring Jeep parked next to her sedan. No one sat inside. Shrugging, she turned back to her car.

"Going to work today?"

She gasped, her ears instantly recognizing that velvet voice. Her body recognized it as well, springing to burning awareness, the skin of her arms and neck prickling. Her purse and book bag fell to the pavement and she fisted her hands at her sides as if she could suppress the inappropriate reaction.

Gideon bent and picked up both bags, his eyes watchful as he straightened and handed them to her. His scent struck her full blast. Wood and man and the faint scent of soap and mint toothpaste.

"You're stalking me," she accused, her voice unnaturally high.

Taking care to avoid touching him lest any of yesterday's longing resurface, she grabbed her bags from his hands and hugged them tightly to her chest.

"You should consider taking a leave of absence until this is all straightened out. I had hoped you reached that conclusion when you stayed home yesterday."

"How do you know I stayed home yesterday?" she demanded, then swiped a hand through the thick air. "Never mind. Don't say it." She glared at him for a moment, her eyes narrowing on the thrumming pulse at the side of his throat. The blood flowed strong and steady within the artery. How she knew baffled her, but she did.

Could see the beating artery as clearly as his hard-lined face before her. "You've been sitting out here casing my apartment since yesterday, haven't you?"

"'Course not. When you came back from your doughnut run I figured you weren't going to work and left." He slid one hand into his front jean pocket and rocked on his heels, the sound of gravel crunching beneath the soles of his shoes scratching the air.

She couldn't help but notice that the hand in his pocket pulled his jeans tighter against a certain part of his anatomy. Desire shot through her, as shocking as yesterday in its unfamiliarity, rushing over her and heating the skin of her face and neck to an unbearable degree. *Why did her eyes automatically have to look there?*

Swallowing, she forced her gaze to his face. "This is harassment." She jabbed the air in front of her with her index finger. "Leave me alone."

God, she needed a latte. Fast. The display of goodies at her local coffeehouse flashed in her mind. And a brownie. A big, fat chocolate brownie. Her stomach growled in agreement.

"Still in denial?" He shook his head. "You're only delaying—"

"Look," she broke in. "I didn't want to do this, but if you don't leave me alone—" She paused, inhaling deeply through her nostrils, the smell of the Dumpster at the far end of the parking lot assaulting her senses. "I'm gonna call the cops."

She waited for his reaction, fully expecting to see him beat a hasty retreat.

Any minute now.

"I'll call the cops," she repeated her threat, using a louder voice this time.

"You could do that." He shrugged one shoulder. "But the police force is full of lycan hunters. Call them and you're as good as dead. They wouldn't waste their time trying to save one infected schoolteacher."

She gaped. Was there no end to his paranoid fantasies? She was going to have to decide how to best deal with Gideon March. He wasn't a student misbehaving in the back of the room that she could pretend not to notice. Staring into his intense gaze, she knew he wasn't going to go away.

"You're insane," she muttered, rubbing her wrist beneath her silver bracelet where it had started to itch.

He propped his elbow on the roof of her car and ruffled his longish hair as if battling frustration. "You keep saying that." He leaned close. Too close. It had been a long time since she had stood this close to a man. Her senses reeled, the musk of him filling her nostrils, making her heart thump against her chest, against breasts that were suddenly heavy and achy.

"I guess it's easier to pretend I'm crazy," he murmured. His eyes gleamed in the dawn air, flitting over her face, as if he was committing her features to memory. "What happens when you realize I'm telling the truth?"

The sound of his voice rolled over her like silk sliding against her bare skin. Claire could hardly make sense of his words, could only stare at his well-carved lips as they moved, imagining them dragging across her flesh. Stepping back, she bumped into her car, stopping her from total retreat. "You're disturbed. Truly. You need help."

His eyes glinted angrily. Even in the dim light, she could count those flecks of gold in his pale green gaze. "Maybe a little," he allowed. "Guess I have to be insane for trying to help a stubborn fool who doesn't want my help."

She ignored his dig and strove for a mild tone, trying not to annoy him further. "I'm going now." She had to step forward to open her car door. Her shoulder grazed his chest and her breath escaped in a hiss. She tossed her bags onto the passenger seat, her movements slow, measured, as if she didn't want to startle the strange animal beside her. "Good-bye." She forced a ring of finality into the farewell.

"Think about what I told you. Time off would be smart. You need to—"

She closed her car door, signaling her disinterest in his words. As discreetly as possible, she pressed the lock button.

He smiled grimly and leaned back against his Jeep, arms crossed over his chest like a man completely relaxed and content with himself and all his paranoid delusions.

Rubbing her stinging wrist, she eyed the lean length of him with admiring disgust. The guy could be a Calvin Klein model. What a waste. Shaking her head, she put both hands on the steering wheel and backed out. Facing forward again, she caught sight of herself in the rearview mirror, the sight startling. The sleek image of herself with the severe ponytail and pewter gaze filled her with unease.

At the first stoplight, she flipped on her overhead light to glare in consternation at her stinging wrist. The skin beneath the silver bracelet was an angry red, almost like it had been burned. She undid the clasp and tossed the bracelet into the cup holder. The light turned green. Stepping on the accelerator, she proceeded, rubbing the inflamed skin absently as she concentrated on putting Gideon March out of her mind.

Gideon groaned when he spotted the familiar Tahoe in his driveway. Its shiny chrome finish glinted in the afternoon sun. He parked alongside the curb in front of his house to make sure he wouldn't block the vehicle from departing.

"It's my damned driveway," he muttered, shifting into park with an angry jerk and killing the engine. "Why doesn't *he* park in the street?"

He wasn't in the mood for this particular visitor. Especially since it called for pretending that everything was normal, business as usual, that his thoughts weren't tangled up in *her*.

Easier said than done. Claire Morgan was one stubborn, aggravating woman. He had said everything he could to convince her, done everything he could. Well, almost everything. Gideon grimaced. He hoped it didn't come to that. He'd spare her that if he could. But how could he help her if she wouldn't cooperate? She either jumped onboard to save her ass or it was over.

Dragging a hand through his hair, he reminded himself that it shouldn't matter, that *she* shouldn't matter. It shouldn't be so complicated. He shouldn't think about his attraction to her, shouldn't think about stripping her naked and entering her in one slick thrust.

The blare of the television greeted him as he stepped onto his porch. Someone had made himself right at home. Gideon unlocked the door and strolled into his living room, eyeing the man relaxing in his overstuffed La-Z-Boy, beer in one hand, remote control in the other.

His voice carried over the din of the television. "It's a comfort to know the local police break in to people's homes these days."

"Not everyone's home. Just yours," Cooper corrected, his eyes never leaving the television.

"What brings you here?" Gideon noted the bag of Cheetos in Cooper's lap—the bag taken from the top of *his* refrigerator. "Besides my food and television."

"Can you believe this guy?" Cooper pointed a Cheeto at the screen, where a young man wearing pants that rode dangerously low stormed off the *Jerry Springer* set. "He just got the DNA test *proving* the kid is his, and he still refuses to believe it."

Denial was a sore subject right now. It reminded Gideon of a particular woman and her own penchant for denying the truth. And she was the last thing he should be thinking about around this man. Cooper McPherson was no fool. He hadn't risen to board director of the Greater Houston Area division of NODEAL by being dense. Even if he did like watching *Jerry Springer*, the man was sharp, suspicious by nature, and one hell of an agent. And he knew Gideon. Damned well. Well enough to know when something was bothering him, but not—Gideon hoped—to know when he lied. Because in the case of Claire Morgan, he was going to have to lie through his teeth.

Gideon eased down on the couch and tossed his keys on the coffee table, uncomfortable and doing his best to hide it. Until now, Gideon had never kept anything from Cooper. They had no secrets. Never had. Cooper was like a big brother. Always around to bully and kick him in the ass when he needed it. Sometimes even when he didn't.

"How can you watch this crap?" Gideon grunted as he yanked a pillow from behind his back to lounge more comfortably. He had to rely on the image of relaxation since his gut was knotted with tension.

"Ah, it's not crap. It's life, my friend." For all of Cooper's jovial air, his eyes were hard and shrewd as they turned on Gideon. "You can learn a lot from watching these shows. They show humanity at its worst. See that fella there ignoring his responsibility?" He waved a hand in the direction of the television. "That's too often the case. Men just don't come through and fulfill their obligations."

Funny, Cooper wasn't looking at the screen as he said this. He looked straight at Gideon. Clearly, he wasn't talking about society. Gideon had to force himself not to fidget. Slow, even breaths.

A long moment passed. They stared at one another. Cooper finally cut to the point of his visit. "Where you been? I haven't heard from you since Friday night's call."

"Busy."

"Yeah? Doing what? 'Cause it sure as hell isn't what you're supposed to be doing. I called all weekend. I had some tips on a new joint I needed you to check out. Where've ya been?"

Gideon averted his eyes from Cooper's piercing gaze. Damn. He shouldn't have looked away.

Gideon covered the slip by snagging the remote and clicking on the channel guide. "Just busy."

Cooper shook his head from side to side. "You wanted this, remember? I warned you. About the demands, always being on call, always available. But you wanted in—"

"Hell, I've been at it for almost fifteen years. I'm no rookie," he snapped. No. Not a rookie. Maybe just burned out? What other explanation could there be for why he wanted to protect Claire Morgan when it was his job to destroy her? He shook off the thought and continued, "I had some deliveries for my grandmother. Not to mention a few orders to finish up," he lied smoothly, nodding toward the door leading to the garage where he did his carpentry work.

Cooper snorted and tossed a handful of Cheetos in his mouth, his jaw flexing as he chewed. "What? Slaying lycans doesn't pay the bills?"

"I need something legit to show the IRS." Thinking the interrogation over, Gideon clicked the channel to ESPN.

"Saw the Dodge parked out back," Cooper commented mildly, referring to the old pickup Gideon used to haul furniture. "I didn't think you could cart armoires, chairs, and the like in the back of that Jeep. Guess you weren't running deliveries today, huh?"

Gideon smiled easily despite being caught in his own lie. A mistake he wouldn't make again. He might owe

Cooper a lot, even his life, but that didn't include a play by play of his every move.

"Fine," Cooper grunted. "Keep your secrets. Just hope you're not getting involved with some chick. You know this lifestyle isn't conducive to that sort of thing. Told you when you got in you could never lead a normal life. No wife. No kids." He leaned forward in the La-Z-Boy as if shortening the distance between them could better convey his next words. He stabbed the palm of his hand several times with his finger. "NODEAL is your life."

Gideon understood perfectly. He always had. "I know." He smiled without humor. "Love 'em and leave 'em. I learned the code from you. You drilled it into me. How could I forget?"

"That's right." Cooper nodded, still looking unconvinced as he settled back in the chair. "Let's talk shop. The body you called in the other night has been identified as one Leonardo Alvarez. Age seventeen. Born in Houston and birth certificate looks legit. Of course, no record of him in the files," he said.

NODEAL's confidential database was used by agents throughout the world for the cataloging of all known lycans, living and deceased. It was no surprise to Gideon that the kid wasn't documented. Gideon already knew he was newly infected.

Leonardo Alvarez. Lenny, Gideon silently mused, experiencing a strange flickering of sorrow for the kid whose last thoughts had been not for himself but his teacher. "He's probably too new to have made it into the database," Gideon murmured.

"What happened Friday? Anything unusual?" Cooper eyed him speculatively. "I sent Foster to run detail and he said everything looked clean. Aside from it being such a young kid. Easy kill?"

"Yeah," Gideon muttered. "No sweat."

Nodding, Cooper asked, "Any leads?"

He hesitated before sealing his act of deception with an indisputable lie. "No." There. He'd done it. Without even a stutter. No going back now. "He operated alone."

"What?" Cooper's brows dipped into a frown. "No buddies?"

Lycans operated in packs—at least two or more. Never, or rarely, individually. That's what made hunting them so dangerous and why inexperienced agents were assigned to a team until deemed fit to hunt alone. Gideon had completed his team training quickly. In fact, he held the record for quickest promotion to IAS—individual agent status. But then, he had something other trainees didn't. A grudge.

"That's right. Solo."

"Unusual."

"I know," Gideon retorted. He wasn't some grunt, new to the ranks. He didn't need Cooper questioning his every answer. Even if they were lies.

Cooper rubbed his bristly chin. "What's your take on it?" he quizzed in his best mentor voice.

"He could have been accidentally infected," Gideon offered, one possibility that couldn't be overlooked, even if unlikely. Lycans didn't run around accidentally infecting people. They fed. And when they fed, they gorged until their victims were dead. Recruitment into their packs was very deliberate, and they didn't abandon their inductees.

"Or . . ." Gideon's voice hung in the air for a long moment.

"Or?" Cooper prodded.

"Or there's a new player in town," Gideon finished. "One who doesn't follow pack tradition."

"My thoughts exactly."

The two men exchanged grim looks. That was NODEAL's worst nightmare. A lycan that infected indiscriminately could be a plague on the city. Or the world. Both men turned and stared unseeing at the television, each absorbing the implication of such a possibility.

Sighing, Cooper stood and brushed orange Cheeto dust from his hands. "I expect you to be available this weekend and taking calls."

Gideon nodded, rolling his eyes. Who needed a wife when you had a NODEAL director breathing down your neck?

For a split second, the by-the-book agent in him considered coming clean and telling Cooper about the teacher, but he quickly squashed that idea. Hell, Cooper would probably put him on suspension. Then he'd track Claire down and destroy her himself. Gideon's personal history with Cooper wouldn't get in the way. Neither would sentimentality. Nor Gideon's vague instinct that Claire Morgan was worth saving. Cooper was hard as nails. From that first meeting in his parents' hallway, his mother's corpse at their feet, that much had been clear. And only became clearer in the following years as Cooper took him under his wing and taught him the trade. Gideon had done his best to model himself after Cooper. A hard man driven by one purpose: to hunt and destroy lycans.

Apparently, Gideon wasn't as tough as he thought.

He owed Cooper his life—his and his sister's. No argument there. He also owed him the truth about Claire.

Unfortunately, it was the one thing he couldn't give him. Not yet.

"You look . . . different."

Claire couldn't help smiling at Maggie's pause as they exited the school together. By the time their conference period rolled around, they desperately needed a little adult R & R. The bagel shop around the corner provided the perfect escape.

Only eleven in the morning and heat already cloaked the city. The smell of baked asphalt, thick and pungent, clogged her pores.

"Different good or different bad?"

"Oh, good! Different good," Maggie assured, a hint of devilry in her smile. "I never knew you had breasts."

Claire chuckled, allowing the tension to ebb from her shoulders. The run-in with Gideon had left her in a foul mood. As a result she lacked her usual patience and had decided to assign book work for her afternoon classes in order to spare them. To top it off, Jill Tanners, Lenny's counselor, was too busy to see her. Claire knew when she was being avoided, but she had no intention of letting Tanners off the hook. It was her job to follow up on Lenny, and Claire intended to pester her until she did.

Her laughter died an abrupt death in her throat the instant she saw *him*. The tension returned, stiffening every muscle as her feet dragged to a stop.

"You've got to be kidding," she muttered under her breath, her heart lurching wildly against her chest.

Maggie pulled up beside her. Claire felt her curious stare scanning the side of her face.

"What is it?" she asked.

Claire couldn't speak. Her attention focused on the maroon CJ-7 Jeep parked in the principal's spot—on the man inside. The Jeep was a far cry from Principal Henderson's Volvo. As was the stone-faced, hard-bodied man behind the wheel.

In the midmorning sunlight, Gideon March sat there like he had every right to park in the reserved space. Big as day and hardly inconspicuous in a vehicle that lacked doors and a roof. Not that his six-feet-plus frame was easy to conceal. A long, lean, denim-clad leg protruded from the Jeep, his Red Wing boot propped on the door frame as he watched her.

What if he got out of the Jeep?

What if he started spouting that ridiculous werewolf nonsense again?

What if—

"Who is *that*?" Maggie whispered in hushed, reverent tones.

Claire shook her head dumbly, her stare never wavering from him. A pair of sunglasses obscured his eyes, but she could feel them burning into her.

"Do you know him?" Maggie pressed.

Claire tore her gaze free, focusing on her car and the prospect of escape. Refuge.

"No." Claire resumed walking, forcing herself not to panic and run.

"Well, honey, I think he knows you. Or the way he's looking, he wants to."

Claire's gaze skittered back to him. Sunlight glinted off his dark blond hair. The nerves along her spine tingled. And not entirely in fear.

"We don't know each other," she insisted, her voice firm.

"Uh-huh. Sure." Maggie smirked at her from over the roof of the car as Claire fumbled for the right key. "Forget about Cyril. You got a hunka hunka burning man over there ogling you."

Claire slid inside the sanctuary of her car, feeling slightly safer now that she could no longer see him or feel his intense gaze. Once Maggie shut her door, Claire hit the lock button. A hysterical laugh bubbled up from the back of her throat. That wouldn't stop him. Not if he wanted to get to her. He had no problem getting into her apartment, after all.

"Now it makes sense." Maggie gave a small, knowing laugh.

Claire started the car and backed out, trying not to notice how her hands shook on the steering wheel. "What does?"

A car horn blared and she slammed on the brakes. Both women lurched against their seat belts.

"Claire!" Maggie shouted, hands slapping the dashboard.

Heart hammering, Claire's gaze flew to the rearview mirror at the car she had almost hit. She waved apologetically at the woman glaring at her through the windshield.

"Jesus," Maggie muttered as the other car drove off in an angry zip. "Now it *really* makes sense."

Once Claire's heart had resumed a steady beat and they had escaped the parking lot, she was calm enough to ask, "What makes sense?"

"The clothes, the contacts, the makeup, your asking for the name of my hairdresser." She counted off on her fingers. "Oh, and the two-car collision we nearly had because you've got your head up your ass."

Claire sniffed, not appreciating Maggie's description. "What are you talking about?"

Maggie nodded thoughtfully, looking so world-wise as she flipped down the visor and checked her heavily applied makeup. "You're gettin' *some*."

Claire could only shoot a puzzled sideways glance at her friend, expecting her to finish the rest of her sentence.

Getting some of what?

Maggie must have sensed her confusion. "God, you're dense. You know." She slapped Claire's arm good-naturedly. "*Some*," she emphasized in heavy, exaggerated tones, waving her hands widely in front of her.

Understanding dawned, and Claire choked, "I am not!"

She hadn't gotten "some" in years. Eight years, actually. Not since Brian—the guy she had thought was her *one*—dumped her for a forty-eight-year-old waitress, who, according to him, made him *feel like a real man*.

"Well, then." Maggie fluttered her hand as if it were

a small distinction. "You're planning on getting some."

Claire shook her head, at a loss for words. It occurred to her that Maggie was exactly the type of girl her mother had kept her from hanging out with in school.

"Hey, I'm not judging. I'm a firm believer in sex. Just ask any of my ex-husbands. Abstinence is unnatural."

Face hot, Claire argued, "Maggie, I'm not—"

"And if that fine specimen back there in the Jeep is a candidate, I say go for it."

Claire was not planning on getting *anything* with *anyone*. Especially not with that lunatic.

But as she pulled up in front of the bagel shop, she couldn't help wondering.

And that was totally unlike her. She simply didn't wonder about those things. Never had.

And maybe the more important question was— Why now?

Chapter Five

Uncharacteristic behavior is a plea for attention; be sensitive to your dog's needs.

—*Man's Best Friend: An Essential Guide to Dogs*

Claire dove onto the couch and hunkered low, peeking above the couch's back to look out the salon's glass-tinted windows.

"Er, can I help you?"

She glanced over her shoulder. A young, beautifully coiffed receptionist angled her head and looked at her with startled, blinking eyes.

Claire turned back to scan the parking lot, dotted with the random assortment of vehicles for a slow Tuesday afternoon, and answered over her shoulder, "I have a five o'clock appointment with Terry."

"Sure," the receptionist said in that cautious tone one uses when dealing with someone unstable. Not unlike the voice Claire had used that morning with Gideon. "Just one moment, please."

She slid deeper into the buttery leather cushions, the

smell far more pleasing than the overwhelming aroma of chemicals stinging her nose. No sign of a Jeep anywhere, even though she had sworn the vehicle followed her into the parking lot. Sighing, she swung around and took a moment to observe her surroundings. The salon looked expensive, from its marble receptionist's counter, to the custom-framed artwork and leather couches. Maggie must live on credit to afford such a posh salon on a teacher's salary with three kids. Another customer watched her warily, magazine forgotten in her hands.

"Claire?" A man stood by the receptionist's desk, garbed in an oatmeal-colored man-gown. His lovely flaxen hair flowed to his shoulders in artful waves. "I'm Terry."

This was Terry?

Maggie hadn't mentioned her hairdresser was a man. And he was definitely male. Even if he wore a dress. Her gaze swept the broad shoulders stretching the fabric.

She followed him, lowering herself into the hydraulic chair he indicated with a wave, bouncing in her seat as he worked the chair higher. Tugging her ponytail free, he examined her closely before fluffing her hair off her shoulders and declaring, "Hmmm, no body. None at all."

She smiled wryly. "I know."

"Okay." He clapped his hands with an air of efficiency. "What we need to do is give you layers for lift—" He fluffed her hair some more for illustration, frowning when it drifted back into place, flat as ever. "—and lighten up all this brown."

"Lighten? As in bleach?"

"Highlights," he admonished. "And with your shade

of brown we can be generous with them. They'll blend in nicely."

Her shade of brown. He meant mouse brown. Not dark enough to be sable. Not light enough to be honey. She regarded herself in the mirror for one long moment, disliking what she saw. A plain woman with plain brown hair sliding prematurely into middle age.

Claire didn't understand what compelled this desire to change, but it was long overdue. She didn't understand why her appearance was no longer good enough, but it simply wasn't.

She nodded decisively. "Do it."

"Great!" Terry beamed, clearly not accustomed to winning such immediate and complete agreement from a client. At least not without more convincing. "You'll be a beauty. Especially with those eyes to set off your new hair."

"My eyes?" She frowned, having no problem focusing on the freakish silver orbs. Although she had tried, repeatedly, she couldn't ignore them. She had let everyone at work assume she was wearing contacts. It was easier than explaining the truth—especially since she couldn't provide that either.

She had scoured the Internet during her lunch break for any explanation of sudden eye color change and arrived at nothing. There was no getting around it. She needed to make an appointment with an opthalmologist. No amount of drugs or allergic reaction to tetanus could change her eye color for this length of time.

Standing behind her, Terry framed her face with broad

hands that looked like they belonged behind a plow and not in a salon. "They're stunning. Do amazing things for your face."

She glared at her reflection.

He didn't understand. The eyes were all wrong. They weren't hers.

In spite of her eagerness to change her appearance, her eyes had changed through no effort of her own. At least when she colored her hair she would know it came from a bottle. That it was her choice. And not a result of something else. What that something else was she couldn't begin to fathom. Wouldn't dare try.

As Terry led her to the back of the salon, she tried to reclaim her earlier enthusiasm, reminding herself that she was going to shop for new clothes after this and not feel the least bit guilty about it.

But a dark, mesmerizing voice insinuated itself into her mind, not to be forgotten, not to be ignored.

On the next full moon, you will shift. And you will kill.

No amount of pampering and self-indulgence could block out that deep voice. Not as long as *he* lurked out there, watching, waiting, a shadow that couldn't be lost. It was just a matter of time before he showed himself again.

Claire stepped through the school's main double doors and squinted fiercely against the blinding sun the following afternoon. It felt like she had stepped into a sauna. Moist heat hugged her and sweat broke out on her top lip.

Students bumped against her as they rushed to escape.

But what did she expect only five minutes after the final bell? Claire usually remained at school at least another hour grading papers. But not today. Today, bobbing in a sea of fleeing teens, she craved escape as much as the students. Even if she hadn't, she still needed to leave right after the bell to make her ophthalmologist appointment.

She walked quickly, eager to put the day behind her. The reactions her new look elicited had grown tedious. The students clearly approved—to an embarrassing degree. By sixth period, she had boys sitting in her class who weren't even on her attendance roster. Their admiration uncomfortably clear, she spent most of the day managing inappropriate behavior . . . and in a far harsher manner than was her tendency. Much to her concern. What happened to her limitless patience? Her forbearance?

Through the horde of bodies, she spied a familiar flash of maroon ahead. Her heart accelerated and her steps faltered.

Her fingers clenched tightly around her keys, indifferent to the steel digging into her tender palm as that familiar face came into view and the day's injustices fled in face of another.

Damn. She still hadn't figured out how to deal with him and here he was—ready or not—parked alongside the fire lane, arms crossed and leaning against the door in a casual pose. She stopped a few feet from him and glared. Students swarmed around her like fish moving downstream. Eyes trained on him, she paid little heed to them as they hurried past.

"Nice hair."

Her hand went to her hair. Terry had done wonders with it. Three shades of gold mingled with her brown strands to fashion a creation that resembled honey struck by sunlight. Sassy layers brushed her cheeks and neck in the softest of caresses.

The hair was only part of her transformation. She watched and waited as his gaze traveled a path from her hair to her face to her new outfit: a short, flirty skirt and sleeveless gold blouse. She felt stupidly eager to see his reaction. *His*. Not a teenage boy's. But the reaction of a flesh and blood man.

Claire could kick herself. Was she really so desperate, so starved for attention, that she craved the good opinion of a lunatic—even if he was good-looking?

The longer he stared at her in that silent, consuming way, the quicker her breaths came. Noisy, jagged little spurts of air that made her face heat up.

She had her answer. *Yes*. She had stooped that low.

"Nice duds." Something in his tone sounded distinctly insincere. In fact, he sounded heartily . . . unimpressed. No, *unimpressed* wasn't the word. She studied his stony, hard-to-decipher face. He *disapproved*.

"What are you doing here?" she snapped.

"Keeping an eye on you."

Fleeing students jostled her closer to him. Conscious of being overheard, she hissed in a low voice, "This has gone far enough." With a deep breath, she bluffed, "I'm going to the police."

"If you were going to do that, you already would have," he replied with a light shrug that said he didn't care either way.

She strove for a smart, pithy reply but came up with nothing. He was right. *Why hadn't she gone to the police?* Despite the return of her purse, he had broken into her apartment. He was stalking her. Threatening her. Turning her insides into knots.

As if he could hear her internal dialogue, he answered smoothly, "You haven't gone to the cops because, deep down, you know I'm right. Your feel it in your blood. That wasn't a dog in the alley. It was Lenny."

She shook her head vehemently and held up both hands as if she could block his words. "That's ridiculous."

Gideon studied her for a long moment, his eyes searching, probing. "You still think he's alive," he concluded, shaking his head.

Since he claimed the dog he killed was Lenny—an absolute impossibility—yes.

"Have you heard from him?" Gideon pressed, his look knowing. "Has he come to class?"

"I haven't seen him," she admitted, "but that doesn't mean anything. Kids skip class all the time. It doesn't mean Lenny is dead or a—" She looked over her shoulder, fearful someone might overhear, but the stampede of students had dissipated to a lone boy, scuffing his sneakers on the pavement as he walked past, oblivious to them. Just the same, she whispered angrily, "Werewolves do not exist."

His green eyes glittered at her with unwavering resolve. "Lycans," he corrected.

"Whatever," she spat back, perspiration trickling down her spine and dampening the small of her back.

"The longer you fight me, the less time we have to find the lycan that infected Lenny. If we don't—"

"You'll kill me, right?" Arching one brow in challenge, she held her breath, hoping he wouldn't agree, that he was just crazy and not truly dangerous.

At his curt nod, her breath expelled from her body in a whoosh. Nothing ambiguous about that. "That's not going to happen," she vowed, her voice barely audible but no less determined. She didn't care that he made her blood race. She wasn't about to let him kill her.

He studied her, his green eyes shrewd, searching beyond her face into her very soul. As if seeing something there, he shook his head regretfully. "The lycan's already gotten to you. It's inside you. Maybe it's already too late."

"Because I won't agree to you killing me?" She pressed a hand to her chest, her voice tight. "That's basic self-preservation."

He smiled, a hint of remorse in the curve of his well-shaped lips. "This isn't you."

"How do you know?" she countered hotly, even more angered because he happened to be right. She was different. Inside and out. "You don't know me." She waved a hand in front of her, encompassing herself with the gesture. "Maybe I'm like this all the time."

"Are you?" he asked in an even, steady voice no less demanding for its mildness.

She lifted her arms wide at her sides. Instead of answering him directly, she exclaimed, "You're threatening to kill me. That might give a woman a bit of an attitude."

The wild urge to strike him overwhelmed her, but that would only confirm his accusations, so she restrained herself and added, "A lot of people would react aggressively."

"Not you. You should have run for help by now. That's what good girls do when they wake up and find a strange man in their apartment." He stepped closer and the scent of him filled her nostrils—fresh cut wood, soap, and male musk. "You're different," he declared, "changed."

Claire found herself struggling to make sense of his words, but the increased pounding of her heart filled her ears, heated her blood, confusing her so that she couldn't help leaning closer, letting her breasts brush his hard chest and her nose fill with the masculine scent of him.

Fascinated, she studied the throbbing pulse at the base of his neck. Calm. Strong. Steady. The mad urge to press her mouth to that spot and taste him seized her. Cocking her head to the side, she lifted her gaze to his. The pale green of his eyes glowed as if lit from a fire within.

His scent altered then. Her nose twitched at the subtle difference. The air around him seemed to color, darkening to a wine-red haze. The pulse at his neck quickened. She licked her lips.

He lowered his head until they were practically cheek to cheek, his breath rasping her ear and raising the tiny hairs on her nape as he whispered, "Can't you feel it?"

Yes, she felt it. Like a fever. A ravaging disease infiltrating and killing the old Claire. She blinked several times, both frightened and exhilarated, before jerking back to focus on his smug face.

"You feel it," he announced, his voice much too satisfied for her tastes. "That's the lycan in you."

Jaw clenched, she stepped back and flexed her fingers around her purse strap. "You don't know anything about me."

"I know more about you than you think."

Ignoring the worry that ambiguous statement elicited, she muttered, "No. You don't."

He couldn't see her. No one saw her. No one knew her. She had spent a lifetime building walls to keep people out, to stay safe and warm inside where pain could never touch her. He couldn't have breached those walls.

"Claire," a faintly breathless voice sounded from behind, as if in a hurry to catch up to her.

She spun around and stopped short of groaning. Cyril advanced, slowing his jog to a slight skip, briefcase swinging at his side.

He stopped next to her. "You're leaving early today. I went by your room." He smoothed a hand over his thinning hair as if the few strands needed taming.

He looked to Gideon suspiciously, asking slowly, "How's it going?" The translation was clear. *Is this guy bothering you?*

"Good. Fine." She forced herself to sound normal, to act as if she was not caught conversing with a dangerous man.

"Hello." Cyril extended his hand to Gideon when it became evident she wasn't going to introduce them. "Cyril Jenkins."

He really was a nice man. An unexciting, nauseatingly nice man. Why couldn't she like him? Things would be so much easier if she could.

"Gideon March."

She watched, tense, as the two shook hands.

"You're a friend of Claire's?" Cyril inquired.

Gideon nodded and draped an arm across her shoulder, the muscle in his jaw flexing wildly.

Cyril's gaze swung back and forth between the two of them. Her face burned as she fought for composure, resisting the urge to wiggle out from under Gideon's arm.

Gideon turned a stunningly white smile on her, transforming the hard lines of his face from broodingly handsome to drop-dead gorgeous. "Don't be surprised if you see me hanging around. Can't stand to be away from my girl here." Leaning down, he grasped her face, long fingers burning an imprint on her cheeks.

Immediately, she felt the cadenced rush of blood through the callused pads of his fingers, a drumbeat reverberating directly to her heart.

She stilled, motionless, as he dipped his head, eyes intent on her lips. His lips settled over hers, warm and firm, a man who knew what he was about. She sighed and he swept his tongue inside her mouth. He tasted of heat and man—sex—and she arched against him. Slanting her head, she drank greedily, her fingers digging into his hard biceps.

And then it was over. Gideon set her from him with a jerk.

Her eyes snapped open. He stared down at her, smiling smugly. Only the muscles bunching beneath her fingers told her he wasn't unaffected.

Feeling stunned and slightly dizzy, she slowly uncurled her fingers from his arms. Dropping her hands at her sides, she gulped a steadying breath. Remembering that they weren't alone, she glanced at Cyril.

"Claire." He nodded, lips tight and unyielding. "I'll see you tomorrow." With a dark look for Gideon, Cyril strode past them.

Leveling an angry glare at Gideon, she hissed, "What did you do that for?"

"You don't need the complication of a boyfriend right now."

"Cyril's not my—"

"Not the point. He wants to be. And whether you realize it or not, you're caught in a dangerous game here. The fewer people involved, the better. Since I'm going to be your shadow from now on, it's easier if people just think we're dating."

"No one will believe we're dating." A dry laugh escaped her at the very idea. Strange how bitter it sounded even to her ears. "They need only take one look at you to know that."

"What's that supposed to mean?"

"Never mind," she muttered, dropping her gaze and staring at her new, open-toed shoes. Her red toenails peeked out at her.

"Tell me," his deep voice commanded.

She looked back up at him in exasperation, readjusting her purse on her shoulder. "I would never date a guy that looked like you."

She thought she detected a twitching of his lips before he responded. "Why not?"

"You—" She waved her hand at him, her voice struggling and sputtering like a dying engine. "Me—"

She was too proud to say what raced through her mind: that he was too attractive, too confident, too everything, to want her. Guys like him didn't date women like her.

His eyes glinted knowingly. He understood. And was amused. Great. It was one thing to feel inferior, but an entirely separate matter to acknowledge it. Humiliating, in fact.

"What's so unbelievable about you and me?" The husky rumble of his voice sparked a shiver in her.

He pulled back so his gaze could trail over her. Her breath caught, suspended in her throat as she suffered his prolonged inspection. From the way his eyes darkened, she somehow doubted he saw the same thing she did. She stopped breathing altogether when he added, "Any hot-blooded man would want you."

Her mouth dropped. Not the most genteel compliment, but she was instantly assailed by an image of them together, in bed, their naked limbs sweaty and tangled as she clutched his dark head to her breasts.

A feeling unlike any she had ever felt pooled like molten lava at her core, its heat spreading to her toes. However, the thrill didn't last. Was quickly replaced by disappointment. Because of all the men in the world that could have turned her bones to liquid, it had to be him. A lunatic.

In a steely voice, she warned, "Stay away from me."

Turning, she marched away, swearing that would be his final warning. No more putting it off. The time had come to take precautions against Gideon March. The man was dangerous. Her hand brushed her lips, still warm and tingling from his kiss. In more ways than one.

Chapter Six

Even the most docile animal can be provoked to attack.

—*Man's Best Friend: An Essential Guide to Dogs*

Nothing had changed. The same carefully laid table bearing the weight of her mother's wedding china and a five-pound pot roast sat before her as it had every Sunday of her life.

Claire looked around the familiar dining room. The smell of lemon-scented Pledge filled her nostrils. Every wood surface gleamed from a fresh polish. The silverware, displayed on a heavily starched tablecloth, winked at her beneath the light of the chandelier.

Her mother looked neat and tidy in a white eyelet blouse and flowing skirt. Her father, on the other hand, had merely donned his bowling shirt over a sleeveless white undershirt. The bowling shirt hung open, unbuttoned, giving her an unrestricted view of his bulging belly pushing against the thin white cotton.

Nothing had changed.

Nothing except Claire.

She felt different—a stranger sitting in a chair grooved and worn from years of family dinners. A lifetime had passed since she last sat at her parents' table. She felt as different on the inside as she looked on the outside.

The gun filling the wide pocket of her cargo pants—its weight a frightening, all-too-real reminder that she wasn't the same person—had a lot to do with it. The gun was solid, a reassuring presence against her thigh. Strange. She had never imagined bringing a gun into her father's house. Hell, she had never imagined *buying* a gun, but that had been the outcome of her last run-in with Gideon March.

Self-protection had prompted her to search the yellow pages for a gunsmith. Texas law enabled her to walk into Carter's Country and walk out an hour later with a gun. No days of waiting. Just a quick online background check.

Next time she saw Gideon March, she would be ready.

Only Gideon had been surprisingly absent the last few days. Even so, she remained vigilant, carrying her gun on her at all times. Her gut told her this wasn't over. He would be back. Like a tiger, he would pounce. Only Claire wasn't a mouse. Not anymore. She would be ready. She would make certain he never made good on any of his threats.

She watched her father's unfriendly face as he chewed. The sight reminded her of a cow working a cud between its teeth.

"Gravy?" Before she could protest, her mother leaned over her shoulder and covered her plate with the thick brown sauce.

"Sure," Claire murmured, watching the congealed grease slither a muddy river over her meat and potatoes. She quickly tried to save her green beans and corn from contamination by scraping them out of range with her fork.

Ladle in hand, her mother slanted her head to get a better view of Claire's eyes. "Very . . . interesting, but—" She paused, wrinkling her nose. "Couldn't you have chosen a different shade? Silver is so . . . so—"

"Weird," her father readily supplied, his voice hard.

Claire sighed, wishing the ophthalmologist had been more helpful. His diagnosis that her eyes were exceptionally healthy had failed to comfort her. He didn't seem to understand that they weren't *her* eyes.

Her mother's slight form flitted around the table like a bird, refilling bowls of steaming vegetables and her father's sweet tea, having yet to take her own seat or eat a single bite of the food she had slaved over all day.

"Glad you could take time out of your busy schedule to have dinner with us," her father grumbled as he swirled the meat on his fork into his mashed potatoes and gravy. He was a brawny man, not particularly tall, with a square frame, square face, and large, square hands. A dying breed—he earned his living by the sweat of his brow working oil rigs in the Gulf. The best thing about his job was that he was gone weeks, sometimes months, at a time. The worst thing? He always came home.

As he shoveled food into his mouth, Claire studied with detached interest those square hands, her father's weapon of choice when she, or her mother, had ever gotten out of line. Fortunately for them, they had learned how to stay in line. Actual instances of physical abuse were rare in her memory, but those few had made a lasting impression. To this day, Claire still ducked when someone raised a hand too quickly. Old habits died hard.

Her mother refilled her glass, squeezing her shoulder in encouragement as she passed. Claire glanced appreciatively into her mother's soft doe eyes. They had learned to communicate silently a long time ago. A touch. A look. A gesture. In her father's presence, all three served as communication.

"I'm sorry about missing dinner last Sunday." She decided to try to explain again. "I caught a bug at school—"

"You could have called." The quickness with which his voice cut in, sharp as a whip, made her flinch. Another old habit.

Her mother eased into her chair, a wobbly smile on her lips as she removed her napkin from the table. "It's all right, Mike. I don't mind—"

"Don't contradict me, Kathleen. You always stick up for her. Your precious little angel over there." He jerked his head in Claire's direction.

Her mother dipped her gaze and fiddled with the food on her plate but offered no further comment. She knew better. For that matter, so did Claire. She hadn't perfected the art of invisibility for nothing, after all.

"You spent all day in there." Her father jabbed his knife toward the kitchen, lips smacking around a mouthful of beef. "And Miss High-and-Mighty can't even pick up a phone. But she sure as hell found the time to fix herself up like some kind of tramp."

She recognized the stark misery in her mother's face, the slump to her shoulders. She had seen it almost every day of her childhood. If not for her mother, Claire wouldn't subject herself to these visits.

"Well. We're glad you're feeling better," her mother ventured to say, darting an anxious glance at her husband, as if seeking permission to speak on his behalf.

He studied Claire beneath hooded eyes as he briskly mixed his beans and corn. "Go to the doctor?" he grumbled as though resenting his concern.

"Yes," she answered, not exactly a lie. After all, she had spent that Friday evening in the emergency room. "I got some antibiotics and only missed work on Monday."

Grudgingly, he nodded and returned his attention to his plate. "A woman your age shouldn't be working at all—"

Claire bit her lip. She could recite the rest of this lecture from memory.

"You should be married." He waved his fork at the empty seats surrounding the dining room table. "I should see some goddamn grandkids sitting in these chairs by now. Have you even once dated since that Brian guy jilted—"

"Mike," her mother interrupted, gentle reproof in her voice as her worried gaze darted to Claire.

Her father threw his utensils down on his plate, the loud clatter on her mother's china making her cringe. Leaning back in his chair, he tossed his hands up in the air. "What now, Kathleen? Can't I speak my mind in my own damned house? What is she? Some goddamned piece of crystal that will break if I mention—"

"Stop yelling at her." Claire's words were barely audible, just a puff of air, a whisper of sound as her hand strangled a homemade roll into crumbs. Yet she might as well have shouted. Her mother gasped.

Her father glared at her, the tic that always warned of a dangerous mood jumping wildly at the corner of his left eye. Claire rubbed the edge of her eye as if she felt it herself, as if she could rub it away. Years had passed since she'd seen the tic, but some things remained permanently etched in memory.

"What did you say to me, girl?" He spoke slowly. Precisely.

Something dark and dangerous unfurled in her belly and this time she had no trouble finding her voice. She lifted her chin. "Don't yell at her. I don't like it." Ignoring her mother's swiftly shaking head, Claire continued. "I've never liked it. And I can't imagine she does either."

"You don't like it!" His face turned a deep shade of red as he leaned forward in his chair, pushing his face close to hers. Too close. Her sensitive nose twitched, revolted by the stink of onions on his breath. "Since when does what you like matter in this house?"

A dull roaring started in her ears, increasing in volume as Claire reached for her sweating glass, needing something to hold, to grasp—to stop herself from hauling back and cracking that square jaw of his with her fist.

Only her father didn't know when to quit. Never had.

His eyes raked her with disgust. “No man even wants you. You’re just a dried-up—”

“Mike!” His name flew from her mother’s mouth sharp with reproach. Her hands slapped over her mouth. But too late.

This time her father offered no warning. He lurched from his chair, hand poised high in the air to deliver a slap to her mother.

“No!” The word erupted from Claire’s mouth, an explosion of sound, freezing his hand midair.

His head snapped in her direction, then, for some reason, swiveled to the wall. He lowered his hand and dropped heavily back into his chair, still staring intently at the wall.

Claire followed his gaze, eyeing the large stain marring the burgundy wallpaper. Shards of glass, almost impossible to distinguish from the melting ice cubes, sparkled like diamonds on the floor.

Still, a long moment passed before understanding sank in—before she realized that she had flung her glass of iced tea against the wall. So quickly. So violently. So abruptly she had not even realized she had moved.

Slumped in his seat, her father fixed wide eyes on her like he had never seen her before, like a stranger sat before him and not his daughter. Varying emotions flitted across his face. Shock. Anger. And, she realized with mingled surprise and disgust, a tiny kernel of respect.

“Claire.” Her mother’s voice broke through the roaring in her head as though from far, far away. “Don’t do this.”

“No more,” Claire ground out, wildly shaking her head. “No more. Do you understand, Dad?”

She had hurled the glass instinctively, thoughtlessly, without strategy, but she wouldn't back down. Something inside her wouldn't allow that. Only one thing was definite: she wasn't afraid. Not of him. Not for herself. Maybe for the first time in her life she was totally, finally, unafraid. And perhaps he recognized that because, incredibly, he started to laugh. The noise sounded strange and fragmented.

"Guess I have to think up a new nickname for you. *Mouse* won't fit anymore." He smiled, or tried to, but something other than humor shaped the curve of his mouth.

Staring into his face, Claire recognized what lurked in his eyes. Could smell the stink of it on the air, taste the faintly coppery twang of it. *Fear*. Her father was nothing more than a bully. A scared little boy. Fitting, considering he had raised her to be a scared little girl. Today, however, that girl was nowhere to be found.

"Looks like you got a bit of the old man in you after all," he declared.

His words filled her with rage, snapping the last of her control. Looking down, she noticed the slim, ebony-handled steak knife clutched in her white-knuckled hand. In one swift motion, she flung it into the table directly in front of him with a soft, vibrating thud. Over the shuddering knife, her eyes locked with the man that had cowed and intimidated her since birth.

"I'm nothing like you," she hissed even though the words sounded foolish. Tossing a knife into the table only proved him right. She was no better than he. A bully.

Unclenching her fist, she let her arm drop to her side. Suddenly, she remembered the gun in her pocket, so available, so ready. Her loose fingers twitched at her side, and she knew she had to leave. Immediately. Before she went too far. She shoved back from the table and fled her father's stunned expression and her mother's muffled sobs.

With a numb heart, she strode through the hallway lined with studio-perfect pictures of a model family, pausing when she came abreast of one photograph. She turned and looked at a younger version of herself. She was maybe six. Outfitted in the customary Christmas sweater with her parents on either side of her. Her father gripped her shoulder, his sun-darkened hand twice as large as the pale smudge of her face. Her smile looked fragile, brittle as glass. That scared little girl seemed a lifetime ago.

Shaking her head, Claire removed it from the wall and walked out the front door into the deepening night, not breaking stride when her mother called her name. She paused at the curb where the garbage waited for tomorrow's pickup, the fetid odor seeming to taint the air in streaks of yellow.

Without hesitating, she dropped the picture into one of the cans, stealing a glance at the charcoal sky as she did so. The moon stared down at her, a small slice of white against the starless night. Gideon March's voice floated from memory. *On the next full moon, you will shift.*

Claire shivered in the warm air and slid inside her car, ridiculously relieved to escape the pale orb's watchful gaze. Sighing, she forced herself not to estimate how many days remained until the full moon.

Her gaze drifted to her reflection in the rearview mirror. The silver eyes glowed back at her, mocking, challenging. There was no hiding from them. Or the stranger she had become. She swallowed the lump in her throat. At least she knew the little girl in the photograph. This woman—she didn't know her at all.

Claire stared out at the sea of familiar faces, doing a quick roll check. The students chatted, the drone of conversation comforting in its normalcy, helping her forget that only two days ago she had stabbed a knife into her parents' table, mere inches from her father's nose. Here, in the bright fluorescent glare of her classroom, her world felt familiar again.

"Hey, Miss Morgan!"

Claire looked up from her attendance folder and smiled warmly at Nina, a pretty, bright-eyed girl who had transferred early second semester. "'Morning, Nina."

Nina neared the podium and whispered conspiratorially, "Still looking hot, Miss Morgan. You gotta tell me who does your hair."

Claire smiled, the girl's syrupy sweet breath making her stomach growl. "Come by after school. I've got the business card in my purse." The peal of the first period bell shook the air.

"Okay." Nina hesitated before taking her seat, her perfect white teeth gnawing her bottom lip. "Have you heard from Lenny?"

The question caught Claire off guard. She had convinced herself she was the only one who cared, the only one hoping to glance up and find him sitting in his seat like any other day.

"No, I haven't."

"He didn't show up for his SAT."

"I know," she replied vaguely, inclined to keep Nina from worrying.

"Something's not right, Miss Morgan."

Claire hedged, dropping her gaze and bending the attendance folder in her hands. "I'm sure he will be back. Wait and see."

Her stomach churned at dishing out such garbage. The same garbage Jill Tanners had spewed to her. The same garbage that had ticked Claire off and prompted the ill-fated trip to Lenny's apartment.

"Last time I saw him, he just walked right on by. Like he didn't even see me."

Claire's gaze shot back up, irrational hope hammering in her chest. "You saw him? When?"

"A couple weeks ago. At Woody's. He was with these creepy-looking older guys. He walked past me without even saying hi."

Claire's shoulders slumped. Nina hadn't seen Lenny. Not recently. Unable to think of a suitable reply, she gestured to Nina's desk. "Let's get started."

Nina nodded and took her seat in the front. Claire sighed, sensing Nina's disappointment and feeling she had somehow let her down. Just like Lenny. She pushed thoughts of Lenny aside, sealing him in the far corner of her mind. Finished checking roll, she placed the folder in the pocket outside her door just as Raymond Jackson strolled into the room with his loping gait. He gave her his signature nod, indifferent to his tardiness.

"Raymond, it's Wednesday. Sure you're supposed to be here?" she asked with an edge to her voice. A few of the students chuckled at her uncustomary sarcasm.

Raymond showed up once a week, usually on Friday, to provide weekend party supplies for his clients. She wondered if his *business*—an enterprise of which the faculty and administration were well aware but lacked proof to stop—had brought him here today.

He answered with a shrug as he dropped his six-feet-plus frame into his seat in the back—no backpack, textbook, or writing instruments anywhere on his person.

Pointing to the blackboard, she began reviewing the day's agenda aloud, stopping to glare at the back of the room where Raymond engaged in a lively conversation with the boy in the row across from him.

Her silence finally drew his attention, and he gave her a belligerent glare of his own, lifting both eyebrows in challenge. But even in that glare, his confusion was unmistakable. Claire never bothered him. All year she had ignored his disruptions, finding it easier than confronting him. She had suffered his presence in her room, telling herself it was only once a week. Yet the sight of him lounging lazily at his desk, carrying on a conversation while she tried to teach, made her blood burn.

"What?" he sneered.

"I'm waiting."

"Waiting for what?"

Something snapped inside her and she heard herself say, "Waiting for you to shut up."

The words flew out of her mouth at missile speed.

Dead silence filled the room. The voice of the teacher in the neighboring classroom seemed unnaturally loud through the partition wall. As did the squeaking wheels of the janitor's cart somewhere amid the school's halls.

The other students exchanged looks, some incredulous, some uneasy, all uncertain.

"What'd you say, bitch?" Raymond demanded. The harsh rasp of his voice scratched the air, reverberating over the gentle hum of the air conditioner.

She moved from behind the podium and strode down the narrow aisle with predatory precision, stepping over backpacks and purses without once looking down. Heads swiveled to watch her progress to the back of the room.

Stopping in front of Raymond, an odd rush of warmth filled her as she leaned down. Her skin simmered, heated by the blood coursing beneath. Impossible as it seemed, she felt herself expand, growing larger and taller than her diminutive five feet two. With hard hands, she grasped the edge of his desk. The simulated wood creaked beneath the pressure of her fingers and she felt certain with only a little more force she could splinter the desk with her bare hands.

Lowering her head, she locked eyes with him and watched in satisfaction as the challenge faded and melted from the dark liquid pools. He dropped his gaze to the top of his desk, shrinking in his seat, the plastic chair creaking from the shifting of his weight. His cockiness evaporated on the air like a wisp of smoke.

His earlier words still ringing in her ears, she growled, "Care to repeat yourself?"

He shook his head, still avoiding her gaze. She reveled in his fear, could smell it, could taste it even, its warm, coppery sweetness flooding her mouth and filling her with a strange hunger. The hunger to hurt.

And that made her stop.

As if burned, she released the desk and looked around at the faces of her students. She read the shock in their eyes and bile rose thick in her throat. Her anger had moved beyond the walls of her parents' house. Today she had an entire audience to witness her behavior. And this time, she hadn't wanted to stop. She had wanted to push further, harder. *Wanted to hurt.*

Digging deep, she fumbled to recover the old, familiar Claire. The orderly, unassuming woman buried somewhere deep inside. The little girl with limp curls in her Christmas sweater. Where had she gone? And most important, how could she get her back?

In a crisp, businesslike tone she instructed the class, "Open your books to page four seventy-six."

Claire sensed Nina's approach, smelled the sweetness of her vanilla perfume even before she felt the slight pressure on her shoulder.

"Miss Morgan?"

She lifted her head from the desk located at the back of the room, where she had collapsed after the student exodus following the seventh period bell. Claire ran her hands over her face tiredly.

Nina stared down at her, the smooth caramel skin of her brow creased in worry. "It's all right." Her fingers flexed on Claire's shoulder in a comforting squeeze. "About time someone showed that jerk up."

Claire briefly closed her eyes and shook her head, not bothering to voice her whirling thoughts. Nina was just a kid, a student. She had no concept of a teacher's duty to treat all students with respect despite how they treated you. And it wasn't Claire's place to burden her with a lesson on professional responsibility.

She stood, the legs of her chair scraping the linoleum floor, chafing her already frayed nerves. "It's after four. What are you still doing here?"

Hurt flickered across the girl's expressive face, and Claire instantly regretted her sharpness. She had been a teacher for almost ten years now, and in that time certain students had undeniably touched her heart. Every year there were a special few, ones she never forgot—ones like Nina who sat forward in their seats with shining eyes, hungry to learn. Students like her were a gift and didn't deserve coldness, even if Claire only craved solitude.

"I had dance practice," she said in a small, wounded voice.

"Oh." Claire glanced down at the shiny purple tights covering Nina's slim legs. Softening her tone, she asked, "Aren't you going to miss the late bus?"

"I got a ride waiting," she replied, her deep brown eyes studying Claire.

"Hello, hello," Maggie chirped as she strolled into the

room, coffee cup in hand. Claire knew it had to be her twelfth cup of the day. Coffee was the only thing that kept her friend going until she could escape work for a cigarette.

Despite her cheerful tone, her eyes appeared guarded and uncertain as they assessed Claire. Nodding briefly to Nina, the concern in her probing gaze was unmistakable. Maggie knew about today. No surprise. Students talked and Maggie had a good rapport with the kids.

Nina picked up her backpack where she had dropped it on the floor. "I'll see ya later, Miss Morgan."

" 'Bye, Nina."

Maggie waited until the girl left before asking quietly, "You okay?"

"Yes," Claire lied. "Fine."

Clasping both hands around her mug, Maggie gently announced, "I heard about today."

"Figured you had."

"Want to talk about it?"

Claire forced a smile and began straightening the papers on her desk. "Nope."

"Hey, we all have those days. One kid goes too far, says the wrong thing, and bang." Maggie snapped her fingers. "It happens to the best of us."

"Right." Claire snapped the day's homework assignment she needed to grade with a large binder clip.

"Only—"

Claire looked up, hearing Maggie's hesitation.

With a small, apologetic smile, Maggie admitted, "*You* never have those days." Sighing, she shook her head and stared into her cup before looking back up. "At least, never before." Her voice softened to ask, "What's going on, Claire?"

Claire sank into her chair and ran her hands over her face. "I don't know, Maggie. I don't know what's wrong with me."

"Did you really face off with Raymond Jackson?"

Claire released a humorless crack of laughter. "Yeah, I did."

Maggie lowered herself into the desk nearest Claire's. "You think that was smart?"

What could Claire say to that? How could she explain that she hadn't stopped to think at all? Just acted. Folding her hands neatly in front of her, she went for honesty. "No."

"A kid like that might want a little payback, Claire. He's gotta save face."

Oddly enough, that didn't worry Claire. Not like it should have. She wasn't at all concerned about her own safety. What worried her was how *she* would react if he did challenge her.

"School will be out soon," Maggie murmured. "You got enough days saved up. Maybe you should take a leave. Come back in the fall. Refreshed."

Claire studied her friend's face before saying, "You think I should?"

"Yes." Maggie nodded slowly. "I do."

Claire drew a deep breath.

A day like today couldn't be repeated. Her students deserved better than a teacher who could no longer control her temper. Snapping at students, taking on bullies . . . all without conscious thought. A stranger to herself, what guarantee did she have that it wouldn't happen again? She couldn't take the risk. Her job required patience and a cool head. Two things she sorely lacked lately.

Today marked the first time in her career she had incited fear in a student. The fright in Raymond Jackson's face replayed itself in her mind like a terrible car crash that she couldn't shake.

She swiped at eyes that burned with unshed tears, hating to admit that she was so changed, that something was wrong with her, that maybe there was something to the ravings of Gideon March after all. That maybe the guy wasn't totally crazy. The possibility rattled her. Because if he wasn't crazy, then neither was her attraction to him.

Chapter Seven

Even the most aggressive dog knows when to turn tail and run.

—*Man's Best Friend: An Essential Guide to Dogs*

Claire slid her key into the lock of her apartment door with practiced speed. In a flash, she was inside, the hard feel of the door at her back reassuring her, closing her off from the rest of the world, sealing her in. Her racing heart steadied. But not by much.

She hadn't seen him, but she felt him, sensed him the whole drive home. Gideon March was close. Her nostrils flared, convinced she smelled the woodsy musk of him. But that was impossible. How could she smell the man when she could not even see him?

Whether he was out there or not, her gut told her she wasn't rid of him. Too many days had passed since their last run-in.

Pushing off the door, she hurried into her bedroom and pulled her suitcase from beneath the bed. Shedding her work clothes, she slid on shorts and a T-shirt. Stuffing garments into her suitcase, she marveled at her impulsive actions, replaying the phone conversation with her mother moments before. As unpleasant as it had been, she had endured her mother's fussing. When she explained she was taking a leave of absence from work, her mother supported the idea and readily agreed to Claire's request to stay at the family lake house.

As she grabbed the needed toiletries off the bathroom counter, she caught a glimpse of her reflection in the dresser mirror and jumped, for a second thinking a stranger stood there.

Wild, honey-hued hair. Flushed cheeks. Strange, glowing eyes. It would take time to get accustomed to the new Claire. Both inside and out. Ready to step out of the shadows, to explore her new self, she slammed her suitcase shut and zipped the top. She was almost out the door when she remembered the cat.

"Molly!" Dropping her suitcase, her gaze scanned the living room. "Here, kitty, kitty, kitty!" No response. Not surprising. Normally affectionate, the tabby had treated her with uncharacteristic hostility lately and spent most of her time hidden away.

Dropping to her hands and knees, Claire peered beneath the bed. As she suspected, her cat glared back with unblinking eyes, baring its fangs in a warning hiss.

"Come on, Molly. Enough. We gotta get out of here."

The tabby responded with another hiss. She tried the serene, soothing voice she used to reason with an obstinate student—well, the voice she formerly used. "You can't stay here. You'll starve. I don't know when I'll be back."

Reaching beneath the bed, she grabbed Molly's collar

to drag her out. A pair of sharp fangs sank into her hand. Claire cried out and let go. Sitting back, she stared at the bite mark on her hand, a haze of red clouding her vision. Rage consumed her, blocking out all reason. Before she knew it, she'd wedged herself back under the bed, her curses filling the air, intent only on wringing that cat's neck.

She was crammed halfway under the bed when his voice penetrated her haze of rage.

"Cats don't care for canines."

With a screech, she wiggled out from under the bed. Once free, she toppled to her side and looked up at his towering figure. Heart hammering, she eyed the man filling her bedroom doorway, Molly forgotten.

Gideon leaned against the doorjamb, arms crossed over his broad chest. With his mussed hair and several days' growth of beard shadowing his jaw, he looked like he hadn't slept in a week.

"How do you keep getting in here?"

He thumbed behind him, the gesture somehow weary. "Sliding glass door. Easy to jimmy. Miss me?"

"No," she snapped, her lips—and other places—suddenly tingling in memory, refuting her words.

His gaze shifted to the suitcase on the floor. "Going somewhere?"

"No."

"I can't let you leave." His words rang ominously. His vow to kill her if she didn't cooperate echoed in her mind.

He stepped fully into the room, his shadow falling over her. His pale gaze slid over her bare legs splayed on the carpet. The air thickened. A ripple of awareness crossed between them and she watched the dark centers of his eyes dilate. The pulse at his neck beat faster. Their gazes locked. A loud drumbeat filled her ears. *His heart.* She knew this, just as she knew it was impossible to hear the pounding of his heart across a few feet. And yet she somehow did.

He advanced until he stood between her ankles. His eyes glowed green fire down at her. He extended a hand. She hesitated a moment before placing her fingers in the warm grasp of his. He pulled her up in one smooth motion, bringing her flush against him, flattening her breasts into his chest. Her nipples hardened, throbbing against the hard wall of him. The corners of his mouth lifted in a knowing smile. Her heart contracted at the sexy curve of his mouth, wanting, craving it on her own, remembering the taste of him.

Cocking an eyebrow, he wrapped one arm around her waist, holding her to him by the small of her back.

"You're hot for it," he mused, his voice a husky rumble.

She shook her head in fierce denial, her hair brushing her cheeks in soft strokes.

"No?" His hand slid around her waist, inching up her stomach and ribs, singeing her skin through the thin cotton of her shirt. Warm fingers closed unerringly over one nipple, testing, measuring, caressing the distended tip through her shirt and bra. She choked back a sob as his fingers played with her, his touch growing firmer until he was rolling and twisting the aroused peak between thumb and forefinger.

"What about now?" he rasped.

Mouth watering, she shook her head, refusing to surrender even if her body already had.

"No?" His hand dropped from her breast. She bit her lip to stop her cry of disappointment.

In one deft move, he popped the button free on her shorts and unzipped her. The backs of his fingers brushed her navel, scorching like fire as he delved inside her panties, his touch swift, sure, taking. He probed between her curls, playing with her, brushing the spot hidden within the folds of her sex. She jerked at the contact, moaning, and parted her legs wider.

He groaned, dipping his head close, long strands of dark blond hair brushing her face. Finding her clitoris, he rolled it between his fingers, exerting enough pressure to make her shudder against his hand.

"Definitely hot for it." He thrust a finger deep inside her. Her head fell back, a silent scream lodged in her throat.

"God, you're tight," he muttered, easing in a second finger, stretching her, the pleasure a sweet pain that built the tension inside her.

"See." His voice rolled over her, drugging, hypnotic. "You don't want to go anywhere."

His words sunk into her brain, a wash of cold where there had been nothing but heat before. She jerked away, his hand slipping from her gaping shorts. The backs of her knees bumped the bed, stopping her from total retreat.

The hand that had caressed her fell limply to his side. For several moments she could only stare at those fingers that had wreaked total havoc on her, longing for them to do so again. Horrified at herself, at her reaction to him, she squeezed her eyes in one tight blink. *Get a grip, Claire.*

"I can't let you leave," he repeated, regarding her with grim resolve, reminding her that while she might have been caught up in her body's reaction, he was still a nutcase who believed she was a werewolf.

Instinct gave way then.

Her leg lashed out with lightning speed, striking him directly between his legs. He hit the ground like a slab of stone. Snatching hold of her suitcase, she ran for the door, not allowing herself a moment of regret.

His groan reverberated on the air and she winced, wondering if shooting him would not have perhaps been more merciful.

Gideon downed the last of the tepid 7-Eleven coffee and wadded the paper cup into a ball. With a curse, he tossed it to the passenger floorboard.

Where the hell was she?

When he got his hands on her . . .

It was his own damn fault, he reminded himself. He let his guard down, forgot what she was. Her sexuality overwhelmed him. Made him forget everything save burying himself in her body. Her lycan instincts were no less at her disposal just because she was unaware of their existence. Her bolting-fast reflexes and powerful kick could attest to that—as did four packs of ice and half a bottle of extra-strength Tylenol.

It had taken him a good while to pick himself off her bedroom floor. Good thing NODEAL agents weren't the settle-down-start-a-family types because he seriously doubted his future ability to father children.

It had been one week since he had picked himself up off Claire's bedroom floor. Panic threatened to swallow him whole at the prospect of not finding her again. That he might have set a lycan loose on the population made him slightly ill. Clearly, this was a lesson. And physically painful as far as lessons went. He should have destroyed her that first night. He should have said something when Cooper placed him on call—five days wasted on cleanup duty when he could have been tracking the lycan who had infected Lenny.

But he hadn't expected her to run, had assumed to find her still in denial, going about her life in blissful ignorance.

He thumped the steering wheel with his fist. That first night had been ideal. Quick. Neat. Painless. Why didn't he pull the trigger then instead of reholstering his gun and going against everything he believed in, everything he had been taught? In one simple act, he had turned his back on the very code that had been drilled into him. The code that he lived and killed by.

Destroy them at any cost.

Sitting outside her apartment, he told himself this wasn't a useless venture. Someone would have to see to the cat she had left behind. She hadn't left out enough food, and he knew enough about Claire to know that she was too responsible to forget about her cat.

Gideon had no idea if her parents lived in the area. It

would take him the better part of a year to contact every Morgan in the greater Houston area. And time was the thing he needed most. Aside from Claire Morgan.

In minutes Gideon could have her complete file in his hands. But at what cost?

Typing her name into NODEAL's database would wave a red flag for Cooper. If Gideon ran a search on her name, she would automatically be listed on the end-of-day activity report Cooper reviewed. Then he'd have some explaining to do. He wasn't ready to admit that his own stupidity had cost him a lycan. Nor was he about to sic Cooper on her. If she had to die, he would take care of it. It was only right. She was his responsibility.

"Shit," he swore under his breath. The new moon had come and gone. Time was running out. If he didn't find her soon, he'd have no choice but to access the database.

From day one, everything had gone wrong. He could see that now. His first mistake had been identifying with the target, connecting with her. He had let her become more than a nameless animal. He had gotten a glimpse into Claire Morgan's life. A life, for whatever reason, that provoked memories of his parents and disturbing *what if* questions. She wasn't like the others. That much he accepted. Otherwise, she would already be dead.

And now she had bolted like a rabbit into the brush. Too late now, but he wished he had taken more aggressive measures to convince her. If he got a second chance he wouldn't screw it up, he would—

He sat up alert in his seat as a woman parked in front of Claire's apartment and stepped out of her Ford Ranger. She rifled through her purse as she shut the door with her hip. She was small, like Claire, and carried herself with a quiet timidity. He caught a glimpse of her profile and instantly recognized her from the photos on Claire's walls. The mother.

He hopped out of the Jeep and followed her to the door of the apartment, where she sorted through a ring of keys.

"Hello there," he greeted, making his presence known.

With a squeak, she jumped and dropped the keys. He bent and picked them up, pasting on his most charming smile. He knew women appreciated his looks, never having a problem gaining female companionship when the need arose. But those were only temporary diversions. An agent's life didn't allow for commitments. Still, he thought it appropriate to exercise some of that charm right now.

"Sorry, ma'am. Didn't mean to startle you." He looked beyond her to the door, striving for a guileless expression. "Are you a friend of Claire's?"

"I'm her mother."

"Really?" Faking a look of shock, he went for the kill. "I thought maybe you worked together. You don't look old enough to be her mother."

Mrs. Morgan blushed, her hands fluttering self-consciously to her frosted hair.

He continued in a smooth voice. "I dropped by to see if Claire wanted to go to lunch." He shrugged, a gesture meant to illustrate both his disappointment and his understanding if this was to be a day reserved for the two of them.

Mrs. Morgan's gaze roamed his face and body appreciatively. "You and Claire are dating?" she asked with undisguised shock.

Had she seen her daughter lately? Yet he couldn't help wondering how much of that magnetism was truly Claire and how much belonged to her lycan blood. The way her gaze devoured him, the way her body moved—if he didn't get to her quick she'd probably end up pregnant. The lycan instinct to seek a mate and procreate demanded it. She wouldn't even know what drove her. But he did. He did, and he needed to stop her before her trouble multiplied. Literally.

"Well, yes, ma'am. You could say that."

"Claire never mentioned—" Mrs. Morgan stopped abruptly, her gaze lowering. "But she wouldn't. My daughter's very private. Mike would just pester her to bring you home for dinner."

And this, he judged by her nervous little laugh, was something both women hoped to avoid.

"I'd love to come over for dinner." Recalling the message from Claire's machine, he added, "I've heard you make a mean pot roast."

"Oh," she laughed and glanced to the door as if it could speak on Claire's behalf. "We'd be thrilled to have you over—that is if it's okay with Claire."

"It might be sooner than you think," Gideon replied, feeling only a twinge of guilt at the hopeful gleam entering Claire's mother's eyes. He could almost see the wedding plans formulating in her head.

"Wonderful. I'll look forward to it." She looked down at the keys in her hand as if suddenly remembering her purpose. "I'm here to get Molly. Claire's at our lake house." Her brow wrinkled. "You didn't know that?"

He made a display of slapping his forehead. "Oh, that's right."

She smiled tentatively, and he wondered if it struck her as odd that an alleged boyfriend didn't remember when his girlfriend went out of town. It certainly would send a red flag up in his face. That Mrs. Morgan didn't possess a discerning nature was fortunate for him.

"Yes, she said she wanted to get away for a bit, and we hardly ever use the place. I sometimes wonder why we even bought it." She shrugged and unlocked the door. "Just glad to see it get some use."

"Sure." He nodded, forcing himself not to ask which lake.

"Well, it was nice meeting you." Mrs. Morgan hovered in the doorway. "I hope Claire brings you around soon."

"Me, too," he murmured, trying to keep the anxiousness from his voice. He had a lead, and as soon as Claire's mother left he could work on developing that lead.

He tossed out a quick good-bye and waited impatiently in his Jeep until Mrs. Morgan stepped back out of the apartment with Molly tucked in her arms. The instant she exited the parking lot he broke in to Claire's apartment by way of the sliding glass door.

This time he inspected her apartment carefully, with deliberation—not the idle inspection of that first night, when he broke inside to rid the world of another lycan menace.

He knew what to look for this time. Knowing the address wouldn't be plastered to her wall, he started with her journal. Finding no mention of the lake house in the pages of painstakingly neat handwriting, he dug through drawers as immaculate and organized as the rest of her apartment. He eventually pulled a floral print box from beneath the bed. Inside he found photo albums. Sitting on the floor, he browsed through pictures, catching himself smiling at Claire in different stages of life. His smile slipped when he came to a teenage Claire on a boat, looking distinctly uncomfortable with a fishing pole in her hands and her father looking on with a critical expression.

He turned the page, the plastic crackling in the silent apartment. His heart skipped when he came to the photo he'd been waiting for. Claire, her parents, and an elderly couple—grandparents, he guessed from their resemblance to her father—posed in front of a restaurant, the name of which was boldly displayed above their heads. Riverside Bar and Grill. He dropped the album, launched himself into her desk, and turned on her computer, tapping his thighs impatiently until the screen lit up. In minutes, he had a list of Riverside Bar and Grill restaurants before him. He narrowed his search to the state of Texas and arrived at two restaurants. One in downtown San Antonio on the Riverwalk and another located in Canyon Lake. Last he heard there weren't any lake houses along the Riverwalk.

For the first time in days, the knot in his chest loosened. A grim smile spread across his face. One more search and he had the address of one Michael Morgan, Canyon Lake, Texas.

"Claire, baby," he vowed, slipping out of her apartment, an excited thrill coursing through him, "I'm coming for you."

Chapter Eight

Even trained dogs need instruction.

—*Man's Best Friend:*
An Essential Guide to Dogs

Arms stuffed with grocery bags, Claire kicked the door shut and weaved her way into the small kitchen. After a morning idly strolling antique stores and then grocery shopping, she had almost convinced herself that everything was normal, that she was on a holiday. Almost.

Unpacking her groceries, she paused to rip open the expensive deli cheese, roll a slice, and take a bite. Her tongue savored the woody flavor as she continued putting her hoard of food into the refrigerator. The blinking red light on the answering machine caught her eye. She punched play and reached for the can of Reddi-wip. Swallowing her last bite of cheese, she tilted her head back, opened her mouth wide, and squirted the luscious whipped cream onto her tongue.

Her mother's voice filled the air, assuring her that Molly was safe and sound. Claire pulled a face at the machine. Disloyal cat. "Should have bought a dog," Claire mumbled, crouching down to store the fresh vegetables in the bottom drawer, fending off feelings of resentment over her cat's betrayal.

" . . . Oh, and I bumped into your friend, Gideon. Such a nice young man, very handsome . . ."

Claire stood so fast her head smacked against the freezer door she had left swinging open.

Rubbing the top of her head, she scowled at the machine, her unease exploding into full panic as her mother went on to say, "I told him you should bring him to dinner when you get back from the lake. . . ."

With her heart in her throat, Claire spun around, desperate to put as much distance between herself and the cabin as possible. Only she collided into a wall. A wall that hadn't been there a moment before.

With a cry, she staggered back, crashing into the open refrigerator door. The bottles and jars lining the door rattled noisily. Had she been small enough, she would have crawled inside the refrigerator and closed the door. But she wasn't. She had nowhere to run. Her eyes lifted and settled on a furious Gideon March.

He twirled a pair of handcuffs on his index finger and took a menacing step forward. "You have no idea how much trouble you've put me through."

Obviously not enough. He had found her. No thanks to her mother.

She darted past him. Hard fingers caught the ends of her hair and gave a yank. Arms flailing, she careened into that familiar wall of muscle. His arms came up to lock around her, squeezing her ribs until she couldn't draw air. Even panicked, she was conscious of the way her breasts rose and fell on top of his forearm, conscious of how heavy and achy they suddenly felt, of how her nipples hardened. The air deepened into shadows of hazy red and purple, mirroring her varying emotions—rage, fear, excitement.

He pressed his mouth close to her ear and growled in a voice that sent shivers down her spine, "We're through talking."

Oh God. He's here to kill me.

Guided by instinct, she flung her head back, crashing it against his chin. With a grunt of pain, he loosened his hold. She broke free and bolted, snatching her purse from a wall hook by the door.

Her hand barely grazed the doorknob before her feet flew out from under her. One moment she was airborne, the next flat on her back—every bone in her body painfully jarred. Dazed, she saw a flash of silver overhead and remembered what had dangled from his hands. Handcuffs. Crouching over her, he grabbed one of her wrists with the cuffs poised in the air, ready to shackle her.

"No!" Her leg shot out, kicking him in the shin, bringing him toppling down on top of her, washing her in the male scent of him. She concentrated on keeping her hands away from those cuffs, concentrated on ignoring the wild need pumping through her bloodstream.

Cursing, he caught one of her flying hands and chased after the other one. An ache throbbed at the center of her thighs. The proximity of his body, the male musk of him, even his rough handling, excited her. *He excited her*. God, she was demented. Or sick.

Pinning both her wrists above her head, he flattened his body along the length of hers. "Enough," he barked.

Nose to nose, they glared at each other, hot breaths mingling, his smell overwhelming her, his hammering heart loud between them.

"Stop looking at me like that," he warned, his green eyes wild. The catch in his voice sent a tremor through her body.

Her breath came in short, rhythmic spurts, each one thrusting her breasts harder against his chest, pressing the hard peaks into his solidness. "Like what?"

"Like you wanna fuck."

Heat suffused her face, rushing through her entire body like a firestorm. Her mouth sagged open. His accusation was ridiculous, absurd, impossible.

"Right," she choked out, trying for sarcasm but her reply sounded more like agreement to her ears.

But it was too late. The damage was done, the fuse lit from the mental image his coarse language inspired. An image she couldn't shake. An image so vivid she wanted—no, needed to make it a reality.

Thrusting her face forward the last inch separating them, she kissed him like a woman starved. She kissed him with a savagery that shocked her. He was still for only a second before surrendering and kissing her back. Releasing her wrists, he grabbed hold of her face and angled her for his slanting mouth. The feel of those large hands on her face, his calluses rasping her cheeks, awakened a hidden Claire, a Claire that felt feminine and desired. Bold and hungry.

Grabbing his shoulders with both hands, she strained

against him, moaning into his mouth. His tongue slid against hers, stoking the inferno inside her even higher.

Desperate, driven by desire, she ran her hands down his back. Tongue parrying with his, she dropped her hands to clutch him, hating the denim that stopped her from feeling the texture of his skin.

Spreading her legs, she let him settle his weight between her thighs, moaning softly into his mouth as he rubbed and ground his hardness against her.

He tore his lips from hers to drag his mouth down her neck. His teeth clamped gently on her nipple through her shirt. She shrieked, bucking against him. Through the thin cotton of her shirt he continued to bite and suck her nipples into turgid pebbles, drawing each deep into his mouth. She brought her hands to his head, tangling them in the long, thick strands of hair. The roll of his tongue over the wet cotton created a delicious friction, drawing mewling, animal-like cries from deep in her throat.

Wild for the taste of him, she shoved at his chest and rolled him over, straddling him with a strength and speed that surprised even her. Something other than desire flickered in his gaze as he looked up at her, but she did not give him—or herself—time to think. Scooting low on his hips, she ran her hands down his chest to the waistband of his jeans. Unzipping him, she found him through the opening in his boxers. Closing her hand around the hard length of him, she gently squeezed. The blood burned through her veins as he pulsed in her hand. She traced her thumb over the silken tip of him, rubbing the bead of moisture that appeared there.

Groaning, he clamped hard hands around her arms and rolled her under him. Slamming his mouth over hers, he kissed her with a savagery that should have shocked her. A growl swelled deep from her throat. He thrust himself against her, driving her into the floor.

Panting, she tore her lips from his. "Please," she begged, writhing beneath him.

She was lost. Mindless. She had to have him. Now. On the floor. She didn't care as long as he was inside her.

"I know," he murmured, hands sliding down her arms to her wrists in an almost gentle hold.

The soft, grinding click did not immediately register. Not until he pulled back. Not until it was too late.

Staring up at him, she blinked in bewilderment, bereft without his hands and mouth on her.

Then it hit her.

"You bastard!"

She tugged her wrists apart, but the steel handcuffs imprisoned her hands together. Fury exploded inside her—and with it an irrational sense of betrayal. He hadn't wanted her at all. Her heart clenched in pain. He had only wanted to distract her. So he could kill her. With a bellow of rage she swung her cuffed wrists toward his head with all the strength she possessed and made contact with a satisfying whack.

Flat on her belly, cuffed to the leg of her mother's antique woodstove, Claire wondered why he hadn't simply killed her. Especially after the murderous look he gave her after she struck him.

Cold steel handcuffs chafed her wrists and she coughed

up dust balls with every inhalation. She cringed at her once white T-shirt, covered in grime from the linoleum floor. Dropping her forehead to the floor, she wished she'd had the guts to shoot him back at her apartment when she had had the chance. Now it was too late. She had missed her chance, and now it appeared he would carry out his threat and kill her.

Heavy footsteps signaled Gideon's return from the bathroom. Craning her neck, she readied her glare. He came into view, dabbing what appeared to be wet toilet paper on the nasty gash above his eyebrow.

Her nostrils quivered as a warm coppery scent assailed her. Her mouth watered and a strange sensation, much like desire, spiraled through her as her gaze narrowed on the dark crimson trickling slowly from the gash on his forehead.

"Hurt much?" She struggled for a bland tone.

"Yeah." He shrugged, his shoulder muscles rippling against the thin cotton of his T-shirt. "Probably needs stitches."

"Good," she replied, unable to suppress her anger.

He scowled, tossed the wad of toilet paper onto the table still holding the weight of several bags of groceries, and planted both hands on lean hips. "Comfortable?"

"No." She jiggled the cuffs for emphasis.

"Good," he returned, tit for tat.

"Look, these are hurting my wrists—"

"Then stop tugging," he advised, looming over her. From her prone position, she felt like an ant at his feet.

Claire couldn't help pressing herself deeper into the

floor. "If you're going to kill me, just get it over with." Her lips quivered despite the brave words.

"There are worse things than death," he replied enigmatically.

She went still, trying to imagine what he could possibly be implying. Her imaginings made her blood run cold. Did he intend to torture her first?

"Get that look off your face. I'm not going to kill you." His soft sigh sounded impatient to her ears and Claire wasn't too sure if his impatience was directed at her or himself.

She eyed him suspiciously, unconvinced. "Then how about taking these off? You can't keep me cuffed to the stove forever."

"You're coming into your strength." He shook his head as if this were a great shame and pointed at the wound above his eyebrow. "You nearly knocked me out. I can't trust you. At least not until you're convinced—"

"I'm not strong. Really." Claire beat her head on the gritty linoleum, no longer caring how dirty the floor was. "I was afraid. It was just an adrenaline rush."

He snorted in clear disagreement. "I'm out of options. There's only one thing left to do."

The hair at the back of her neck prickled. She didn't like the sound of that. Lifting her head, she watched warily as he moved back into the bathroom, out of view.

"W-where are you going?" she stammered, straining her neck to catch a glimpse of him.

He emerged from the bathroom holding his holstered gun. At the smooth sound of the gun sliding from its leather home, her throat constricted.

He took aim.

"No," she choked, the word weak and strangled as she struggled to sit up despite the uncomfortable pull on her arms.

"I didn't want it to come to this." His lips thinned into an unforgiving line. Hard malachite-green eyes looked down at her, and she knew hope was useless. "It'll be quick," he promised.

Jamming her eyes shut, she tried to shrink into the smallest ball possible in anticipation—

The gun didn't explode in her ears. Not like in the movies. A soft zing stabbed the air. At first, she felt only pressure. No pain. Claire opened one eye. Then the other. Gideon stood in the same spot, observing her with mild interest as he unscrewed the silencer.

Then came the pain, washing over her in undulating waves of hot, then cold. Bracing herself, she sucked in a breath and looked down. Blood soaked the front of her shirt, making it impossible to tell exactly where she had been hit. So much blood. The coppery scent overwhelmed her.

"Oh God," she wailed, turning accusing eyes on him. "You really shot me."

Only moments ago she had kissed him, drank passion from his lips, his body, reveled in the feel of his callused hands on her face. Hands that had now delivered her death. The betrayal hurt more than the hole in her chest. Which only made her a fool since she had known he was dangerous from the first moment they met and failed to do anything about it. She glanced back down at the blood spreading across her shirt like an orchid in bloom and cursed her stupidity. Why hadn't she gone to the cops? Or used her gun?

But she knew the answer. She hadn't truly believed him dangerous. In spite of everything, something about him had always struck her as . . . reasonable. Not a killer.

"You really shot me," she whispered.

He nodded.

Tears blurred her vision.

"Sorry." He nodded again, looking only faintly apologetic. "It'll be over soon."

She strained against the cuffs, overcome with the need to free herself and staunch the wound.

"Uncuff me! Let me at least die with my hands free."

"You're not dying," he said a touch impatiently.

"It burns," she groaned, even as the burning sensation seemed to ebb. Numbness was setting in. Death must be near.

"It's the healing sensation."

Claire blinked several times. "What?"

"Your cells are regenerating."

For a moment, she allowed herself to hope, but then concluded this must be part of his plan to torture her before she died. No way could she survive a chest shot. She looked away, dismissing him, having no wish to stare into the eyes of her killer as she drew her final breath.

"Look." He crouched down next to her and pulled her shirt up. Horrified at the mutilated flesh she was sure to see, she squirmed away.

"Stop wiggling." He yanked her shirt higher. "See?"

Claire couldn't resist looking.

Gideon swept his hand over her belly and ribs, wiping the blood away. Something clattered to the floor with a ping. She stared at her torso. To her astonishment, no gaping hole stared back.

"See, it already sealed itself." Picking up whatever fell to the floor, he displayed a small, crushed piece of metal between his thumb and forefinger. "Now if this had been silver, we wouldn't be having this conversation. You'd be dead."

"My God." Her eyes focused on the bloody bullet, and her eyes finally accepted what her mind could not.

Gideon unlocked her handcuffs. Claire's hands roamed over her chest and stomach. She felt nothing beyond the slipperiness of blood.

"I'm not shot." She looked back at the bullet, undisputable evidence.

His lips twisted into a semblance of a smile. "Oh, you were shot. You're just not dead."

Tearing her gaze from that tiny chunk of metal, she searched his face, her eyes scanning every line, every nuance, missing nothing. She suddenly saw him for what he was. Sane. "Tell me. Tell me everything."

He nodded slowly. "Get cleaned up first."

On unsteady legs, she moved to her suitcase. Her hands shook as she rummaged for clean clothes. With her mind reeling, the simple act took far longer than it should have. Once alone in the bathroom, she took a moment to lean against the door and let herself shake at will. She deliberately avoided looking in the mirror as she stripped, unwilling to look at her eyes now that she understood the reality behind them.

Standing under the showerhead, she tilted her head

back and let the water pelt her face, thinking over everything Gideon had told her, everything she had once refused to believe yet now knew to be true.

Lenny was truly dead. She couldn't pretend otherwise anymore. Yet she couldn't blame Gideon for killing him. If he hadn't, she would be dead. Still, she gave in to the grief, to the tears, letting them disappear in a rush of water down the drain. She told herself that once she stepped out of the shower she wouldn't waste another moment to tears. Lenny was gone, but she was still here, and she needed to figure a way out of this nightmare.

Shutting off the water, she stepped from the shower. As she wrapped herself in a towel, her gaze slid to the mirror, to the stranger staring back, pewter eyes gleaming with a hunger that she now understood.

Without thinking, her hand snatched up the first thing it could find—a small vase of dried flowers on the back of the toilet—and let it fly. The mirror shattered with a loud crash. Shards of vase and glass rained down on the counter and floor. Still, those lycan eyes were visible, distorted through the fractured mirror. The eyes of a beast, mocking, laughing at her display of pique.

"No," she raged, wanting to gouge them from her face.

Her hand closed around the ceramic toothbrush holder just as Gideon burst into the bathroom. He caught her arm before she could let it fly.

Prying the toothbrush holder from her clenched fist, he tugged her away, his grip warm and firm on her arm. Shards of glass cut into the bottoms of her feet and she winced, stumbling against his chest.

Gideon looked down. "Damn," he muttered, sweeping

her into his arms and carrying her out of the bathroom. Claire soon found herself on the bed, her feet propped in Gideon's lap as he plucked glass from the soles of her feet, his hands surprisingly gentle.

She watched him silently for a moment before asking, "Why are you doing this?"

His brow creased as he concentrated on her feet. "You might be a lycan, but it's still gonna hurt to walk around with glass in your feet."

Claire wet her lips. "I mean, why are you helping me?"

He looked up, studying her for a moment before returning to his task. "We'll head back to town today. We don't have a lot of time, so you're going to have to help. I need to know everything about Lenny. Family, friends, where he liked to hang out. There's a good chance he knew the lycan who infected him, so we'll start by retracing his movements of the last month."

Claire considered him for a moment before nodding. He was helping her, trying to stop her from turning into a bloodthirsty monster. A killer. She shut her eyes and gave her head a slow shake. That was all that mattered.

Opening her eyes again, she asked, "What happens when we find the one who infected Lenny?"

"I'll kill him." He said it so simply, like he killed all the time, and it was then that Claire finally accepted that he did. All except her, a small voice in the back of her mind reminded her.

"After you kill him, the curse will be broken."

At this, Gideon hesitated, his hand hovering over her foot. "If he's the alpha, yes."

"Alpha?"

"Each pack has one alpha and every lycan can be traced back to that alpha, either through birth or infection."

"So if you kill the alpha, the rest of the pack will become human again?"

"No." His eyes cut directly to hers. "Only those who aren't damned." Lowering his head to examine her foot closer, he explained, "If you kill and feed, you're damned. It doesn't matter if your alpha is killed or not. The curse can't be broken after you've fed. There's no going back after that."

Claire shook her head. "What if we can't find Lenny's alpha?"

"You'll shift on the next full moon. And you'll kill."

Claire sat motionless, too horrified to even flinch as he plucked a chunk of glass buried deep in the arch of her foot. His words rolled over her, too horrible to believe. Except she was past denial.

"Even if I don't want to?" she asked, trying to keep the desperation she felt from rising in her voice.

"Lycan instinct is too powerful. You won't have a choice."

Gideon slid her feet from his lap, his eyes locking with hers in a silent message. *And neither will I.*

Claire nodded. The words hadn't been spoken aloud but she understood. She understood that the man who had saved her life in a dark alley might very well become her executioner. Gideon March would not spare her life twice.

Gideon buried his hand in his pocket, rolling the silver bullet between his thumb and forefinger. The bullet he had originally planned for her.

He had tracked her down intending to end it once and for all. His lips twisted wryly. That he had nearly taken her on the floor only confirmed in his mind that he had gotten way too involved with his target. He had lost all objectivity. Time was running short and she was a ticking time bomb.

Only face to face with her, he couldn't go through with it. Unbelievable. After all the trouble she put him through, he couldn't do it. At least not yet.

He watched her collect her things from around the cabin. Her movements were quick, purposeful. Her feet padded silently over the floor, all sign of injury gone. She clearly didn't realize what a mess her feet had been. The average person would have needed stitches. He grunted, sliding his hand out of his pocket. Hell, she took a bullet in the chest. The average person would be dead. He might as well face the fact that there was nothing average about Claire Morgan. Or his feelings for her.

Determination etched her features as she packed. Misplaced determination. But then that was his fault. He was only prolonging the inevitable. Giving her hope he had no right to give. He ran a hand over his bristly jaw, asking himself what the hell he was doing.

The odds were against her. Lenny had been alone. With no clues to go on, it would be hard enough to locate the lycan responsible for infecting the kid—and next to impossible to track his alpha. But it was a chance. A chance Gideon's parents never had.

His gaze drifted to her mouth, instantly distracted, instantly reminded that Claire was not like the others he had destroyed in one very big way. He'd never kissed the others. Never felt such a bone-deep want for them, not even when the females had turned their considerable wiles on him in an effort to save their wretched lives.

She was a lycan now, without control. Soon to be without conscience. He should have known better. He had succumbed to that soft mouth, to those breasts, to her hands on his cock, before reason asserted itself and he slapped the handcuffs on her wrists. A moment of weakness. *That's all*. What sane man could resist a taste? Hell, she was one ball of raging hormones right now. No man was safe from her. A point he wouldn't forget again.

She must have felt his stare. She ceased shoving garments into her bag and looked up at him.

"What?" she asked, her voice whisper soft. Her eyes reminded him of a wounded animal's.

"Nothing." Looking out the window at their two vehicles, he drew a deep breath and willed a return to the cold practicality that had ruled him.

He had killed hundreds of lycans in his life. Sometimes two, three in a single week. Only he had never hunted a particular one before. Never had to. But then it had never been necessary.

"We'll leave your car here," he announced. "On the drive back you can go over everything you remember about Lenny. Starting with his family."

"No problem," she muttered, pulling her suitcase off the bed and dropping it to the floor with a thud. "He didn't have one."

Claire leaned across his lap and yelled into the intercom, "A bacon triple cheeseburger and large fry and—"

"And?" Gideon echoed.

A warm flush crept up her face. She could have pretended she wasn't hungry and ordered a fast-food salad of wilted lettuce and dry, prepackaged chicken, but she had missed lunch and couldn't deny her rumbling stomach.

Her gaze scanned the menu. Swallowing her pride for the sake of her hunger, she finished her order. "And a large order of onion rings, a large chocolate shake . . . and a large Diet Coke."

"Diet?" He lifted an eyebrow, his voice mocking as he asked, "You sure about that?"

"Yeah." She sat back in her seat, her tone daring him to comment further as he drove up to the window. She might be seriously hungry, but she still liked her Diet Coke.

"Diet Coke," he muttered, shaking his head as he passed her drink and shake to her.

She secured them safely in the double cup holder and looked at him blankly when he extended his own soda into the air. He looked down at the occupied cup holders and back at her.

"Can't you hold it?" she asked.

"And drive?" he grumbled, wincing as he secured his ice-cold soda between well-muscled thighs. "Sure. No problem."

She looked out the plastic window of the Jeep's Bikini top as they waited for their food, her dark thoughts lingering like the gray, low-hanging clouds in the sky. On the next full moon she would succumb to an instinct that demanded she feed on human life.

Bile rose in her at that, and she glanced at his hard profile. Only he wouldn't let that happen. He would make certain it never came down to that. One way or another. He would destroy her first. He hadn't said as much, but she knew, she understood, and she didn't blame him. Claire looked back out the window at the impending night.

There was still a chance. Claire swallowed hard and nodded in conviction, clinging to that belief. They'd find the alpha and break the curse before Gideon had to resort to such measures. He must believe it possible. Otherwise he would have already killed her.

And why hadn't he? The question continued to bat around inside her head. What was his motivation for helping her? Was she his good deed of the year? A single altruistic measure to break up a long line of kills?

"I haven't told you thank you."

The soft beat of his thumbs on the steering wheel abruptly ceased. "For what?"

Claire looked at him again. "Helping me."

His lips thinned. "I haven't helped you yet."

"I think you have." Claire recalled what he had said about the police force being full of hunters like him. "Those other hunters you mentioned, would they do what you're doing?"

"No. They'd have destroyed you that first night." The muscles in his jaw knotted and his eyes grew intense, burning as they looked at her. "I guess I'm just growing too soft for this job." There was both sarcasm and anger in his voice. Claire wondered to whom it was directed.

Gideon turned, relieving her of his intense gaze as

he accepted the bags of food through the window. She took the warm bags, the aroma of fried food tantalizing. He shifted the gear stick and they were soon speeding along the frontage road. Even with the top attached, the air hummed loudly around the vehicle as they merged onto the interstate. Grease soaked through the white paper bags balanced on her lap, singeing the tops of her thighs. But she didn't care. A burger in one hand, she shoved fries into her mouth, hardly chewing before she swallowed.

"Mind handing me my burger?"

"Oh," she mumbled around a mouthful of hot, salty fries. She fumbled in the bag for his burger, unwrapped half of it, and handed it to him, avoiding the overwhelming temptation to take a bite.

"So," she asked, biting into an onion ring, "how does one become a lycan hunter?" Silence stretched, so she pressed. "I mean it's not exactly the kind of job you find in the classifieds."

"I've been training since I was a kid," he offered.

She ate another onion ring, waiting for him to elaborate. When he didn't, she sighed impatiently. "What? Is it the family business or something? Was your father a lycan hunter, too?"

"No. Just another victim of its curse."

Her gaze shot to him, the onion ring in her mouth suddenly dust. "He was infected? Like me?"

His jaw knotted again. "No, my mother was. My father merely her dinner."

"Oh, my God," she whispered, nausea churning her stomach. "That's why you do this." It was personal.

Cursing, he jerked a hand from the steering wheel to run through his hair, tousling the sun-kissed locks. "Christ. I don't talk about this. With anyone. I don't know why I am now."

"Maybe you need to talk about it," she suggested.

He slid her a bitter look. "Let's get a couple things straight. Just because I'm helping you doesn't mean we get friendly. We don't chat and share life histories." His gaze cut to her, penetrating, demanding nothing less than total agreement. "We're *not* friends. Get it?"

"Yeah." Claire understood. Even as his words undeniably stung. It should have occurred to her sooner. In the event they didn't break the curse, killing her could be awkward, difficult, if they formed a friendship. "So how many like me have you helped before?" she asked.

He slanted her an unreadable look. After a long moment, he finally replied. "None."

"None?"

"Look, my job is to destroy lycans. That's the code. Whether you've fed yet or not doesn't matter. You're infected. Every agent in the country—hell, the world—would snuff you out rather than let you draw another breath."

"Codes? Agents?" She shook her head. "What are you, the FBI?"

"Underground societies. I'm an agent for NODEAL, the National Organization for Defense against Evolving and Ancient Lycanthropes. Europe has EFLA, the European Federation of Lycan Agents."

"Werewolves are that rampant?"

"Like damned locusts. And their numbers have been

growing. Especially in the States. There's been a lot of rumbling in the ranks. NODEAL's considering merging with EFLA. They're better at controlling their lycan population."

"That many people are being infected by werewolves?"

"Actually, no. Lycans are very discriminating. They prefer to breed within their packs. A single lycan female can successfully procreate for a generation or two."

"If they're so discriminating, then why was Lenny infected?"

He frowned, staring straight ahead at the two-lane highway. "I don't know. Rogue lycan, perhaps. Or maybe the kid got away before they could finish him off."

Fighting back the brutal image that evoked, she swallowed down the tightness in her throat and asked, "So what else can I expect?" Besides turning into a monster and feeding on human flesh?

He was silent a long moment. "Heightened senses—taste, touch, smell, sight. You're stronger. Faster. Quick to anger. Quick to react."

She nodded. Her temper had certainly been hair-trigger lately. And her senses had been sensitive. To a distracting degree. She had tried to dismiss it. Rationalized it away, pretended not to notice.

"You're the one living through it. You can probably better describe it."

Moistening her lips, she volunteered, "I eat a lot."

"You're burning more calories now."

Her head swiveled to look at him. "What?"

"Your metabolic intake has increased because lycans burn energy faster."

"You mean I can eat like this and not gain weight?" She glanced at the discarded bags on the floorboard, her lips twisting. "Guess that's one perk."

"This isn't a joke."

"Am I laughing?" she snapped. "Trust me, I'm hanging on by a thread here." Hearing the wobble in her voice, she blinked burning eyes and stared out at the pasture-land flying past, knowing soon she would be back in a concrete jungle full of flesh-hungry beasts.

And she was one of them.

Chapter Nine

Dogs come in all shapes and sizes; know your type.

—*Man's Best Friend:*
An Essential Guide to Dogs

Nibbling on her straw, Claire surveyed the house beneath the muted glow of streetlights. "This is your house?"

"Yeah." He pulled her suitcase from the backseat before she had a chance to grab it herself.

The narrow, redbrick two-story with a deep front porch was an older home, circa 1940s. An inviting swing swayed in the night breeze on one end of the porch, and a pile of firewood sat on the other end. A large magnolia tree shaded the house, its thick leaves rustling. Inhaling, she caught its sweet, almost lemony aroma.

A family house. For a family man. Definitely not the house she had imagined him residing in.

Come to think of it, she really couldn't imagine him having a home at all. He had taken on such mythical proportions in her mind that she couldn't imagine him putting down roots anywhere. She visualized him living out of his Jeep, never sleeping, simply passing his time cruising the city streets, frequenting seedy bars as he hunted and destroyed werewolves. Silly. Despite his extraordinary vocation, he was just a man. No more. No knight in shining armor sacrificing his life in pursuit of a grand quest.

She followed him into the house and up the stairs, their footfalls deadened by the faded runner covering the wooden steps.

"The couch folds out," he explained in crisp tones, dropping her suitcase on a couch in a small, wood-paneled room. She moved to the window and parted the curtains with one hand, looking down at the front yard, its grass rippling in the late-night breeze.

"The sheets are already on. I'll bring you a blanket."

"Thanks," she murmured, her gaze following the streak of light on the wood floor to its source. The moon sat high overhead, beyond half full. It wouldn't be long before it was completely full.

"We don't have much time left. Eight days," he said as if reading her thoughts.

Eight days? His words struck her like a blow. Struggling for breath, she let the curtains fall back in place. "Where do we go from here?"

"It's late. Get some sleep. We'll start tomorrow by going back to the bar where I first saw Lenny." He paused at the door. "You'll need to dress the part." Gesturing to her person, he seemed to struggle for the appropriate words. "Look, you know . . . done up."

Done up?

"Okay," she answered slowly, uncertainly.

He left, his footsteps thudding down the hall.

Alone, she glanced around the room, noticing the rolltop desk in the corner. A computer much newer than her own sat on top of the worn walnut surface. She stepped closer. Personal papers littered the desk, a few bills, a book. A very worn, dog-eared book. She picked it up and read the title: *Man's Best Friend: An Essential Guide to Dogs*.

The skin at her nape prickled.

Curious, she opened the book, her gaze falling on the inscription inside the cover.

Gideon, welcome aboard. May this book aid you as it has me.

It was signed *Cooper*.

Stomach in knots, she carefully set it back on the desk. *A dog book.* She pressed a trembling hand against her mouth, afraid that she was going to be sick. Her changing behavior could be studied and learned from a dog manual? It was galling, it was degrading . . . it scared the hell out of her. She jerked her hand from her mouth and flipped the book over on the desk, hiding its cover.

More determined than ever to win back her life, she unzipped her suitcase and began rifling through clothes, searching for an outfit that qualified as "done up." Still, her gaze kept straying to the book, a taunting reminder of the lycan blood coursing through her. It didn't matter that she couldn't see the cover. She could see the book lying there, read the title in her mind.

Fed up, she strode over to it and flung it in the top drawer, out of sight. But not out of mind.

• • •

Claire stayed in her room most of the following day. Availing herself of the computer on the rolltop desk, she searched for any reference to lycans or werewolves. Instead of giving her a clearer picture, her head ached from trying to sort through a myriad of myths.

Gideon didn't show himself. She heard the back door slam early that morning and watched as he jogged off down the street. She noted his return an hour and a half later, drenched in sweat, muscled biceps gleaming in the morning sun. The sight made her breasts tighten against her shirt.

At eight o'clock she headed downstairs. A quick survey revealed the living room and kitchen empty. No sight of Gideon anywhere. She inspected the fridge. Typical bachelor fare. All the drinks she could want: orange juice, Gatorade, Diet Coke, beer, beer—she pushed aside a carton of expired milk—more beer. Aside from a box of baking soda there wasn't anything to eat.

Hands on her hips, she called out, "Gideon?"

"In here," came a muffled reply.

She followed his voice, opening the door that led to the garage. No vehicles occupied its stifling confines. A large fan whirred in the corner, the only thing circulating air in the enclosed space. The scent of freshly cut cedar and oak assailed her. Suddenly she knew she knew why he always smelled of wood.

The garage teemed with machinery: a table saw, drills, and other tools she didn't know the names for. A large workbench scattered with various hand tools lined one side of the garage. Two rocking chairs, one large bookcase, and a dresser filled most of the remaining space.

Gideon sat on a stool, chest bare and glistening with perspiration as he sanded one of the rocking chairs. Her mouth dried as she watched his biceps flex and ripple in a fascinating dance of muscle and sinew. Her palms itched to touch that tanned skin. Instead, she rubbed her hands together to stop from reaching out.

"Hey." He leaned back on the stool and wiped the back of his hand across his brow, revealing the slightly paler underside of his muscled bicep.

Oh God. She swallowed. The skin would be soft as velvet there. Her gaze roamed the faint pattern of blue veins, wanting to trace them with her fingers.

His gaze flickered over her, and she held her breath, waiting for his reaction. She wore a shimmering turquoise halter top that dipped low and loose between her breasts. Shocking attire for a woman who never once wore a bikini at the beach. Her low-rise black slacks hugged her hips. The entire ensemble made her feel bold, sexy, and a little bit like the teenage girls in her class who flaunted their bodies so they could twist boys into knots.

Not that she hoped to twist Gideon into knots. She was only following orders. Still, it would have been nice if he noticed, if he showed a hint of reaction. Instead, he returned his attention to the chair, not giving her a second glance. Apparently, if she was waiting for his approval, she had a long wait ahead.

Stepping nearer, she stroked one of the chair's curved arms. "Beautiful," she murmured. "So, this is what you do when you're not hunting werewolves?"

He paused without looking up, his jaw flexing. "Lycans," he corrected.

She rolled her eyes. "Semantics."

He resumed sanding, the rhythmic scratching sound filling the air. "My grandmother owns an antique shop in Rosenberg. She sells my work out of her store."

Claire moved to inspect the mahogany dresser, marveling at the intricate carving on each of the drawers. "You're an artist," she mused.

He snorted, sanding away vigorously, his dark blond hair, brown with sweat, falling in a sweep over his forehead. "Hardly. My dad was a craftsman, a true artisan. People from all over the country wanted his work."

She rubbed the smooth surface of the dresser as if easing the pain she sensed inside him. Still, she couldn't help feeling a stab of envy. Even in his few words, she knew he'd had the kind of relationship with his father she never would have with hers.

"And he taught you everything he knew, right?" Because she knew that's what fathers did. Good fathers anyway. The only thing her father had taught her was that invisibility was safer.

"Yes."

"And your mother?" she asked, wincing the moment the question slipped out.

His mouth tightened. His movements became more vigorous. She felt his tension, palpable as waves of heat radiating on the air.

"My mother was a music teacher. In her free time, she was the choir director for our church. She was a good Catholic. Fish on Fridays—and not just during Lent. No excuses. We were front pew every Sunday. Christ," he snorted, "she didn't exactly lead the type of life that attracted lycans." His bottle green gaze cut to her. "She never took a stroll down a dark alley."

Claire stiffened. "Are you saying I brought this on myself?"

His well-carved mouth twisted almost cruelly. "I'm not saying anything, Claire."

Disliking the implication that she had brought this on herself, she suggested, "I thought we could get something to eat before we go out."

He grunted.

"What?" she asked—then remembered.

Eating out together, socializing—those were taboos. He didn't want to get too close. No doubt he had avoided her all day for that very reason.

"Sorry to trouble you," she snapped, hating the pout in her voice, the pang of loneliness in her heart. Turning to leave, she called over her shoulder, "I'll just go and eat the box of Arm and Hammer in your fridge."

She was halfway to the door when his voice stopped her. "What'd you have in mind?"

"Texadelphia," she replied, salivating at the image of a beefy steak-and-cheese sandwich as big as her arm. She usually avoided them. Too many calories. But who was counting now?

He stood, wiping his hands on his worn jeans. A wave of his scent hit her, sweat and man, and her body sprang into aching awareness.

"Give me a sec to shower."

She nodded, trying not to imagine his naked body

beneath a spray of hot water—or her hands sliding over his large body, lathering soap over every hard inch of him. Her belly clenched and she rushed from the room, desperate for a moment alone to rein in her aberrant yearnings before facing Gideon again.

As they sat in a back booth, Kid Rock blasting from the speakers above, Claire eyed the collegiate-looking couple sitting in the booth across from them.

She smiled and nodded her head at them. "First date."

An arm stretched casually along the back of the booth, Gideon eyed the kids. "How can you tell?"

Her gaze skimmed the little black dress with spaghetti straps the girl wore. "She's way too dressed up for this place."

A smile twitched at his lips. "You're not one to talk about being overdressed."

She glanced down at her cleavage. He had noticed after all. Yet nothing in his face showed whether he appreciated her efforts or not.

"This is overdressed?" she asked.

"No. I guess I'd call it *under*dressed."

He leaned forward and rested his elbows on the table, dark blond hair falling over his brow. "Why do I get the feeling that you, Miss Morgan, never owned an outfit like that before?"

"So maybe I went on a little shopping spree." She shrugged, sipping her drink.

"And what about your other changes?" His gaze skimmed her face and hair.

His implication was clear. It was nothing he hadn't

already said. He chalked up her makeover as a side effect of the curse.

"Give me a break." Unwilling to admit that he was right, she said, defending herself, "I had the same hairstyle since fourth grade. A haircut was long overdue."

Pride stopped her from conceding that anything other than her own free will brought about the changes in her appearance.

"You're not a very good liar." Those light green eyes glittered knowingly.

She dropped her gaze and plucked at her paper napkin.

"The new you definitely impressed your boyfriend," he added in a low voice.

She lifted her gaze, her brow creasing. "What boyfriend?"

"Your teacher friend."

"Cyril?" She grimaced and waved a hand in the air. "We had one date. Besides, I don't think he would like the new me."

He smirked. "He did from where I stood."

"Maybe on the outside. But he likes his women—" She searched for the right word, fingers pinching the air as if she could grab hold of it.

Gideon readily supplied it. "Wimpy?"

"Yeah," she confessed, nodding. "You could say that."

"In my experience, wimpy guys only go for two kinds of women: wimpy or bossy. There's no in between."

"How do you figure?" She set her drink aside and leaned her elbows on the table. It had been a long time since she had had a stimulating conversation. Even longer since she'd been with a stimulating man.

"Wimpy men like women who make them feel stronger. Or they like the bossy types that can tell them what to do. It's lead or be led." He tilted his head, cool green eyes assessing her. "Like with lycans."

She frowned. "How so?"

"With lycans you're either an alpha or a beta—a leader or a follower. One pack, one alpha."

So he was saying Cyril liked her because she was spineless and could be led? Claire had spent a lifetime watching her father bully her mother. Had she turned out the same way? As submissive as her mother? Attracting men like her father? Ready to impose their will on a woman so that they could feel stronger?

Shaking her head, she bit out, "How do you know Cyril didn't like me because I was the other way? Bossy?"

He seemed to fight back a smile. "Just a hunch."

Her nape grew hot and she lifted her hair to let air cool her skin. "You're wrong. I'm not a wimp."

"Not now," he allowed.

"Not ever." Not entirely true, but she didn't care. It would never be true again.

Their food arrived then. Claire grabbed her foot-long cheese steak out of the basket. The waitress barely pulled her hand out of the way in time. Sinking her teeth into it, she groaned at the explosion of moist steak and gooey mozzarella in her mouth. Hot juice dribbled down her chin. She wiped at it with the back of her hand and took another bite without having even swallowed the first.

Wide-eyed, the waitress left, glancing over her shoulder, clearly amazed at the speed with which Claire devoured her sandwich.

Lifting her gaze, she watched the slow movement of Gideon's well-carved lips as he chewed his dinner. A different kind of hunger sparked in her blood.

"What about you?" She set the remains of her sandwich back in the basket, her voice low and sultry in a way she had never spoken before. "What kind of woman do you like?"

"Me?" The question clearly caught him off guard.

"How do you like your women?" she repeated. "Someone you could easily lead? Or do you like a woman to take charge?"

Suddenly she saw herself unzipping his jeans as she had at the lake house. Running her thumb over the engorged head of him. Except this time she was lowering her mouth, playing her tongue over him . . .

Their eyes clashed. The air sparked with electricity and she knew he was seeing the same thing, too.

"Not wimpy," he said at last, voice strained as he broke eye contact and leaned forward to grab a chip from his basket of food.

"I thought so," she murmured, picking up her sandwich again.

He wanted her. As much as she wanted him.

Only her satisfaction was short-lived.

Because the reality of it was that Gideon March would never give the *true* Claire Morgan the time of day. When all this was over and the curse was broken he'd forget all about her.

Staring into her glass, she studied the melting ice cubes and felt a frown pulling at her mouth. She didn't want to revert to the mouse again. The submissive. True, she could have continued through life timid and afraid, without ever knowing what she missed. But now she knew.

She knew what it felt like to stand up to her father. To take control of her classroom. To go after what she wanted. Now she knew, and she could never go back. Didn't want to go back. She smiled wryly. Although she could do without the loss of her soul and feeding on humans every full moon.

He stared at her from across the table, his eyes hard, shrewd, almost as if he could read her thoughts. "Don't get too comfortable, Claire. You can't stay like this."

Of course not. She knew that.

Not if she wanted to live.

Yet a small voice rose up inside her. *Were you even alive before you became a werewolf?*

Chapter Ten

A pack species, dogs are social creatures.

—*Man's Best Friend: An Essential Guide to Dogs*

"Now what?" Claire asked, eyeing the long length of weathered bar—stained and sticky from unidentifiable fluids—for its dish of complimentary peanuts.

"We wait," Gideon replied, scanning the room without glancing her way. He thrust a beer into her hand with a terse "Drink."

Wrinkling her nose, she looked askance at the beer in her hand. She never drank beer. Occasionally, a glass of wine. But never beer. Her father drank beer. By the truckloads.

She stared at the bottle in her hand as if it might sprout teeth and bite her. Looking up, she caught the hulk of a bartender leering down her cleavage from behind the bar. He smoothed a hand over his forest of a goatee and blew her a kiss.

Stifling a shudder, she turned and watched Gideon take a swig from his bottle. Growing up, she usually closeted herself in her room when her father sat drinking in front of the television. A safe place to avoid the path of his red-eyed gaze. Of course sometimes not even the barrier of her door protect her.

"I hate beer," she muttered, her father's slurred insults echoing in her mind. Her nose twitched, almost smelling his foul beer breath hissing in her face.

"And why's that?"

She shrugged. "When my father wasn't working on a job, he was home. Drinking." She nodded. "And that was pretty much it." She snorted, a pained smile curving her lips. "God, we couldn't wait for him to leave."

Silence fell between them, filled by the din of the bar. She wondered what had inspired her to bring up her father. She never talked about him. Not with anyone. Not even with her mother.

"Was he a mean drunk?" The question fell hard from his mouth, almost startling her.

"Mean better describes him sober. Drunk, he's something else." Something worse. "I learned to stay out of his way." She crossed her arms, rubbing flesh that suddenly felt chilled as she remembered the times she had not escaped his notice. "For the most part."

He stared out into the bar, the rigid line of his profile resembling carved stone. Suddenly, he said, "The timid little mouse suddenly makes such sense."

Heat crawled over her cheeks. Their conversation at dinner flooded back over her. "I'm not a wimp, remember," she snapped. "Not a mouse."

He turned his gaze on her, eyes a cool and steady green.

Dropping her arms, she met his stare directly, challenging.

"If you are—were," he amended, gaze flicking over her, taking in her shiny halter top, slowly roaming over the swells of her breasts, "it sounds as though you had good reason."

"To be weak?" she growled. Vulnerable? Submissive? *Her mother?* She shook her head fiercely.

"No," he countered, eyes burning as they drifted back to her face, drilling into hers. "To be human."

Human. Something she could no longer lay claim to either. At that moment, he must have realized the same thing, too.

His eyes changed, the green deepening, assessing her with a burning intensity. The air between them altered, grew charged. Hunger pumped through her veins and her nipples hardened against the thin, satiny fabric of her top. The muscles along his square-cut jaw knotted and she scented his reaction to her—visceral and immediate, earthy, a spicy musk on the air.

He tore his gaze from her and looked out at the bar again, severing the moment.

She gripped the cold, wet bottle and did her best not to shatter the glass in her hand. Studying him, she tried to steady her breathing and suppress her annoyance that he no longer looked at her, that he had clamped down hard on the desire flaring between them, snuffing it out like a flame between his fingers.

Leaning his elbows back on the bar, he took another long swig of beer. Casual. Calm. She watched, mesmerized by the play of muscles in his throat. God, he was . . . incredible.

Tearing her gaze away, she tried to shake off this damned attraction for him. In a very short time, she'd either be dead or wimpy again. In either case, Gideon didn't fit in to the equation, so there was no sense getting worked up over him.

The Eagles crooned "Take It Easy" in the background, mocking her tension. Taking a delicate sip of beer, she wet her lips and asked, "What are we looking for?"

The small sip of the Texas-brewed Shiner rolled down her throat in a bitter trail. She tried to hide her wince, wanting to appear tough, the kind of woman who hung with the guys and tossed back a few bottles. The kind of woman he might like.

He scanned the smoky bar steadily filling to capacity. Attention trained on the room, he pointed his bottle at a distant table. "Look, I'm going to sit over there—you sit there."

She looked at the two tables he indicated—so very far apart. Her stomach clenched.

"Why?" she asked, alarmed.

"They're more likely to approach if you're alone."

"How do you know they'll even approach me?" She forced a sip of beer into her suddenly dry mouth, surprised to find that it didn't taste so bad anymore.

He looked down at his boots. The action was almost guilty—if she could ever apply such an improbable emotion to him, which she couldn't. There was nothing the least repentant about him.

"They will," he answered, still avoiding her eyes.

Claire studied him as he rubbed the back of his neck beneath his hair. She got the feeling he hadn't told her everything.

What was he hiding? And what made him so certain they would approach her?

Shaking her head, she asked, "Why would they waste their time if I'm not in their pack?"

"They will. Trust me."

She eyed him uncertainly, but accepted his answer. She had wasted too much time already refusing to believe him.

Another question burned on her mind. "How do I know whether someone's like me?"

"Their eyes will be the first giveaway, unless disguised, but even then you should sense them."

At her frustrated look, he elaborated. "It's not something I can explain. I only know that lycans seem to recognize each other on a primal level." He smiled wryly. "I've never experienced it myself. Maybe you can fill me in later. When you're back to normal."

Back to normal. After she encountered her first werewolf. After they killed the alpha. After this was all over and she returned to her old self. *The mouse*. While that didn't exactly excite her, the prospect of staying alive did. Just hearing him say those words so calmly, so confidently, reassured her that she was going to come out on top.

Gideon stepped from her side, and she resisted grabbing his arm. *Don't be a coward. Just tap into all that newfound confidence*. That bolstered her for the barest second.

Until she realized these other lycans would be confident too, and aggressive, and experienced. Not to mention they had strength in numbers, since, according to Gideon, they traveled in packs.

She knew he did this sort of thing for a living, but how could Gideon contend with multiple creatures possessing unnatural strength?

He must have sensed her anxiety because he turned back to her, pale eyes glowing in the smoke-thick air. "Don't worry about knowing who they are. They'll know you."

"That's what I'm afraid of," she muttered as he walked away and left her at the bar.

Once he took his seat at the designated table, he sent her a wink. A small comfort considering how suddenly, terribly alone she felt—like a dingy cast adrift from its mother ship. She moved slowly to her table.

The bar attracted a young crowd, and she hoped she didn't run into any students but knew it likely. Gideon had last seen Lenny here, after all. She'd heard students mention the place before. Apparently the management didn't care too much if they allowed minors inside.

"Hey there."

She looked up at a guy not a day over twenty, his face blotchy with acne. Claire scrutinized him intently, opening her senses for a sign, anything that would tell her one way or another.

He glanced over his shoulder to where a group of equally unappealing guys mouthed encouragement and sent him indiscreet thumbs-ups.

"Hello," she returned, darting a glance at Gideon, sitting with a sudden alertness in his chair.

"Can I buy you a drink?" he asked abruptly, his manner that of a man unaccustomed to picking up women.

Clearly, the question was intended "to pave the way," considering she held a three-fourths-full beer in her hand. She snuck another glance at Gideon and caught him shaking his head no. Apparently he had reached the same conclusion. This guy wasn't a werewolf.

"Ah, no thanks." She lifted her beer in the air. "Already got one."

"Uh, like some company, then?"

"I'm waiting for someone." Not exactly a lie.

"Sure," he mumbled a touch resentfully before returning to his friends.

A glance around revealed several eyes focused on her. Many of which belonged to pimply-faced prepubescents like the one she ran off. Any of those eyes watching her could belong to a lycan, she reminded herself. Ageless eyes, disguised in a youthful shell. Still, she found it hard to remember this when—

Whoa, there. A man walked her way. Not a kid. Claire leaned forward as he approached in all his black-leather-pants-and-turtleneck glory. She rested an elbow on the table and set her chin in her palm, her body warming and tingling as he approached.

"Where've you been all my life?" he asked.

God, guys actually said things like that? Sadly, it didn't sound that bad coming from his lips.

Flipping her hair over her shoulder with a flirtiness she never knew she possessed, Claire patted the seat beside her and opened her mouth, ready to invite him to sit down. Then she remembered her purpose tonight. Darting a glance across the room, she met Gideon's unhappy gaze head on. His eyes glittered dangerously. Swiping one finger swiftly beneath his neck in a cutting motion, he indicated she should end the conversation and set this one loose.

With a sigh of reluctance, Claire repeated her earlier excuse, "Sorry, I'm waiting for someone."

With an odd sense of frustration simmering inside her, she watched him walk away. She turned a glare on Gideon. He stared back at her with a glare of his own, shaking his head side to side as though disgusted.

What's wrong with basking in the admiration of an attractive man? She wasn't getting any attention from Mr. Lycan Hunter over there. At least not the kind her body craved. She was the one looking death in the eye. If she wanted one last hurrah, who was he to stop her?

They walked silently through the parking lot, their feet crunching over loose gravel, the distant thrum of Aerosmith beating steadily behind them. The air was thick and balmy, the loss of the sun doing nothing to ease the stifling humidity.

"We'll try again tomorrow," Gideon said.

She nodded and forced a smile despite the defeat lodged deep in her chest.

Her skin began to hum, prickling with awareness. Her smile slipped. They were in a particularly dark part of the lot, the last security light several feet behind them. Her feet skidded quietly to a stop. She scanned the parking lot, her vision adjusting to the night, flitting over the hoods of cars and trucks, seeing well despite the darkness.

Gideon stopped ahead of her, apparently realizing she wasn't walking next to him any longer. He turned to face her. "Claire?"

She wet her lips and inhaled deeply, smelling . . . something.

The tingling in her skin intensified, the tiny hairs on her neck standing on end. Turning her head left and right, she peered at the shadows lurking in the far end of the lot, feeling the eyes that watched her every moment.

They weren't alone.

Then she heard it. Feet flying like wind across the parking lot. Gaze flying to Gideon, she opened her mouth to cry a warning. Before she had the chance, a dark blur flashed between them, knocking Gideon down.

A clammy hand slammed over her mouth, smothering her scream. She tasted the warm saltiness of sweat and animal over her open mouth. An arm snaked around her waist and lifted her off her feet.

She struggled, kicking, jabbing, thrashing as she was heaved higher off the ground.

Gideon's grunts and curses came from somewhere below her kicking feet.

Her captor was strong. Too strong. Far stronger than she. And intuitively she knew.

He wrenched her around to face him. He was young. And yet not. The way his gaze scoured her face and body, so knowingly—it was as though he knew her intimately. That look spoke of years lived. She had never seen him before, yet she knew him. Just as he knew her. As a species recognizes one of its own. In one startling instant, she realized just how well she knew him. *She was him.*

"Claire," Gideon shouted.

She tore free of her captor's gaze, no less magnetic for his brown-colored contacts, and searched for a glimpse of Gideon again. She spotted him rolling on the ground, locked in struggle with another lycan.

"Don't worry about the human." Hard fingers dug into her cheeks, forcing her to face her attacker again. "Tony will take care of him. Right now I want to get to know you better."

Fabric ripped. It was an ugly sound. Frightening. Violent. Her hands dove for the tattered scraps of her halter top.

"Why are you fighting it?" he demanded, seizing her hands and squeezing the bones of her wrists until she feared they would snap.

"Come on, baby. I could smell you a mile away." He cupped her chin, cold fingers fanning her cheek possessively as he nuzzled her neck, his wet breath rising hot and rancid to her sensitive nose. "You're hurting for it. Let me make you feel better."

His mouth covered hers, his fetid tongue pushing past her teeth. Claire gagged, her stomach rolling at the disgusting taste of him. Hands, hard and cruel, grabbed her waist and hefted her on top of a nearby hood. She cried out as her bottom slammed down on unforgiving steel.

A strange, animal-like cry rose up from deep in her

throat. She raked her nails down his face in a savage swipe, his blood coating her palms. He snatched hold of her wrists and yanked them high above her head.

A fierce instinct burned through her blood. With a growl, she bared her teeth and sank them into his arm. Cursing, he dropped her wrists. She took advantage, curling her hand into a fist and striking him so hard his head snapped back. She surged against him, trying to throw him off her. But he was strong. Shoving her down on the hood, her head smacked steel, stunning her motionless as he fumbled with the hook at her waistband. His triumphant cry stabbed the air. Her zipper sang out as he tugged at her pants, his jerks frantic. The fabric was too tight to slip off with ease, so her body slid up and down the hood with each rough yank.

A million stars stared down at her, the twinkling dots of light mocking her as her head cleared and she renewed her struggles.

This isn't happening. This can't be happening.

A sudden crack of gunfire shattered the air. Her gaze sought Gideon. He stood several feet away, his gun in his hand, a lifeless body at his feet.

Her attacker spun around between her thighs, a deep growl vibrating from him at the sight of his fallen comrade. "You'll beg for death before I'm through with you," he ground out.

Before he could make good on the threat, she sprang on his back. Wrapping her arms around his throat, she squeezed with all her strength. He thrashed side to side, trying to toss her off him.

Suddenly another shot split the night. Both she and

the lycan fell back from the force. Air rushed from her lungs. Pinned beneath the dead weight of him, Claire pushed at his body, struggling and choking on a mouthful of scraggly hair that fell in her face.

With a grunt, she flung him off her and sucked in sweet gulps of air as she zipped her pants back up.

Gideon snatched her hand and pulled her off the ground. Her gaze landed on the sprawled bodies. She lifted her gaze to him.

Eyes on the building in the distance, he spoke quickly, "I didn't have time to attach the silencer. We gotta get out of here."

The warm hold of his hand on hers felt wonderfully reassuring and she tightened her grip, hurrying alongside him, glancing one last time at the two bodies. "What just happened?"

"We were ambushed."

"You killed them," she murmured as they neared the Jeep.

"No. I didn't," he said without breaking stride. "They were already dead."

She released his hand when they reached the Jeep and barely had both feet inside before he gunned the engine to life. They tore out of the parking lot, tires spinning and gravel flying.

"Their fate was sealed the second they became infected," Gideon said. "A long time ago, I'm guessing."

She looked away from the road to stare at his profile, absorbing his words before she announced, "Then I'm dead, too."

He glanced at her, the lights of an oncoming car casting the hard lines of his stern features into relief. "Not yet. I wouldn't help you if you were."

She shook her head and stared ahead, the streetlights narrow streaks of rainbow flying past. "I don't understand. Why are you helping me at all?"

"Maybe I've gone soft. Maybe I've gotten tired of killing and felt like saving a life instead. Maybe you're . . ."

"I'm what?"

He shook his head, whatever he thought to say held in check.

Claire hugged herself, her fingers digging into her arms as she recalled the brutality of her attack. "I'd rather be dead than become like them."

"If it comes down to that, I'll pull the trigger myself."

She glared at him. "So you've said."

He was so cold. So calculated. And in that moment, she hated him for it. Even if she knew he couldn't afford to be any other way.

Gideon glanced at her as she crossed her arms in a noisy huff, clearly offended by his bluntness. He sighed. It wasn't as if he would enjoy ending her life. Not hers. Not Claire.

There had been a time when he enjoyed the hunt, relished the kill. Each successful mission avenged his parents. At least when he started out, when he was young, that was the case. He hardly slept, hardly ate—only hunted. His sole purpose had been to hunt and destroy. And standing over each of his kills, he had imagined that dead lycan to be the one who infected his mother.

Lately, that driving need to annihilate lycans had vanished. Partly because he now accepted that they could never totally be eradicated. His efforts only added sand to a constantly widening hole. Lycans had walked this earth for generations. They were a finely honed species, built to endure the expanse of time, built to withstand NODEAL and the other underground societies created to hunt and destroy them.

The most he got out of the hunt anymore was a minor sense of accomplishment. That he had performed a small, necessary service for society. Gideon realized, however, that he wouldn't even have that peace of mind if he destroyed *her*. He would only feel failure. And, he admitted, a sense of loss.

Because Claire Morgan had gotten under his skin.

She had infiltrated his resolve to keep their relationship impersonal. He wanted her. He pounded the steering wheel with his fist and pushed the impossible thought from his head.

Tonight, when she'd hinted at the abuse she had suffered at the hands of her father, he had experienced a violent impulse no less savage than that which drove lycans. He wanted nothing more than to drive across town and beat the shit out of the bastard with his bare hands. For hurting Claire, for reducing her to a ghost that clung to shadows rather than stepping into the light, for failing to be the father he should have been, the kind that made her know how special she was. He took a curve a bit too fast, hugging the guardrail, his back right tire lifting.

Sitting rigidly beside him, she looked nervously between the road and him, as if expecting him to crash into the guardrail. Realizing how fast he drove, he eased his foot off the accelerator. No sirens chased them. They were safe. For now.

He shook his head in disgust, thinking back to the two lycans. They mustn't have been in the club. They carried themselves like predators, like lycans. The sight of them would have immediately put him on alert.

"I killed them both," he spat out. His goal had been to keep a lycan alive for questioning. "Now we've got nothing." She jumped beside him when he hit the steering wheel a second time.

This was going to be even harder than he had first thought. Their only lead was Lenny, a dead lycan. What could Gideon do? Go around town killing as many lycans as possible in hopes of nailing the right one? That would never save her in time.

He pulled his cell out and stared at the glowing face for a long moment, debating whether to put in the call. He had left two dead lycans behind. Questions would arise within the organization. Shoving the cell back into his pocket, he muttered another curse. Too bad. He couldn't risk it. Not with Claire.

NODEAL could cope. He cringed, imagining Cooper on a rampage, searching for a rogue agent when he discovered two dead bodies with silver bullets lodged in the corpses. Two dead lycans and no one claiming the job. Cooper would go nuts.

"You okay?" he finally asked, glancing at her. She clutched the tatters of her halter top to her chest, her black satin bra peeking out. He forced his gaze back to the road, both disturbed and tantalized by the sight.

"Sure," she said slowly, appearing to weigh his question. "I just had a werewolf—"

"Lycan," he automatically corrected.

"Semantics," Claire snapped, glaring at him before continuing. "I just had a *werewolf* try to rape me on the hood of a car, but I'm swell."

"Sarcasm doesn't suit you," he replied.

"Yeah, well, I'll deal with this my way." Her brow scrunched and this time her voice came out subdued when she asked, "Why did he say I wanted it?"

He stared at the road, lips pressed tightly together as if he could hold back the truth.

"It wasn't just talk," she insisted. "He really *believed* I wanted it."

At this point, he knew he couldn't keep the truth from her any longer.

Considering the vibes she put out, the lycan hadn't been far off. She did want it. She just didn't realize it yet. Had it only been yesterday that they had nearly fucked on the floor of her family's lake house? It had taken every ounce of restraint to reject what she so eagerly offered and slam those cuffs on her wrists.

It was foolish, even unrealistic of him, but he had hoped to avoid telling her. There had been enough revelations yesterday. She didn't understand her urges. But he did. He had seen the way she responded to Mr. Black Leather Pants in the bar. The woman needed a chastity belt with one very big lock.

Hell, she could be lying on her back under him right now if he only crooked a finger. That image made him shift uncomfortably in his seat and his hands clenched the steering wheel. No way around it. He had to tell her. Then maybe she would understand. Maybe she could fight it. Because, God help him, he found it harder and harder to resist her.

"What aren't you telling me?" she demanded, her voice cracking.

"Lycans follow . . . primitive urges," he began, searching for the appropriate wording.

She waved impatiently for him to continue.

"They feed and they procreate. The objective being to further the species." He shrugged and flexed his hands on the steering wheel. "Simple, really."

Her look told him she disagreed.

"What are you saying?" She shook her head. "I don't understand."

And that, he guessed, was because she didn't want to. He knew her well enough at this point to realize she had a hard time accepting ugly truths.

"It's not conscious. It's instinctual," he elaborated.

"Procreate?" she echoed.

"You know, to reproduce—"

"I know what it means," she snapped.

"They're a pack society. A lone female of childbearing years, without any other lycans—male lycans—protecting her, is a prime target."

She leaned back in her seat, her head bouncing against the headrest several times. "Unbelievable. I'm a sex target," she muttered. Her head shot off the seat, apparently struck with a sudden thought. "And you sent me out tonight without telling me any of this?"

"I wanted you calm."

"I could have better prepared myself."

"It would have gone down the same. You were already freaked out enough. Now look at you. You're hysterical."

"I am not hysterical," she said tightly, trying, he guessed, to keep herself from yelling and lending credence to his claim. "So you're saying that as long as I'm without a pack, every werewolf we come across will want to jump my bones?"

"Pretty much."

"Great."

"And you haven't exactly helped the situation."

"What is *that* supposed to mean?" she demanded, her look indignant.

"You've . . . embraced your urges." He wondered why he even mentioned it except that he was annoyed at her total naïveté. Was she completely unaware of the signals she put out—how she looked, how she moved, how she affected him?

"How?" Her lips worked like a fish's, searching for words. "I don't have any urges."

He laughed as he turned into his driveway. "Oh, yeah?"

"Yeah," she countered.

He shut the motor off and faced her, the leather creaking beneath his shifting weight. "Yes. You do."

She shook her head again.

"And I suppose you still think this change in appearance—" He waved a hand over her person. "—is just coincidental?"

Her eyes flared wide, the brilliant silver glowing even brighter. She jabbed a finger through the air accusingly. "You told me to dress provocatively!"

"You changed your looks before I made any suggestion about how you should dress tonight."

Her knuckles whitened where they held her top together. "You got me to dress like this when you knew they would come after me."

"I didn't know you were going to dress like Pamela Anderson. You're the one who sent that lycan into overload."

"Oh," she squeaked, face flushing a vivid red.

Before she could arrive at a more dignified answer, he hopped out of the Jeep. Heading toward the back door, he called over his shoulder, "That lycan was right. You want to give it up."

Gideon bit the inside of his cheek, stopping himself from adding that he wanted to be the one to receive it.

Chapter Eleven

> A dog in season is subject to variances of mood; be sensitive to your pet.
>
> —*Man's Best Friend: An Essential Guide to Dogs*

Claire stepped into the kitchen and let the door slam behind her. "You make it sound like I'm in heat," she accused.

Propping her hands on her hips, she waited for him to assure her otherwise, waited for him to say she wasn't actually a dog, that she couldn't be ruled by base, primitive urges.

He cocked an eyebrow at her as he shrugged out of his jacket and removed his holster. She translated his look to mean, *if the shoe fits*.

All the ways in which she had recently changed flashed across her mind: heightened senses, quick temper, wardrobe, hair, makeup, renewed interest in men.

"Oh, my God." She sank into a chair, propping her elbows on the kitchen table and burying her face in her hands. "I *am* in heat."

"You're not in heat," he said as he opened the refrigerator to peer inside.

She peered through her fingers, staring at him hopefully.

"Well," he amended, "not exactly."

She dropped her face back into her hands with a moan. Not only was she a werewolf, but a werewolf whose biological clock tolled for a litter of her own. "I'm not stepping outside this house ever again."

"Yes. You will," he countered with annoying certainty, head still inside the fridge, rear end displayed to full advantage in his well-worn denim.

Jamming her eyes shut against the sight, she fought back a wave of lust. Oh God. Did *he* drive her wild with need? Or was it simply an instinctive need to fornicate? She snuck another glimpse at his ass, refusing to believe that she had lost all dignity, all self-control—that sex, regardless of the partner, would suffice.

She leaned back in her chair and crossed her arms over her chest. "Maybe it's not a good idea to flaunt myself all over town."

"We're not any closer to finding the alpha of your pack. You're going out again. You have to."

"My pack," she snorted in contempt. "I don't have a pack, remember? That's why everything on four legs wants a piece of me."

Gideon's lips twitched.

She glared at him and uncrossed her arms to wag a finger in warning. "Don't you dare laugh."

"Believe me, I find no humor in the situation." His mouth fell into an uncompromising line. His eyes dropped and he cleared his throat. "You can change clothes. Unless you enjoy exposing yourself to me." His voice sounded tight and strangled.

She followed his gaze. Her top gaped open, revealing her black push-up bra. She felt her nipples tighten beneath the black silk and grabbed at the tattered fabric.

"Maybe I'm trying to seduce you," she flung out with far more bravado than she felt. Face flaming, she scooted back in her chair back and added, "I am in heat, after all."

Deciding it best to flee—before she made a fool of herself and succumbed to the base impulses tormenting her—she stormed out of the kitchen.

She was not an animal. *Not a dog in heat.* She alone controlled her body. Even if she did want to pick up where they left off at the lake house. Gideon was the only one to affect her that way. Only he made her forget that the two of them were a very bad idea.

Thankfully he had control enough for both of them.

Claire stared at the shadows flickering across the ceiling, thoughts of tonight and Gideon keeping her awake. The purr of a diesel engine growled in the night. Kicking back the covers, she hopped off the uncomfortable pull-out and moved to the window.

Parting the curtains, she watched a man climb out of his truck and stride up the front walkway. Something about the purposeful way he carried himself, the quick way he canvassed the area, reminded her of Gideon.

Footsteps pounded down the hall—the smack of Gideon's bare feet on the house's old wood floors. Apparently, she wasn't the only one awake and aware of their late-night visitor.

The door to her room flung open. Gideon stood there bare-chested. She devoured the sight of him, the stranger outside forgotten. His eyes settled on her with an intensity that sent heat rushing to her face. His jeans hung loose and unbuttoned on his waist. The enticing line of hair disappearing below his navel made her throat constrict. Tousled hair, dark in the room's shadows, brushed his naked shoulders. She felt herself take a step forward, fingers twitching at her side, itching to touch that hair, recalling its softness in her hands.

She froze, rooting her feet to the floor, telling herself to get a grip.

He pointed an imperious finger at her. "Stay here."

The back door opened and slammed shut below.

"Gideon," a voice boomed out.

Gideon gave the smallest flinch.

Goosebumps sprang to life over her skin. "Who is it?" she whispered.

"My boss. Don't make a sound," he cautioned, his eyes glowing bottle green in the shadows. "Not unless you want it all to end right here, tonight."

His meaning left no doubt. Shivering, she nodded.

He turned and walked back out of her room, closing the door behind him.

For a long moment, she held her breath, almost afraid the sound would carry downstairs and give her presence away.

His boss? The low rumble of their voices barely carried

from the bottom floor. The drumming pulse at her neck gradually slowed. They couldn't hear her from up here.

Easing the door open, she stuck her head out into the hall. The voices were no clearer, still a faint murmur on the air. She crept down the hallway on silent feet and lowered herself to the top step, well out of sight but in perfect hearing range.

"Two dead lycans and no one's claiming them. Know anything about it?"

"Why would I?" Gideon's voice rang out.

"The whole thing smacks of a rogue hunter. You know I won't tolerate that. Not in my town."

"Yes. I'm well aware of our policy regarding non-sanctioned hunters."

She bit her lip. What would happen if his boss realized he lied? Worse yet, what would happen if it were discovered that Gideon sheltered her? She could guess at her fate, but what about him? Until that moment, Claire hadn't realized just how much he was putting on the line for her.

A long pause followed Gideon's flip response. She strained forward on the step, waiting.

"Seen your sister lately?"

Biting her bottom lip between her teeth, Claire hugged her knees to her chest.

"Not much. She's busy with school and work."

"Right."

Even from her position high on the stairs, she detected the man's skepticism.

"You know what I think?" he continued.

"I'm sure you're going to tell me," Gideon retorted.

"Your sister's been trying to get into NODEAL for as long as I can remember."

"So?"

"So, maybe she's decided to do a little freelancing."

Gideon's rich laughter rippled through the air. "I don't think so. Between classes and tending bar, she's pretty busy."

"I want to talk to your sister—"

"Then talk to her. You don't need my permission."

Even from where she sat, Claire could picture his lips curving in that mocking smile.

"Oh, I'll do that. But if I find out she's involved in this—"

"You'll what, Cooper? Slap her on the wrist. So what if she did the world a favor and took out two lycans? Big deal."

Cooper? Her gaze darted back to her room, remembering the inscription in the book tucked away in the drawer.

"You know the rules, Gid. We don't let women in."

Interesting. Werewolf hunters were sexist. Guess they didn't have to worry about the ACLU filing suit. Not when the world was ignorant of their existence.

"And she's not," Gideon returned. His voice sounded closer. The soft fall of footsteps signaled their advance into the living room. Her heart jumped and she cautiously rose to her feet, hands pressing flat against the wall on either side of her. If Cooper departed through the front door he would pass the stairs. One glance up and he would see her.

"I know *you* understand, Gideon. Just make sure your sister does, too."

The step groaned beneath her shifting foot. Panicked, she dropped back down—and the step creaked in protest a second time. Her heart froze.

"What was that?" Cooper asked.

She bit the knuckles of one fist, welcoming the pain, deserving it.

"What?" Gideon asked, voice calm, even a touch bored.

"Do you have someone upstairs?" Cooper asked, his tone disapproving.

Claire jammed her eyes shut.

Gideon laughed dryly. "Would I be down here talking shop with you if I had someone upstairs?"

"Ah, hell. Suppose not."

Stupid, stupid, stupid. Dropping her face into her hands, she shook all over.

"I'll call you tomorrow," Cooper announced.

Their footsteps faded back into the kitchen.

She waited and listened to their muffled good-byes, too afraid to move, to breathe, until she knew Cooper was out of the house.

Suddenly, Gideon stood at the foot of the stairs, glaring up at her with blood in his eyes. One hand gripped the railing. Her eyes penetrated the dark, noting the whitening of his knuckles the moment before he swung himself up the steps toward her.

With a hiss of alarm, she spun around on the balls of her feet. His hand closed around her ankle just as she reached the landing. He dragged her back down into the stairwell and flipped her on her back. A deep throbbing started in her abdomen, spreading outward, turning her limbs to mush.

Hands digging into her shoulders, he demanded, "What didn't you understand about keeping quiet?"

He gave her a little shake. Claire grabbed the back of her head where it bumped a step. "I only wanted to know what was going on."

"So you eavesdropped?" he growled, his mouth so close their breaths mingled, fusing into one shared gust of air.

"You know a better way for me to find out what's going on? You only tell me half-truths."

His legs slid between her bare ones, the rough denim scratching the sensitive skin of her inner thighs. Her breathing hitched and she forgot about the stairs digging into her back. Forgot about everything except the wonderful weight of him bearing down on her. *Damn primitive urges.*

"Do you know what would happen if he found you?" He grabbed her face in both hands and his voice sounded strange to her ears—hoarse and uneven. "Nothing in the world could help you, then." His eyes searched hers, glittering with an emotion she could not name. "He'd kill you."

Her belly tightened at the feel of his broad, callused palms against her face. "Would you have stopped him, Gideon?"

He inhaled a ragged breath that shot through her like a bolt of high-powered voltage. His voice fell to a hush. "Don't make me choose."

She let the tips of her breasts brush against his chest,

keenly aware that only the thin cotton of her T-shirt separated them. "Haven't you already?"

He groaned, his look tormented, making her heart clench inside her chest.

"Don't look at me like that," he rasped before his mouth swooped down on hers. He swallowed her moan, took it deep inside his mouth as his hands dove beneath her, pulling her off the uncomfortable steps and pressing her close to his chest, to the wild beating of his heart.

This time it was all about them. It wasn't a ploy to get a pair of handcuffs on her. He kissed her because he wanted to. Had to. And she reveled in that knowledge. Like a bird released from its cage, her heart soared with the awareness of her feminine power.

Mouths meshing, limbs tangling, her body somehow ended up on top of his. Her hands roamed his naked chest, palms grazing the hard pecs, the narrow indentation of his sternum, the flat plane of his stomach. She exulted in the freedom to touch, to feel all that hard, bronzed flesh.

She slid down the length of him, her lips trailing kisses across warm, quivering skin. The sound of his panting breath reached her ears, filling her with triumph. She pulled the opening of his jeans wide. The tantalizing line of hair trailing below his navel pointed like an arrow to the hard heat of him she remembered. She pressed a moist, open-mouthed kiss at the lowest point visible.

Moisture rushed between her legs, dampening her panties. Needing satisfaction, she growled and yanked at his waistband urgently.

He made a rough sound and slid from beneath her.

Rising to his feet, he loomed above her on the landing, that glorious bare chest lifting in deep, ragged breaths. Sitting on a step, she clutched the bottom of her T-shirt in each fist, twisting the fabric against her knees, fighting the impulse to spring at him.

She knew as she stared at him that the moment had come. He would either take her, accept the fire that existed between them, or turn and walk away.

He dropped his hand, extending it to her. The gesture signified his decision had been made. There would be no going back now.

Helpless to her desire, to the need he roused within her, she placed her hand in his and rose to her feet. As long as the lycan curse grasped her firmly in its clutches, she was helpless to resist. At least that's what she told herself as she drank passion greedily from his lips.

Her arms snaked around his neck, his skin smooth and warm beneath her arms. He ravaged her mouth, never breaking the kiss as he lifted her in his arms. She was hardly aware of the slight jarring motion as he carried her up the stairs.

He followed her down onto his bed, trapping her between the soft mattress and his hard body, their lips fused together.

Desperation simmered just beneath the surface, making their movements rushed, feverish, their handling of each other rough.

Their clothes melted away. He slid between her legs with expert precision and everything slowed as she stared at this too beautiful man in the moon's glow. Her breath caught at the sight of him looming above her, the heat of his gaze, the impossible breadth of his shoulders, the narrow waist and sculpted belly.

He traced her collarbone, the slope of her shoulders, the swells of her breasts. His touch gentled, reverent as a prayer as he forged a burning trail with the callused pads of his fingers, exploring each rib, feeling their length and width, driving her mad, frantic. His thumbs drifted upward, grazing the undersides of her breasts in teasing strokes.

"Gideon," she moaned.

He kissed her again and she felt his smile against her mouth as he took her swollen mounds into both hands. She gasped as he squeezed, testing their fullness. He bent, sucking her nipples until they stood pebble hard. A low keening moan rippled from deep in her throat. The sound more animal than woman. Desire, white hot, shot through her and she arched under him.

He broke away to crush his mouth over hers. Their kisses grew wild, starved for the taste of each other. She thrust her hips against him. He answered by nudging her thighs farther apart with one knee.

Sliding her hand between them, she gripped him, flexing her fingers around the thick length of him. His harsh gasp excited her and she stroked him, fingers gliding over him in fast strokes.

He moaned into her mouth, the rigid length of him pulsing in her hand. She teased his head against her opening and he nudged the tip against her. Panting, her fingers dug into his shoulders.

He sat up and placed her on her knees before him, his hands smoothing over each rounded cheek before biting the tender flesh. A growl ripped free from deep in her throat at the feel of his teeth on her. The ache inside her grew, throbbing, burning, and she spread her thighs, thrusting herself back and rubbing her bottom against his erection.

Her hands dug into the bed covers. He pulled her back by the hair, kissing the arch of her throat. She reached behind her and grabbed his cock, stroking the engorged shaft, running her thumb over its plump head, guiding him toward her.

He groaned, a deep animal sound of need.

He probed at her opening from behind, parting her slick folds with the swelled head of him. Unable to stop herself, she pushed back, impaling herself on him.

He locked one muscled arm around her waist and held himself there for a moment, buried in the tight heat of her. His warm chest rested against her back, his heart beating fast and strong into her, a distant drum that echoed the pounding of her own pulse.

He swiped free the hair from her neck and pressed an open-mouthed kiss to her nape as he began to move. His hand sought her breasts, cupping them as he plunged into her. Again and again.

"Harder," she begged, rocking back to meet his every thrust.

His hands carried their own special heat, branding her, singeing her breasts as he fondled and squeezed her nipples as he moved in and out of her.

Her flesh rippled with heightened sensation. Waves of searing heat flowed through her body like rolling lava. Her fingers went numb where they clutched the covers, tearing the fabric. She whimpered, beyond pleasure, beyond pain as the movements increased, grew more frenzied.

"Oh God," she groaned, her skin burning, the ache in her growing, expanding.

This wasn't normal. It had *never* felt this good before. She would have remembered. She moved wildly, slamming back against him, aching for . . . something.

His hands tightened on her breasts.

His thrusts grew harder. Faster. Fierce. This was no gentle joining. Her body demanded a desperate, furious union of flesh. Nothing less. She tilted her hips, clenching her inner muscles around his sliding heat, trying to get more, trying to reach that elusive hurdle.

His fingers slid from her breasts to dig into her hips. "Go on," he rasped. "Come. Come for me."

Whimpering, she dropped her head, letting herself relax into the steady build of tension tightening through her. The pressure increased, building. He swiped the hair from her shoulders again and dragged his mouth over the sensitive skin.

Every muscle in her body suddenly squeezed and contracted. She cried out as shudders racked her, took her soaring over that final precipice. Arched under him, she stilled, his back a hard wall at her back, the only thing grounding her to earth.

His hands circled her waist and he bucked behind her, thrusting several more times, pouring his liquid heat inside her. His groan rumbled through him into her as if they were one. And in that moment, they were.

Panting, she collapsed into the bed bonelessly, the hot length of him still inside her.

His body came down over her, a crushing, delicious weight, the fan of his breath warm against her spine.

Never more sated or content, her eyes drifted shut.

The gentle tapping of rain on the window woke her. She stretched, spine arching, her hand seeking out the warm body beside her. Her palm flattened over the supple skin of his back. She could feel his lifeblood rushing just below skin and sinew.

He had held her a long while before rolling onto his side. She hadn't known the rapture could last, that a man's strong arms could feel so good around her. Better in some ways than the actual sex. With Brian there had been no cuddling after sex. To be honest, there'd hardly been sex.

Sighing, she slid her hand off his back and slipped out of bed, for some reason moved to do so. Guided by a force she could not identify, she stopped before the window, standing where the rug didn't reach. Her feet shifted on the wood floor, absorbing the cold. Through the part of the curtains, she looked up at the night sky, at the object calling to her. Gray clouds scuttled across the black night, but the moon glowed a hole right through them. It loomed large and godlike overhead, its beam seeming to locate her specifically. Almost full. Only a sliver more and it would be a complete orb. She shivered and hugged herself.

"Come back to bed." His voice sounded behind her, thick and scratchy with sleep.

Wordlessly, Claire turned and slid back into bed. He tucked her against his side and she marveled at the strangeness of it all. She'd shared a bed with a man before but not like this. She didn't remember this intimacy, this—

Her mind shied away from the word *love*, but there it was, intruding and insinuating itself into her heart and head where it had no business being. Not without the possibility of a future.

She shifted beside him, smiling at the twinge of soreness between her legs, a tantalizing reminder of all that had occurred. Her smile slipped as a thought occurred to her.

"Gideon," she began. "We didn't use protection."

"No worries. You can't get pregnant. And I'm disease free. NODEAL requires yearly physicals. They test for everything—from cancer to STDs. An agent has to be in peak physical condition."

Claire nodded, tracing small circles over his chest. "And why aren't you worried about getting me pregnant?"

"Lycans and humans cannot procreate. It's like trying to breed two different species. A lycan and human can never produce offspring. If it were possible, it would already have happened. Sadly, plenty of lycans have raped humans. Such a savage act goes hand in hand with their vicious nature."

"I see." Hearing herself lumped into the *nonhuman*

category sent a chill to her heart. Her gaze drifted to the window, at the nearly full moon looking down on them.

"You can't help but look at it, can you?" His deep voice, faintly sad, resigned, jarred her and it took a moment for his meaning to sink in.

"I feel like it's calling me," she confessed. "I want to wipe it from the sky."

"I know," he sighed. After a long moment, he added, "Crazy how we know next to nothing about the very thing that controls our lives."

"What do you mean?"

"Well, the moon controls the tides, affects the weather, crops, our moods—"

"And now my soul," she added bitterly.

"Yes." He sighed. "Ironic that she only reveals herself to us in part, isn't it? We only ever get to see one side of her. We never see the dark side of the moon. No one has."

"The dark side of the moon," Claire whispered. She didn't even want to see the side visible—the side growing more visible with every passing moment. As far as she was concerned, the dark side could stay just that. Dark. Unknown.

Pushing thoughts of the moon away, she splayed a hand over his washboard belly, enjoying the way his muscles contracted beneath her fingers. Pressing her ear to his heart, she listened to the strong, steady beat and asked one of the questions that had plagued her. "Do you know how your mother got infected?"

His heart thumped harder beneath her ear and she

felt his stomach muscles dance and ripple under her palm. A long moment passed. Claire bit her lip and waited.

"I'm not sure. She never showed any signs of being attacked or bitten." The rich rumble of his voice vibrated against her ear. She felt him shrug. "Sometimes I wonder if Cooper knows more than he's telling. He said an anonymous tip brought him to our house that night. It's all very suspicious, but I don't know." He paused before adding, a note of bitter finality to his voice, "I'll never know."

That pregnant pause told her so much. It told her how badly he wanted to know. It told her how he had devoted his life to searching for the truth, for answers to a mystery that had robbed him of his family.

"You've killed a lot of lycans," she guessed.

"Hundreds," he confirmed, voice flat, without remorse.

"You could have already killed the one responsible," she pointed out.

"Believe me, I've thought the same thing. I've never killed a lycan without asking myself that very thing. *Is this the one?*"

"After your parents died, where did you go?"

"My grandmother took us in. Although I can't say she wanted to. It was all very hard on Kit. A little girl needs love. More than what I could give. A woman's touch, you know. My grandmother was finished raising children." He laughed dryly. "I'm not sure she even wanted my mother. They were never very close. My parents, my sister, and me. We were it. We were everything. Until that night, I couldn't have asked for a happier life."

She closed her eyes, saddened at what he and his sister suffered, what they lost. His mother had killed the man she loved, the father of her children. Gideon knew firsthand about savagery and death.

"That's why you joined NODEAL?"

Vengeance. She could understand such a motive. Which is why she couldn't understand his willingness to let her live. She was only grateful for it.

He nodded. "It's all I've ever wanted to do."

"Destroy lycans?"

Again, he nodded.

"But not me?" she questioned, her confusion clear. How could he even stand to be with her, much less hold and touch her?

He said nothing. His hand moved over her hair, caressing the strands. "I want to give you the chance my mother never had."

"How old were you when your parents died?"

"Sixteen."

"My God," she breathed against his chest.

"My sister was only eight," he continued in a hollow voice. "I always felt guilty that she didn't have more time with our parents. That she only had eight years to remember."

Claire propped her chin on his chest and looked up at him. He traced her eyebrows lightly.

Her heart clenched as she thought of the boy who lost both parents in one night, about the allegiance he must feel to the man that saved him and his little sister. "Must be hard to go against Cooper like this."

"It is and it isn't."

"What do you mean?"

"It's hard to accept that I'm breaking policy and betraying Cooper. He saved my life. And he gave me a goal, something to live for when I wanted to die right alongside my parents. I needed a purpose in life." He cupped the side of her face with one hand, his voice velvet smooth as he murmured, "But it would be harder to destroy you."

Her throat muscles tightened suddenly, so much that it hurt to breathe. And in that moment, she knew she loved him. Loved this man who had already given her so much. Given his past, he should have wanted nothing to do with her. Unable to speak past the emotion clogging her throat, she climbed her way up his chest and did the only thing she could. She kissed him. Like her soul depended on it. Like it was the final kiss she would ever have from him.

He rolled her onto her back. Claire closed her eyes and concentrated on what his mouth was doing to her and not the ever-increasing moon outside the window.

"Hello—who are you?"

The question sent Claire lurching up in bed, tearing her from disturbing dreams filled with threatening shadows and silver-eyed creatures that both terrified and tempted her.

Through the tangle of hair shielding her face, she eyed the young woman standing at the foot of the bed—a Krispy Kreme box balanced on one palm, one chocolate glazed doughnut in the other hand. She was small, slim, almost girlish in appearance except for the keen, world-wise green eyes beneath high arching eyebrows.

"Kit," Gideon groaned next to her, his muscled arm warm and solid beside hers.

Kit took a dainty bite, casually surveying her brother in bed with Claire. "I thought you liked brunettes, Gid."

"Christ," he cursed, adjusting the covers around his waist. "Just walk right in."

His sister paused to take another bite. Her tone faintly accusing, she cocked her head and gave him a coy look as she reminded him, "You gave me a key."

The smell of chocolate made Claire's stomach rumble.

"Hungry?" The blonde clamped her doughnut between pearly white teeth and poked through the contents of the box with her free hand. Stepping forward, she sat on the edge of the bed and extended a doughnut to Claire as if she visited her brother in bed with strange women all the time.

Pushing back the hair from her face, Claire reached for the offering, but Kit's sudden scream made her jerk back. Falling back on the bed, she looked around, half expecting to see a giant rat or snake slither across the floor.

Gideon cursed beside her.

A chocolate doughnut smacked Claire in the face, snapping her head back in surprise.

"Kit!" Gideon scolded as Claire wiped the sticky chocolate from her face.

"Are you crazy?" His sister charged, flinging the box of doughnuts on the floor, sending them tumbling in all directions. "You're in bed with a lycan!"

"She's only infected. She hasn't fed yet."

"Yet," she snarled, the baby-smooth lines of her face tightening.

"Kit," Gideon said, sitting up. "You're going to have to trust me. I know what I'm doing."

"How could you forget?" she demanded, her voice thick with emotion, green eyes so like Gideon's sparkling with fury.

"I'll never forget," he returned. "How could I? Maybe I want to give Claire the chance Mom never had."

"Right." She snorted, her gaze cynical. Her gaze turned on Claire then, and the full blast of venom there could be felt as keenly as a slap to the face. "*Claire*. Since when do you care about anything or anyone except killing a lycan?"

Shaking her head fiercely, she stormed out of the room. Her feet pounded down the stairs. A door slammed, the sound reverberating through the old house's thick walls.

They sat side by side for several moments, tension humming thickly on the air.

Claire turned to look at him and her mouth watered at the sight of his lean, sinewy chest. The morning light streaming through the window only highlighted the perfection of his body. She thought only movie stars had bodies like that. No man she knew did. Brian had been pasty and pale, with legs and arms skinnier than hers. Gideon's arms were tanned bands of muscle.

Averting her eyes, she murmured, "That didn't go over well, did it?"

He dragged a hand through his shaggy, sun-kissed

locks. "Not too bad actually. She didn't go for my gun and try to shoot you herself. Guess we're lucky it wasn't Cooper again this morning," he grumbled.

Claire could only nod, finding little positive about the encounter. Kit had seen only a monster when she looked at her. A monster that needed destroying. "Will she tell Cooper?"

Rubbing the back of his neck, he considered her question. "Kit's loyal. And Cooper pisses her off. Has ever since she was a kid. We lost our father and Kit didn't want him for a substitute. Resented what she thought was him trying."

"That's enough to keep her from running to him? She was pretty upset."

"Yeah. And Kit has always wanted to be an agent, but Coop won't consider it. Another reason she resents him."

"Maybe she'll decide to take me out herself, then."

"I can handle Kit." He patted her knee through the thin sheets.

The touch did anything but reassure her. Her skin sizzled from the contact. He must have realized what he had done because his hand stilled, molding to the curve of her knee. Her breath caught, trapped in her chest as their eyes locked. Last night flooded back. And with it came the hunger.

His pale green eyes deepened to a darker shade, reminding her of a forest after rain. Her skin grew warm where his hand rested.

His fingers flexed over her knee. "We really should get up."

She slid down on the bed. He came over her, the smooth expanse of muscled chest irresistible to her hands. Her fingers rounded over his firm shoulders, curling around the bulge of his biceps. He moved his hand from her knee and up over her thigh.

"We should," she agreed, gasping when he came to the juncture of her thighs. His fingers rubbed her moist folds through the thin cotton sheets, dampening the fabric with her desire.

"Later," he growled against her mouth, wrenching the sheets free and sinking his member into her with one thrust, filling her completely.

Gideon was still smiling when he stepped from the shower. Not until he wiped the mirror with his towel and stared at his face did the fool grin slip from his face. He swept his wet hair back from his face and stared starkly at himself, wondering just what the hell he was doing grinning like a love-struck fool over a woman under a death sentence.

If Claire was going to have a chance, he had to end this thing between them now. He couldn't languish away the time in bed with her, no matter how good she made him feel. For the first time in his life he could forget. *She* made him forget. The ugliness of his parents' deaths, the long years of killing, the blood. He had killed so much that when he closed his eyes he saw nothing but blood. With Claire, all that vanished. He saw only her. He felt only peace.

But any peace he found would be lost forever if he had to destroy her. Determined to keep her at arm's length, he sighed and secured the towel about his waist. Opening the bathroom door, he braced himself as though walking into battle. Facing Claire and keeping his hands to himself would require more strength than even he was accustomed to.

He froze at the sight of her. Humming softly, she stretched over the bed, pulling the covers the last of the way up and plumping the pillows. It was a purely domestic scene. The kind of task one's wife performed. The kind of thing his mother had done.

"What are you doing?" he demanded.

She looked up and bestowed a bright smile on him. At his glower, her smile grew hesitant. "Making the bed."

Turning, he marched into his closet and proceeded to dress.

"Is something wrong? Gideon?" He heard the confusion in her voice and fought back his impulse to reassure her, to take her in his arms and kiss her until he forgot what she was, what he had to save her from becoming.

"Nothing," he replied, strapping on his holster and gun. "We have a lot of ground to cover today. Let's get going."

Chapter Twelve

Dogs are proud creatures and often find it difficult to back down from a challenge.

—*Man's Best Friend: An Essential Guide to Dogs*

With his bleary eyes and slurred speech, Lenny's foster father was undeniably human. A sorry excuse, but human nonetheless. No way could he be the lycan responsible for infecting Lenny. Claire had hoped, at the very least, that he might have some information, some clue to send them in the right direction. The two friends of Lenny's they had visited earlier that morning—boys she had often seen him talking to at school—had been of no help either.

But the foster father knew even less of Lenny's habits than his friends had.

"Where's your wife?" Gideon demanded, shaking him by the shirtfront when it looked like the guy might pass out.

"She took off with some guy. Weeks ago."

Gideon let go of his shirt. The man slumped back into

the couch, his bloodshot eyes drifting to Claire. *The Price Is Right* blared loudly behind them from the tiny television. His head swayed side to side as he asked, "You that teacher Lenny always talked about? Miss Whatsit?"

"Miss Morgan, yes."

"Coulda jammed my fist in that kid's mouth for all his yapping about you." He took a swig from a can of beer. Several other crushed cans littered the chipped and stained coffee table. "Miss Morgan this, Miss Morgan that. Had a real hard-on for you. Coulda puked the number of times that kid tossed your name out. Stupid kid," he mumbled, shaking his head in disgust as he fished the remote control from under a couch cushion.

"Come on, Claire." Gideon grabbed her hand. "Let's go."

But she couldn't move. His slurred words rooted her to the floor.

"Len thought you were gonna save 'im." Throwing his arms wide, his voice cracked with harsh laughter. "Take 'im away from all this and turn 'im into a college boy. Well, how's he doing now, teacher lady?"

Claire took a deep, shuddering breath, willing her feet to move, to walk out the door.

"Let's go. Don't listen to this jackass." Gideon tugged on her hand, finally managing to pull her out the door. It slammed behind them, stinging her ears.

Claire barely registered walking, much less climbing into the Jeep. She gazed blindly through the windshield, gnawing her thumbnail to the quick before she realized the Jeep sat parked, motor silent and still.

Glancing at Gideon, she asked, "Why aren't we moving?"

Gideon gestured to the apartment building with a flick of his wrist. "Don't let that guy get to you." A flash of light lit up the sky followed by a rumble of thunder.

She shrugged one shoulder and faced the front again, the leather seat creaking as she settled her weight and leaned her head against the headrest. "He's right. I didn't help Lenny."

"Maybe. But I didn't see any other teachers in the alley putting their asses on the line for a kid that night." His voice turned hard and angry as he started the Jeep. "Maybe if you had worried a little less about Lenny and a little more about Claire, you wouldn't be where you are now." He gave the gear stick a rough yank. "I think you've sacrificed plenty, more than Lenny ever wanted or expected—"

"How do you know what Lenny thought? He probably thought I didn't—"

"He knew you cared. His last words were of you."

Her mouth snapped shut. Nothing could have shocked her more. Lenny spoke of her at the end? Pressing a hand to her chest, almost afraid to ask, she whispered, "What did he say?"

She watched Gideon's jaw tense, the muscles flexing. A loud crack of thunder fractured the silence.

"What did he say?" she repeated over the thunder's echo, staring at the fast-darkening sky through the windshield.

"He told me to help you." His gaze flicked to her, then back to the road. "He made me promise to help you."

"And that's why you're doing this?"

Another pause. Then he answered, "No."

Her brow furrowed. "Why then?"

"I don't know why," he explained, his voice impatient.

At that moment, the sky opened up and rain poured down in torrents, angrily pounding against the windshield and beating noisily on the Bikini cover. The windshield wipers worked overtime, fighting the onslaught of water.

They drove on the congested four-lane highway in silence before she dared to announce, "Could we get something to eat?"

She scanned their surroundings. A myriad of restaurants blended together through a veil of rain, indistinct shapes dwarfed by tall gray buildings and taller billboards, but none were what she wanted. "There's a place called Angelo's near my apartment, and I could pick a few things up while we're there."

Thirty minutes later, a red-checkered vinyl tablecloth separated them. Gideon opened a plastic-coated menu, his hair glistening and slightly wet from the five-foot hurdle to Angelo's covered portico.

"Everything's good," she volunteered, fluffing her own damp locks with her hand.

The waiter soon arrived and Claire placed her three-course order. Gideon didn't blink an eye, no doubt accustomed to her unending eat-fest.

"Maybe we could go grocery shopping after this and get some things for the house."

His eyes shot to hers over the rim of his glass, wide and unblinking in his expressionless face. He took his time setting his glass back down on the table before saying quietly, "I don't think so."

"It'd be nice if—"

"It'd be nice," Gideon interrupted, "if you stopped trying to play house with me."

Heat flooded her face. "I only suggested we buy groceries so we don't have to keep eating out."

"You made my bed," he cut in.

Claire jerked, not foreseeing that complaint. "So." Thank God he hadn't caught her inhaling his scent on the sheets and pillows, closing her eyes as love for Gideon washed over her unchecked. She fisted both hands on the tabletop.

At that moment the food arrived. A strained silence fell. Tension crackled on the air. The waiter looked from one to the other uneasily before making a quick escape.

Gideon motioned between the two of them. "This has got to stop."

"What?"

"This thing between us. It's distracting me from what I need to be doing . . . which is focusing on finding the alpha to break your curse."

"I thought that's what we've been doing."

His green eyes sparked fire. "I suppose we are. When we're not fucking. Or when I'm not thinking of fucking you."

She blinked at his coarse words. Unbidden, the image of them sweaty and tangled in his sheets rose in her mind. Body tingling, she traced the rim of her glass. "What are you saying?"

"If I'm not going to put all my energy and attention into helping you break this curse, then I might as well destroy you now."

Claire sucked in a deep breath and sank back into

the leather bench, tossing her napkin on the table. "So you scratched your itch and now you're wondering why you're keeping me around anymore, is that?" She swallowed down the hot lump rising in her throat.

"Claire, that's not—"

"What are you waiting for?" she asked, her voice shockingly calm. "You think I need to be destroyed. Go ahead, then."

Their gazes clashed in silent battle. Belatedly, she realized that she'd thrown down one hell of a dare.

She waited for him to say something, to refute her taunt by saying that he couldn't do that. That he didn't want to, that what he felt for her would never permit him to do such a thing. Instead, he just stared at her with cold eyes.

Even knowing he could offer no such assurances—that it was unfair to expect him to soothe her with false promises—she felt a flash of anger. She had given more than her body to him. It was not just some curse, some animal instinct that drew her to him. Her hunger forgotten, Claire bolted from the table and fled the restaurant.

She heard him call her name, but didn't stop.

Pushing the door open, she fled into the rain. She hurried along the uneven sidewalk edging the road, enduring the splashing water from passing cars. One stopped. A Jeep. A maroon Jeep. The passenger door flung open. Gideon leaned across the seat, shouting, "Get in!"

"No," she shouted back and continued walking in stiff strides, hands shielding her face in a feeble effort to ward off the rain. A pointless endeavor. She was already soaked.

With the passenger door swinging open, the Jeep sped ahead and drove up onto the sidewalk, jerking to a stop several feet in front of her and blocking the driveway to her dry cleaner's. Claire stopped and stared at those red parking lights warily. The driver's door thrust open and Gideon climbed out. He marched toward her, his lean figure cutting through the rain like a blade, eyes unblinking against the deluge of water sluicing down the hard planes of his face. Hands fisted at his sides, he stopped in front of her. Her head fell back to glare at him.

"Are you getting in?"

She hesitated, staring at the unyielding set of his mouth and reading the determination in his face to have his way, to win. He wouldn't accept anything less than her total surrender. She knew that. Just as she knew she could not—would not—give in to his bullying. She'd been bullied enough in her life. No more.

She found the will to lift her voice over the pounding rain. "No!"

Gideon had seen this in a movie before. Girl won't get in the car. Guy demands she does. Girl tells him to go to hell right before guy flings her over his shoulder in a caveman display of dominance. If Claire wanted to play that girl, then he would be more than happy to oblige her and play his part.

Bending, he grabbed her by the knees and flung her over his shoulder. She screeched and pummeled the backs of his thighs with her fists. He was well aware she didn't hit like a girl—not with the lycan blood coursing through her veins—and that first blow nearly brought him down.

"Let me go!" she demanded over the steady beat of rain.

"Can't." Grinning, he adjusted her more comfortably on his shoulder and suffered her punches. "You'd fall on your head and break your neck."

She jabbed a fist into his back, grinding her knuckles into his spine and nearly upsetting his balance on the slippery sidewalk. He delivered a loud smack to her rear end. "Stop that or we'll both fall and crack our heads."

"Well, that wouldn't kill *me*, would it?" she retorted.

"Smartass," he grumbled, dumping her in the passenger seat.

He was half-afraid she would bolt when he left her to walk around to the driver's side, but she wisely stayed put. Slamming his door shut, he turned to look at her. With her wet hair plastered to her head, she reminded him of a drowned cat. Her chest rose and fell with ragged breaths, her dusky nipples pebble hard through her soaked shirt. His hands itched to take hold of them, to taste them through her wet bra and shirt.

She stared ahead, not looking his way, ignoring him.

He rested both hands on top of the steering wheel, palms and fingers slippery wet against the leather, grappling for control. What the hell was he doing? Getting in too deep, his mind was quick to reply.

Simultaneously, they turned and looked at each other.

He didn't know who moved first. Whatever the case, he was kissing her, his hands cupping her wet cheeks, his fingers tangling in the soaking strands of her hair. He crushed her to him, swallowing her moan into his mouth, frustrated by the uncomfortable gear stick between them. God, he felt like he was back in high school again, making out in the front seat of his grandmother's cramped Honda. Only she wasn't some teenage tease. And he wasn't some fumbling, desperate boy. Well, maybe he was desperate. He had to be. Why else was he so damned attracted to her? A lycan? One overexcited nip from her and it all ended. At least for him. Like playing with fire. And even that knowledge couldn't make him stop, couldn't keep him from delving his tongue deeper into her mouth.

Her little mewling sounds drove him wild and he strained against her, hungry to get his hands and mouth on the soft mounds crushing into his chest.

The sound of a horn startled them and sent them flying apart. He looked wildly about, realizing he had caused a minor traffic jam.

A woman in a Cadillac was stopped halfway in the road, halfway in the driveway, honking madly on her horn. A line of cars honked behind her, all unable to move forward.

Ignoring the way his hands shook, he shifted the gear stick and sped off. His tires locked for a moment on the wet road, sending his Jeep into a fishtail. Claire gasped beside him until he gained control of the vehicle.

He didn't speak until they pulled up in front of her apartment a minute later. "I thought we could dry off and you could get the things you wanted."

At that precise moment the aroma of melted cheese and rich marinara sauce hit him in full, tantalizing force, reminding him of what he had in the backseat.

"What's that smell?" Apparently, Claire hadn't missed it either.

"Our lunch."

She looked over her shoulder at the bags of food sitting in the back. Taking one bag, he handed her the other. Arms shielding their precious cargo, they darted through the rain to her apartment, which was dark and stale from lack of use. Flipping on the light, she set her bag on the table. He placed his bag on the surface as well. She looked around her apartment, surveying everything with an air of sadness, as if seeing it for the first time. And in many ways it was the first time, he reasoned. She saw it through new eyes. The eyes of a woman who didn't know how much time she had left.

Damn, there he went again. Connecting with her. Empathizing with her. Wanting to pull her into his arms and kiss her fears away, to bury himself in her heat until both of them forgot the world around them.

He had to keep personal feelings for her at bay. It would only make destroying her harder—if it came down to that.

Her eyes widened as he pulled his sodden shirt out of his jeans and over his head.

"What are you doing?"

"Getting undressed. Got a towel?" he asked.

She nodded jerkily and disappeared into her room, returning seconds later with a towel in her hands. "Why don't you throw your clothes in the drier." She pointed to what looked like a closet tucked behind her kitchen table. "I'm going to change."

He waited until the bedroom door shut behind her

before removing the rest of his clothes. Standing naked in the middle of her living room, he used the towel to rub himself dry. That done, he secured the towel around his waist and dumped his wet clothes in the small drier. The machine's rumble soon filled the air, accompanied by the occasional clinking against the metal drum.

By the time she joined him, wearing a pair of gray sweats and a Texas A&M T-shirt, he sat at the kitchen table unloading their food. Her gaze shot to his bare chest, her hungry gaze chipping at his resolve to keep things impersonal between them.

"Do you understand what I was trying to say at the restaurant?" he blurted, compelled to reach an understanding with her . . . with himself.

She bit her bottom lip and his gaze focused on those small white teeth sinking into the moist pink flesh. Releasing the lip, she replied, "Yes."

"No more intimacy. From now on, what we have is strictly a working relationship. Our only focus is on getting you out of this mess. It's the only way."

"Of course." She nodded.

They ate in silence. Exactly what Gideon preferred. No more talk of grocery shopping. No more behaving like a couple, like lovers. Silence. Distance. No threats to the walls he struggled to erect between them. She finally understood how it had to be between them.

A heavy weight settled in his chest, part remorse, part resignation.

He was halfway through his spaghetti when Claire gave a small gasp and looked up. "Woody's," she blurted, clutching her spoon tightly. "Lenny hung out at a place called Woody's. A student mentioned seeing him there shortly before he attacked me. She said he was with some creepy older-looking guys."

"Woody's? In the Village?" he asked. Instead of relief that they now had a lead, he felt a flash of anger. "Why are you only now telling me this?"

"I just remembered," she said in defense, shrugging. "It's not as if I kept it from you on purpose."

"'Course not," he replied in clipped tones, annoyed all over again and feeling suddenly validated. Maybe she would have remembered sooner if he hadn't been busy getting her flat on her back. "Anything else you forgot to mention? Any silver-eyed students? A colleague exhibiting uncharacteristic aggression?"

Her eyes shot icy daggers at him. "Very funny."

"Because it's only your life on the line here."

Claire's voice trembled. "I've got more at stake here than you. Next time you're worried about growing too attached to someone you might have to kill, remember that I'm the one needing the killing."

She surged to her feet, her silver eyes shadowed with raw emotion. "I'll be in my room getting a few things."

Alone, he stared at her door, contemplating whether he should knock and check on her. Then he shook his head, hardening his heart. Distance, he reminded himself. It was the best thing. For both of them.

Chapter Thirteen

A dog's instinct never fails.

—*Man's Best Friend: An Essential Guide to Dogs*

The gun felt heavy in her hands. Heavier than the one she had purchased—the one she had intended to use on Gideon when she thought him a dangerous lunatic. Strange how things had changed in such a short time. She no longer thought him a lunatic. Just dangerous. And mostly to her heart.

"Standard NODEAL issue. Forty-four revolver. Custom-made silencer," Gideon explained, stroking a finger along the barrel. "Cock the hammer with your thumb."

Claire pulled the hammer back, the grinding click an oddly satisfying sound, empowering. A good feeling. Just what she needed for the night ahead.

They were venturing out to Woody's. It was strange, but she felt tonight was it. The night they would find the alpha. The night she would be returned to herself. But perhaps that was just desperate hope.

"Then you just pull the trigger. Your aim doesn't have

to be great, just make sure you hit your target. The silver will do all the work." Gideon nodded in approval as she repositioned the cold, hard steel in her hands and aimed at the wall of his living room. "Looks like you have some experience handling guns."

Claire shrugged. "A little." She didn't bother telling him about the gun she had purchased. Ever since leaving her apartment they spoke only when necessary. He had made it clear they weren't friends—not lovers—merely cohorts united for a like purpose. It didn't matter that she wanted more, that she wanted him. It was an odd sort of irony. He couldn't let himself want her, because she might not live out the week. But she wanted him all the more, desperately, because of that same fact.

Gideon took the gun from her, flipped the lever on its side, and with a flick of his wrist demonstrated how to open the cylinder. He pointed at the flat faces of six silver bullets before turning the gun and emptying them into his palm. His movements were deft and practiced, those of a man long accustomed to handling firearms. "If you empty the rounds tonight, reload—immediately. Never be caught with an empty cylinder."

Claire nodded. Gideon tossed the bullets in his hand. "Customized Colombian silver bullets." They clinked together lightly. "Okay. This is the hard part."

Her gaze shot to his grim face, arching a brow in silent question.

Seizing her hand, he dropped the bullets into her open palm. "Reload."

Claire hissed in pain and dropped the bullets that scorched her flesh. They clattered noisily to the wood floor, spinning and whirring in wide circles at her feet. She stared down at her open palm, at the angry red welts rising on her skin—exactly six in number.

"Pick 'em up."

"They burn."

"You're a lycan. Silver burns. Now pick them up."

"What about gloves—"

"You'll look strange wearing gloves in ninety-degree heat, and you can't take the time to put on a pair of gloves when you need to be quick and reload."

Claire sucked in a deep breath and pressed her wounded palm against her denim shorts in an attempt to reduce the sting. Flexing her other hand around the gun, she squatted and stared down at the innocent-looking cylinders, bracing herself to pick them up.

"If you can't load the gun, you can't defend yourself," Gideon said above her. "You might as well quit right now."

Quit. He meant die.

Swallowing, she poised her hand over one bullet. With a deep breath she grabbed it, ignoring that it felt like fire on her fingertips. Trying not to fumble, she slid it into one chamber. Her hand dove for the next one, afraid that if she stopped she would never finish. Sweat broke out on her forehead, and the smell of burning flesh seared her nostrils. After the fourth bullet, she looked at her hand. The fingers were badly blistered. Tendrils of smoke drifted above her palm and she gave a strangled cry, horrified at further evidence of her descent into a nightmare from which she could not wake.

"Move," Gideon growled next to her ear. She hadn't

even noticed when he dropped down beside her. "Don't stop, damn it. Move."

Tears blurred her vision as she finished loading the last two bullets. She forced herself to grip the gun in her throbbing hands. Lifting her chin, she glared at him defiantly, her chest lifting in pride. "I can do it."

"Good," he announced in a flat voice, his look frustratingly blank. "Just be ready to do it again tonight." He turned and left. Her heart sank as she listened to his fading footsteps.

Claire sank onto the couch and set the gun beside her. Outside, the sun dipped behind the treetops. Another day gone. Tonight would be the night. It had to be. She flexed her sore hands open and shut. Already the pain was starting to ebb, the lycan ability to heal working its magic.

Only the pain in her heart lingered.

Woody's catered to a wide spectrum of patrons: from high school adolescents eager to test their independence to hard-edged thirty-somethings. Music pulsed over the air, a heavy, discordant throb emitted from a band that appeared to be strung out.

It wasn't long before Claire spotted Nina through the haze of smoke, in a skirt much shorter than any she ever wore to school.

Claire pointed across the dance floor to the girl. Gideon followed her finger, his gaze running over Nina in cool assessment.

"What's her story?" He spoke over the bar's din, his first words since he left her standing in his living room.

"She's a good student." Claire studied the crowd surrounding Nina. Some were recognizable from the hallways. "Transferred in last January. Can't recall where she came from exactly."

"Maybe a little of everywhere?" he asked grimly.

"Yeah," Claire said in surprise. "Something like that. I think her dad is in the marines. How'd you guess?"

"Packs move around. It's not their nature to feed in one area too long. Long-standing impulse—don't deplete the food source."

Claire swung her gaze from Gideon back to Nina. "You're not suggesting—"

"Why not? She knew Lenny and could easily have infected him." He shrugged. "I'm not getting a read on her either way, but the more experienced lycans are harder to detect. Especially the females. They're more adept at blending in."

"She's just a girl."

"For all we know, she could be five hundred years old. Lycans can live a very long time. The longest on record is twelve hundred years."

She felt her eyes widen. "There's a twelve-hundred-year-old werewolf out there?"

"We *think* he's still out there. He's either dead or been lying low for a couple centuries. If he's dead, it's through natural causes. Otherwise NODEAL would have a record."

She silently wondered how NODEAL could efficiently monitor the comings and goings of every single werewolf, but she let the matter drop, refocusing her attention on Nina and the possibility that her prize student might be a werewolf.

The notion troubled her, and not simply because she cared for Nina. "A female alpha?" She felt her brow scrunch.

"Alphas are frequently female."

"Really?"

"Sure. Don't females rule many species? Ants? Bees? Even ancient human cultures bowed before woman."

Claire nodded. She supposed a lifetime of watching her father subjugate women—including her—made her question the notion of female empowerment.

Still, Nina?

"Last night I felt those other two. Before they even attacked us. I've never felt anything around Nina."

"She could be that good." At her skeptical look he elaborated, "Alphas are the wisest, strongest lycans out there. They are masters of camouflage. You may never sense them. But let's find out if you can."

They cut through the dance floor, skirting gyrating couples as they made their way to the predominantly teen section. Heavier smoke. Fewer bottles. Apparently not everyone possessed a fake ID. Their presence definitely earned a few stares. Especially Gideon's. He towered over boys who had yet to reach full development, and the girls openly drooled.

She tapped Nina on the shoulder.

"Omigod! Miss Morgan!" The girl crushed Claire in a hug.

The hug felt good. Surprisingly good. Even amid the heavy smoke, she inhaled the clean, fruity scent of Nina's shampoo, overcome by the realization that this might be the last time she saw her. She squeezed Nina closer. Claire gave herself a mental shake. Now was not the time to walk that dark road. She needed to concentrate on other things. Like whether or not Nina could be the werewolf that infected Lenny.

Claire didn't sense anything, didn't *feel* anything beyond the bittersweet emotion that welled up inside her. Arms locked around the girl's slight frame, she knew Nina couldn't be anything other than what she appeared: a sweet, innocent girl.

"Where have you been?" Nina pulled back to demand. "We have this awful sub! She assigned us seats and I have to sit next to Eddy Case!" She noticed Gideon then and her eyes widened. "Is this your boyfriend?" Before Claire could answer, Nina rushed on, her words tumbling out excitedly, "I heard a rumor you were dating Mr. Jenkins, but I didn't want to believe it." Her lip curled in distaste. "He's bald."

Claire rolled her eyes. That one date was going to follow her for the rest of her life.

"Mr. Jenkins and I are *not* dating."

Nina waved a finger back and forth between Claire and Gideon. "So this is your boyfriend."

"Yes," Gideon answered smoothly, slipping an arm around her waist. Claire stamped down her streak of pleasure at the feel of that solid arm holding her close.

Nina grinned and winked at her, mouthing, *"Nice."*

Deciding a change of subject was in order, Claire asked, "How's school?"

"Almost over. Thank God."

They chatted for a few more minutes until Gideon caught her eye and motioned for them to move on. With a hug, she pulled away. Gideon led her to the bar at the far end of the room.

"Well," she asked, "what do you think?"

"More importantly, what did you think? Feel anything?"

She shook her head, her gaze shooting back to the group of teenagers. "Nothing. Not from any of them."

"Maybe it's no one from school. Maybe it's someone in his family."

"He only had foster parents." She sighed, resisting the hopelessness threatening to swallow her. "And we already checked them out."

"The mother wasn't there."

"He said she took off," Claire reminded him.

"Yeah, that's what *he* said." Gideon shook his head.

A cold weight settled in the pit of her stomach. The alpha could be anyone in the entire city. The entire state, for that matter. It could have been a random infection; it didn't even have to be someone Lenny knew.

"Hey." He turned her to face him, his fingers whisper-soft on her chin. The gentle look in his eyes tormented her, made her want what he would not give. It was easier when he treated her like a stranger. Easier to not want him so badly that way.

He continued in that velvet voice, "I haven't given up. Don't you quit either."

Her thoughts in a jumble, she forced a wobbly smile.

Suddenly, her nape prickled. Her eyes cut across the room, knowing what she would find staring back at her.

"Over there," she squeaked, her gaze trapped by two pairs of silver eyes. One male. One female.

Gideon followed her gaze across the room through the haze of smoke. "Bingo."

"They're—"

"Lycans," he supplied.

"They're not wearing contacts," she added, wetting her lips nervously.

Their eyes glowed bold and obtrusive amid a crowd of ordinary faces. Claire shivered.

Tight red leather molded the female's body like a second skin, hiding nothing of her sleek, lithe form. They watched her intently, two hungry predators.

"They're not trying to hide." Gideon nodded grimly. "Confident bastards."

No, not hiding. It was more like they were advertising themselves. Her skin sizzled where their gazes trailed, eliciting a strange longing, an unremitting ache that throbbed deep within her. She resisted their pull by turning her back on them. Her eyes darted wildly ahead of her, instinctively searching for an escape route.

"It's okay," Gideon murmured against her ear, clearly sensing her anxiety. "See that exit in the back." His breath, soft as a feather, ruffled her hair. Claire inhaled a shaky breath, looked to the red exit sign in the distance, and nodded.

"I'm going to leave out the front. Wait five minutes and take the back exit," he instructed.

"You want me to lead them outside," she concluded, briefly shutting her eyes against the panic rising hot and bitter in her throat. Her last experience with these creatures was still fresh on her mind. The thought of being alone with them even for a moment had her shaking her head.

Gideon grabbed her face and forced her to look at him. "You can do this, Claire. You have a gun. Use it if you need to."

Her hand went to the leather handbag against her hip where her gun slumbered, loaded by her own hand.

His green eyes gleamed with determination. "I won't let them hurt you." His fingers pressed into her cheeks, injecting her with some of his courage.

Her eyes drank in his face, absorbing his words and letting them fortify her. "All right," she agreed.

"Good girl." Before he dropped his hands from her face, he planted a hard kiss on her mouth. She had no doubt in her mind it was just for show, for the benefit of watchful eyes, when he muttered against her lips, "Leave one of them alive for questioning. Give me time to get in position. When they follow you, don't look back. Talk to them. Distract them until I make my move. You won't see me, but I'll be there."

Then he was gone. She closed her eyes briefly, inhaling the lingering scent of him, suppressing the sudden stab of loneliness at not having him at her side.

Chapter Fourteen

Dogs possess a keen sense of smell.

—*Man's Best Friend: An Essential Guide to Dogs*

Gideon lowered himself behind a stack of crates, muscles stretched tight as he peered between a crack in the wood slats. Pulling the gun from its holster, he screwed on the silencer. Tonight would be different. Tonight they were ready. Prepared. No more surprises. No more ambushes.

He trained all his attention on that door, waiting breathlessly for Claire to emerge. Unfortunately, he was too focused. He didn't notice he had company until he heard the shoe scrape over loose gravel behind him. He spun, dropping to his belly, leveling the gun on the slight figure at the mouth of the alley.

"Kit!" He rose to a squatting position and lowered his gun.

She stood over him, one of his guns, a ridiculously large .357, in her hand. "Hey, big brother."

He yanked her down, glancing over his shoulder at

the club's back door. Satisfied that they were alone, he demanded, "What the hell are you doing here?" He nodded at the too-large gun in her hands. Kit took after their mother. At five feet, she barely reached his shoulder. The gun looked obscene in her slight hands. "And where did you get that monster?"

Readjusting her fingers around the gun's bulk, she ignored his question. "Thought you could use some backup."

"Since when do I include you on my hunts?"

"Since when do you shelter lycans?" She stuck out her chin the same way she had done as a determined two-year-old, dead set on buckling herself into her own car seat even if she hadn't figured out how to work the belts and clasps. "Considering you've taken it upon yourself to break a few rules, I figured I could, too."

Cursing, he jumped to his feet and dragged her after him out of the alley. He wasn't about to risk his sister's life. Legally, she might be an adult, but he was still her brother. Hell, he was more than a brother. Since their parents' deaths, he was her sole parent. Their grandmother had fed and sheltered them, but at sixteen Gideon had known she viewed them as a yoke about her neck. At sixty-five, she had finished raising children and only did the bare minimum parenting.

Kit tugged against his hold. Clearing the alley, he released her and shoved her ahead of him into the parking lot. "Go home, Kit."

"No." She propped a fist on her hip.

"You can't stay." He waved to the sea of cars. "Leave." He glanced over his shoulder, hoping Claire hadn't stepped outside yet.

"Let me stay."

"You know why you can't. NODEAL prohibits female agents for a reason."

"Yeah, and it's bullshit."

"No, it's proven fact. Menstruation makes females more vulnerable. We need agents that are not only strong but more difficult to detect."

Kit pointed at herself. "Well, if Cooper is going to accuse me of hunting lycans and read me the riot act for something I didn't do, then I might as well get in on the game."

He sighed and looked up at the sky. *Cooper.* Gideon should have guessed. She did the opposite of whatever that man said. "He came to see you, huh?"

"Uh, yeah." She said with heavy sarcasm, nodding as if that much was clear. "He tore me a new one."

"He's under a lot of stress," Gideon found himself defending him. "Never forget how much we owe him, Kit."

"What about you," she accused, arching an eyebrow. "You seem to have forgotten. You're the one breaking code behind his back."

Her words hit home, igniting a guilty flame in his heart. He dropped his hand and said flatly, "Go home, Kit."

"When are you going to stop treating me like a child?" Green eyes so like his own glinted up angrily at him. "You're not my father, Gid. If I want to do this, you can't stop me."

Gideon squeezed the bridge of his nose. He didn't have time for this.

Clasping the gun in both hands, elbows bent, she

faced the alley. Gideon nearly groaned, remembering that while his friends' sisters had played with dolls, his had wanted to play cops and robbers. Just his luck she never outgrew the habit.

"I'm the closest thing to a father you've got. If our father were here, he'd tell you to go home, too."

"And I'd tell him exactly what I'm telling you. I'm staying."

Gideon stared up at the sky again, pleading for patience before shooting another glance behind him. He couldn't waste any more time arguing with his sister. Claire needed him.

"Don't follow me," he warned, jabbing his thumb behind him. "I mean it."

At the stubborn jut of her chin, he used the one trump card he held, even if he found the notion of blackmail distasteful. "You want to pay your own way through school?"

Her eyes narrowed.

He didn't like threatening to withdraw his financial support. Even if she did change her major every semester, she was smart and he wanted her to finish school, to get the education he didn't have. He wanted her to go places. To be somebody—not an agent chasing vengeance like him.

At the mutinous twist of her lips, he knew he had won. He pointed to the parking lot behind her. "Get in your car."

She scuffed her shoe against the pavement, reminding him of the little girl he used to send home when she tried to tag along with him and his friends. Only she wasn't a little girl anymore. She was a grown woman with more courage than sense. Like it or not, Gideon couldn't protect her forever. If she was dead set on becoming an agent like him, there was little he—or Cooper—could do about it. Honestly, he'd rather have her go through NODEAL training and start out with a team than set out into the world as a vigilante and get herself killed.

He released a pent-up breath. "If you leave now, I'll talk to Cooper for you."

Her gaze, glowing with hope, shot to him. "Promise?"

Gideon nodded, feeling the frown pulling at the corners of his mouth. He didn't like it, but Kit's stubbornness gave him little choice. "I promise. Now go."

"You're awesome!" Grinning, she spun around, her fair hair tossing about her head. "You won't regret it."

Gideon scowled. He already did.

She closed the door firmly behind her, drowning out the heavy thrum of music. Rotting refuse from the Dumpsters tainted the air, and she pressed a hand over her sensitive nose. She was reminded of another alley not so long ago. Only this one was darker and smelled worse. And there was no guesswork involved. She knew what would be joining her. Had felt their eyes on her back as she exited the bar.

Her eyes scanned the narrow space stretching in front of her, searching left and right for a glimpse of Gideon. The opening leading to the parking lot yawned far ahead.

With a few quick steps, she distanced herself from the door. Inhaling, she braced herself, waiting, staring in silence at the dark steel door. She lifted her face to the night sky. The moon shimmered through swiftly moving clouds, a beautiful, frightening thing, bathing the alley in an iridescent glow. Watching, waiting, biding its time. Barely a week remained.

A heavy blare of music signaled the door's opening. Claire dropped her gaze and watched them step out one by one. The door shut behind them, once again muffling the music and noise from the bar. Their number had grown to three. The third to join possessed arms the size of tree trunks. Her chest rose and fell a bit faster, the beating of her heart in sync with the distant thrum of music.

That familiar sensation, warning of nearby lycans, tingled at her nape, far more intense than the night before. Was it because there were three of them? Or because they were stronger, more powerful, than last night's lycans?

Her tongue darted out to wet her lips. She pulled her purse in front of her, her hands worrying the strap, letting it act as a shield.

A spark of hope flared to life, worming its way inside her fear-clogged heart. Maybe one of them was the alpha they sought. Maybe it could end here, tonight. Lenny had frequented this place. It wasn't an impossibility that one of the three could be the alpha she sought.

The youngest-looking of the three smiled almost kindly, his teeth a flash of white against his tan face. "You look lonely, dear." He extended an elegant long-fingered hand to her. His black Italian silk shirt rippled over his finely sculpted chest with the movement. "There's no reason for one of our kind to ever be lonely."

Claire's feet shuffled back a step, her heart hammering wildly in her chest. That coaxing voice and smile mesmerized her, summoning her nearer as if pulling her by an invisible thread.

She felt his power. Recognized instantly he was the leader among the three. The strongest.

"You're alone," the female in red stated.

Claire nodded. "I'm looking for someone."

"And who would that be?" she asked.

At this, Claire hedged.

"Who turned you?" the leader asked, his voice smooth as silk.

Claire's gaze locked with his, recognizing at once that he understood. He knew she sought the alpha responsible for her curse. "A boy named Lenny."

"I don't know him. Careless of him to turn you and then leave you to your own devices. Lycans are careful at initiating into our pack."

"Yes," the female chimed in with a sneer. "We don't let any trash off the streets join us."

"Come, Bianca," the leader chided. "Be hospitable. Our lovely friend here is one of us now and she appears to be in need of guidance."

"I'm not one of you." Claire slid her hand inside her purse and curled her fingers around the gun.

"Is that what you think?" The leader's kind smile turned almost cruel then. "Pity. We shall have to convince you, then."

"Join us." Bianca stretched out her hand. Claire stared at that slender hand with its perfectly manicured nails and a strange sense of detachment settled over her.

Something cold and evil glittered in the female's steel gaze. Malevolence shadowed the curve of her mouth, and Claire knew there wasn't anything friendly about her.

The newest member to the trio growled his impatience. "Enough talk." He smoothed a hand over his slicked-back hair, fingers sliding down the dark length of his tight ponytail with an anxious energy. "Let's take her and show her what it means to be a lycan."

Claire's skin crawled as she watched him run his tongue over fleshy lips. *Take her.* She knew he meant more than coercing her to join their pack. Instantly, Claire marked him the wild card. The impatient one.

He started toward her, his silver gaze glowing brilliantly, startling and otherworldly against his swarthy face.

Gideon, where are you?

Unwilling to wait any longer, she slid the gun from her purse, flexing her hand around the textured grip, cold and abrasive in her hand.

The beefy lycan paused, staring in confusion at her gun before his lips peeled back into a feral grin. He shook his head slowly, wagging a long, thick-nailed finger.

"Ah, ah, ah," he said as if they played a game, as if she weren't serious, as if she didn't have every intention of blowing a hole through his black heart if he took one more step. "First rule of the pack is to stick together."

"I'm not of your pack."

"A lone female—breeding as you are," the leader inserted. "You have to belong to a pack. It might as well be ours. Accept what you are. There is no other choice. You are one of us. You can't undo it."

His words hit her hard, as no blow could.

The brawny lycan continued his advance.

"Stop." Her thumb pulled back the hammer, the grinding click loud on the air. "I mean it," she warned, her finger curled around the trigger.

She aimed at his chest and shook her head side to side in determined avowal. "I swear to God I'll shoot."

The leader's voice continued, rolling over her, seductive and mesmerizing, softening her will. "Everything's confusing right now. We can make things easier. Come with us. We'll show you how incredible life can be."

"I'm not one of you," she muttered in a harsh whisper. Jamming her eyes shut, she squeezed the trigger. The gun bucked in her hands. The acrid smell of cordite stung her nostrils.

She peeked one eye open, then the other. The brawny lycan stood frozen, rooted in place just inches from her. He looked down at his chest and back to her face in shock.

She watched as he toppled to the ground. She felt no rush of victory. Only shock. She had killed someone—no, not someone. She had destroyed a lycan. Yet it was hard to remember the distinction as the silver faded like a wisp of smoke from his eyes, leaving a very mortal shade of brown behind.

A flash of movement caught her eye. Too late. She didn't have time to lift the gun and aim before the shrieking female charged her. Claire landed on her back with a teeth-rattling jolt. Her gun clattered against the pavement, skittering several feet away. Pinned, she couldn't budge as razor sharp nails attacked her neck and face, scratching and slicing in a flurry of motion. Saliva dribbled down onto her face from the crimson lips snarling above her.

With a howl of rage, Claire caught one of the flying wrists and gave it a vicious twist. The female hissed and brought her other hand crashing against Claire's face.

Surging against her, Claire flipped the female off her. Snarling, she jumped into a crouching position, readying herself.

"Enough, Bianca," the leader's voice declared.

"She killed Marcus. She has to die." Bianca jerked her head in the direction of Claire's gun. "Let's give her a taste of her own poison."

The lycan crossed his arms over his silk shirt and murmured, "Then we would have two dead instead of one."

"She killed her own kind," Bianca snarled, body flexing beneath the red leather as if she would spring on Claire again. "She has to die."

Claire's stomach churned and her eyes darted back and forth between the two lycans discussing whether she lived or died.

"I don't think so." He rubbed his chin. "She is new. Confused. She hasn't been properly schooled."

"She used a silver bullet, Ian." Her manicured hand motioned to Marcus's corpse in disgust. "She knew what she was doing. She must pay."

"There are ways she can serve the pack. She's breeding. In a year she can give back a life for the one taken."

Bianca growled her disagreement. "The decision isn't yours." In a flash, she was up and heading for the gun, muttering over her shoulder, "You can't stop me."

A definite edge entered his voice as he softly threatened, "Pick up that gun and you deal with me."

Bianca halted and looked over her shoulder.

The air changed, altering imperceptibly. Claire waited breathlessly, observing the silent exchange between them. Indecision flickered across Bianca's face. Her gaze drifted longingly to the gun before sliding back to Claire. "You just want to mate with her." The words spewed from her red lips like venom.

"Now, now, kitten," Ian chided, his tone conciliatory. "Benedict will decide—it's his right."

Because he was their alpha? Claire's pulse jumped hopefully against her throat. Could this Benedict be the one?

"Fine." Bianca glared at her, making it clear she would never be fine. Not as long as Claire lived, anyway.

"And Bianca." Ian waited until he had her full attention again. "Benedict will agree with me. So put aside your petty jealousies. She will be one of us."

Bianca's lips peeled back from her teeth in a sneer. "No one will forget she killed Marcus. I won't."

Ian flicked his wrist and released a little sigh. "Marcus wore too much cologne. Besides, she is far prettier."

Bianca strode past Claire, managing to sneak a kick to the ribs with the pointed toe of her boot.

"Watch the hooker boots, would you?" Claire hissed.

Bianca's eyes narrowed to slits, the silver glowing like light spilling from a shutter.

Suddenly, the music from inside the bar grew louder, announcing a new arrival. Claire glanced up at the heavy clang of the club's back door, praying to see Gideon, but her hopes were dashed when she met another silver-eyed gaze. Her heart plummeted to her stomach. Where the hell was Gideon?

The newcomer assessed their tableau before his gaze settled on Claire with unnerving intensity. Dressed all in black, his face was hard as granite, his square jaw unmoving, framed by hair as black as his clothing.

He studied her for a long moment before commanding, "Come."

"She's ours." Bianca declared. "Don't interfere—"

He flashed a broad hand in the air, silencing her. "Step away if you wish to live." His speech was oddly formal.

Bianca blinked at this edict and looked to her companion uncertainly.

"Who are you?" Ian asked.

"Someone you don't wish to challenge," he answered, never once looking to Ian. His steady gaze stayed on Claire with searing intensity.

"And why is that?"

"My name," the newcomer paused, finally looking to the nervous pair, "is Darius."

A change swept over the two lycans, an anxiety that had not been there before. She could taste their fear, coppery and metallic as blood in her mouth.

"Leave her and go," Darius repeated, his voice a rasp of sound on the air.

Ian and Bianca exchanged looks. Finally, a touch of defiance to his voice, Ian announced, "Darius is dead."

The one claiming to be Darius smiled. A strange smile. Like it didn't belong on his face. Like it hurt his cheeks to do so. "Is that what is being said?"

"Does she belong to you?" Bianca demanded. Ian grabbed her arm and gave her a warning glance.

"Let's just say I'm making her my concern."

"She killed one of our pack." Bianca shrugged free of Ian's hand and pointed to the corpse, heedless of her cohort's silent warning. "In accordance with pack law, we demand recompense."

"Very well." Darius's voice was cold, curt, void of emotion, his unfamiliar accent enunciating each word crisply. "I shall recompense you by letting you live."

Bianca's mouth parted in a small O of surprise. Apparently Claire wasn't the only one breaking pack customs.

Darius motioned at Bianca. "Rein in your bitch lest you lose two members of your pack this night."

Bianca looked prepared to argue, but Ian clamped a hand down on her arm, saying in a tight voice, "Shut up, Bianca."

"There's only one of him," she hissed, trying to wriggle her arm free. "He can't be who he claims."

"I'm leaving." Ian's guarded gaze never left Darius. "Come with me, or stay here and find out if he's really who he says. Just know you'll likely die for your efforts."

Bianca nodded reluctantly and allowed Ian to lead her away. Claire's mouth was suddenly desert dry as she faced this new threat, suppressing the urge to pursue the departing lycans and press them for more information about Benedict. An instinct she was fast learning to heed told her not to turn her back on Darius. His icy gaze bore into her, relentless as a blizzard snowfall.

Her gaze flew to her gun several feet away, muscles tensing, ready to dive when his voice stopped her cold.

"You'll never make it in time."

She lifted her gaze to his, shocked to see that his eyes had begun to glow. Brighter than silver. Like two beacons of light scorching her to the spot.

His brow furrowed. "You're—" he broke off as if suddenly seeing her—truly seeing her. "You're not damned yet."

Claire opened then shut her mouth, seeing no reason to deny the charge.

"A lycan with a soul," he murmured. "For how long, I wonder?"

"There's nothing to wonder about. My soul's not going anywhere," Claire vowed, sliding one step closer to her gun. "So you can forget about me joining—"

Zing.

She barely heard the gun's muffled echo, suspected she wouldn't have noticed it if she didn't know the sound so well, but she did. It was a sound she would never forget.

Claire spun around in time to see Bianca fall and Ian throw himself at Gideon. She lunged for her gun with a strangled cry, sure that at any moment Darius would stop her, but she still had to try, had to help Gideon.

She ran the length of the alley, stopping several feet from the struggling pair and leveling her gun. Still, a clear shot eluded her. Squinting one eye shut, she took aim at the moving pair.

"Come on," she muttered under her breath, her heart rising in her throat as every second passed, "give me an opening."

The gun was suddenly plucked from her hands.

She yelped and tried to snatch it back.

"A friend of yours?" Darius asked mildly.

He didn't wait for her answer. Stepping in front of her, he took aim. She launched herself at him, raining blows upon the broad expanse of his back, desperate to protect Gideon.

A second shot punched the air, its soft zing a stab to her heart. Claire jumped off Darius, exhaling thickly as she watched Ian crumple to the ground. Not Gideon. Relief washed through her, consuming her, blinding her to all other concerns. Forgetting about Darius and what he would do when he realized he had missed and shot one of his own, she raced ahead.

Gideon was alive. That was all that mattered. She grasped him by both arms and looked him over. "Are you hurt? Did he bite you?"

Gideon shrugged free of her arms, assessed himself, clearly checking for any open wounds where Ian could have infected him. "I'm fine."

His gaze lifted beyond her and before she knew it, he thrust her, stumbling, behind him. Apparently he had noticed they weren't alone. Gideon's gun lay a yard away and Darius held hers in his hand. Unarmed, Gideon stepped back, taking her with him, hands splayed on either side of her hips.

Darius studied them, following as they inched down the alley. "What are you doing with her, lycan hunter?" He nodded his dark head at Claire peeking around Gideon. "She's not for you." His eyes lingered on her for a moment, his gaze oddly intimate, possessive.

"How does he know you're a lycan hunter?" she whispered into Gideon's ear, flattening her palms against the rigid muscles of his back.

"I can always spot a lycan hunter," Darius answered. "A useful survival skill."

Claire swallowed and wet her lips nervously. Gideon tensed beneath her hands.

Darius continued conversationally, gaze trained on her. "They have a distinctive smell," he explained. "Haven't you noticed your keen sense of smell?" He tapped the side of his nose and shook his head indulgently, a light smile curving his lips. "I have much to teach you."

"Like hell," Gideon swore.

"What do lycan hunters smell like?" Claire couldn't help asking, intrigued. Gideon had only ever smelled wonderful to her. Man and soap and fresh cut wood.

"Claire," Gideon warned in a low voice. "Would you mind keeping quiet?"

"They've got a certain stink to them," Darius answered, his voice laced with undeniable amusement. "The sour smell of righteous honor."

His hands tensed, squeezing her hips even tighter.

Silence fell as Gideon and Darius assessed each other.

Finally, Darius repeated his question, all amusement gone from the clipped velvet of his voice. "What are you doing with her, lycan hunter?"

"Keeping her from becoming like you," Gideon returned.

"Ah." The fathomless silver pools of his eyes reflected nothing. And his face, carved of stone, was equally impassive, but his voice held a certain amount of contempt as he asked, "And you think you can succeed?"

At this, Gideon said nothing. She glanced at the back of his head, frowning as she waited for him to say that they could succeed. That they would. After all, what was the point of all this if he didn't believe she had a chance?

"And you, my little dove?" Darius's glowing gaze drilled into her. "You think this killer of lycans will save you?"

Claire opened her mouth but no words came. How could she claim what Gideon himself could not?

"Interesting." He tossed the gun down with a noisy clatter. "You are both full of confidence. I'll leave you to it." His gaze hovered on her a moment longer. "Maybe we'll meet again."

"Don't count on it," Gideon replied.

Smiling vaguely, Darius turned.

"Wait!" Claire cried, rushing around Gideon.

Darius looked back over his shoulder, a dark brow arched.

"I was infected by a boy." She held her breath, searching his face, hopeful. "His name was Lenny."

"And you want to find him?"

"No. He's dead."

"Ah. You want to find his alpha, then."

She nodded jerkily.

His silver gaze shifted to Gideon, then back to Claire, assessing, measuring. "I don't know anything about a boy named Lenny. Or the alpha you're looking for. What you're trying to do is impossible. You'll never find and destroy the alpha you seek before the next moon. You'd best adjust to the fact that you're a lycan now."

"A monster?" she cried, his words filling her with a keen sense of hopelessness. "Never!"

"A monster," he echoed, cocking his head to the side. "Yes." A humorless smile curved his lips. "I am that. And so are you."

That said, he stepped back through the club's door, his words ringing in her ears. *You'd best adjust to the fact that you're a lycan now.*

Claire stared at the door he had disappeared through. "Why would he let us go?"

"I have no idea," Gideon muttered, his expression troubled as he stared at the door Darius had disappeared through.

"He called himself Darius."

"What?" Gideon's gaze shot to her face with startling intensity. "Are you sure?"

"Yeah, why?"

Gideon snatched up both their guns. After reholstering his gun and stuffing hers into his jacket pocket, he grabbed her hand and dragged her into the parking lot.

"Gideon," she demanded, running to keep up with his long strides and trying not to sound panicked. "What's going on?"

"Remember that lycan I told you about? The old one?"

Claire thought for a moment before recalling the twelve-hundred-year-old lycan he'd mentioned. "The one rumored to be dead?" she asked, a tight knot forming in the center of her chest, making it difficult to breathe.

"Yeah. His name's Darius."

A shudder ran through her and she nearly tripped

over her feet. His hand tightened around her fingers and he increased his speed, pulling her along faster.

"But if that's him, why would he let us—"

"I don't know, but we're not going to test his charity tonight. He's a killer. We couldn't even fathom the number of lives he's taken over the centuries." Gideon looked left and right as if he expected Darius to pop up from behind a parked car. They headed deeper into the parking lot, Gideon's strides swift and angry.

"I don't think he'd let us go just to come after—"

"The way he looked at you—" Gideon broke off, shaking his head. "I'm surprised he walked away."

"Maybe we should go after him."

"Let him go."

"Why? Those other lycans mentioned a Benedict. I think he's their alpha. Maybe Darius knows—"

"No, Claire. He may have shot one of his kind, but he's not inclined to help us. And I don't like the way he looked at you. Next time he may not let you go."

"So what, then? Another night and no leads?" she demanded. "I'm going after him." Spinning around, Claire stalked back down the alley.

Gideon's hand clamped down on her arm, whirling her around. His green eyes glittered. "You want to give him a go at you? Is that what you want?"

A deep growl rose up in her throat. "Exactly. I'm a creature of passion, remember?" she mocked, wrenching her arm free and stepping back. Blood pumped through her veins thick and fast. He made a grab for her arm again and, without thinking, she brought her palm cracking against his cheek. His head jerked from the force of her blow.

Her hand flew to her mouth, drowning out her gasp. Even in the murk and gloom of the alley, she made out her handprint, white and stark against the swarthy skin of his cheek, evidence of her rage, a proclivity for violence that gripped her in its throes.

His furious gaze roamed her face, leaving a trail of fire in its wake. When his gaze settled on her mouth, heat swept over her. Claire started to tremble, the familiar wanting sinking deep in the pit of her stomach and spreading outward. Helpless, she leaned in.

He grabbed her by the back of her neck and hauled her against him, slamming his mouth over hers. She parted her lips, groaning at the sweep of his tongue inside her mouth.

His hands dropped to clench her hips, wedging her against him, his erection a hard ridge prodding her belly. She ground against him, wanting that hardness elsewhere, buried inside her.

A soft voice intruded. "Want me to shoot her for you, Gid?"

Claire spun around to face Gideon's sister, aiming a gun that looked much too large for her slight hands.

"Kit," Gideon groaned. "Put the damned gun away before you hurt someone."

Kit lowered the gun. "I know how to use it." Her green gaze narrowed on Claire. "And I know who to use it on."

"Kit," he growled in warning.

"No, Gid," she snapped. Facing Claire, she demanded, "What the hell are you doing? Besides putting my brother at risk? Take some responsibility. If you care at all for my brother, you will end this before he gets hurt."

"Kit, that's enough," Gideon barked.

Claire stared at the young woman's face, feeling the truth of her words like a razor blade to her flesh.

"This is why I was late getting to you," he explained, waving a hand at his sister. "She showed up and wouldn't leave. She wants to hunt lycans," he quickly explained.

"And he won't let me because I'm a woman," Kit retorted. "Have you ever heard of such crap—"

"Because you're too young," Gideon insisted.

"I'm twenty-four! Not some teenager." Kit waved her gun in a small circle, sending Gideon and Claire ducking.

"Give me that thing." Gideon snatched the gun from her hand.

Claire shook her head, wondering how she ended up in the middle of a sibling squabble.

Gideon tossed a wary look over his shoulder, no doubt still worried about Darius. He pointed to a Cyber Green Volkswagen bug parked next to the Jeep and growled, "Get in your car and go home, Kit. I don't want to worry about you for at least another twenty-four hours."

She scuffed her shoe on the ground, kicking up a cloud of dirt. "Don't forget your promise to me."

"I won't forget. I'm just not going to do anything about it tonight. It's not safe. Now get of here."

Apparently satisfied with whatever promise Gideon had given, Kit ducked inside her car. Claire followed suit and climbed inside Gideon's Jeep.

Another night with no leads. No information. No closer.

Gideon slid in beside her. She glanced at the rigid lines of his profile. Her heart ached with the need to touch him. She smoothed her hands over her jeans to keep from reaching out. He didn't want her touch. Didn't want closeness from her of any kind. Moonlight spilled through the windshield, gilding the hair at his brow a silvery blond. Her gaze followed the light to its source, to the ticking time bomb in the sky. *There is no other choice. You are one of us. You can't undo it.*

The small flame of hope that she nurtured deep in her heart sputtered out.

Chapter Fifteen

Like humans, dogs may suffer bouts of depression.

—*Man's Best Friend: An Essential Guide to Dogs*

Claire didn't utter a word the entire drive home, and from the glances Gideon sent her way, her silence unsettled him. He might not know what to do or how to deal with a quiet, brooding Claire, but she did. She knew exactly what needed to be done.

"Want something to eat?" Gideon asked when they entered the kitchen.

She shook her head. Surprisingly, even food didn't appeal to her. Ever since the lake house she had resisted voicing the one question burning in her mind, too afraid he might reconsider helping her. But that didn't matter anymore. She had to know the truth. Lifting her face to stare him directly in the eyes, she asked, "Why haven't you killed me yet?"

He blinked, clearly caught off guard.

"Why haven't you killed me?" she repeated, her voice

insistent. She dug her nails into her palm, waiting for his response, determined to have it.

Gideon flexed his hands into fists beside him.

"Claire, I—" He stopped abruptly, leaving whatever he was going to say unfinished as he shrugged out of his jacket with jerky, agitated movements.

She watched as he laid his jacket over the back of a chair, her gun clearly outlined in the pocket. She buried her hands in her pockets, curling her fingers into tight fists. Turning, he stalked out of the kitchen without a word, ignoring her question.

Claire followed him into the living room. "Other agents would have. Hell, your sister would have."

He stopped in the middle of the living room and turned to face her. "I intended to destroy you."

She nodded, wrapping her arms around herself as she sank to the couch. "That night in my apartment. You were there. You were going to kill me, then."

He stared out the front bay window that faced the street, nodding. "I had the gun in my hand," he said quietly, touching his fingers to his mouth. A mouth that even right now she would like to press against her own, to kiss until the nightmare faded. *Insanity.* That was the only word for it.

"I put the barrel right to your head." He tapped his temple with his index finger.

"You should have ended it then." Before things got carried so far with them.

Claire drew a deep, shuddering breath at the image of him standing over her as she slept, a gun pressed to her head. She would never have known what hit her. Never have even seen his face. Never have felt the things she did for him. Kit's words blew through her like an arctic wind. *If you care at all for my brother, you will end this before he gets hurt.*

She lurched from the couch, throat thick with emotion. What was she waiting for? Some lycan out there to rape her? For Gideon to gather his nerve and destroy her? She swallowed past the thickness in her throat. She cared for him too much to do that to him.

He took a step toward her. Claire lurched back and held up a hand to ward him off, afraid that he would touch her. If he did, she'd fall apart, crumble right in front of him. Shaking her head, she released a short laugh that sounded strange and brittle. "I bet you wished you had."

"You have no idea what I feel," Gideon growled. "Until you, I was fine. I never questioned what I did," he exploded, green eyes flashing like emeralds in sunlight. "But you're different. You're . . ."

Claire dropped back onto the couch and lowered her shaking forehead into her palm. "Please, Gideon. Stop." She couldn't hear it. Couldn't bear to hear him say he cared for her when she knew it couldn't go anywhere. She had to protect him—and the world—from herself.

"No," he broke in. "I won't." In two strides he stood before her, wrenching her to her feet. "I'm not soft. I've killed others. Too many to count. And I've watched those I loved destroyed right before my eyes . . . my mother, my father." His eyes scanned her face, and she gasped at the pain visible there. "If I need to, I will kill you."

Claire couldn't help thinking he sounded as though

he were trying to convince himself and not her. And right then, she vowed it would not fall to him. He'd suffered enough pain in his life. She would not add to it.

She pressed her lips into a firm line. The waxing moon outside demanded she do something. She had no intention of waiting. No more lying to herself. Those lycans tonight had known the truth. So did Kit.

His green gaze clashed with hers. Tension crackled on the air like electricity, palpable and frightening.

She wiggled free of his hold. "It's late."

His hands groped air. For a moment, she thought those hands would grab her and pull her back into his arms. And a part of her desperately prayed he would. She wanted to feel his hands on her again. One last time.

Instead, they dropped listlessly to his sides. "Good night, Claire," he said, his voice flat, lifeless.

Her throat constricted and she nodded mutely, unable to return his good night. Not when it really meant good-bye.

She fled before she could collapse in a pile in front of him. Upstairs in her room, she stared at the couch. There was no sense pulling out the bed tonight. She wouldn't be sleeping. Sinking onto the couch, she rested her head on the pillow, nuzzling it with her cheek, seeking what comfort she could as she waited. A few minutes passed before she heard his solid tread on the stairs. He stopped at the top and she held her breath, heart aching, imagining him standing there, imagining him looking at her closed door. Silently, she begged for him to enter, to give her one more memory, a taste to take into eternity with her.

At last he moved on, his footsteps receding down the hall to his bedroom. She would wait a little longer. Until she was sure he slept. He would never hear her creep down the stairs. Never realize what had happened until it was over.

In the still of the kitchen, Claire stepped toward the chair where her gun slumbered peacefully in Gideon's jacket, waiting. She slid her hand inside the pocket and wrapped her fingers around cold, hard steel. Now that she had reached the decision, she was anxious to get it over with. She wanted it to be over. While she still had the courage.

As she pulled the revolver out of the pocket she wondered if gunmetal ever felt anything but cold. Her thumb pulled back the hammer. Her finger curled around the trigger like a ribbon furling itself. She studied the black steel in her hand. *What am I doing?* The answer came back quick and firm. *Ending it*. For Gideon. For herself. For the world. It was the right thing to do—the responsible thing, even if it went against every instinct of survival she possessed. Deep in his heart, Gideon knew that. She had seen the truth etched in the hard lines of his face. She would spare him the burden of shooting her.

Claire lifted her trembling arm and pointed the barrel to her temple, the kiss of the gun cold on her skin. The gun wobbled so much she brought her other hand up to grasp her wrist to still the shaking. Jamming her eyes shut, her finger started to squeeze.

"You're going to make a horrible mess in my kitchen."

Claire gasped and spun around.

There was a flash of movement as Gideon knocked

the gun from her hand. It clattered to the floor several feet away.

She looked from the gun to Gideon, fury choking her. Yet a small thread of relief niggled beneath the fury.

His eyes glittered in the darkened kitchen, his tall, athletic figure limned in moonlight spilling through the kitchen window above the sink. "Never took you for the cowardly type."

With a ragged cry, she flung herself against him, beating his chest, arms, face, anything her fists made contact with, for once indifferent to his bare skin and loose pajama bottoms that revealed too much for her senses.

He had no idea how much strength it took for her to lift that gun to her head. No idea how much she wanted to live. Especially since she had never truly lived before he came along. It took every ounce of courage she had to lift the gun, every drop of love in her heart.

"Damn you," she hissed, hot tears pricking her eyes.

He grappled for her flailing hands. Giving up, he folded her into his arms and jerked her against him, chest to heaving chest. She struggled until they fell to the kitchen floor.

"Why are you doing this?" she sobbed, the linoleum cold and unforgiving beneath her back. "If you can't do it, just let—"

He silenced her with a hard kiss.

She surrendered, helpless to her desire, to the need he roused within her. Her arms snaked around his neck, his skin warm and supple beneath her arms. He ravaged her mouth, never breaking the kiss as he swung her into his arms and carried her up the stairs.

He followed her onto his bed, covering her with his hard body, sinking into her softness as his mouth devoured hers. His hands moved over her, swift and feverish, breaking their kiss for only a moment to yank her T-shirt up and over her head.

Then his hands were everywhere. Her breasts, her hips, seizing her panty-clad bottom in his hands to pull her against him and grind his erection against her crotch.

She shoved him back, forcing him on his back. Hungry, starved for the taste of him, she slid his pajama bottoms off and straddled his thighs. Never taking her eyes off him, she dipped her head and closed her lips around his thick shaft. Tongue swirling around the plump head of him, she sucked, her hand squeezing gently at the base of him, delighting as he surged off the bed, thrusting himself deeper into her mouth.

Groaning, his hands fisted in her hair as he worked his hips. She sucked harder, working her tongue over the delicious length of him, salty and warm.

With a growl, he wrenched away from her and tossed her on her back, his mouth claiming hers again as he tore her panties in one savage jerk.

He impaled her in one hard thrust. She screamed at the engorged heat of him filling her. She grabbed a fistful of his hair, tugging his head back so that she could kiss his arched neck, licking and nipping at the tendons stretched taut along his throat.

He groaned, a deep animal sound of need. Pulling back, he drove into her again, the force sinking her deep into the mattress. He grabbed her hands and placed them on his warm chest. His heart thumped beneath her palm, a distant drum that echoed the pounding of her own pulse. Those green eyes glowed with an intensity that stole her breath.

His lips took hers again. His hands carried their own special heat, branding her, singeing her cheeks where he held her face and better angled her mouth for his questing tongue.

Her flesh rippled with heightened sensation as he dragged himself in and out of her. Waves of searing heat flowed through her body like rolling lava. Her hands fell limply beside her head and she whimpered, beyond pleasure, beyond pain. He grabbed hold of one leg, his hand a searing brand behind her knee as he stretched her leg back, angling her for deeper penetration. Her head flew off the pillow, a shuddering cry rising from deep in her chest.

She groaned, her skin burning, the ache in her belly twisting tighter. Each thrust left her writhing beneath him. Her hands grabbed his shoulders, his back, his buttocks. She moved wildly, searching, aching for the building climax.

He grabbed her hands, trapping them on the pillow on either side of her head. His fingers laced through hers. Palm to palm, their eyes locked, his eyes gleaming down at her knowingly.

His thrusts grew harder. Faster. Intense. She tilted her hips, shifting beneath him, trying to get closer, trying to take more. He wrapped an arm around her waist. In one fluid motion he flipped her so she sat on top.

"Go on," he commanded, fingers digging into her hips, urging her to move. "Ride me."

She didn't wait for another invitation. Instinct took

over and she rode him hard, hands pressed against his chest for leverage. Whimpering, she dropped her head and worked her hips furiously, laboring until a fine sheen of perspiration coated her body. Her hips never ceased their frenzied dance. She took him in and out of her body in hard, rapid-fire pumps. The pressure increased, building. He swiped the hair from her face and dragged her mouth down to his for a bruising kiss.

Every muscle in her body suddenly tightened and contracted. She tore her mouth away and cried out as shudders racked her, took her soaring over that final precipice. Arched over him, she stilled, her hands slippery where they clutched his chest.

His hands circled her waist and he bucked beneath her, thrusting several more times. His groan rumbled through him into her. Panting, she collapsed against his chest, never happier than at that moment to be alive.

They spent the day making love, napping, and making love some more. No mention of the future. No mention of the time remaining, of the six days left to them. Night would come soon enough and they would have to rise and confront the world. Regret and recriminations could come later. Right now, Claire in his arms was all that mattered.

At noon, Gideon ordered two large pepperoni pizzas and watched in awe as Claire devoured one whole pizza herself.

Licking tomato sauce off her fingers, she caught him staring at her. “What?” she asked, looking adorable in his too-big shirt and with her mussed hair.

"Finished?" he asked.

She inspected the empty pizza box on the bed before nodding.

"Good." He swiped the pizza boxes off the bed with one arm and tossed her on her back.

"Gideon!" She laughed up at him, a rich, throaty sound that rippled through the air and wrapped silken chains around his heart.

Holding her face in his hands, he stared down solemnly at her. "I've never heard you laugh." His thumbs stroked her finely arched brows almost tenderly. "Not truly."

"I haven't had a reason lately."

He frowned, not liking the reminder of all that was wrong, of all that stood between them.

"Until you," she added, gazing at his mouth. Her fingertips traced its curve, almost as if she wished to erase the frown from his face.

Her tongue darted out to wet her lips. "It feels good."

"It sounds good," he whispered, tugging her hand away so that he could kiss her deeply. An emotion very much like satisfaction tightened his throat at the sinuous way she arched against him. Satisfaction . . . and something else.

He realized he hadn't felt this good in a long while either. And Claire was the reason.

The sound was soft, barely discernible—just a click. With her heightened senses, it might as well have been a foghorn blaring in her ears for all that it jarred her awake, pulling her from Gideon's warm arms and a comfortable slumber.

Someone else was in the room with them.

Her senses hummed with awareness, but she waited silently, eyes closed. The wood floor creaked close beside her. Too close. Her eyes flew open, blinking rapidly at the black hole floating directly in front of her eyes. A gun barrel. And beyond it, a grim face of stone. Cooper.

Claire eyed him. Dark haired. Dark eyed. Thin, ruthless lips set in a narrow face. He gripped the gun with familiarity, like it was an extension of his arm. Not an ounce of softness detectable anywhere. There would be no reasoning with him. No pleading. He wanted her dead.

Funny. She would have willingly placed herself before his gun last night to spare Gideon. But not now. Things had changed. She had changed. Even if she had only a few more days, those were days she could spend with Gideon.

"Gideon." She tapped the chest beneath her cheek with her fingers.

His chest moved beneath her cheek, alerting her to the fact that he was already awake.

"Put the gun down, Cooper," he said quietly.

Claire didn't breathe, didn't move. Her fingers curled around Gideon's bicep.

"Point that gun somewhere else." Gideon's voice lifted, rumbling beneath her ear, the command unmistakable.

Cooper glowered at her like she was something dirty on the bottom of his shoe. She self-consciously pulled the bedding higher to cover her nudity.

"Could have seen this coming with other agents." Cooper's cold gaze cut to Gideon. "But never you."

"She hasn't shifted yet. Hasn't taken a life. She's still got a chance. We can save her." His hand gripped her shoulder, more to reassure him, or herself, she couldn't guess.

Cooper gave a bitter laugh. "What chance?" His gaze swept over her, cold as winter sleet. She tightened her hold on the sheets, pulling them to her neck. One look in those eyes told her this man wasn't interested in saving her. No matter what Gideon said in her defense.

Cooper frowned thoughtfully. "I had plans for you, Gideon. Saw you taking over after me. Just never would have pegged you—" He paused to shake his head fiercely. "You seemed impervious to a pretty piece of ass. Guess I was wrong. Hope she was good."

A growl rumbled from deep inside Gideon's chest. He tucked her more closely against him. So tight she could hardly draw air. It suddenly hit her that he was trying to make it impossible for Cooper to get a clear shot at her. At least not without risk to himself.

"You're not killing her," Gideon announced.

"Gonna stop me, Gid?"

"If I have to."

She looked between the two men, her chest tight and hurting as if a heavy weight had been placed upon it. They had a long history. They were more than friends. Almost family. Claire couldn't come between them.

Gideon tried again, saying, "If you would listen—"

"Oh, I understand perfectly. You've lost your edge. Too busy thinking with your cock." His hard stare swung back to Claire. "Move away from her."

"No." The single word fell into the charged air, a gauntlet tossed down.

Her gaze met Cooper's over the barrel of the gun and she read cold-blooded determination in the dark depths. He wouldn't stop until she was dead. Even if it meant hurting Gideon. The hairs on her nape stood. She couldn't let that happen.

Cooper widened his stance and trained his gun on what he could see of her. His gaze swung to Gideon. "Move out of the way, or I'll shoot the silver-eyed bitch dead in your arms."

He meant it. She knew it just as she knew Gideon wouldn't budge from her side. If anything, he would shield her and take the bullet himself. She recognized that in the sudden way he tensed, his muscles taut like a bowstring.

Knowing what she had to do, she drew a deep breath, surged to her feet, and tossed the comforter over Cooper's head.

Gideon took advantage of the opportunity and tackled Cooper to the floor, locking his arms around him and pinning him down. His gaze met hers over the kicking and thrashing comforter.

"Go! Take my Jeep!" His eyes burned green fire. "Go!"

She hesitated, the pounding of her heart loud in her ears.

"Gideon," she whispered. "I . . ."

At that moment Cooper heaved violently beneath him and Gideon roared, "Go! Get the hell out of here!"

Naked, she fled downstairs, through the living room, and into the kitchen. Something crashed upstairs, sounds of the battle Gideon waged on her behalf. Heart hammering, she danced in place near the door before grabbing Gideon's jacket and slipping it over her nakedness. Snatching his keys off the table, she darted out the back door and into the yard.

In the fading glow of dusk, she faltered and looked over her shoulder. She bit down hard on her lip, loath to abandon Gideon. No matter that he ordered her to go, no matter that she risked a silver bullet if she stayed, she worried about what Cooper would do to him.

The hairs on her nape tingled, a warning that was growing all too familiar.

She swung around just as twin bands of muscle locked around her, hauling her off her feet and sealing her in. Her eyes shot up to meet a pewter gaze and her stomach pitched. Opening her mouth, Claire screamed.

Chapter Sixteen

Dogs are destined to seek out other dogs for companionship.

—*Man's Best Friend: An Essential Guide to Dogs*

Gideon ducked Cooper's swinging fist and charged, throwing his shoulder into his middle and sending them both crashing to the floor. They rolled, jabbing their fists against each other, knocking into furniture and banging into walls.

Suddenly, Claire's scream shattered the evening air.

Gideon froze. His first fear was that Cooper had brought reinforcements, other NODEAL agents.

He flew off Cooper and sprang to the window overlooking the backyard in time to see Claire flung over the shoulder of the lycan from the alley last night. Darius. He would rather he looked down at a yard full of agents.

"Claire!" he shouted through the glass, fingers clenching the window's wood frame.

At Gideon's shout, the bastard looked up, winked, and gave Claire's bottom a little pat.

A growl rumbled low in Gideon's throat. Without thinking, he plunged his fist through the window, oblivious to the pain, oblivious to the thick blood streaming down his knuckles in warm rivulets. Shoving past Cooper, he took off downstairs.

By the time he arrived outside, the yard was empty. A car sounded in the distance. He ran alongside the house to the front yard, where a metallic SUV pulled away from the curb and peeled down the street. Gideon ran, legs and arms pumping. Heedless of his nudity, of the stinging smack of his bare feet on hot asphalt, he sprinted down the middle of the street, trying to read the license plate. The vehicle swerved around the corner, tires squealing, before he could note the numbers.

"Claire!" Panting, he skidded to a halt in the middle of the street. Indifferent to the setting sun warming his nude body, he stared blindly ahead. His hands sliced through his hair, clutching the shaggy locks at the back of his head until he came close to ripping them out by the roots. Throwing back his head, he hollered at the sky.

He fucked up.

Claire was gone. In the hands of a lycan who would put her through God knew what. And in five days, she would shift. She would kill and feed.

He ran his hands over his face roughly. Claire had been right last night. He should have simply let her pull the trigger. His own desire, his selfish need for her had stopped him, sentencing her to God knew how many lifetimes as a lycan—a veritable hell on earth. And if the day arrived when some other agent did what he failed to do and actually destroyed her—she would face an eternity of damnation.

The sound of his name came to him from far away. He turned to see Cooper standing on the curb, one hand pressed against his rapidly swelling split lip. "You're naked, man." With a grimace of disgust on his face, Cooper gestured to the house. "And bleeding. Come inside before your neighbors call the precinct."

Gideon inspected his hand and numbly noted the blood trickling down his fingers to the street. Dropping his hand, he marched past Cooper, cutting through the lawn still warm from the day's relentless sun. "Go to hell."

Cooper followed. "You know, I'm the one who should be angry here."

Gideon yanked the back door open and stalked inside, going straight for the bottle of whiskey on the pantry's bottom shelf. "Put it in a letter."

"How about putting some clothes on?"

Gideon glanced down at himself.

"Probably need stitches," Cooper added, nodding to Gideon's hand.

Unscrewing the cap, Gideon downed a mouthful of liquid fire and continued to ignore the man he felt like pummeling to the floor. It wasn't Cooper's fault, he reasoned. He had no one to blame except himself. He felt hollow, dead inside. The whiskey burned its way down his throat, warming his belly.

"So, that's it?" Cooper crossed his arms. "You're going to get shit-faced now?"

The disgust in Cooper's voice was only a measure of what Gideon felt for himself. He wrenched a paper towel from the holder and wrapped it around his hand. It would have to do. He wasn't taking his sorry ass to the emergency room.

Bottle in hand, he took the stairs two at a time, trying to ignore the fact that Cooper followed.

He snatched his jeans off the floor, feeling Cooper's glare. "She wasn't damned yet, hadn't taken a life," he snapped, sliding into his jeans.

"Doesn't matter. You know that."

"That's how you see things. I disagree."

"Since when?"

It was on the tip of his tongue to say since Claire, but he held back. He didn't want Cooper to know he'd fallen for a lycan.

Yet it seemed Cooper had reached his own conclusions. "Since you tripped and fell into bed with her?"

He pinned Cooper with his gaze. "Careful, Cooper."

Cooper stared at him for one long moment before rolling his eyes. "Shit. Even better. You're in love with her."

Gideon pulled his shirt over his head and stuck his arms through the sleeves in rough, angry movements, not bothering to answer. He didn't know what to say. Didn't know if it was true. Did he love Claire? It certainly explained why he couldn't bring himself to kill her.

"Where are you going?" Cooper asked as Gideon tugged on his socks.

"To find her," he answered simply.

"You need to get that hand stitched up," Cooper repeated, his voice grudging, as if he hated to reveal that he cared.

Gideon glanced at his hand as he took another swig

from the bottle. Blood already soaked the paper towel, but it didn't matter. He'd live. Claire, on the other hand . . .

His gut clenched. "Your concern is touching, but I've got shit to do."

"You mean find her?"

"That's right."

"Did you get the plates?" Cooper asked.

"No."

Cooper shook his head. "You're not using your head. How are you going to find her? You might need a little more to go on than a silver Tahoe."

True. Gideon didn't know anything beyond the legend of Darius. But he couldn't just sit around and wait. "NO-DEAL has records. I can run through the profiles in the database—"

"No," Cooper cut in. "You can't."

Gideon cocked his head. *No?*

"You're suspended, Gideon," Cooper decreed, his mouth a hard, unsmiling line. "Until further review. You're denied access to the database."

"I have to find—"

"Oh, we will find her. We'll find both of them. NO-DEAL will take care of business. Like always. Only without you," Cooper assured him, nodding. "Your involvement in the organization ends here."

Gideon flung the whiskey bottle across the room. It shattered against the wall with a loud crash. Glass rained down on the floor. The amber liquid would undoubtedly stain his white wall, but he couldn't rouse any concern.

"Was her fate ever in doubt?" Cooper asked quietly. "Did you really think you could save her?"

"How would I know? I've been trained to destroy. Not help."

Cooper inhaled slowly. "She's not your mother, Gid."

"No, my mother's dead. And damned," Gideon snarled. "No one tried to help her. Oh, except you. You were there, ready with a bullet."

"Maybe I didn't save her soul. But I always took comfort in the fact that I helped you and your sister. I thought that meant something." Cooper lifted one shoulder in a shrug and pushed off the door. "Use the time off. Think things over." He tapped his head. "Like what you want to do with the rest of your life. Because your days at NODEAL are over. There's no way the board will keep you on."

"I don't give a shit about the board. I don't need their sanction to—"

"Gideon," Cooper's hand grasped his shoulder, his eyes hard. "We don't tolerate rogue operators."

Gideon shrugged free of his hand. "I will find her."

Cooper shook his head. "You'll fail. Maybe even get yourself killed in the process. Then I'll find her and destroy her." Cooper's dark gaze drilled into him. "And until then others will die." He jabbed the air inches from Gideon's chest. "All because of you."

Gideon looked Cooper square in the eyes. For years, he had revered him, emulated him, wanted to be just like him. Only very recently his wants had taken a drastic change.

"I'll find her," Gideon vowed. "She's my responsibility."

Cooper turned into the hallway.

Gideon's voice stopped him at the top of the stairs. "And Cooper—stay out of my way."

Wordlessly, Cooper disappeared down the stairs. Moments later the back door slammed.

Alone in his room, Gideon stared unseeingly at the amber liquid running down his wall and dribbling to the floor. He didn't doubt that if he didn't find Claire, Cooper would. That's what he did best—hunt lycans.

Gideon couldn't let that happen. He was responsible for her. Curling his bloody hand into a fist, he made a decision—hard as it was. No one would destroy Claire but him. Even if in destroying her, he destroyed himself.

Cooper or any other agent would do it mechanically, coldly, without compassion. Just another assignment. Since that first night the job belonged to him. Claire belonged to him. As much as he belonged to her.

No more. She deserved compassion at the end. She deserved to be held in someone's arms when she died. In the arms of someone who loved her. Yet as he grabbed his holster, hope niggled in the back of his mind, a stubborn ember that wouldn't cool and die.

Maybe. Just maybe there was still a chance.

Claire leaned forward in her seat as the vehicle slowed. She clutched the dashboard in both hands, watching as a uniformed guard waved them through wrought iron gates. Turning around in her seat, she stared back at the guardhouse fading in the distance. The gates clanked shut, the sound echoing in her ears.

As they drove up a winding drive she couldn't help

noticing several dogs, rottweilers and Doberman pinschers, roaming the grounds. How would she ever get past them?

"You can't escape," Darius announced as if he could read her mind.

She tugged at the bottom of her jacket, trying to cover more of her naked thighs. Gideon's familiar scent reached her nose, creating a deep pang in her heart. The sound of him calling her name from the street still rang in her ears. She hoped he was all right, hoped Cooper hadn't hurt him.

Darius parked in front of a sprawling limestone mansion with a Spanish tiled roof. It loomed at least three stories high. He came around to open her door for her and she bolted, prepared to take her chances and try to outrun the dogs. She had to try. Once inside that house, she might not get another chance.

She didn't make it far before he yanked her back by the collar of her jacket and flung her over his shoulder. Claire found herself staring at the ground again, the bones of his shoulder digging uncomfortably into her stomach.

He carried her through the front door. A man held the door open for them, watching blandly as Darius hauled her upstairs like a sack of potatoes. On the stairs, a maid clutched a broom and dustpan in one hand and stepped aside as they passed, eyes averted in deference. No one seemed the least bothered to see her slung over Darius's shoulders.

"Help!" she cried out.

He carried her down a long hallway lined with portraits that looked museum quality. She studied the burgundy runner as she bounced on his shoulder, wondering if he led her to the rest of his pack.

He entered a room and tossed her on a bed. She shot to her feet and scanned the rest of the room, searching for others. Her eyes met nothing save a well-appointed room with bars protecting the window.

Sighing in relief, she pulled Gideon's jacket tighter around her only to catch another whiff of him. Her heart constricted at the clean masculine smell laced with that faint hint of freshly cut wood.

Squaring her shoulders and taking comfort in Gideon's scent, she faced Darius. "What a lovely jail. You'll have to give me the name of your decorator."

"I want you to be comfortable," he said politely, gesturing to the room with an elegant sweep of his hand.

"So that your pack of wolves can ravish me in luxury?"

"There are no other lycans here to save us."

"I'm not like you," she shot back, motioning at him with a desperate wave.

"I know." His gaze raked her. "That's why I want you."

Her bare toes curled into the plush carpet and she inhaled deeply, steeling herself against that hungry appraisal, more terrified by that one look than all his manhandling. There was no mistaking the carnal interest blazing in those icy eyes.

He advanced on her slowly, like a cat stalking its prey. "I couldn't forget you. You're different. You're not like the others—"

"What about your pack?" She moved back a step for every step he took in her direction. "Werewolves aren't monogamous. You want me, but that means I would have to—" She struggled to say it. "Mate with the others." She shook her head vigorously. "No thanks."

He nodded as though he approved. "Someone's been teaching you about lycans."

"That's right." She bumped into a dresser and slid along it, her hands feeling the smooth wood drawers behind her. Still moving, always moving. "I know enough to know that I won't be one of your kind—"

"You already are."

"No! I won't mate like a dog in heat with your pack—"

"I told you. I'm the only one here. And I'm not sharing you with anyone." He lips curved. "I'm keeping you for myself."

She frowned. "What do you mean you're the only one? Every wolf has a pack."

"Not me."

A lone wolf? Without a pack? Gideon had never mentioned such a possibility.

She angled her head suspiciously. "Why not?"

"Like you . . . I'm different."

"Different how?"

"I don't feed."

Despite everything Gideon had explained to her about the nature of lycans, hope unfurled in her chest. This lycan didn't feed? Maybe Gideon didn't know everything. Maybe a lycan could resist the insatiable need to kill. Maybe she could live as a werewolf and avoid eternal damnation. Maybe she and Gideon could be together.

She edged closer to Darius, hands clasped as if in prayer. "You've *never* fed?"

His smile vanished and his silver eyes shone with an almost angry light. "I didn't say that."

She dropped her hands and took a step back, disappointment welling up inside her again. "Then you're no different. You're a killer. Damned. An animal like the rest of them."

He was in front of her before she had time to register he had moved at all. Hard hands circled her arms. He wasn't as tall as Gideon but broader. An unbreachable wall.

"*I am different*. My last kill was a long time ago." At her look of disbelief he added, "Three hundred years."

Okay. That qualified as a long time ago. She wet her lips nervously. But did it matter how many years had passed? A life taken was a life taken. From what Gideon had told her, his soul could never be redeemed. "How old are you?"

His hands loosened, but he still held her. Suddenly, he looked tired, the hard lines of his face stark. "Too old."

"Why don't you have a pack?

The corners of his full mouth curled. "Being that I don't kill, I don't play well with the other lycans." His fingers flexed lightly on her arms. "It's a lonely existence." He scanned her face as if memorizing every feature, every detail. "I can't live among humans. I can't live among my own kind. And I refuse to infect an innocent and make them like me just so I can have a companion. But you—" His gaze roamed her face. "You're already infected. You don't have a pack and don't wish to feed. I'd say that makes us perfect for one another."

He had to be kidding. He wanted her to be his girlfriend?

"But I don't want to be a lycan at all. I want to be human again." Desperate, she tried to wriggle free. "The man you stole me from was helping me find the alpha responsible—"

He snorted. "Any luck there?"

She stopped struggling, the truth hitting hard. "You could help me."

He shook his head, the blue-black strands of his hair grazing his chiseled cheekbones. "The full moon is almost upon us." Darius released her and walked toward the door. "Joining me is your only option."

She moved to the bedpost, grasping the smooth wood in her hands as the significance of his words washed over her. "And what if I refuse?"

"On the eve of every full moon I lock myself in a steel-walled room. Then, on the new moon, a trusted member of my staff unlocks the door and frees me. You will be with me in that room."

She closed her eyes and sagged against the bedpost, weak with relief. She would not kill. No matter what happened, she wouldn't take an innocent life. At least there was that blessing in this nightmare.

His voice intruded on her musings and she opened her eyes to find his pewter gaze locked on her knowingly.

"I think you understand the forces that drive lycans. Those forces are already alive and well in you. We may not be able to kill and feed in that room. But we will mate. Instinct will demand it."

Relief suddenly gone, Claire slid to the floor, stricken, her hands clinging limply to the bedpost. His voice rolled over her like a fog that she could not outrun.

"Considering the alternative, eternity as my mate won't be such a bad fate. I'll see that you at least keep your soul."

"No! Never!"

Smiling at her as if she were a child to be indulged, he slipped from the room as silently as a curl of smoke.

Considering the alternative, eternity as my mate won't be such a bad fate. I'll see that you at least keep your soul. Perhaps. If only she wasn't already in love with someone else. If only the thought of another touching her did not make her want to curl into a small ball and die.

Chapter Seventeen

Just because one dog rejects another doesn't mean mating won't occur.

—*Man's Best Friend: An Essential Guide to Dogs*

The shadows on the walls lengthened, taking on frightening dimensions. Like the monsters of her childhood dreams. Only the barest amount of moonlight filtered past the tree branches outside her window. With one hand beneath her cheek, she watched as the shadows grew and stretched. She stayed as she was, curled on her side as the night deepened, wondering if Darius's sour-faced housekeeper would return for the tray of food she had left at lunchtime.

Initially, Claire had vowed not to eat, not to touch a morsel of food brought to her. Pathetically, her resolve had not lasted beyond breakfast. She had managed to turn up her nose at the fresh fruit and steaming oatmeal, but not the heaping mound of creamy pasta salad strewn with shrimp and sun-dried tomatoes. Claire couldn't resist. Nor could she leave the thick wedge of chocolate cheesecake uneaten. Only further proof that the lycan instinct overpowered her will. Her stomach rumbled and Claire couldn't help wondering when dinner would arrive.

As if in answer to her thoughts, the door opened.

Claire lurched from the bed, bare feet sinking into the plush carpet as she braced herself. She still wore Gideon's jacket but had wrapped a chenille throw around her bottom half in an attempt at modesty.

The housekeeper stood in the door's threshold, her sherry brown eyes glittering with malice. Not lycan eyes. That was some comfort at least. "Time to shower," she announced gruffly. "Follow me."

Claire followed. Willingly. Locked up since yesterday, she felt sticky and welcomed the prospect of a shower. It would feel good to be clean again. Even better if she had fresh clothes.

Thinking that it wouldn't hurt to have an ally, Claire hurried to walk beside the stern-faced housekeeper. "What's your name?"

The woman stared straight ahead, the slight thinning of her lips the only indication she even heard the question.

"I'm Claire," she volunteered.

After a long moment, the housekeeper offered her name. "Helen."

"Helen." Claire stopped her with a hand on her arm and searched the woman's apathetic face for some hint of emotion. Her cold, flat gaze never even blinked. "You know what he is, don't you?"

Helen quirked her eyebrow in silence.

Claire pressed a hand to her chest. "What I am?"

"Yes," she answered coldly.

"Then, you know I need your help."

Stone-faced, Helen stepped around Claire and continued down the hall. "That's what Master Darius is doing. Helping you."

Claire scowled and fell in step beside her. "No, he's not."

"He's saving you from hurting others . . . and from damnation." Helen stopped and pushed open a door, gesturing inside. "You should be thanking him."

"You're brainwashed," Claire accused. "You know what will happen when we're locked together—"

"Have you taken a good look at Darius?" Helen's eyes raked Claire coolly, critically. "You could do a lot worse."

"Of course," she mocked. "I should drop down and kiss his feet in gratitude."

Loyalty burned with bright fervor in Helen's eyes. And something else. Not just loyalty. "Watch how you speak about Master Darius."

With a jolt, Claire realized the middle-aged woman was in love with him.

As if realizing she had revealed too much, Helen straightened and said defensively, "He saved me. Twenty-five years ago. I used to be a real looker then." Her eyes swept over Claire scornfully. "Better than you. I begged him to turn me, but he said he would not corrupt an innocent."

Helen's coldness suddenly made sense. She was jealous. Of Claire.

The housekeeper went on, "One night walking home from work a lycan got it into his head to take me home with him. I was to be his dinner. But first I was his toy—" She shrugged abruptly, as if it were a simple ordeal, but Claire knew it had to have been traumatic. "Darius saved me," Helen finished. "I owe him everything. I chose to devote my life to serving him."

Claire studied the older woman's face, easily detecting a former prettiness buried beneath the sagging skin and age lines. She also saw something else. Heartache. The pain of unrequited love. She released a deep sigh. No wonder Darius appointed this woman his watchdog. She was his disciple. As loyal as they come. Claire would get no help from her.

Sighing, Claire walked past Helen and entered the bathroom, closing the door behind her. Once inside the spacious cream-tiled bathroom, she turned on the shower, dropped the chenille throw, and removed Gideon's jacket, instantly missing his familiar scent. Steam gusted out of the shower, but as she turned to step inside she caught her reflection in the mirror.

The sight startled her. Those eyes—she refused to think of them as hers—stood out starkly against her pale face, a haunting reminder of what she had become. Of what she was becoming. Her hair was a wild tangle about her shoulders and body. And her body . . . well, it looked different. Thinner, leaner. Amazing considering everything she had been eating lately.

She splayed a hand across her rib cage in awe. She'd never been exactly overweight, but her ribs had never jutted out from her skin before. She angled her head, inspecting herself further in the fogging mirror. It wasn't only the weight loss, she decided. Her body seemed toned, muscles sharply defined. A certain vitality hummed from her skin. Not a bad thing, she concluded, then frowned. No, not bad. But not *her*. Not Claire. It had to be the lycan, readying her body as the full moon drew nearer.

Everything was different. She was different. The woman Gideon made love to wasn't the real Claire Morgan. That conclusion soured the sweet memories as nothing else could. What would happen if the curse were broken? If she returned to her old self? A shadow everyone overlooked? A shadow Gideon would overlook? No. Her hand curled into a fist at her side. She would hang on to this new Claire . . . while ridding herself of the curse.

Stepping into the shower, she let the water pound against her skin. She sniffed the salon shampoo before applying it to her hair and working it into a thick lather. Time vanished as she stood beneath the water's spray, letting the liquid warmth permeate her body.

Shutting the water off, she stepped out and wrapped herself in one of the fluffy white towels. She grabbed a second one off the rack and rubbed her hair. It took a moment to realize the jacket and chenille throw were missing. Gone. Someone had entered the bathroom while she showered and taken them.

A sexy little black number hung from a hanger on the back of the door. On the counter sat a tiny pile of black lace. With two fingers, she lifted the impossibly small panties. G-string. Briefly, she considered rebelling and not wearing the clothes left for her. But then she reconsidered. Why not look her best and use her wiles to get what she wanted from Darius? It might go a long way in convincing him to help her.

She slipped into the lingerie and black dress, towel-drying her hair before using the mousse on the counter to tame her locks. She availed herself of the cosmetics displayed on a glass tray. Stepping back, she assessed herself, pleased with the smokiness of her eyes and glossy pout to her lips.

Minutes later the door opened and Claire couldn't help wondering if Helen had been listening for the water to stop.

Helen's gaze flitted over her, narrowing in displeasure. Claire guessed she hadn't been in charge of her wardrobe. "This way," was all she muttered.

Claire followed her downstairs to a large dining room and a linen covered table set for two. Darius stood with his back to her, the profile of his coldly handsome face gazing emotionlessly out a set of French doors overlooking a garden. Claire felt a stab of relief. Here was her chance to reason with him.

He turned, his frosty gaze skimming her in approval. "Thank you, Helen," he said softly. "That will be all."

Helen nodded and departed.

"Do you like the dress?" Darius asked, approaching her with his pantherlike gait, his broad chest and shoulders rippling against his black shirt. "I chose it especially for you. You look beautiful." He held out her chair for her.

She stared at where his broad hands rested on the back of her chair, noticing they were marked with several scars—clearly from his previous life. His life before he became a lycan. She moved and lowered herself into the seat. Swallowing, she opened her mouth and began. "I want you to let me go."

He settled into his chair. "To return to your lycan hunter?" Uncorking a bottle of wine, he reached for her glass. "He will kill you, you know."

"He was trying to help me."

Darius lifted a dark brow skeptically. "Is that what he was doing when I found you and saved you?"

She flushed. "He could have killed me long ago."

"I'm certain," he smoothly cut in, adding, "and taking you to his bed is all part of his plan to save you."

Claire reached for her wine glass, suddenly needing to do something with her hands. "What I chose to do is none of your business."

He chuckled softly. "But it is. We're bonded, Claire. Linked in a way that you will soon understand."

She sipped the dark, sweet red wine. It was good and she was thirsty. She had to stop herself from gulping the entire glass down. She needed her wits tonight if she was going to convince Darius to let her go.

He set his glass back down and covered the top of her hand with his own. "Lycan agents kill lycans. They don't save them. They don't bend. Has it occurred to you that he might be toying with you?"

"No." Despite the denial, she felt doubt sink in. She slid her hand from beneath his.

Sighing, he stood and removed a gleaming silver lid from the serving platter to reveal a roasted rack of lamb.

"Let's consider your chances," he said as he served her, his movements elegant and smooth. "The lycan who infected you is dead."

She stabbed a succulent-looking new potato with her fork without answering.

"Any idea who infected him? What pack he belonged to? The alpha of his pack?"

She shook her head.

"Then how is it you think this lycan hunter can save you?"

She hated his even, placating tone, as if he were trying to prove something logical to a child who failed to see reason.

"What other hope do I have?"

"Me," he volunteered, his gaze drilling into her, his arctic gaze intense.

With his earlier avowal that they would mate ringing in her ears, she said, "No, thanks."

"I'm offering you protection. I can keep you from killing. Your soul doesn't have to be lost."

Claire split an oven-warm roll in half, tendrils of steam rising from it. "Like yours is."

He nodded. "No one ever offered me such a chance. It wasn't even available to me when I first turned."

"And when was that?"

"The year 790. I was a monk at Lindisfarne Abbey."

"A monk?"

His lips curved. "I suppose that would be hard for you to believe. A servant of God now damned for eternity." His smile slipped. "We often took in pilgrims. We asked little of them, simply provided them with food and shelter. One night we took in a group. They were lycans. They attacked us in our beds. It was a blood orgy."

"What happened to the other monks?"

He lifted one shoulder in a shrug. "Historically, Vikings were attributed with razing the monastery to the grounds."

"And that first full moon you fed?"

"Yes. And for countless moons after. I was lost to the curse."

"What made you stop?"

He averted his face, staring toward the French doors and the branches dancing in the breeze. "Someone died that shouldn't have. I extended my protection to a human, made it known within my pack that no harm was to come to her."

"And your pack killed her anyway?"

His silver gaze cut back to her. "No. But they made certain I did."

A chill blew through her heart at his words. "Can you guarantee I'll never escape? That I'll never infect someone else, even accidentally?"

"There are no such guarantees."

She leaned back in her chair, dropping her fork onto her plate with a clatter, frustration getting the better of her. "Then let me go. If Gideon can't help me, I'll gladly let him kill me. I won't risk innocent lives. You should understand that."

"It's your heart talking, not your head." He shook his head fiercely, black hair shaking wildly. "I won't release you. The day will come that you will appreciate what I'm doing."

"Stop treating me like a child who doesn't know any better."

"Then stop acting like one."

"If you do this to me . . ." Claire paused to gain control of her wavering voice. "I'll hate you every day that we're together."

"I'll take that chance."

There was no getting through to him. Despite the hunger still rumbling in her belly, she pushed back her chair and stood. "I'm going to my room." She turned to leave, but his voice stopped her cold.

"You're in love with him."

She stiffened but didn't turn around.

He continued, his voice cutting across the distance like a whip. "You think he can save you. That he'll stop anything bad from happening to you. He won't. He only used you, putting off what he always intended to do. He will—"

"Kill me?" she snapped.

"That's right."

"Let him," she declared, forcing her feet to carry her out of the dining room even as she marveled at how she could say those words. Because in her heart she didn't mean them. She didn't want Gideon to kill her. No. She wanted him to love her.

Gideon sat in Cooper's leather desk chair and pulled up the profile archives. A rare breeze fluttered through the curtains at the open window and ruffled his hair. He stopped and listened for a moment, the sound of a diesel engine outside increasing in volume. The drone faded, blending in with the evening's other midtown traffic, and he relaxed.

Gideon's fingers resumed flying over the keyboard.

He would have broken in to Cooper's house sooner—yesterday, when that bastard first took Claire, but Cooper had been home.

Only board administrators like Cooper had home access to the NODEAL database, and this was his best shot at finding Claire. Logging on with Cooper's password had been easy. He'd seen Cooper type it in countless times.

Typing the name Darius into the search engine, he instantly accessed an extensive file—one that also linked to the files of several other lycans. Gideon's stomach plummeted as he scanned the information, confirming what he already knew. Darius was one old son of a bitch. Circa 800 AD. Last spotted 1870, New York City. Pack: unknown. Current whereabouts: unknown.

Hell, Gideon knew more than that. At least he knew what city the bastard lived in.

Had Claire already suffered untold indignities at his hands? His throat thickened. It was his fault. With a leaden heart he shut off the computer and crawled back out the window.

Chapter Eighteen

Females are selective when it comes to choosing a mate, even when in season.

—*Man's Best Friend: An Essential Guide to Dogs*

Helen entered without knocking.

"Good afternoon," Claire said dryly, propping herself up on the bed with her elbow, smoothing her sundress around her legs. "Come to glare again?"

"Darius wants you to walk the gardens with him."

Claire looked out the window as if considering the idea. It was a beautiful day. Not a cloud in sight. The blue so bright it hurt her eyes. The idea of stepping outside held its appeal. She'd been cooped up for two days. But his steadfast refusal to help her still pricked her temper. "No." Her voice came out hard, clipped, implacable.

"No?" Clearly, Helen had not expected a refusal. She shook her head, scowling. "Darius wants you to walk with him. You have to come."

"I don't *have* to do anything." Leaning back on the bed, she folded her arms behind her head.

Helen clenched her fists at her sides and looked inclined to physically toss Claire off the bed.

Confident that she could overpower the woman, Claire lifted an eyebrow and challenged, “Think you can make me?”

With a grunt, Helen spun around and marched out of the room. The lock sounded behind her.

Seconds passed until Darius’s arrival. Claire eyed his scowl, feeling a flash of satisfaction to see she had cracked his implacable exterior.

His lips pressed into a hard, inflexible line. “Walk with me.”

“No,” she shot back. “I want to go home.”

“This is your home now.”

“No!” Tired of everything in her life being out of her hands, she pounded a fist against the mattress. “I can spend eternity in these walls, but it will never be home to me.”

He strode across the room and yanked her off the bed, reminding her just how strong he was, how dangerous.

“I’ve been patient with you thus far.”

“I can think of several choice descriptions for you—*patient* isn’t one of them.”

“Indeed?” His gaze crawled over her face, studying her as if she were some strange creature, a bug under a microscope that he’d never seen before. “Would you like to see me truly impatient? Make a comparison?” His voice was soft. Too soft. The hairs on her neck prickled. She wiggled to get free, alarmed at the change in him, as if something had been unleashed.

He brought her flush against him, his hands rough.

"I don't have to wait for the full moon, you know. Four days is a long time to wait for something I want . . . for something I can have right now."

She struggled harder, realizing she had been foolish to provoke him. He had lulled her into thinking he was nonviolent. A packless lycan that chose not to feed, not to kill. She had pushed him too far. He was still very much a wild animal. Soulless.

Darius shoved her back on the bed, his body following her down, crushing her into the mattress. She whimpered at the heavy weight of him driving her into the bed and beat against his chest and shoulders.

"I'd rather have you human anyway," he muttered against her throat, his lips warm, surprisingly soft. The beast within her stirred and she knew in that instant she could let him have her, take her physically, and not hate it.

But he wasn't Gideon. Her heart would not be involved. Her heart beat solely for Gideon and it always would.

The clipped velvet tones of Darius's voice rolled over her. "Shifted, we don't always remember things clearly—I want to remember you."

Her hands stung from pounding him. He was a brick wall. Impenetrable muscle. She ceased struggling, allowing her hands to fall limply at her sides. Shutting her eyes, she forced herself to lie motionless, for the beast not to respond.

He stilled over her. Slowly, she opened one eye, then the other. He climbed off her to stand at the side of the bed. Looming over her, his chest lifting with deep, angry breaths, he stared at her in the strangest way. As if he didn't see her at all. As if he saw someone else when he looked at her lying there.

"Go." His voice was so low she wasn't sure she heard him correctly.

Claire lifted her head off the mattress. "W-what?"

"I don't want a corpse beneath me." He pointed to the door. "Go," he said more loudly, his voice a crack of thunder on the air.

She scrambled off the bed, distancing herself warily. "Really?"

"Get out of here before I change my mind!"

She flew to the door, looking over her shoulder when he reminded her, his voice as forbidding as a rumble of thunder on the air, "In three days you'll shift."

The anger had dissipated from his face. Looking tired, he said, "Try to break your curse. I'll come for you when you realize you can't."

She started to shake her head, to tell him not to bother, to forget her, but he was on her so fast she never saw him move. His hands clamped down on her arms and shook her until her head snapped back. "Don't do anything stupid. Don't kill yourself. Don't give up when you realize your lycan hunter can't save you."

Her eyes met his steely gaze and she wondered if her own eyes could possibly be that penetrating, that frightening. Or was it just him?

His hands fell from her arms. "Now go." He stepped back from her, arms falling to his sides. "I'll come for you before you shift, and I expect you to join me when I do."

For the first time, Claire considered what he offered—

while avoiding the thought of what would occur alone with him in that room once they had shifted. Her mind and heart couldn't contemplate such a thing. Not after Gideon.

Still, it would give her more time to find her alpha and break the curse. No one would be hurt. She would be alive. Her soul would be safe. Even if her heart wasn't.

In a barely audible voice, she agreed. "Okay."

Worrying about her heart was a luxury she could no longer afford. Not when her life and soul were on the line.

Claire sat behind the wheel of the car Darius had loaned her and waited for the red light to change. She thrummed her fingers on the steering wheel, trying to decide her next move.

It wasn't safe to return to Gideon now that Cooper knew about her. She had to stop relying on him. She had to put her wants and desires aside and cease being the fool Darius claimed she was, holding out for the impossible dream that Gideon could save her.

The car behind her honked, spurring Claire to both drive and reach a decision. Who was she kidding? Nothing could keep her away from Gideon. Not common sense. He at least deserved to know she was okay.

Half an hour later, she slowed to a stop alongside the curb of his house, resting her foot lightly on the brake. Leaning forward, she propped her chin on the steering wheel and studied the quiet house. His Jeep was gone. She stifled the deep sigh welling up inside her. It was selfish to ignore the danger she brought down on his head simply because she couldn't resist seeing him again. She lifted her foot off the brake.

A sudden movement to her right caught her eye. Claire turned—

The passenger-side window shattered. Glass rained down on the passenger seat, several pieces striking her face and arms. Screaming, she ducked and hit the gas with her foot.

The car surged forward blindly. She felt the tire bump the curb and quickly straightened the wheel, whipping down the street and running the stop sign. She risked a glance in the rearview mirror to see a man standing in the middle of the street holding a gun.

Claire drove several blocks at breakneck speed until her heart stilled enough for her to ease her foot off the gas. Once on the freeway, she let the tears roll down her face in hot trails, unchecked.

Clearly, that guy had been a NODEAL agent running surveillance on Gideon's house. Did Gideon know? Or was this all Cooper's handy work? Either way, it was time to leave Gideon March alone. She didn't need to complicate his life more than she already had. She had to let him go. For both their sakes.

She swiped the back of her hand against her wet cheeks and glanced down at the passenger seat. Amid the shards of glass, a dark silver ball winked at her in the sunlight. Must have bounced off the seat belt buckle. Keeping one eye on the traffic, she stretched out her hand and flicked it to the floor, out of sight.

A short time later, Claire turned into the parking lot of her apartment complex. She scanned the lot cautiously, her eyes lighting on a familiar four by four parked in front of her building. Cooper himself sat behind the wheel. Sinking low in her seat, Claire zipped past and exited the parking lot. Uncertain whether he recognized her, she glanced several times in the rearview mirror to make sure he didn't give chase.

After a few minutes she sighed, confident she wasn't being tailed, then sighed even deeper when she realized she was out of options. She couldn't go to Gideon's. Couldn't go to her place. And yet she wasn't ready to return to Darius.

Grimacing, she drove until she reached her parents' house. Once there, Claire sat parked behind her father's truck in the driveway for several minutes, staring in silence at the two-story brick house framed against the smoky gray of early evening. The house looked different, smaller than she remembered.

"What the hell," she muttered, getting out of the car. After facing down lycans, her parents should be a piece of cake.

Claire usually entered the house without warning, but after her last visit she thought it wise to knock.

The door swung open following her three swift raps.

"Dad," she greeted, her voice tight.

Genuine surprise etched his blunt features. "Claire," he returned. "I thought you were at the lake house."

"I came back sooner than expected."

He looked over her shoulder. "New car?"

Luckily he couldn't see the shattered window from where he stood.

She waved at the shiny Buick. "Just a friend's."

"Your car's not running? I can take a look at it for you."

Claire blinked. Although mechanically inclined, her father had never bothered to look after her car for her. Never even bought her a car. She bought her first car herself, in college, and he always left the care of it to her. Maybe this was a sign. Her father's way of offering an olive branch?

Bitterness rose from the back of her throat to fill her mouth. It was clear he was trying, but she couldn't help wishing he had tried years ago when she was a girl in need of a father. The irony wasn't lost on her. Three days before the end and they suddenly had a chance at a relationship.

"My car's fine. I just left it at the lake."

He opened his mouth, and then shut it again, as if he had decided against prying.

She heard herself explaining anyway, out of habit, "My friend met me up there and we wanted to drive one car back instead of two." She shrugged lamely.

He frowned. "You left it at the lake house?"

Nodding, she held her breath, waiting for him to heap his usual criticism upon her head. Instead, he continued to nod, accepting her explanation.

"Claire?" Her mother hurried past her father to embrace her. "What a surprise." Ushering her inside, she glanced up at her husband. "Isn't this a nice surprise, Mike?"

Claire's father nodded in agreement.

Her mother eyed her closely, reaching up to brush the hair back off her forehead. "I tried calling you at the lake house all week."

Claire couldn't think up an excuse for that. At this point, her father would usually dive in with some comment about her being inconsiderate and selfish, but he remained oddly silent as he followed them into the kitchen.

Her mother stuck her head in the fridge and began sorting through the leftovers. "We have some ham—"

"Sounds good," Claire replied numbly, feeling strange standing in her old familiar kitchen, her parents on either side of her. The last time she'd been in this house she had felt different, changed, but she hadn't known the reason.

Her mother set a platter of sliced ham on the island countertop. "You want a sandwich?"

Claire nodded and began munching on a slice of ham as her mother reached for the Wonder bread. Her mother moved about the kitchen with boundless energy—a humming vitality that Claire had never seen in her before.

"Can't say I'm sorry you've come back early." Her mother pulled two jars from the fridge.

Claire arched a brow and licked the salty taste of ham off her fingers.

Her mother dipped her head, color flooding her cheeks as she dug a butter knife out of the drawer. "Your father and I have been playing with the idea of getting away." Removing a plate from the cabinet, she glanced almost shyly at Claire. "Are you finished using the lake house?"

Claire nodded, frowning at both her parents. They seldom used the lake house.

"Good." Her mother set a napkin next to her plate,

giving it a cheerful little pat. "We'll head up there this weekend, then." Glancing at her husband, she suggested, "Maybe we can rent one of those paddleboats."

Claire nearly choked on a bite of ham. Certainly her father would shoot that idea down. He would want to float in a paddleboat about as much as he wanted a root canal.

"Sure," he murmured, giving Claire wide berth as he moved to the fridge, further astounding her when he got his very own beer.

Claire looked her father up and down incredulously. *Who was this man?*

"Miracle Whip or mayo?" Her mother held up both jars.

Blinking and wondering who these impostors were, Claire pointed to the jar of mayonnaise. "Give me the real stuff."

Her mother lifted an eyebrow at her choice. No doubt thinking of all the calories. Claire usually chose the fat-free Miracle Whip.

"You're all bones," her mother clucked, slathering a generous amount of mayonnaise on the bread. "Oh," her mother added as if suddenly remembering, "the reason I've been calling you up at the lake is because your friend Maggie contacted me."

"Maggie?" Claire echoed.

"Yes, she said that the school's been trying to get hold of you because they're using your room for summer school. She's said it's important you come clear out your things. She also said Jill Tanners was looking for you.

Had some information on a kid you were worried about. A boy named Lenny?"

Claire drew a deep breath. "Lenny?"

Her mother nodded.

What information could the counselor possibly have? Whatever it was, it was worth investigating. And if she didn't go, she risked losing all her teaching resources it had taken years to accumulate. If she didn't fetch her things, it was as good as admitting she was dead. Claire wasn't willing to do that. Not yet. If she were, she might as well drive back to Darius and offer herself to him. "The building's already closed for the day. I'll have to go tomorrow."

Her mother handed her a large bag of potato chips and placed a fat ham sandwich before her. "So how is that boyfriend of yours?"

Avoiding her mother's eyes, Claire grimaced and swiped her finger along the edge of her sandwich where the mayonnaise threatened to spill out. Licking the creamy goodness off her finger, she said, "Gideon's fine, Mom."

Fine. Safe. As long as she ignored her heart and stayed far away from him.

Chapter Nineteen

Should you find yourself in the company of a strange dog, be sure to make no sudden movements.

—*Man's Best Friend: An Essential Guide to Dogs*

Claire was bent over, rifling through her last box, still fuming over her conversation with Jill Tanners. The woman wanted to be the first to let Claire know that Lenny was dead. No doubt gang related. She cursed beneath her breath. No one would ever know the truth. That Lenny had been a good kid, a victim.

"Claire!"

She glanced up and grimaced to see Cyril in her doorway, an expression of mild surprise on his otherwise bland face. "What are you doing here?"

"Packing up," she replied, trying to keep the annoyance from her voice. What did it look like?

Stepping inside her classroom, he eyed the boxes. "The rumors are true, then? You've resigned?" he asked with a frown.

She smiled wryly. The teacher's lounge really should be banned. The faculty gossiped worse than the students. "I haven't resigned. They're using my room for summer school." She couldn't help wondering what other rumors circulated about her sudden leave of absence.

As if answering her wonderings, he said, "You didn't elope and move to Europe?"

"Is that what everyone is saying?" She shook her head, lips stretching in a rueful grin. "Nothing as exciting as that, I'm afraid."

Only more, she silently added, thinking about the turn her life had taken. She had had enough adventure in the past few weeks to last a lifetime. She paused, fingers closing around a heavy brass apple paperweight a student had given her years ago. But to say she regretted it all would mean she regretted meeting Gideon. And that, she couldn't claim.

"Ah." Cyril nodded, looking somewhat relieved. "I should have known to take what I heard with a grain of salt, considering the source."

"The faculty lounge," Claire guessed.

He nodded. "You're coming back in the fall, then?"

She hesitated, unsure how to answer that. She settled for the truth. "I don't know."

"Oh." His shoulders slumped in disappointment. His reaction seemed out of place. For God's sake, they'd only had one date. And if he liked her so much, why had he switched his attention to Jill Tanners?

He stuffed his hands into his pockets. "I hate to lose you."

She looked up sharply from the box she organized. Why did he sound like he meant more than professionally?

"Miss Morgan!"

Nina. Just in time. His intent stare was beginning to creep her out. What had ever inspired her to go out with Cyril in the first place? On their date, he had seemed as bored as she was. Yet she knew the reason. She had agreed to go out with him because she felt she should, because it had been years since anyone had asked.

Cyril frowned as Nina hugged her.

"I was hoping you'd be here." Nina, all teenage bubbliness and smiles.

"What are you still doing here?" Claire asked. "Yesterday was the last day of school. Shouldn't you be out having fun?"

Nina motioned to the bulging backpack slung over her shoulder. "I still had to clear out my dance locker."

Claire nodded.

Nina's gaze roamed over the boxes surrounding Claire's desk. "You're not coming back?"

"No." Claire shook her head, then quickly amended, "I mean, I don't know yet." She finished placing the last of her curriculum binders into a box.

Cyril lightly coughed, reminding her of his presence. He shot an annoyed glance at Nina, clearly wanting Claire to get rid of her.

He must have gotten the clue that Claire wasn't going to chase the girl off, because he finally announced, "I guess I'll be going. Enjoy your summer." He hovered in the doorway for a moment, hands deep in his pockets, almost as though expecting her to stop him.

"You, too," Claire replied with a light wave of her hand.

As he left, Nina plunged back into chatter. "So you are coming back, right?"

Claire hefted one box into her arms. "Maybe."

Nina motioned to the boxes. "You're carrying these to your car? I'll help."

They took the ramp downstairs rather than risk missing their footing on the steps. Nina chatted happily at her side about her summer plans as they stepped outside, the afternoon air pungent with the smell of baked asphalt and rotting vegetation.

"I'm going to lifeguard at my neighborhood pool. Can you believe they're going to pay me to get a tan?"

"I think you actually have to do more than tan while you're on duty," Claire said in amusement as she set the box on the trunk of the car and unlocked the door.

"Yeah, I gotta stop little kids from dunking each other." Nina shrugged. "No biggie."

"And don't forget you have to whistle every half hour for adult swim time," Claire teased as she picked the box back up.

Nina laughed. "Yeah, that's right."

Claire set the box into the backseat, shoving it to the far end to make room for the others to come. She pulled her head from the car's interior, a flip comment about lifeguarding twisting into a gasp as agony exploded in the back of her head.

Clutching the base of her skull, she first assumed her head hadn't cleared the door frame, that she had accidentally bumped it. But as she staggered back from the car, she was struck a second time from behind.

Nina. Her instincts about the girl had been wrong.

A third blow brought her to her knees. She grabbed the car door. Her hands latched onto it, trying to pull herself up. She was almost to her feet when a quick, sharp pain penetrated her shoulder, dropping her to her knees again.

Convinced she had been shot, Claire clutched the back of her shoulder, expecting to feel blood. Instead, she pulled something from her flesh.

She held a needle in her hand, staring at the steel tip in bewilderment until she began to sway. The syringe slipped from her open palm and she watched it fall through the air, her vision growing cloudy, then black as it dropped.

She never saw it hit the asphalt.

Claire struggled against the black, pushing past it, fighting the heavy twin weights of her eyelids. Gradually, she felt the cold stinging her cheek where it pressed into freezing concrete. Her eyelids parted to discover a tilting, shifting, careening world of gray. Jamming her eyes shut, she waited for the dizziness to pass. Moments later, she tried again. Blinking several times, she rubbed her eyes until her vision cleared.

Claire pushed herself to a sitting position. Four dull gray walls surrounded her, one dirty window positioned high up, out of reach. A chalky concrete floor stretched out beneath her, disappearing into shadows. She wiped drool from her chin with the back of her hand and inhaled deeply, but there was only the stink of mildew and stale air. She looked up. The window allowed in a single beam of early morning light where tiny motes of dust shivered, trapped.

Morning? She brushed her fingers against her aching head and forced herself to recall how she got here. She had been loading things into the backseat, talking to Nina, when someone struck her from behind. Claire closed her eyes tight, drawing in a hissing breath. *Nina.* Gideon had been right.

Biting her lip, she looked up at that lone window. If she even managed to reach it and break the glass, she could squeeze maybe one leg through the space. Someone chose this jail cell deliberately, with great care. Most Texas homes didn't have basements.

A groan sounded nearby, startling her, alerting her that she wasn't alone. Tensing, she squinted into the gloom. A crumpled form lay at the bottom of the wooden stairs, a dark stain against the floor. Claire inched closer, making out the black hair pooling on the floor in an inky puddle.

"Nina?"

Claire hesitated. She crawled toward the girl, the cold concrete hard and unforgiving on her knees. Her hand stretched out, finding her pulse. Erratic but strong.

Lying in a haphazard fashion at the base of the stairs, one arm at her side, the other flung above her head, Nina didn't appear much of a threat. She resembled a limp rag doll, forgotten and discarded where she had been tossed. Claire eyed the steep incline of stairs. A closed door loomed at the top, sealing her in from the rest of the world.

Skirting Nina's inert body, she clutched the rail and climbed the steps. At the top, she closed her hand around the doorknob. Locked.

She jiggled the knob and beat on the steel-framed door with her palm, crying out until she grew hoarse and her hand stung.

A small voice chirped from below. "Miss Morgan?"

Claire spun around. Far below, at the base of the stairs, she noted a slight movement. Nina was awake. A single hand lifted, fingers outstretched as if searching for a lifeline. The movement must have cost her because she cried out in pain, her hand dropping.

Claire hurried down the steps in a flurry of pounding feet. "Nina!" She dropped to her knees and gently rolled the girl onto her back. The arm stretched above her head plopped down on her chest lifelessly. Nina's pretty face twisted in pain. Her mouth opened wide in a silent scream and her eyes glazed over, losing focus before fluttering shut.

"Nina!" Claire tapped her cheeks. "Come on. Stay with me."

Her eyes remained shut as she rasped, "I think my arm's broken."

Claire eyed the arm across her chest. It rested at an awkward angle, oddly limp. Scanning the rest of her slight body, Claire asked, "Are you hurt anywhere else?"

Nina's lips barely moved as she spoke. "My whole body hurts . . . from the stairs."

"Stairs?" Claire's gaze traveled up the steep incline of steps. "You fell down the stairs?"

Her tongue darted out to wet her lips. "Pushed."

"Pushed?"

A push down those stairs could have killed her. If she only suffered a broken arm and a couple bruises, she was lucky.

Claire hesitated to touch her in fear of aggravating her injuries, but she wasn't exactly able to get to a phone and call for help. She might have no choice but to move her.

She smoothed a palm over Nina's forehead. Despite the basement's chill, the skin felt clammy. "What happened, Nina? Who pushed you?"

"Hit you. And stabbed you with a—"

"Sshh, I know." Claire leaned close to Nina's mouth to better hear, asking, "Do you know who it was?"

Just then the door above opened and a beam of light shot down on them. A dark figure stood at the top of the stairs, outlined by the light.

Finally, the figure stepped down, revealing his face.

"I believe you're asking about me."

Gideon splashed water on his exhausted face and lifted his gaze to his reflection. Bloodshot eyes stared back at him, the haggard lines of his face hardly recognizable.

He had not slept during the last three days. He had returned to Woody's countless times and scoured other clubs, all known hangouts of lycans. No sign of the bastard anywhere. Or Claire.

He pulled the hand towel off the bar and rubbed it vigorously against his face. Tossing the towel on the counter, he headed downstairs. Opening his fridge, he went for a power drink, hoping the sugar and caffeine would revive him. After gulping down a bottle, he grabbed his keys and headed for the door. Ready for another day of searching. Even if the odds were against him, it kept him from going mad with thoughts of Claire . . . suffering at the hands of Darius.

He blinked against the morning sunlight and slid his sunglasses in place. The dark sedan parked across the street immediately caught his notice. Lips tightening, he crossed the street in long strides. With a flick of his wrist, he tapped a knuckle against the driver's side window.

The window rolled down in response.

"Tom," Gideon acknowledged. "This is how it is now?"

The agent shrugged one shoulder and grimaced. "Just following orders."

"Right," Gideon grunted. Turning on his heels, he marched to his Jeep, more convinced than ever that his days at NODEAL were over. He wanted nothing to do with a group that discounted his years of loyalty and service, that trusted him so little, condemning him for trying to save a single innocent life.

His throat constricted and an invisible hand squeezed around his heart. Pain like he had never known, not even when his parents drowned in their own blood, washed over him as he realized Claire probably wished he had followed NODEAL's exacting codes.

"Cyril?"

His lips stretched into an oily smile. "Good morning, Claire. Sleep well?"

Blood rushed to her head as she looked up the steps. His eyes glowed unnaturally, like highly polished silver.

Instantly, she knew he was more than a lycan. He was the alpha she sought. What she had failed to see before became glaringly clear.

The dropout rate had increased since Cyril's arrival. And now she knew why. Those "at risk" kids were the perfect targets. No one blinked an eye when they went missing. They were the perfect food supply.

"You infected Lenny."

He sighed heavily. "Yes. That was an accident, I'm afraid. I never meant for him to get away."

Fury and hate filled her. "He was my student," she growled.

Cyril walked down the rest of the steps, ignoring her words. "I'm quite selective, you know. I haven't initiated a new member to the pack in years." He said this with pride, like a father preening over his family. "But I've given you a lot of thought, Claire. You're not the type I would normally choose to join our ranks—"

"Then why did you ask me out?"

He laughed lightly. "Not to recruit you. I wanted information. More than I could get in a file. Kids like Lenny adore you. You're the mother they don't have." He smirked. "And you so love them. Don't you remember that night we went out? What we talked about?"

She searched her memory. They'd talked shop, of course. Work. Common ground. Claire thought he had shared her interest in reaching the more unfortunate students, but apparently he had just been pumping her for information. Regret washed over her. She had talked about Lenny. About his situation at home, about his neglectful and disinterested foster parents. She had told him how special Lenny was to her—that she had managed to reach him.

"You used me to get him to him, you bastard!"

Smiling, he nodded. "Indeed. I used you to get to all of them."

She folded Nina's trembling hand in her own, taking comfort as much as she gave it. "Why are we here?"

"As I've said, I've given it a great deal of thought and what's done is done. You're one of us now. I've decided to keep you." He nodded decisively. "It will amuse me to watch your development. You were so skittish before, such a mouse." His gaze raked her appraisingly. "Already you've changed. For the better."

"I won't join your pack."

"You don't have a choice." He motioned to Nina, who watched them with wide, haunted eyes. "That's what this little pigeon is for."

She glanced to Nina, then back to him.

"You'll stay down here until tomorrow. Until moonrise." He nodded at Nina. "And she's going to keep you company."

Claire's eyes shifted to Nina in horror. Nina blinked, bewildered, confused, evidently failing to grasp Cyril's implication. But Claire understood perfectly.

He pointed at two jugs of water near the foot of the stairs. "So you don't dehydrate. Be sure to give the girl some. We don't want her to perish before you get the chance for a fresh meal." His lips curved in a mocking smile. "You should be starving by tomorrow night."

"Please, you can't do this." She looked over her shoulder

at Nina, her face frighteningly pale beneath her caramel-toned skin. "Anyone else. Not her."

He looked amused. "Ah, you will be a delight to train. I'm anxious to see how long it takes you to lose this . . . sensitivity after you've had a taste."

Turning, he started back up the steps. Claire flew after him, her feet a blur beneath her. Snarling, she launched herself at him, legs wrapping around his waist, fingers clawing down the sides of his face.

He plucked her from him as if she were weightless. Hard fingers closed around her face, lifting her off her feet. "Careful now, Claire. You're no match for me."

"I'll kill you," she hissed.

Laughing, he flung her down. She hit the concrete floor. Hard. He called down to Nina. "You don't happen to be a virgin, do you?" He shook his head in mock disgust when Nina failed to answer. Clucking lightly, he addressed Claire again. "These girls today just don't know how to hang on to their virtue. I can't tell you how long it's been since I tasted a good virgin. The blood is always—" He pinched the air as if seeking the right words. "Sweeter."

The bile rose in the back of her throat.

Still laughing, he ascended the stairs. The door clicked shut behind him, the sound magnifying in her ears.

"Miss Morgan?"

Claire looked down at her student, the silent plea clear as day in those espresso-colored eyes.

Nina stumbled for words, her brow creased in worry. "You're not really going to kill me, are you?"

Chapter Twenty

Don't be fooled by appearances; sometimes
the scrawniest dogs are the most dangerous.

—*Man's Best Friend:*
An Essential Guide to Dogs

Gun ready, Gideon yanked open his door and took aim. "Where is she?" he asked with deadly calm, his barrel a mere inch from those silver eyes. He looked away for the briefest second to scan the street. Tom, who had diligently dogged Gideon's trail, was nowhere in sight. *Guess Cooper called off his watchdog.* Or Tom got lazy and went on a food run.

His gaze flicked back to Darius, the very bastard he had spent endless agonizing days hunting. The lycan didn't appear the least bit ruffled to have a gun in his face. He lifted a dark brow and asked mildly, "She's not with you, then, I presume?"

Desperate for answers, Gideon flung his elbow against Darius's throat and pinned him to a porch pillar. He pressed the gun to the center of his head. "If you touched her—"

Darius's lips curved in clear amusement. "I didn't hurt her, if that's what you're worried about. Or didn't she assure you of that herself?"

"Why would she be with me? You took her."

"I let her go. Days ago."

"You let her go?" Gideon's finger loosened on the trigger and he eased his arm from the lycan's throat, shocked and a little skeptical at this unexpected news. "Why?"

"Because that's what she wanted." Darius shrugged lightly, as if even he couldn't make sense of it.

"She didn't want to go with you in the first place," Gideon reminded him, finding it hard to believe that this lycan would take Claire's wishes into consideration.

"Yes," he agreed, angling his head. "But I thought I could persuade her to stay with me. We lycans are social creatures, you know. We enjoy companionship. I thought Claire would come around."

"What about your pack?" Gideon sneered. "They're not company enough?"

"I don't have a pack."

At this Gideon could only stare. Every lycan had a pack.

"No pack. I had hoped Claire could be my pack," he said in a soft voice. "She's all I need."

Gideon aimed the gun again, beyond tempted to blow this lycan away. "Sorry, she's not yours."

"So I learned." Once again, Darius appeared unperturbed. "Appears she's not so easily persuaded. Someone got to her before me." His gaze cut to Gideon meaningfully, making it clear to whom he referred.

Darius sidestepped Gideon and entered the house. "Despite my best efforts to convince her otherwise, she thinks you can save her." He smiled that cold smile again. "But we both know differently. Don't we?"

Gideon was still grappling with the news that this lycan had freed Claire. Where was she? Why hadn't she come to him?

"You let her go?" Gideon demanded, rotating where he stood, his gun following the lycan strolling through his living room.

"You sound suspicious. Bad experience with others of my kind, I presume." Darius stopped, hands clasped behind his back, and rocked on his heels, saying, "Is that why you became an agent?"

Gideon stiffened. He wasn't about to share his personal history with this bastard. It made no difference that he was steadily breaking every preconceived notion he had about lycans—Gideon still didn't trust him.

"Ah, sore subject, I see. Would it do any good to tell you that I too share your dislike for my kind? My intentions toward Claire are honorable."

Gideon snorted. "Right. That's why you flung her screaming over your shoulder and abducted her."

Darius's silver eyes narrowed. "*I* offer her life. What do you offer her? A one-night stand and a silver bullet?" The criticism in his voice cut like a whip.

"Shut the hell up." The bitter taste of rage flooded his mouth. His finger curled around the trigger, so tempted. "I'm trying to help her."

"I'm sure you are." Darius nodded his dark head, but his voice sounded less than convinced. "All you agents have the same solution for the world's lycan problem.

Destroy. Kill. It never crossed your mind that there may be a better way to help Claire?"

Gideon pounded his fist on chest. "I'm trying to help her find—"

"Yes, but you're going to kill if you don't. Correct?"

Gideon opened his mouth several times, finding himself at a complete loss. In all honesty, he couldn't answer that question any longer. He had vowed no one would end her life save him, but when it came down to it, could he even do it?

Then it hit him that he didn't owe an explanation to this lycan. "This is between me and Claire."

"I don't think you want her to die," Darius announced, his look thoughtful. "What if I told you there's a way to protect her soul and let her live as a lycan?"

Gideon stepped closer, Darius's words fanning the flame of hope sheltered deep in his heart. Then common sense prevailed and he muttered, "That's impossible."

"Such a pessimist." Darius clicked his tongue, looking disappointed as he headed for the door. "It seems Claire misplaced her faith in you, otherwise you'd at least hear me out. No matter. I'll find her without you. I promised her my protection, told her I'd come for her today."

Anger unfurled low in Gideon's belly. What exactly went on between Claire and this lycan to make her trust him? "Why would she trust you?" he demanded, refusing to believe that she would turn to a lycan for help over him.

"We have an understanding."

Gideon had no reason to feel betrayed. He and Claire

had exchanged no words of love, made no promises. He shouldn't feel betrayed that she accepted the help of another, of a lycan—but he did.

"What kind of understanding?" he growled.

"Whether you believe it or not, I'm not your typical lycan."

Gideon had no trouble believing that. So far this lycan had displayed behavior far from customary. The fact that Gideon was talking to him and Darius had not tried to rip out his throat said a lot.

Darius went on, "I lock myself up during every full moon so that I won't feed."

"Right," Gideon snorted. He didn't know what was more unbelievable. That Darius claimed to lock himself in a room or that he didn't *want* to feed. Once a lycan fed and tasted human blood he lost all conscience. The beast ruled him. "No room can hold a lycan in the throes of blood hunger."

"I've built one that can. A tank couldn't crash through these walls. It's impenetrable."

Gideon stared at him. It couldn't be that easy to save Claire. Could it? True, he had never thought how one might save someone from shifting. Before Claire, he had never wanted to.

"Don't believe me." Darius shrugged. "Claire does, and I promised to keep her safe."

Darius's words ripped through him like a bullet, reminding him that where he had failed, this lycan had managed to deliver.

Then he remembered one important fact. "Locked up with you is safe?"

"The rest of the world is safe from us, yes."

"But she's not safe from *you*." Gideon was no fool. He knew what would happen between them in that room once they shifted, and he couldn't stomach the thought.

"She is what she is. As am I." He waved a hand at Gideon. "She doesn't belong with you."

"But she belongs with *you*?"

"I'm a lycan. She's a lycan. You are not. Think about it. I'm offering her a chance, a way out without risk to others or her soul."

Gideon struggled against Darius's offer, wanting to deny it, wanting to reject it as a possibility, knowing that releasing Claire meant giving her up—that she would belong to Darius. He couldn't deny his feelings for her any longer. He loved her. He wanted her to live. Even if it meant living without him. Even if it meant giving her to this lycan.

He lowered the gun until it hung loosely from his fingers.

"All right. Let's find her."

"Gideon." Kathleen Morgan sounded frantic over the phone line. "I'm so glad you called. Have you seen Claire? We haven't seen or heard from her since she left here."

The knot in his gut tightened, twisting. "When was that?"

"Tuesday afternoon."

"Did she say where she was going when she left there?"

"She needed to clear out her room at work," Mrs. Morgan explained. "The school is using it for summer school classes. And a teacher needed to talk to her about a student."

His fingers tightened about the phone. "Did she mention the student's name?"

"Lenny, I think."

Of course Claire would have gone to hear what the teacher had to say. "Don't worry. We'll find her."

Less than an hour later he walked the halls of Roosevelt High School with Darius at his side. A handful of faculty still roamed the building, but it had the air of an abandoned ship. Most doors lining the halls were closed, the panels of glass next to them revealing darkened caves within. Summer vacation was well under way. He stopped a lone student, a boy lugging a saxophone case, and got directions to Claire's room.

Her classroom was unlocked. He flipped on the lights, blinking against the sudden fluorescent glare. The room was empty save for the uniform rows of desks. One box sat on her desk and several more littered the floor.

"She never finished," Darius announced, peering into a box.

Gideon's gaze swept over the room. "She was interrupted," he surmised aloud.

Darius lifted a backpack off the top of a desk with two fingers. A Hello Kitty mirror hung off the backpack's zipper. "Hers?"

"No," he answered, pulling her chair out from her desk, discovering her purse discreetly stashed on the cushioned seat. "She wouldn't have left her purse."

"Now what?" Darius asked.

"Let's check the office downstairs. Maybe someone talked to her. Saw something."

Darius pushed himself off a file cabinet and followed. As they neared the front office, they passed dozens of large photos displaying championship football teams, drill teams, and other school clubs.

"Hey, hold on a minute."

Gideon stopped again and looked impatiently over his shoulder at Darius. "What?"

Darius stared intently into one of the large frames. "You ever see this guy before?"

Gideon moved beside Darius to stare at a district championship photograph of the school orchestra.

Darius tapped the glass above Cyril's face. "Know him?"

"I've met him. Claire introduced me. Cyril Jenkins."

"He's a lycan."

Gideon looked back and forth between Darius and the photograph, his chest constricting, suddenly painfully tight. "It's just a photograph. How can you tell?"

"I know him." Darius's expression grew strained. "It's been a while, and his name wasn't Cyril then, but I would never forget his face."

Gideon could only stare at the bland, unassuming features of Cyril Jenkins and fight back the urge to fling back his head and howl in rage. He'd met the man and had never even suspected. All this time the alpha they sought had been under their noses. And now he had Claire.

"You couldn't have known. He's very old—wise enough to know how to disguise himself from agents."

Claire had dated him—sat across from him at a restaurant. Worked with him every day. The thought made his fists clench tighter. Apparently his hunch that the geeky band director had been interested in Claire wasn't far off. Damn straight he was interested in her. She was a member of his pack.

"There's your alpha," Darius pronounced, reading Gideon's mind. "At least we know who has Claire now."

"Yeah, but not where," Gideon clarified, looking toward the office and nodding at the secretary talking on the phone behind her desk. "Think she can be persuaded to give us his address?"

"Never question a lycan's ability to enthrall." With a tiny salute, Darius pushed through the glass door.

Gideon paced outside the office, trying to keep his thoughts from Claire and what Cyril could be doing to her. Those thoughts would drive him mad and make him useless. Darius soon emerged, a slip of paper in hand. "Got it."

Gideon nodded, grim determination filling him. *Claire, baby, I'm coming.*

Chapter Twenty-one

When a dog is hungry enough, it will eat anything to survive.

—*Man's Best Friend: An Essential Guide to Dogs*

Gideon watched the double doors of the gray two-story building impatiently. He understood Cooper was angry. But their history alone should have guaranteed him an audience instead of the desk sergeant's curt "Yeah, he's in, but said if it was you not to bother him."

"He caught you in bed with a lycan," Darius's rich, clipped tones rumbled from beside him. "You're a lycan hunter. Somewhat flies in the face of what you do, doesn't it?"

"I'm aware of that," he snapped, not bothering to explain that he and Cooper went way back. Far enough back to make certain allowances.

"Yet you expect him to overlook that? How is he going to react with me by your side?"

Gideon didn't care what Cooper thought. He would team up with the devil himself if it helped save Claire. Jenkins lived north of Houston on forty acres. They had already cased the property that afternoon. With its thick foliage, the house was undetectable from the road. An ideal setup, a virtual compound for Jenkins's pack. Who knew how many numbers they were pitting themselves against? It was beyond risky, even with Gideon's experience and Darius at his side. Their combined skills wouldn't be enough. They needed Cooper.

"There he is." Gideon leaned forward in his seat as Cooper made his way to the employee parking lot on the side of the building.

He shifted into drive and rolled out of the parking lot several cars behind Cooper. Cooper lived close to work, preferring a short drive, and that appeared to be where he was headed. A few minutes later, Gideon pulled into the driveway behind Cooper.

"Wait here," he instructed Darius, swinging out of the Jeep with one hand gripping the door frame.

Cooper stopped and braced his legs apart in the driveway when he spotted Gideon. "You're suspended, Gid. Go home."

"I know where she is."

At this announcement, Cooper lifted an eyebrow, asking flatly, "Where?"

"Her alpha found her and took her to his pack. He goes by the name of Cyril Jenkins—"

"Have you checked the calendar lately?" Cooper cut in, shaking his head and waving a hand at the late afternoon sky. "Tonight's moonrise. You know they're ten times stronger once they shift. Forget it. I'll run surveillance next week and send agents to pick them off. Safely. One at a time."

"Next week will be too late for her."

"It's already too late for her," Cooper thundered, the veins throbbing on his neck. "I don't know what's happened to you to make you think you can help this one, but you can't."

Gideon clenched his hands at his sides, not bothering to explain whatever it was that had set Claire apart from the start, making it impossible to destroy her, making her the one woman he couldn't resist, the one woman to infiltrate his heart. It wasn't something he could explain. It was something he felt, something he could not control. Like the beating of his heart. "I'm going. With or without your help."

"By yourself?" Cooper's lips twisted in a semblance of a smile, clearly thinking Gideon joked. "It'd be suicide."

"I've got backup. A partner." Gideon nearly choked on the word.

"Yeah?" Cooper snorted. "Who? No agent would be stupid enough."

Gideon jerked his thumb behind him.

Cooper squinted at the figure sitting in Gideon's Jeep. "Who's that?"

"A lycan."

Cooper went rigid, the lines and angles of his narrow face tightening. "You've totally lost it. This goes beyond breaking code—"

"Hear me out—"

"That's a lycan sitting there calm as you please?" He shook his head, face screwing tight. "Man, you think I'll team up with one of their kind to help you?"

"Cooper, listen—"

"Get the hell off my property."

Gideon held his ground, reining in his temper. "Cooper, we go way back—"

"Which is why I don't shoot your ass and that son of a bitch right now." He threw his arm wildly in the direction of the driveway. "Didn't I teach you anything?"

"Yeah, you taught me. A lot. You taught me how to think, not just follow dictates mindlessly when they don't make sense."

Cooper's eyes bulged, his face dangerously red. "What are you talking about?" he demanded. "What doesn't make sense about killing the bloodthirsty fuckers?"

"It's always been NODEAL policy to destroy the infected. Without even trying to save them. Without even considering other alternatives."

Cooper stared at him for a long moment. "What alternatives?"

Thinking of Darius's special room, he said, "Come with me. If we don't kill Claire's alpha, I'll show you the other alternatives."

For a moment, something flashed in Cooper's eyes. Uncertainty. Consideration for what Gideon was proposing.

His gaze steady and unblinking on the man he called a friend for half his life, he appealed one last time. "Help me. Together we can save her."

"And him?" Cooper pointed a damning finger to where Darius waited in the Jeep. "Something tells me that cold-eyed bastard watching us can't be saved. So what are you doing with him?"

Gideon frowned. "He's not your run-of-the-mill lycan.

He doesn't have a pack and he doesn't kill." Even as Gideon said the words he winced at how unbelievable they sounded.

Cooper snorted. "Right. And he's helping you out of the goodness of his heart." He choked out a derisive laugh. "Come on, Gid. You're not that gullible. What's in it for him?"

Gideon swallowed and confessed, "He wants Claire."

Cooper threw back his head and laughed. "Priceless." He turned and cut through his lawn with swift strides, calling over his shoulder. "You two called a truce in order to save a woman you're going to duke it out over later."

On his front stoop, Cooper turned to face him. He stared right through Gideon, his look quelling. "I don't help lycans." He turned around and unlocked his front door, calling out just before the door slammed behind him, "Or their friends."

The waning afternoon simmered all around him as he fought through the thick growth of trees and brush. The air hugged him, dense and moist as Gideon swung himself over the fence. Locusts roared dully to each other in the trees, their calls growing in frenzy. He inhaled deeply, trying to steady his pulse and clear his head. Hard to do when his thoughts were full of Claire and what she must be enduring within the lycan's compound.

The tang of pine was sharp in the steaming air, making his skin itch. Sweat trickled down his spine as he led the way, leaving the road and world behind.

It was a prime piece of real estate. Close enough to commute to the city but remote and private enough that no one would note any suspicious comings and goings. Leaving the property uncleared had been a deliberate move. It took half an hour to reach the house through the heavy undergrowth.

The woods finally gave way to reveal a rambling structure that looked more like a dormitory than a house.

Gideon dropped to his stomach and crawled as close as he dared to the compound. "There." He pointed to a second-story window positioned above an outside air conditioning unit. That was their way in.

Darius crawled up beside him and nodded in unspoken agreement.

Two lycans chatted beneath the front portico—one male, one female. They looked almost normal, pushing back and forth on a swing, chatting companionably. At one point the female laughed, throwing back her head in delight. The sound rose over the locusts and slithered through the air.

Darius tensed beside him. He pointed to the woman. "That's Jesslyn."

Gideon eyed Darius, noting his stony expression. The tight compression of his lips said it all. "Old friends?"

Darius nodded. "She was a prize breeder for the pack three hundred years ago."

"Doubtful she still is," Gideon observed, knowing a female lycan's fertility had a limit. It varied, but most were purported to breed for only two to three hundred years.

Darius cut him a sharp glance. "You've done your homework."

"It's part of the job."

"Saving would-be lycans part of the job, too?"

Gideon shrugged, uncomfortable discussing Claire with a lycan who wanted her for himself. He felt the old familiar scorn surfacing. He didn't fully understand why Darius chose to lead an atypical existence, but it was too late for him. Darius was damned. He had murdered countless innocents. There was no redemption in store for him.

"Jesslyn was a particular favorite of Cyril's. At least when I—" Darius stopped and shook his head.

A sneaking suspicion began to take root that Darius's past was tied up with Cyril and this pack.

To verify, he asked, "Anything you need to tell me before we go in there?"

"Yes. I want to take her and Cyril out myself."

Gideon cocked a brow. "Bad blood, huh?"

"I owe them."

"How's that?"

Darius's dark brows drew tight over his pewter gaze as he gazed at the female lycan he wanted to kill. "For almost a thousand years the beast ruled me. I lived to feed. Then, one day, I met a girl—a woman. The daughter of an Indian shaman. She had her father's gift. Though she was still young, untried, she used her powers to try to break my curse." He shook his dark head, a tinge of awe in his voice as he murmured, "She was not afraid of me. Even invited me in among her people. Can you imagine that? She knew me for what I was and was not afraid. She wanted to help me."

"You loved her?"

"I could have," he allowed, jaw clenching. "The pack never let me."

"They killed her?"

"No." Darius turned silver eyes on him. "But they forced me to." Turning, he faced forward again.

Gideon stared at the lycan for a long moment, seeing him perhaps for the first time and realizing that they had something in common. The curse had cost them. Something more precious than their own lives. The lives of people close to them, loved ones that died horrible, undeserving deaths while Gideon and Darius remained behind to suffer the memories.

A blue conversion van with tinted windows pulled up in front of the house then, drawing his attention. Doors slammed. Three lycans exited the van and walked to the back, opening the rear doors. The two on the porch joined them. Although they moved slowly, calmly, an air of eagerness simmered just beneath the surface. One by one, they hefted several unconscious bodies into their arms. Gideon counted a total of five. Three girls and two boys.

"Looks like they're dining in tonight," Gideon pronounced grimly.

"With only five bodies to feed on, they can't have more than half a dozen lycans inside. The rest probably ventured out to hunt, leaving the others behind to keep an eye on Claire."

Darius grimaced as if struck by a troubling thought.

"What?" Gideon prodded.

"The first time—" Darius paused, clearly uncomfortable. "The first few times a lycan shifts, things can get out of hand. They can wreak a lot of damage, lose control. It's often pack custom to mate with the initiate after they feed."

Gideon's hands dug into the earth in front of him, the moist soil slipping underneath his nails and filling his palms. The thought of Claire shifting, turning into one of them and enduring orgy sex filled his throat with bile.

The image of his mother fully shifted flashed across his mind—the gore on her face, his father's blood on her monstrous hands. He hadn't allowed himself to consider Claire actually shifting before. Not in reality. It was never supposed to come down to this. He had meant to either save her or destroy her. Now it appeared neither might occur. He shook his head and cleared his thoughts of all emotion, zeroing in on the mission at hand, slipping into his familiar role of hunter.

His gaze drifted back to the house, sizing up the lycans as they carried the bodies of their victims inside.

Gideon motioned to the window at the side of the house. "Let's go."

Darius grabbed hold of his wrist, stopping him. "It grows late," he announced in that oddly formal speech of his.

Gideon followed Darius's gaze to the purpling sky, the brilliant streaks of red and gold a painter's dream. The sun had already disappeared below the treetops, forsaking them to the coming night.

Darius's voice was no less firm for the quiet solemnity with which he spoke. "If we're not out of here in time—"

"Don't worry," Gideon cut him off, giving a quick, single nod. "I'll kill you."

Darius lips twisted in a crooked smile. "Somehow I thought you'd say that."

"No prob." With a small amount of wonder, he realized he wouldn't relish destroying the lycan. Hell, first Claire, now Darius. He might as well forget about being a lycan hunter and go into the business of lycan preservation.

"Let's go." Gideon crawled through the grass, calling over his shoulder in hushed tones, "With any luck you'll be back in that room of yours before moonrise."

Claire dozed in and out of sleep with Nina's head cushioned in her lap. She had quickly gotten over her fears of touching Nina and used a length of rope to bind Nina's arm to her chest. The basement grew colder as the day faded, disappearing into shadows, and she covered Nina with a tarp.

"Miss Morgan," Nina whispered in the stillness.

"Hmm?" Claire asked, trying to fight the hunger pains clawing her stomach.

She trailed her fingers through Nina's hair, soft as a child's. With a pang she realized Nina was just that—a child. Sometimes she forgot that her students, trapped in their almost grown bodies, were still children. Lenny had been only a boy. A lost boy whose sad life met an even sadder end. She blinked at the tears springing to her eyes.

Her inadvertent role in Lenny's death pressed down on her chest, an invisible weight. No matter what happened she would never forget how Cyril had used her. Even if she succumbed to the curse and lost her soul, she would remember. Somehow she would cling to a shred of humanity, a bleeding scrap to bury deep and pull out one day when the chance arose. On that day she would make Cyril pay for all he had taken from her.

"Does it seem darker to you?"

Claire glanced at the single window. The muted beam of light was higher now, hitting the wall and not the floor.

"Just a bit." Her voice quavered on the lie.

"I've been thinking about the way I'm gonna die—"

"Nina, don't—"

"Please, let me say what I have to." Nina grabbed her hand. Claire gasped at the unexpected coldness of her slight fingers. Her dark stare demanded she listen. "You could kill me before you change."

She shook her head and pulled her hand free of Nina's grasp, the horror of what she asked too much to contemplate.

Before she could voice her protest, Nina rushed on to say, "Over there. Take one of those."

Claire followed her finger to where several pipes lay stacked near an old furnace. Instantly, she understood what Nina would have her do.

"One strike—"

"No," Claire broke in, shaking her head from side to side, horror wringing her heart. "I'm not a killer."

"Listen to me," Nina insisted in a surprisingly steady voice, her sad, solemn eyes so adult as they looked up at Claire. "It could be over. Quick. It's better than—" Her voice lost its steadiness and she choked on a sob. She covered her face with her one good hand. "I don't want to die that way."

"Sshh, I know." Claire stroked her long hair, the strands silk under her hand.

Nina swiped her wet cheeks with the backs of her

fingers and sniffed, her voice rising strong again. "The pipe."

Claire shook her head, strands of hair clinging to her tear-soaked cheeks. "I can't."

"You have to." She squeezed Claire's hand with her chilled one. "You owe me that. Don't let me die the way he intends." She shook her head side to side vehemently. "Not that way."

Claire stared into her face for several moments, the weight on her chest now too tight to draw air into her lungs. How could she refuse Nina a humane death?

Standing, she made her way to the pile of pipes, her heart an aching throb beneath her breastbone. Bending, her hand closed around the smooth steel. Staring at it in horror, she tested its weight in her hand.

Oh God, how can I do this?

She recalled her fright when Lenny attacked her. The horror, the pain. And Nina would endure so much more than that. Claire couldn't put Nina through that. Not if she could help it. Claire had to offer her whatever relief she could—even if that relief was a swift, merciful death.

With slow, measured steps, she approached the girl, the heavy pipe clutched tightly in her hands.

Chapter Twenty-two

Dogs possess exceedingly long memories;
they never forget a kindness or a wrong.

—*Man's Best Friend:*
An Essential Guide to Dogs

Gideon stripped off his shirt and wrapped it around his hand. With one plunge he sent his fist through the window, the cotton fabric of his shirt muffling the sound of shattering glass. He dropped back down on top of the air conditioning unit, shaking shards of glass from his shirt before shrugging back into it. Pressing his back against the house, he waited, breath suspended.

Below him, Darius crouched in the dirt. Satisfied they hadn't been discovered, Gideon went first, rising up on the faded green unit to peer through the window. A narrow, empty hallway stared back. As quietly as possible, he cleared the remnants of glass from the window and slipped inside. His booted feet thudded quietly on the carpet. Darius followed, dropping down silently beside him. They stood side by side, tense and vigilant as two jungle cats.

Shadows crept along the long length of hall. Dusk

hovered in its final farewell, fading from the window behind them, casting a red pall over the shadowed interior of the house.

Muscles tense, Gideon stepped forward. Then he stopped, freezing as a pair of rottweilers rounded the corner. They stood together, legs braced wide apart, glossy black hair standing on end as they bared their teeth and growled.

"Uh, Darius?" Gideon spoke between unmoving lips, eyes never wavering from the dogs.

"Did I mention packs frequently use dogs as protectors of the den?" Darius asked in an offhanded air.

"You left that bit out."

"Sorry. Don't let them get their teeth around your neck," Darius advised just before the dogs charged, nails clattering against the hardwood floor.

The dog on the left flew through the air toward Gideon. Bracing himself, he focused on the snarling one hundred forty pounds coming his way.

The beast slammed into him with the force of a tank. Stumbling back several steps, Gideon grabbed the dog by the head just before his steel-trap jaws clamped down and tore his nose from his face. He twisted the animal's ears and felt a stab of satisfaction when a sharp whimper pierced the air.

Gideon glanced over his arm to see Darius snap the other dog's neck. "Mind helping me?" he grunted.

Darius stepped over the dead dog and strolled toward Gideon as he might on a walk in the park. Bending, he wrapped his hands around the dog's neck and broke it like a toothpick.

Gideon shoved the dead animal off his chest. Looking back and forth between the two prostrate dogs, he felt himself grin. "Damn glad to have you with me."

Darius pulled Gideon to his feet, motioning to the dogs. "There may be more."

Suddenly, a soft, melodious voice spoke. "Normally I would be quite put out with anyone who killed my pets—"

Gideon's head swiveled in the direction of the voice. Jesslyn stood in the hallway, two lycans framed on either side of her.

"Do you know how long it takes to properly train them?" Jesslyn gestured to her pets, her look aggravated. "It's all in the breeding, really." Her silver gaze flowed over Darius, warming to dark pewter. "But since it's you, Darius, I'll find the forgiveness." She held out both arms. "Welcome home, darling. It's been a long time."

"Jess," Darius acknowledged, staying put.

After a moment she dropped her hands, her plump lips pouting, marring her lovely features. With a light shrug, she shifted her attention to Gideon and smiled again. "Lovely. I see you brought a snack." Her gaze swept over Gideon in appraisal. "A bit more than a snack," she amended, a hungry gleam entering her silver eyes. "He looks like Brad Pitt. Delicious."

"You know who I've come for," Gideon announced.

"Indeed?" She tossed her thick blonde hair over her shoulder. The fading sunlight cast her face in a fiery glow. "Our Claire is the popular one. Cyril is quite taken with her, too."

Her gaze swung to Darius, and Gideon heard the jealousy in her voice when she asked, "Don't tell me you've come for her as well? Perhaps I should take lessons from our little Claire. She attracts mates like bees to the honey pot."

Impatience reared its head. Gideon pulled the gun from his holster. He was finished chatting. "How many of you have to die before I get what I've come for?" Lifting the gun, he fired.

The lycan to Jesslyn's left hit the floor with a howl. The other one charged, and Gideon fired a second time, watching numbly as he collapsed at his feet. He swung the gun back at Jess, cocking an eyebrow. She stood cool and composed.

"Where is she?" he asked, his words dropping like heavy stones into the charged air.

She stood calmly, as if members of her pack were wiped out in front of her every day. Her glittering gaze turned on Darius, ignoring Gideon entirely. "You've come to kill us? Your brethren? Your old pack?" she accused, her voice low.

Darius lifted one shoulder in a shrug. "Should have done it a long time ago. Would have if I'd known where to find you."

She made a clucking sound with her tongue and thrust her bottom lip out. "You're still angry. Over *her*."

"No," Darius corrected. "I don't feel anger anymore. I don't feel anything at all. I am quite content on my own."

"All this time? You haven't fed?" She shook her head in wonder and laughed, the sound brittle. "Fool." Smiling, she tilted her head, gaze narrowing thoughtfully. "And have you found salvation yet, Brother Darius?"

Darius didn't answer.

"Of course not." Her smile melted away and she gestured to the fallen two, her gaze drilling into Darius. "You'll stand by and watch this human annihilate us?"

"No," Darius responded quickly.

She smiled in satisfaction, but Gideon glimpsed the hint of relief behind that smile. She extended a hand to Darius, elegant fingers curling in a beckoning wave. "Welcome home, my love. I've missed you."

Darius plucked the gun from his hand. Before Gideon had time to react, Darius pulled the trigger.

"Sorry I can't say the same," he replied, his voice flat.

Jesslyn fell to her knees, a hand pressing over the hole in her chest—as if she could staunch the blood blooming on her cotton print dress. "Darius?" she whispered, her look bewildered.

"I haven't come to *watch* him kill my old pack." Stepping closer, he pressed the gun to her forehead. "I've come to help." Then he pulled the trigger. Her body jerked and hit the ground in a soft thud. Turning, he tossed the gun to Gideon. "Better reload. They know we're here."

Gideon reloaded and tossed it back to him. "Looks like you're going to need one, too."

Pulling out a second gun, he stepped around the bodies. They resumed walking down the hall, opening every door they came to, systematically searching the rooms, closets, and adjoining bathrooms.

"Is it possible he's not here?" Gideon asked as he opened yet another door, this one leading to a linen closet. They had to find Cyril. Cyril was the key.

"Oh, he's here. Lying in wait." Darius nodded grimly. "I can feel him."

They descended the stairs, stopping before a large sunken living room. Empty. A large rock fireplace dominated the corner of the room. Gideon motioned with his gun to the large sectional couch. Darius nodded in understanding. They moved to opposite ends of the couch and peered over it. Nothing but carpet.

Gideon heard a strange scrabbling sound and looked over his shoulder. Nothing. But the sound grew louder. He swung around the precise moment a lycan dropped down into the hearth from inside the chimney, stirring up a huge cloud of soot. With an inhuman shriek, he launched himself on Darius.

Coughing through the foul air, Gideon squinted and aimed, praying he didn't miss.

The cold seeped through Claire's clothes, numbing her skin and penetrating her bones as she knelt on the floor beside Nina. She carefully set the steel pipe beside her—gently, softly, so Nina wouldn't hear the steel clank against the concrete floor. No need for an audible reminder of what was to come.

Despite Nina's brave front, she was tense as a board, staring up at Claire with wide eyes.

You can do this. You promised Nina.

"Relax." She smoothed a hand over Nina's brow. "We have a little time."

Some of the tension eased from Nina's rigid shoulders. "You'll let me know when it's coming?" she asked.

"Of course," Claire lied, easing the worry lines from

Nina's forehead with her fingers, determined to make her relax and drop her guard. Her skin was soft. Like a newborn's.

Claire watched the gentle rise and fall of Nina's chest. When Nina's eyes drifted shut, Claire knew the time had arrived. Her hand closed around the pipe. Ever so slowly she lifted it, her fist tightening around the pipe until her fingers ached. She raised the pipe high above her head. Sucking in a silent breath, she jammed her eyes shut and prepared to swing.

God forgive me.

The door at the top of the stairs flung open the second before she brought the pipe crashing down. Claire froze and watched Cyril descend.

"There's been a change in plans." The wood steps creaked beneath his weight. Two other lycans followed behind him. "We've decided to join you."

He stopped at the bottom of the stairs, his gaze landing on the pipe in her hand. "Claire," he said, tsking, shaking his head in reproof. "What are you doing? Depriving yourself of a warm meal? We can't have that. I know you must be starving. Perhaps we should show you how it's done."

Nina clutched her wrist in a bruising grip. Claire looked down, translating the silent plea in Nina's gaze. *Kill me.*

A plea she couldn't refuse.

With an agonized cry, Claire swung.

Damn. Gideon couldn't get a clear shot through the haze of soot, and he couldn't afford to miss. Not with a gun loaded with silver bullets. If he so much as clipped Darius in the shoulder, he'd be dead.

He watched, eyes stinging from the polluted air, waiting for his chance as Darius and the other lycan crashed through the glass coffee table. Glass rained down on the carpet, crunching beneath them as they rolled in the shards. Finally, Gideon got his chance. Praying he didn't move at the last second, he squeezed the trigger.

"About time!" With a grunt, Darius threw the body off him. Standing, he dug a jagged piece of glass out of his arm and flicked it to the carpet like it was a piece of lint.

"Come on." Gideon strode out of the living room, Darius fast on his heels.

A sound reached his ears. He paused, angling his head to the side. There it was again. A thudding noise. Like someone banging on a wall. Or door.

"What's that?" Darius looked at Gideon.

Hope, desperate and burning, swelled to life in Gideon's chest.

Claire.

They ran in the direction of the sound, following it through a swinging door that opened to a large, airy kitchen outfitted with an industrial-size stove and stainless steel fridge. An old medieval-style trestle table with a battered and scarred surface stood in the center of the room, at odds with the rest of the very modern, utilitarian kitchen.

The back door hung open, swinging lightly in the still air, as if someone had just rushed past it. The slow creak of its hinges raised the hair on his arms. Gideon rotated on the balls of his feet, the barrel of his gun sweeping the kitchen. He took careful note of that open door, half expecting a lycan to charge through it.

The pounding grew louder, accompanied by shouts. The racket came from a bolted pantry door. Gideon flung back the bolt. The breath rushed from him in disappointment.

Darius stepped beside him to eye the pantry's occupants. Amid several twenty-pound bags of dog food, two teenagers stared up at him with mixed expressions of fear and hope. The other three were still unconscious on the pantry floor.

"Help us!" A girl with badly smeared black eyeliner glared up at him.

"We'll get you out of here," Gideon promised.

Her face softened in relief, and she hugged the weeping girl beside her.

"But you need to wait here a little longer."

She shook her head fiercely. "No! You have to get us out of here now!"

Gideon waved a hand in the air to calm her. "I promise I'll get you out of here." He pressed a finger to his lips. "For now you have to stay quiet, okay? No more pounding."

"Hell, no! Listen, you asshole—"

He closed the door on her protests and set the bolt back in place. The pounding resumed with gusto.

Gideon's gaze shot to the open door. The air outside had deepened to an opaque purple. Time was up.

"We're not going to get me home in time," Darius announced, his words echoing Gideon's grim thoughts. "You're going to have to kill me."

Gideon turned to face Darius, leveling his gun at him as he did so.

Darius held up both hands, saying mockingly, "I didn't mean just this second."

"Can you feel it coming on yet?"

"Yes." A muscle in his jaw twitched, the only sign of his tension. Of his unwillingness to die. "We have a little time. You still need me—I'll let you know when it's time."

"We've searched the house." Gideon ran his hand through his hair roughly. "What's left?" He refused to believe Claire wasn't here somewhere. She had to be. Just as Darius could feel Cyril, Gideon could feel Claire. He knew she was here. His heart felt her.

Darius pointed. Gideon followed his finger to the back door just as the wind blew it shut—and revealed another door.

A steel-framed door.

Chapter Twenty-three

Never underestimate a dog's survival skills.

—Man's Best Friend:
An Essential Guide to Dogs

Gideon turned the doorknob and stepped onto a small landing overlooking a basement. The air was several degrees cooler than in the rest of the house. Darius stepped beside him.

It didn't take long for his eyes to adjust to the dimness and zero in on Cyril standing below, arms wrapped around Claire and a girl, the student she'd hugged at Woody's. He had not counted on seeing the girl.

His eyes sought Claire, drinking in the sight of her, checking to see she was unharmed. Apart from her wide, anxious gaze, she looked in one piece. He breathed easier.

"Gideon!" she cried out, trying to step forward.

Cyril pulled her back, one hand tightening around her neck. Gideon lurched forward, ready to go to her, but Darius flung out an arm to stop him. They exchanged looks, the message in Darius's eyes clear, urging patience, caution. Gideon took a deep breath and collected himself. If they wanted to get out of this alive, he couldn't let his emotions rule him. He needed to keep a cool head.

"Darius!" Cyril called out in greeting, his voice ringing with false warmth. "What a pleasant surprise!"

Darius's gaze swept the basement and its three inhabitants. "Isn't this a familiar scene?" he muttered dryly. "Guess some things never change. If a lycan doesn't want to kill, you'll find a way to make sure they do."

Chuckling, Cyril shook his head.

Gideon fought to control the anger spiking through him at the sight of that bastard's paws on her. The way his fingers dug into Claire's skin—he had to force himself not to fly down the steps and wrench her from his arms.

"Still miffed about that?" Cyril queried.

Instead of answering the question, Darius's voice rang out in quiet command. "Let them go."

"You're not in charge anymore, remember?" Cyril taunted. "We voted you out unanimously. I rule this pack now."

Darius started down the steps. Gideon followed.

"Still the good monk?" Cyril continued with a shake of his head. "Why can't you just accept what you are, Brother Darius?"

They were halfway down the steps, Gideon's gaze glued to Claire, when two hands shot from between the steps to grab hold of Gideon's and Darius's ankles. A hard yank pitched them forward, sending them tumbling down the unforgiving steps and onto the concrete floor in a tangle of limbs.

Two lycans flew from beneath the stairs. Crouched on his hands and knees, Gideon struggled to rise, battling his dizziness. Hard steel struck him in the back once, twice, forcing him to the floor with a jarring thud. Pain thrummed through every inch of his body. Groaning, he struggled to rise again.

Claire screamed, the sound piercing his soul.

He twisted around in time to see the pipe descending to his head. Rolling to the side, the pipe grazed his shoulder. His hand brushed cold metal. His gun. Grabbing it, he swung around and fired at the lycan swinging a pipe. Once. Twice. The lycan's body hit the ground.

Crouching, Gideon ignored his dizziness and spun around, searching through the murky air for the second lycan. He spotted him springing through the air toward him. Gideon fired again, jerking out of the way as the lycan collapsed to the ground beside him.

His gaze sought Darius then, finding him restrained with a pipe through his chest, impaled to one of basement's support beams.

"One move and I snap her neck," Cyril called out, recapturing his attention.

Gideon swung his gun in the direction of Cyril.

The alpha held Nina before him, two hands wrapped around her neck. "Toss the gun down."

Gideon's gaze moved beyond Cyril to where Claire hunkered, clutching at her chest, breathing abnormally fast.

"Claire?" he called, dread consuming him. *No. Not yet.*

Her frightened gaze met his, mirroring the dread welling up inside him.

Cyril glanced over his shoulder at her and an evil smile curved his lips. "You're too late. It's already begun. She's mine now."

Claire struggled to steady her breathing as her gaze shot back and forth between Gideon, Darius, and Cyril. She straightened, trying to still the wild thumping of her heart with deep, calming breaths. It did no good. Her heart felt ready to explode from her chest.

The gun in Gideon's hand wavered and she knew he was going to do what Cyril said and toss down the gun.

"No," she cried out, trying to step around Cyril, but he moved and blocked her.

Claire watched Gideon lower the gun and acted fast. Her foot lashed out at the back of Cyril's knees. He stumbled and she grabbed Nina's wrist, yanking her free from Cyril's hold. She flung Nina with more force than intended, forgetting her strength. Nina hit the wall with a cry, her injured arm taking the brunt of the impact. Cringing, Claire watched as Nina crumpled to the floor in an unconscious heap.

Damn. Claire started toward Nina but whirled around at a shout.

One of the fallen lycans clutched Gideon's ankle. She watched, horrified, as the lycan sank his teeth into Gideon's calf, penetrating the denim and reaching skin. She heard Gideon's flesh tear, heard the lycan's teeth sink into muscle and sinew.

Claire screamed, surging forward with her hand outstretched. Her fingers strained to reach Gideon even as she realized it was too late.

Cyril recovered quickly, striking her across the face. She toppled back from the sudden blow, clutching her cheek.

A shot rang out.

Pushing herself up with one palm, she watched Gideon shoot the lycan clinging to his leg. Shaking the creature off, he lifted his gun. But it was too late. Cyril was on him. Knocking the gun from Gideon's hand, he grabbed him by the throat, lifting him several inches off the floor.

Cyril studied Gideon's reddening face for several seconds before saying, "I'm not going to kill you right away. Killing is too good for you, too easy. I'll keep you alive. Make you a slave to the pack, feed you the scraps."

Cyril's voice sounded strange. Thick, almost strangled. A glance at his face revealed why. He was beginning to shift. His face altered, the bones elongating and stretching as the skin darkened to a deep gray. Fur sprouted over his entire head in a thick reddish brown mane.

She raised a trembling hand to her own face and felt that she had started to shift, as well.

"Oh God," she whimpered, her voice strange and unnatural.

A gnawing hunger flared to life in the pit of her belly. Her heart still hammered at a frantic tempo, the air rushing out of her mouth in spurts. Dipping her head, she moaned low in her throat. A scratchy, tingling sensation overwhelmed her body. Powerless to resist, she threw back her head and arched her spine, moaning louder.

Clutching her cheeks, she felt her bones shift, stretch, grow. Fur sprouted from her pores and filled her palms where she clutched the sides of her face.

The hunger grew, eclipsing all else. Claire struggled to hold on to herself, to what she knew, but it grew increasingly harder as her body twisted inside itself.

She heard her name as if called from a great distance and vaguely recognized Gideon's voice.

"Claire! Claire, fight it! Get the gun," he shouted.

Staggering toward the gun, she lifted it in her hands and turned, her gaze finding Gideon. Clutched in Cyril's giant paws, his eyes met hers. She watched Cyril's nails grow, stretching into huge talons that dug into Gideon's face, drawing blood.

"Pull the trigger!"

Cyril looked back and forth between her and Gideon, the slow turn of his head unhurried, unconcerned. He didn't see her as a threat.

She doubled over, clutching her belly at the sudden cramping.

"Claire!" Gideon cried out. "Shoot him!"

She shook her head savagely.

Straightening, she willed herself to follow his command, but the hunger was staggering, washing over her in hot, undulating waves, increasing with every second. She wanted to fling the gun down, tear off her skin, and . . .

Suddenly, she caught sight of Nina, stirring into consciousness. Every one of Claire's heightened senses zeroed in on her, aware of every breath, of the rapid beating of her heart, of the sweet blood rushing just beneath the surface of her warm, caramel skin. She looked so . . . tempting, smelled so sweet.

Claire no longer saw Nina. She saw food. And she

knew the blood would taste delectable. She could almost imagine it flooding her mouth, rushing through her teeth and over her tongue, its warm nectar sliding down the back of her throat. Saliva pooled inside her mouth. Claire couldn't resist. She took a step toward her.

"Miss Morgan?" Nina whimpered, scuttling farther away along the wall. Claire stopped, squeezing her eyes shut, battling the urges that washed over her, threatening to consume and swallow her whole. She flexed her hands, startled to feel the dig of claws cutting into one palm . . . and the forgotten gun in the other.

"Claire!" Gideon shouted, his voice reaching out to her from the fog. "Claire, don't! Claire, I love you! God, please, don't!"

She lifted the gun, gazed at it in her hand. From somewhere deep inside her, she found the will to spin back around and level the gun on Cyril.

Cyril dropped Gideon to his feet and faced her, his silver eyes gleaming, his claws contracting open and shut at his sides. Releasing a low growl, he circled her, clearly no longer confident of her intentions.

He lunged.

She squeezed the trigger, uncertain if the anguished howl splitting the air belonged to her or Cyril. Claire fell to her knees the same moment Cyril collapsed before her.

Head bowed, chest heaving with great swallows of air, she dropped the gun and watched her hands gradually reduce to their normal size. The wiry hair receded back into her pores and her heart ceased to thump so violently in her chest.

Suddenly, she was caught up in Gideon's arms, crushed in a tight, suffocating hold. Closing her eyes, she reveled in it.

"You did it," he whispered against her hair. "God, I don't know how . . ." His voice faded on a sigh.

Tears slipped from her closed eyelids. She felt the warm wetness roll down her cheeks. Yes, she had done it. She had ignored the hunger, ignored the pull, and mastered the beast inside her.

A low growl interrupted the moment and they both turned, suddenly remembering Darius pinned to the post. Only it wasn't Darius any longer. It was a fully shifted lycan, larger and more frightening than Claire could ever have imagined. Whereas Cyril had been reddish brown, Darius was black. A huge black-furred monster even her nightmares couldn't have summoned.

"Oh. My. God." Nina's hushed voice floated from behind them where she pressed herself into the wall—knees tucked to her chest—and once again passed out.

"That's one big mother," Gideon marveled beside her.

"Big?" Claire echoed, head falling back to take in all of Darius. As a man he easily stood six feet tall, but now, fully shifted, he was closer to seven. With a howl of rage, he wrenched the pipe from his chest.

Gideon dove for the gun Claire had dropped and swung around in one fluid motion. Frowning, he aimed and muttered, "Sorry, my friend."

Claire closed her eyes and looked away, sick at the prospect of Darius's death. With a soft prayer on her lips that his soul would be granted a second chance—that he would receive some chance at redemption—she waited for the end.

Gideon curled his finger around the trigger, heart heavy with the burden of his task.

Darius had known the sacrifice in coming here, had known the odds, and had taken the risk for Claire's sake. Still, it didn't make it any easier.

Suddenly, the muffled zing of a silencer cut through the air. Then another. And another. Gideon thrust Claire behind him.

Cooper stood at the top of the stairs, face grim, gun aimed at Darius.

Darius staggered several steps before dropping to his knees with a great thud. His face smacked the concrete floor in a loud crunch of bone.

"What are you doing here?" Gideon demanded, anger bubbling inside him as Cooper started down the stairs. Cooper had made it perfectly clear he could expect no help. If he had changed his mind, he could have done it sooner, before he nearly lost Claire.

"Thought you could use a little help." Cooper shrugged.

"Too little, too late." Gideon waved his gun at Darius's body. "I could have handled him."

Cooper assessed the bodies littering the basement with mild interest. "You've been busy." His gaze cut to Claire peeking from behind Gideon. "Guess you found her alpha."

"No thanks to you," Gideon snapped.

"I did my part." Cooper said, defending himself and

motioning to where Darius lay fallen. "Not that I should have."

"Yeah, big help. You shot the lycan I already had in my sights." Shaking his head in disgust, Gideon turned to Claire. He ran his hands over her arms, relishing the feel of her.

"What about him?" Cooper's voice broke in, ringing like a drill sergeant.

Gideon looked over his shoulder. Cooper pointed at Darius. Irritated, he started to ask what he meant, then stopped, realizing that Darius hadn't shifted back to his human form yet.

Curious, he left Claire's side and stepped nearer. A thick pelt of black hair still covered Darius's body. Lycans always returned to their human form in death. Darius's chest rose and fell with deep, silent breaths. He wasn't dead. Gideon's bewildered gaze shot to Cooper.

A smile tugged at the corners of his mouth. Turning the gun side to side, he said, "Don't know how strong these tranquilizers are. Gave him enough to put out an elephant. Still, you might want to get him wherever he's supposed to be."

Claire demanded, "He's not dead?"

"No." The way Cooper's mouth tightened, Gideon knew he didn't exactly understand why he hadn't killed Darius, but Gideon did. He'd done it for him. Trusted him enough to believe that Darius might be worth saving.

"Yeah, and if this ever gets out my career's over."

"My lips are sealed." Gideon pretended to zip his lips.

"Just get the hell out of here." He nodded to Darius. "And take pretty boy with you."

"What about Nina?" Claire asked, motioning to the unconscious girl.

"Oh yeah," Gideon said, suddenly remembering. "And there are some kids upstairs in a pantry—"

Cooper waved a hand and sighed deeply. "I'll take care of the kids. Know just which cops to call."

Gideon had a good idea, too.

Cooper shooed at them with his hands. "Leave it to me. You get out of here. I don't want to explain your presence."

Gideon nodded, recalling the night of his own parents' death. He and Kit hadn't opened their mouths once. Cooper handled it all. Just as he would undoubtedly handle this. He was an expert at covering up the truth. Then and now. Gideon would probably read a story in the *Chronicle* tomorrow about a police raid on a cult in North Houston and the rescue of several abducted teenagers by law enforcement officers.

Conceal and cover up. Keep the knowledge of lycans hidden from the rest of the world. It's what Cooper did best.

Suddenly weary from it all, desiring a little peace and normalcy in his life, Gideon would gladly leave him to it.

Grabbing Claire's hand, his eyes met hers, startled by the pools of brown staring back at him. The knowledge that she was safe, free of the curse, hit him hard then.

It was too dark in the basement to study the exact

color and nuance of those eyes. But he would. Later. A leisurely inspection. He had all the time in the world to study them. He had plenty of time to discover the real Claire Morgan, assuming she gave him the chance.

The cold, hard truth revealed itself in the unearthing of her wide brown eyes, and Gideon couldn't ignore it.

It was over. Claire no longer needed him. The question remaining was whether she wanted him.

Chapter Twenty-four

> The devotion between human and dog is often reciprocal; sometimes a dog is just as much master as pet.
>
> —*Man's Best Friend: An Essential Guide to Dogs*

After depositing the still unconscious Darius to a much-relieved staff, they headed home. Or to Gideon's house, Claire silently amended. When had she started thinking of Gideon's house as home?

An uncomfortable silence filled the air during the drive. She twisted her fingers in her lap until they were white and bloodless. What now? What did one say when all reason for conversation vanished? When their whole purpose for meeting, for interacting, had ceased to be?

Claire knew one thing for certain. She wasn't sticking around to find out. She couldn't bear facing him the day he realized she wasn't who he thought, the day he discovered she wasn't the woman he had so brashly claimed to love in that basement. Not even close.

She entered the house ahead of him. Squaring her

shoulders, she turned to face him. Best to end it now. She preferred that to witnessing his regret later when he realized she was just a woman. A plain, unexciting woman who didn't inspire feelings of love.

"I'll go upstairs and get my things. My parents must be really worried. They expected me to come back home after I got my things from school." She tried to smile, but felt her lips wobble. "My mom's probably called missing persons—"

Frowning, he interrupted her. "Claire—"

She threw up a hand to silence him. "I really appreciate everything you've done for me. I'm lucky you found me and not some other agent."

His eyes narrowed and he took a menacing step toward her. "Claire, don't even say—"

"I'd be dead if it weren't for you. I won't ever forget that." She backed away, afraid of what he would say if she let him. "I hope NODEAL takes you back. I know how important—"

He grabbed her by both arms and wrenched her against him. The anger in his eyes stopped her speech cold. "I don't want your damned gratitude."

Then he kissed her.

Claire stifled a moan of pleasure at the hard pressure of his lips on hers, forcing her lips to remain still and lifeless beneath his. His hands moved to her waist, slipping beneath her sundress to caress her back. The rough pads of his fingers feathered along her spine. Her skin broke out in goose bumps.

The blood pounded in her head, urging her to respond, but she couldn't give in. Not this time. She no longer had an excuse. There wasn't a beast within her anymore demanding she obey primitive sexual urges. It was time to think logically and behave rationally.

She shoved at his solid chest with the heels of her palms, arching her spine. His hands slid around to cup her breasts through the lacy cups of her bra, knocking her hands away. Her nipples hardened and puckered against his palms. His fingers dipped inside the lace, rolling over the tips until her breath quickened. She gripped the edge of the kitchen table behind her for support, gasping when he bent his head and lifted first one breast to his mouth, then the other, laving his velvet tongue over each rigid point before sucking them fully into the warmth of his mouth.

Nothing could come of this.

He didn't really want her.

Lifting his head, he kissed her again. She sealed her lips tightly against his. Her lips trembled from the effort. She had to stop—

"Damn it," he rasped against her mouth, "kiss me." His fingers tightened on her shoulders. *"Kiss me."*

That broken plea was her undoing. With a strangled cry, she surrendered, looping her arms around his neck and returning his kiss. Just one last time. As the real Claire. Not the lycan.

One more time, she vowed, and that would sustain her through the years ahead.

Lips meshing, tongues tangling, he wedged his hands between them. He slid her panties down until they dropped to her ankles. Freeing himself from his jeans, he grabbed her waist and effortlessly lifted her off the floor.

With one arm around her waist, he dropped her on the kitchen table, impaling her with one slick thrust.

She gasped at his sudden fullness inside her, flattening her palms on the table and tilting her hips to meet his thrusts.

He panted, fingers digging into the soft flesh of her hips as he thrust into her again and again.

He dipped his head for another kiss, drinking long and deep from her mouth. Heat spiraled from within her, reaching every nerve ending in her body. They moved against each other wildly and her gasps grew louder, twisting into moans.

"Come," he growled into her ear, biting the lobe with his teeth. She shivered. Reaching between their bodies, he found her clit and rubbed. She shrieked, bucking beneath him. His fingers persisted, worked the sensitive spot as he moved in and out.

The knot of tension within her burst. She collapsed back on the table in a shuddering heap, replete, sated, head spinning.

Gideon surged inside her one final time before his head dropped against her neck. Neither moved for several moments. Claire wasn't sure how long she stayed there, Gideon's moist breath against her throat, the warm, musky scent of him filling her nostrils, *him* filling her. Her fingers trailed through the silky soft hair that brushed his neck.

He pulled off the table, taking her with him, his voice a low rumble in her ears. "I know someplace more comfortable."

Claire didn't object as he carried her upstairs. She

studied the lines of his profile, the dark fringe of lashes, his square jaw, committing it all to memory. Pulling back the covers on his bed, he placed her in the middle and slid next to her, tucking her against his side.

For a long time no words passed between them. She smiled dreamily and traced circles on his hard belly, afraid to break the spell. Closing her eyes, she let herself pretend this was permanent, forever, that this was home.

Suddenly, he moved from her side to flip on the light. Then he was back, looming over her, staring at her so intently she felt her smile slip.

"What?" She fidgeted nervously, feeling exposed and vulnerable beneath the light.

"Your eyes."

Frowning, she pulled the covers up to her neck. "I know. Boring brown."

"No," he said slowly, studying her eyes closely. "They have tiny flecks of gold around the center." He pointed as if counting each tiny speck. "Amber," he pronounced. "You have amber eyes."

No one had called her eyes amber before. No one had ever even bothered to look. She felt herself smile. Grabbing his face in her hands, she kissed him soundly.

When she released him, he tugged her closer, deepening the kiss, his tongue sweeping inside her mouth as he shoved the covers aside. Cupping her bottom in both hands, he positioned himself between her thighs. She felt him hard and ready, nudging at her entrance.

"Gideon," she gasped when he ground himself against her. "Again?"

Instead of answering, he lowered his head and took her nipple into his mouth. She arched, moaning as he tormented her with his tongue and teeth.

"Gideon," she begged, grabbing fistfuls of his hair.

His hands slid along her thighs, guiding her legs around his waist, opening her wider. Slowly, he sank inside her. Her head flew off the bed with a gasp. He rested his forehead against hers, the searing intensity of his gaze penetrating her as thoroughly as his body did. Her heart swelled.

This would be enough. This memory, this time with him would be enough. It had to be.

She savored his body over hers, in hers, as he made love to her. Her hands and mouth caressed him, loving him, worshipping every line and hollow of him until they were both spent, exhausted. He flipped the light off before settling back into bed. Wrapping an arm around her waist, he spooned her.

Her eyes drifted shut and for several moments she allowed her breathing to match his, the fall and rise of her chest mimicking his. Never in her life had she felt this close, this intimate, with another soul.

"I love you, Claire." The words were a whisper against her hair, barely audible, but she heard them, a painful echo of her heart's sentiments.

Only he didn't really love her. How could he when he didn't know her? He fell in love with the lycan. A wild creature of instinct. Not Claire.

She waited until his breathing grew even and slow, certain he slept. Cautiously, she crept from the bed, freezing when a spring squeaked. She glanced at his profile. God, he was beautiful.

When he didn't stir, she gathered her clothes and left, slipping silently from the house and vanishing into the moonlit night.

"Cooper," Gideon greeted, halting his flight down the stairs as he spotted his friend kicked back in his recliner eating the last of his Pringles.

"You're out of Cheetos," Cooper complained.

Gideon glared at him and forced himself to stroll into the living room like nothing was wrong. Like Claire hadn't crept off in the middle of the night. Like he hadn't woken up to a cold, empty bed. "I haven't been to the store lately."

Cooper's gaze narrowed as he eyed Gideon. "You look like hell."

Gideon snorted and plucked the can of Pringles from Cooper's hands. "It hasn't even been twenty-four hours yet. You could have waited a little longer before dropping by."

Biting into a chip, Gideon dropped down on the couch and tried to pretend as if nothing was wrong, that he wasn't suffering, that Claire's leaving didn't hurt. That he wasn't dying inside.

"I suppose wiping out half a pack of lycans in a single evening might zap your strength."

Gideon stuck another chip in his mouth, shrugging. "I had some help."

"Yeah, your lycan buddies."

"Claire's not a lycan." Gideon was quick to interject.

"Yeah, not anymore." Cooper glanced around the living room. "So, where is the woman of the hour?"

Again, Gideon shrugged, forcing his eyes to the television. He didn't want Cooper to glimpse any of the torment that simple question elicited.

"You don't know?" Cooper scratched his head. "After everything you did for her, I thought you two would be setting up house, picking out tea towels, china patterns. That's actually what brought me here." Cooper leaned forward in his chair. "You know NODEAL doesn't allow married agents. No live-in girlfriends. Emotional entanglements can jeopardize security. So let's clear the air now." Cooper paused, his look grave. "How serious are you about her?"

Gideon looked at Cooper blankly, wondering what he would think if he knew Claire had left him already. Instead of directly answering, he said, "I didn't really think *staying* an agent was an option. Didn't you fire me?"

Cooper shook his head as if it had all been a misunderstanding. "If you want back in just say the word."

Gideon mulled over Cooper's words before saying, "No. I'm finished."

Cooper leaned back in his chair, rubbing his chin thoughtfully. "Mind telling why?"

Gideon leaned back on the couch, his stomach churning at the thought of giving up all he had ever known. If not a lycan hunter, then what was he? Vengeance had been his companion for so long now. But a life of destroying lycans left him hollow inside. Helping Claire, falling in love with Claire, had filled him with a purpose. Shit. And now she didn't even want him.

"If I were to continue hunting, things would have to change. I couldn't do things NODEAL's way anymore. I wouldn't want to simply destroy. If the chance arose, I'd want to save the infected, too."

Cooper leaned forward, punching a button on the remote control. The television snapped off. "What's really eating you? I'm not surprised about your wanting to quit NODEAL. You've broken every code, done everything possible to sabotage your job." He looked around the room again, this time his tone insistent as he asked, "Where's Claire?"

Gideon stared at his bare feet propped on the coffee table, hating the vulnerability gnawing at him as he confessed, "I don't know. At her apartment, I guess. She left last night."

"Uh-oh. What'd you do?"

Gideon blinked. "Me?" He pointed to his chest. "I didn't do anything." At Cooper's skeptical look, Gideon added, "I told her I love her."

"And she took off?"

"Yeah."

Cooper grunted. Shaking his head, he stood up to leave. "You went through a lot of trouble to keep that woman alive." He paused, his eyes drilling into Gideon relentlessly.

"Guess she doesn't want anything to do with me now that the curse is broken," Gideon said, despising the anguish he heard in his voice.

Cooper shook his head. "Sure looked like she loved you from where I stood."

"Yeah, well, you know about love as much as I do."

Cooper approached him and squeezed his shoulder. "Stop being an ass. Love makes people do stupid things, even run from the person they want most. Now go get her."

Claire stood in her apartment doorway and stared at the deliveryman in front of her, a heavyset, balding man with a thick Italian accent who pronounced her last name with a silent *g*. *Moron*. Sadly appropriate.

What had she been thinking last night, going to bed with Gideon? She might have fallen in love with him, but he hadn't fallen in love with her. Not the true her.

Depressed, Claire took solace in food—even as she knew her days of unlimited eating were over.

She took a risk ordering delivery from Angelo's since they never got the order right, but she hadn't felt like leaving her apartment. Just to be safe, Claire had made the old lady repeat her order over the phone. Maybe this once it would be right.

As she studied the green paper receipt in her hand and read the scrawling handwriting, her hope died a swift death. Once again, she didn't get what she had ordered. As in life.

She wasn't going to dig into her favorite baked ziti and Caesar salad. Nope. Instead, it was to be veal Parmesan and house salad.

Claire fumbled inside her wallet, her movements jerky. The telephone started to ring, but she ignored it.

Suddenly, she paused, fingers tightening on the bills as she looked up at the bored-looking deliveryman holding out the brown paper bag of food to her.

"You know," she began slowly, "I ordered baked ziti and a Caesar salad." She held out the green paper receipt to verify her claim.

He took it from her and squinted. "Says here you ordered the veal."

"Yes, I know what it says," she drew out her words, "but I know what I ordered. Baked ziti and Caesar salad."

He looked from the receipt to her again, asking in his thick accent, "You're saying you don't want it?" He held up the bag of food.

"I want ziti," she clearly enunciated each word, hoping to get her point across.

He frowned and grumbled, "What am I going do with the veal?"

"I don't know," she snapped. "Use it to wax your car for all I care. All I know is that I ordered baked ziti. I'll *pay* for baked ziti. I'll *eat* baked ziti." She pointed to the bag. "Not that."

Maybe it was silly to take a stand over such a trivial thing, but she'd suffered enough disappointments lately. A woman nursing a broken heart had a right to the comfort food of her own choice. And if Claire couldn't take a stand over something so minor, then she really was the same old mousy Claire.

"I'm not coming back here again tonight," he warned, waving the bag of food between them. "Take the veal, lady, or—"

"I'm not," Claire said between her teeth, "taking the

veal." That said, she firmly closed the door in his face.

She stood there a moment, leaning against the door's solid length, breathing unusually fast, knowing that she had just done a hell of a lot more than take a stand over an incorrect order of food. Staring down at her shaking hands, she felt a smile tug her lips. Suddenly, she was seized with confidence.

I'm fine. Strong. Not the mouse. But not the beast either.

For the first time in her life, she was exactly what she should be.

Herself. The person she was meant to be before she allowed fear to rule her. Maybe turning into a lycan, even for a short time, had been a blessing. She'd been given the gift of herself. She'd been given Gideon.

That had been the real Claire who shot Cyril, the real Claire conquering the beast that urged her to feed. The lycan had tried to claim her, but she won.

And she was the woman Gideon wanted. Even loved. At least before she snuck off in the middle of the night like a coward.

Pushing off the door, she headed for the shower.

She had just concluded she wasn't a coward.

Time to prove it.

"Claire!" Gideon pounded on her apartment door until his knuckles stung.

The neighbor across the way cracked open his door to glare at him.

"What?" Gideon snapped with enough heat to send the neighbor ducking back inside his apartment.

"You can't avoid me forever," he called through the door, hands braced on either side of the frame. "Open the damn door."

With a growl, he went around the back and entered her apartment through the sliding glass door—again. The sight of Claire walking out of her bedroom, rubbing her wet hair with a towel, greeted him.

She spied him just as he slid the door shut. "Gideon!" She hopped in surprise. "You nearly gave me a heart attack. Can't you knock like a normal person?"

"I did knock."

She blinked those wide amber eyes of hers at him. "You could have waited for me to answer then."

He marched toward her, immediately catching a whiff of clean shampoo and raspberry soap. "I've been out there for five minutes. I waited long enough."

He scanned the terry robe—the same one she wore that first night. God, was that only a month ago? He'd lived a lifetime since then. He'd let go of the past, of his need for solitude, and fallen in love. With Claire. With beautiful, feisty Claire. He couldn't let her go. He should have known it would come down to this that first night. His inability to pull the trigger had been the first clue.

She tugged the towel from her head. "What are you doing here?"

He focused on her face, resisting the urge to tear the robe off her and do what his body longed. They needed to talk first. Then they could move on to more pleasurable activities and get on with their lives. Together.

"You didn't really think we were finished, did you?" At her blank look, he continued. "No good-bye, no note, no phone call. Nothing. I woke up and you were gone." He hated the hurt and accusation in his voice, hated to reveal his vulnerability.

She turned away and sank down on the couch, holding her robe carefully together at her shapely knees. With a searching look, she asked, "Why are you here, Gideon? Because I didn't tell you good-bye?"

"Claire, I—" He swallowed and tried again. "I—"

She waved a hand to silence him. "Don't. You don't have to say anything. I shouldn't have taken off like that. It was wrong. Cowardly." She took a deep breath. "In truth, I was coming to see you."

"You were?"

She stood up and paced the small living room, twisting her fingers. "To apologize," she explained. Her amber gaze reached inside him and twisted his guts even tighter, bleeding his heart dry. "You've done so much for me, you deserved better than me taking off like that."

Shit. More gratitude. Gideon thought he might be sick. He didn't want her damned gratitude. She made it sound like he had provided some kind of service for her. Everything he had done was because he wanted to, because he had to . . . because he loved her.

"No," Gideon pronounced, voice hard and firm. In two long strides he crossed the short distance separating them, grabbed her by the shoulders, and gave her a little shake, "Stop being so goddamned grateful." He dropped his forehead to hers and inhaled deeply. "I know you, Claire Morgan."

Her wide eyes blinked at him, but she didn't say a

word. He gave her another small shake, willing her to speak. "And you're not getting rid of me."

He claimed her lips in a fierce kiss, as if he could kiss her into complying, into loving him. He came up once to repeat, "I know you." He inhaled again before continuing. "And I can't live without you. I'll love you until the day I die."

He waited for her to say something, anything, but she simply stared at him with those warm amber eyes. So different from the cold silver of before.

The eyes were different, but she wasn't.

"Well." She paused to moisten her lips, saying softly, "If you know me so well, then you know my response."

He felt himself frown. Uncertainty gnawed at him, but he spoke anyway, daring her to contradict him. "You love me." If his words came out like a command, he didn't care. He wasn't letting her run off on him again. His voice grew more determined, insistent. "You're crazy about me. You can't live without me. You want to marry me."

He held his breath as she lifted her chin and looked him squarely in the eyes. "I do love you." Lowering her head, she smiled, her cheeks turning pink as she added, "I'm so crazy about you I even do stupid things like run off in the middle of the night."

Grinning, he reprimanded, "You better lose that habit quick."

"And you," she countered, tapping him on the chest, "better be serious about that proposal, 'cause I'm not letting you take it back."

He pulled her flush against him. "Oh, I'm serious."

Dipping his head, he bit the soft skin of her neck before kissing it gently. Cupping her backside, he pulled her tighter against him. She responded by growling low in her throat.

"Hey," he muttered, teasing, "I thought you weren't a werewolf anymore."

"Lycan," she corrected.

He smiled against her mouth. "Semantics."

Turn the page for a sneak peek
at Sharie Kohler's

KISS OF A DARK MOON

Available from Pocket Books

Leaning forward, Rafe glanced through the windshield. Fingers of red and gold clawed at the graying sky. He inhaled deeply, lowering his gaze back to the building he had been watching for the last half hour. Watching and waiting. Time was running out. Blood already laced the air, rich and pungent as freshly tilled earth.

The barís front door swung open. A lone woman stepped out. Petite with a mass of short blonde curls, she headed down the sidewalk alone, her short strides quick. His gaze shot to the seat next to him, to the file there, which he had memorized. The photograph within was black and white and not of the best quality, but he would recognize her anywhere. He recognized her now. Kit March. He'd been sent to terminate her.

He frowned. Two days until the full moon and the beasts ran restless, almost as dangerous as when the moon beamed brightly overhead, gorged and hungry against a dark sky. He'd observed such nights before. Countless times. He knew what was to come, the carnage when hell's foot soldiers were granted free roam, their bloodlust unleashed.

He assessed his surroundings, his nostrils flaring. Almost as though his thoughts had called them forth, the door to the bar swung open again and *they* emerged.

Three big bastards stepped out into the dusk. Even across the street's distance, their eyes glowed a familiar silver. Pack creatures, bold and deadly. They stood still for a moment, not speaking as they lifted their faces to the air, no doubt catching the scent of the female who had gone ahead of them. In moments, they were moving, following her with avid, feral eyes as she turned into an alleyway.

Little fool likely had no idea there were three beasts on her tail. She would be overpowered in an instant.

Rafe opened his car door and stepped into the humid night. He couldn't let them get to her first. *If she were attacked . . .*

He blinked hard, refusing to contemplate the prospect. He would not allow that to happen. For all their sakes. Quickening his pace, he approached the alley, the sweet scent of vanilla filling his nose as he followed in Kit March's wake.

Kit scanned the area ahead of her, nerves stretched taut as wire as she turned down an alley three blocks away from the bar she had just quit. The steps behind her were undetectable amid the busy city sounds, but she knew they were there nonetheless. Just behind her. She had baited her trap. If she knew how to do one thing well, it was get their attention. After all these years, it had become instinct to her.

She imagined the sour heat of their breath on her neck and wiped one sweaty palm against her skirt. Her pulse thrummed hotly at her throat and she fought to steady it, knowing they could sense her adrenaline. A quick glance up revealed a sun-streaked horizon battling the murk of impending night. Dusk.

She cursed to herself when she thought of the date she left behind at the bar, sitting alone now with his glass of chardonnay as she strolled between twin brick walls of a shadow-shrouded alley, grade-A scum hot on her heels.

The loneliness had gotten to her and she had let her friend Gina set her up. Loneliness. That growing ache for a connection, like the kind her brother had found with his wife . . . the kind the whole world seemed capable of forming except for her. Why should her determination to hunt and destroy lycans preclude her from leading a normal life? From finding intimacy with another human being? Having an honest-to-God love life? Her brother was able to combine both worlds, and she vowed to do the same.

Dan seemed like a decent guy. At least from what she could tell after five minutes. They hadn't made it very far past introductions when she had sensed their presence.

The heels of her boots clicked sharply over the broken concrete. In the cavern-like depths of the alley, the heavy tread of their steps rose over the night and she knew it was time to make her move. A hot gust of air expelled from her lips as she began to dig through her purse. Nearing a Dumpster, she slowed her steps, feigning ignorance of the three dark shapes closing in behind her.

Her date forgotten, she tensed for the fight.

Bring it, scumbags.

Slipping one hand inside her purse, she wrapped her

fingers around her gun, the cold metal reassuring in her hand as she flicked off the safety. Her lips moved, silently, feverishly, as she issued a quick prayer. The same prayer she always muttered. A silent plea that they not suspect, not realize *who* she was—*what* she was—until it was too late.

Faking a little stumble, she hunkered low and reached for her boot as though her heel had come loose. Dropping her purse, she pulled her gun free and whirled around in time to see the three lycans lunge, teeth bared in a hiss, eyes glowing a preternatural silver.

She fired. One spun from the bullet to his chest. Caught off guard, the other two stopped, looking in shock from her to the corpse at their feet.

Without blinking, she used her advantage and fired again, dropping another one. They never expected a woman to be armed, to fight back. It never crossed their minds that she could be a viable threat, an actual lycan hunter. Feed and fornicate—nothing else filled their heads. To them, she was merely fresh meat.

Forgetting his comrades, the remaining lycan charged her with the speed known to his cursed species. He launched himself at her, a dark blur on the air. Before she could squeeze out a third shot, he knocked the gun from her hand. It skittered across the filth-covered pavement. Out of reach. He struck her a brutal blow, and her head snapped back, sharp pain exploding in her cheek. She staggered, the coppery taste of blood filling her mouth.

Her breath escaped in a hiss of pain. Recovering her balance, she put her training to use. Swallowing down blood, she lashed out with her leg and kicked the lycan coming at her, following with a quick jab of her fist to his face. All diversionary tactics; she could never hope to outfight a lycan. She only hoped to buy enough time to reach her gun.

With a dive, she slammed to the ground. A hard hand clamped around her ankle, dragging her back over loose gravel and jagged concrete. She clawed for a handhold, straining toward her gun. Ignoring the sting of her palms, she flipped onto her back and kicked the lycan squarely in the face with the heel of her boot. Once. Twice.

Blood streaming from his nose, he grappled for her flailing feet. She stretched an arm behind her, groping for her weapon.

"Need some help?"

Kit looked up at the sound of the thick, gravelly voice. A stranger stood over them, his face in shadow, the light pouring from the mouth of the alley limning his large physique. He lifted his arm.

A gunshot zipped through the air, a muffled hiss of sound. Blood sprayed her boots and legs. The lycan collapsed at her feet. Without hesitating, she kicked the heavy weight of him off her and snatched her weapon off the ground.

Even as she rose to her feet and faced the stranger, her chest heaving with serrated breaths, she knew he had to be another hunter, even if she didn't recognize him. No one else would have been ready with silver bullets. And only silver could have killed her attackers. Dread filled her. Most of the agents in the area knew her—or *of* her. And most disapproved, buying into NODEAL's policy prohibiting female hunters. The fact that he had saved her ass would only confirm in his mind that she had no business hunting lycans.

Dusting loose gravel from her stinging palms, she stared into the demon dark eyes of her savior. *Savior?* Not a chance. She would have gotten herself out of the situation. She'd been in bad jams before—and still made her kills. She didn't need anyone to save her.

Inky lashes much too long for any man to possess framed those dark eyes, watching her intently.

"Thanks," she bit out, moving to scoop up her purse. Shoving her gun into it, she added, "But I had it under control."

"Right," he replied, his well-carved lips twisting. A hint of an accent, rich and throaty, laced his voice, the origin indecipherable to her ears.

Eyeing him warily, she fished her cell phone out of her purse, and left a quick call on Cooper's voice mail. Even unofficially sanctioned to hunt, she reported to him after every kill.

The agent continued to watch her, his dark gaze oddly intent. Dropping her phone into her purse, she tossed out, "Thanks again."

Turning, she strode away even as she felt his stare drilling into her back. Stepping onto the sidewalk, she glanced regretfully to the doors of the bar and back down to herself. Splattered in blood, palms and knees a scraped mess, resuming her date was out of the question. If Dan was even waiting anymore. Another botched attempt at a love life . . .

Watching for cars, she crossed the street, eager to put as much distance between herself and the other hunter as possible.